PRAISE F[illegible]
JOHN[illegible]

"From page 1, you'll be caught in this gripping, taut thriller . . . five stars." —Larry King, *USA Today*

"The author writes with a tough authority and knows how to generate suspense." —*Kirkus Reviews*

"Vivid characterizations . . . Clever twists . . . Relentless."
—*People*

"Suspenseful . . . Keeps the reader guessing with unexpected twists." —*Publishers Weekly*

"Attention-grabbing . . . Briskly paced." —*Chicago Tribune*

Too Far Gone

Chosen as one of The Strand's Twelve Best Books of 2006!

"*Too Far Gone* offers terrific characters caught in the grip of kidnapping, murder and a deadly storm. Every moment is real enough to touch. The twists are truly surprising, and the pacing never lets up. It simply doesn't get better than that." —John Gilstrap, author of *Six Minutes to Freedom* and *Scott Free*

Side by Side

"A fantastic action thriller that starts off at light speed and just accelerates until the shocking and exciting finale... John Ramsey Miller writes a strong crime thriller with espionage and military overtones filled with plenty of guts and heart." —*USA Today*

"*Side by Side* demonstrates that the best books are entertaining and education AT THE SAME TIME... A compelling story of hillbilly bad guys, steroid-enhanced villains, technologically brilliant information-gatherers, FBI agents, espionage, thieves and international mobsters. It was only when the alarm clock went off that I realized I'd read the whole night." —*Contra Costa Times*

Upside Down

Nominated for Best Paperback Original for International Thriller Writers Award

"The book is a tense cat-and-mouse game, with neither Faith Ann nor Massey sure whom to trust. Faith Ann is a great character, resourceful and poised beyond her years."

—*Kansas City Star*

Inside Out

Nominated for a Barry Award for Best Paperback Original

"*Inside Out* is a great read! John Ramsey Miller's tale of big-city mobsters, brilliant killers and a compellingly real U.S. marshal has as many twists and turns as running serpentine through a field of fire and keeps us turning pages as fast as a Blackhawk helicopter's rotors! Set aside an uninterrupted day for this one; you won't want to put it down." —Jeffery Deaver, author of *The Vanished Man* and *The Stone Monkey*

"A compelling and exciting action thriller starring a likeable protagonist, a widower raising his blind son who still misses his wife who died in the same accident that injured their son." —*Midwest Book Review*

The Last Family

"A relentless thriller." —*People*

"Fast-paced, original, and utterly terrifying—true, teeth-grinding tension. I lost sleep reading the novel, and then lost even more sleep thinking about it. Martin Fletcher is the most vividly drawn, most resourceful, most horrifying killer I have encountered. Hannibal Lecter, eat your heart out."
—Michael Palmer, author of *Silent Treatment*

"Martin Fletcher is one of the most unspeakably evil characters in recent fiction . . . A compelling read." —*Booklist*

"First-time novelist John Ramsey Miller's *The Last Family* is another attention-grabbing thriller that likely will find a home in Hollywood. The briskly paced page-turner pits former DEA superagents against each other in a taut dance of death and revenge." —*Chicago Tribune*

"This is a right fine debut thriller based on a great idea." —*New York Daily News*

"Miller provides enough action for any Steven Seagal movie. . . . Some of Miller's plot twists look like a long, easy pop fly coming at you in center field, only to dart around and pop you in the back of the head." —*Charlotte Observer*

ALSO BY JOHN RAMSEY MILLER

Too Far Gone
Side by Side
Upside Down
Inside Out
The Last Family

Available from Bantam Dell

SMOKE & MIRRORS

JOHN RAMSEY MILLER

A DELL BOOK

SMOKE & MIRRORS
A Dell Book / April 2008

Published by
Bantam Dell
A Division of Random House, Inc.
New York, New York

This is a work of fiction. Names, characters, places, and incidents either are the product of the author's imagination or are used fictitiously. Any resemblance to actual persons, living or dead, events, or locales is entirely coincidental.

Cover design by Flamur Tonuzi

Book design by Steve Kennedy

ISBN 978-0-440-24310-6

Printed in the United States of America
Published simultaneously in Canada

www.bantamdell.com

OPM 10 9 8 7 6 5 4 3 2 1

For my sons, Christian, Rush Lane, and Adam, each a unique and spectacular human being

Acknowledgments

Special thanks to Tunica County, Mississippi, Sheriff K. C. Hamp for giving of his time and allowing me a close look at his department. Thanks to David Crews of Oxford, Mississippi, for his continuing assistance. Thanks to my super agent, Anne Hawkins; my editor, Molly Boyle; and my publisher, Nita Taublib, for their hard work and constant support. And finally, thanks to my family, my friends, and my readers.

I have been interested in handguns since I was a teenager. I never write about a weapon (other than military ordnance and explosives) unless I am personally familiar with it, and seldom about one I haven't either owned or field-tested. When I began writing Winter Massey, he carried a SIGSauer 226, which I still believe is the finest and most accurate mass-produced handgun in the world, and which was, at that time, the service weapon of the U.S. marshals, and a gun most other federal agents carried. When Winter Massey retired, he was able to carry whatever weapon he chose. The Reeder custom handgun Winter carries in this book is a gun I had the pleasure of playing with for several weeks. Of all the custom handguns I have ever fired, the .45s made by Kase

Reeder of Flagstaff, Arizona, are the finest I've had the pleasure of handling. The artisans at Reeder have been kind enough to let me play with several of their 1911 creations so I could put them through their paces to see which one Winter Massey, whose life depends on a single piece of equipment, would select as his carry piece. He decided on the "Rekon Kommander."

Finally, as I am a native with both friends and family residing there, I spend a lot of time in Mississippi, but I am not a gambler. I had never been to the casinos outside Tunica until I decided I wanted to bring Winter Massey home for an adventure. I am of the opinion that gambling is an industry that takes away far more from people than it gives in return. While the impoverished Tunica County I knew as a young man has become prosperous, it has come at a cost. All casinos prey on human frailty, and the by-product of gaming in terms of human tragedy is real and immeasurable. The men and women who run the casinos, legitimate businesspeople or men like my fictional Pierce Mulvane, are exploitative: no amount of civility, bright lights, glitz, and glamour changes that.

1

THE MISSISSIPPI DELTA
SOUTH OF MEMPHIS
THURSDAY

RIFLE CASE IN HAND, A SOLITARY FIGURE MOVED among the trees and scrub brush made leafless by the season. The still, predawn air made fog as the man exhaled. The cold stimulated him. It brought back memories of the glacial eastern European mountains where he had spent his youth learning the art of murder.

Dressed entirely in camouflage, the man slowly and silently made his way through the woods on the damp leaves. Not that there was any danger here in this remote place. No enemy awaited him—only a target of his choosing, who was at that moment taking in and expelling a few last breaths. But being careful was reflexive. Caution made the difference between life and death.

The killer moved to the hide he had selected at the edge of the forest line—a sweet gum tree that had been felled by autumn winds. Kneeling behind the tree, he set his rigid case on the ground, unbuckled its latch, and lifted out the Dakota T-76 Longbow rifle topped with a powerful scope.

Although he much preferred operating at close range, he could nevertheless place a .338 Lapua Magnum round through a cantaloupe at twelve hundred yards. At three thousand feet per second, the bullet would punch a .34-caliber entrance hole in the target's skull, whereupon the hydrostatic pressure would literally hollow out the cranium, filling the air downrange with a vapor comprised of brain tissue, bone chips, and blood. Surviving such a cranial event was about as impossible as threading a needle in the confines of a dark closet while wearing boxing gloves.

The shooter gently leaned his rifle against the fallen tree's trunk. Reaching into the case, he pulled out a sand-filled canvas bag. Using the back edge of his right hand, he chopped a channel into the center of the bag before setting the gun's stock into the groove. A squirrel climbing the trunk of a nearby tree became aware of the man and chirped, its tail flicking nervously.

Taking up the gun, he opened the bolt and pressed it forward, watching as the brass case of the topmost shell slid from the magazine and vanished into the firing chamber. The mechanism sounded like a vault door closing in the quiet woods. Bringing the butt firmly against his shoulder, he lowered his cheek to the cold synthetic stock and looked downrange through the scope.

Ready now, the man behind the tree had only to wait for the morning light to gather so he could get a line of sight across the expansive field. Even after ninety career kills—not including collateral damage—the assassin felt the old mix of anticipation and adrenaline growing within him. He held out his hand and smiled to see that his fingers were as rock-steady as those of a surgeon.

Of all the people the man had neutralized, only three of them had been dispatched for personal reasons. Until two years earlier he had only killed because he was ordered to by the state, or, after the wall fell, had been paid handsomely to kill. He had come here to make one more personal kill, to clip one final loose string hanging from the fabric of his life.

The man had never failed to carry out an assignment because, unlike other professional killers, he always had an insurmountable advantage. It wasn't merely that he was more intelligent than his targets or their protectors, or that his lethal-arts skills were vastly superior—although those things were true enough. The killer's real edge was his vision of each assignment as a chess match—a game of strategy and deception, wherein he laid and sprang elaborate traps, always ending with a vanquished king. Because the stakes in his games were absolute, he always controlled the board, only making moves to spark his opponent's reaction. There was never any question as to the outcome.

Taking a toothpick from the open rifle case, he clenched it between his teeth, chewing on the tip until the faint taste of clove filled his mouth. Daylight was imminent, and as the hunter peered through the scope with his finger outside the trigger guard, a calm enveloped him. He knew—as surely as the sun was rising at his back—that this shot would kick-start the most challenging game of his career.

2

SITTING IN A DEER STAND FOURTEEN FEET IN THE air, Winter Massey looked at Faith Ann Porter, a tall, skinny, fair-skinned thirteen-year-old with large blue eyes and reddish blonde hair.

Two high-powered rifles leaned against the rail in front of them.

As the sun rose, the woods surrounding the field came slowly into focus. The field, planted with rye, clover, and alfalfa, formed a natural basin bordered by two ridges that ran east to west. At one edge of the field, a line of tall bamboo created a natural wall.

Faith Ann smiled excitedly at Winter, her cold-reddened face surrounded by a camouflage fleece hood. Far to the north, another hunter's gunshot pealed like dull thunder. The shot was followed a few seconds later by another.

To his right, Winter spotted four deer moving cautiously down the slope among the trees. He placed a hand on Faith Ann's narrow shoulder and silently pointed to the animals. Nodding solemnly, she slowly lifted her rifle and, using the still to steady the weapon, looked through the scope at the animals. Using his binoculars, Winter watched a large buck trotting after the does, head up, ears flickering, nose sampling the air, steam issuing from his nostrils. Winter's heart quickened as he studied the antlers and counted the points.

"Is he a shooter?" she asked in a whisper.

"Eight-point," Winter said. "Take your time and pick your shot when he's between trees. Make sure of your sight picture, and—"

"I know. Squeeze, don't jerk."

Faith Ann put her cheek against the stock and her eye behind the scope. She flicked off the safety, keeping her finger out of the trigger guard as Winter had taught her.

The buck stopped fifty yards away, broadside to the stand. Faith Ann, doing as Winter had instructed her, used this opportunity to fix the crosshairs of her scope on the area just behind his shoulder, where the heart and the lungs were nestled.

Winter watched Faith Ann release her safety as a rustling sounded across the field. He turned to see a second buck breaking from the wall of bamboo. The huge deer's coat was dark, almost black, and the golden antlers growing from his skull looked like tree limbs glued onto his head, held up by a swollen neck.

"Hold your shot," Winter whispered. "Safety back on."

"Don't shoot?" she asked.

"Very slowly, look out in the field to your left."

Faith Ann turned her head and exhaled when she saw the animal.

Like a stallion, the buck trotted straight into the middle of the field toward the nervous group of does standing at the edge.

Faith Ann moved with deliberate slowness, careful not to make any noise or movements the deer might spot. A rutting buck would be less wary than usual, but anything out of the ordinary would spook him.

Winter held his breath and placed a hand on his rifle. If Faith Ann missed or couldn't bring herself to shoot—which happened even to seasoned hunters faced with such a trophy—he could make the shot for her. If she missed, he would have a second or two before the animal bolted, and he would fire before it took off.

Winter had never witnessed bucks in combat, but he knew that was exactly what was unfolding before them. Winter counted the points on the rack of the larger deer. Twelve points with such elegant symmetry was a rarity.

The eight-point marched into the green field, placing himself between the does and the mature interloper. Like gladiators, they circled each other slowly, heads low. The larger buck had perhaps three years and forty pounds on the eight-point, whose antlers were half as massive. The older deer's muscles were better defined, his neck twice as thick, and his muzzle turning gray. It was like a hound facing off with a mastiff.

The more experienced animal charged and although the eight tried to sidestep at the last moment, the larger deer hit him in the shoulder with his broad chest, knocking him off balance and skidding him sideways into the soft ground. The eight-point spun, lowered his head, and struck the larger animal head-on, locking antlers. With muscles tensed, they twisted their horns like wrestlers for advantage. The harsh clicking of antlers went on for a long minute until the smaller buck lost his footing and tumbled to the ground, expelling his breath in a hiss.

The bigger buck backed up and lowered his head. As

he tensed for the rush, the other deer quickly made it to his feet and shook his head.

Lurching, the eight rushed the twelve. The sound of their antlers colliding was like a gunshot. The twelve's weight sent the eight reeling, and he whirled and lowered his head again, but the larger buck raked a blow down his length that opened the hide on his back leg like a razor. The smaller deer was breathing hard as his grizzled elder circled him carefully, seeking a vulnerable spot to ram.

Winter was watching the battle with such intensity that the unexpected clap of gun thunder raised him off the bench.

3

A DULL BOOM IN THE DISTANCE BROUGHT SEAN Massey to full consciousness. It took her a second to orient herself to her surroundings, enough to realize the sound was actually a rifle report. Morning light gave the closed curtains inside the motor home a warm yellow glow. She yawned and looked at the splayed toddler sleeping peacefully on her back beside her. Winter and Faith Ann had managed to get up and get out of the thirty-two-foot-long motor home before dawn without waking her.

She slipped out of bed and dressed in a flannel shirt,

jeans, and ankle-high muck boots. Closing the bedroom door behind her, she looked out into the galley where Rush Massey, her fourteen-year-old stepson, sat at the table, dressed warmly for the day ahead. He had his fingertips on the page of an open book, the paper blank but for the raised dots of Braille. He tilted his head as his bright blue eyes seemed to focus on Sean.

From under the table, Nemo, Rush's Rhodesian ridgeback Seeing Eye dog lying with his chin on his forepaws, turned his eyes on Sean and wagged his heavy tail.

"Morning, Sean," Rush said cheerfully. "You hear that shot?"

"I sure did."

"I bet you a dollar it was Daddy's ought-six. I bet Faith Ann couldn't shoot one," Rush said. "I bet Daddy had to do it."

"You think that was them shooting?" Sean asked, taking a box of cereal off the counter and filling a bowl. "There are a lot of hunters around here."

"I know it was. The direction was right and the loudness too."

"And you think Faith Ann doesn't have what it takes?"

"She *is* a girl," he replied. "No offense. Girls don't shoot like men and they don't kill either."

Sean smiled. *If you only knew.* "None taken. You want breakfast?"

"I ate right after they left," he said. "I washed my bowl. I know it was them since the stand is east of here and about four hundred yards away." He pointed over his shoulder. "It was definitely from that direction. We're parked on a northeast by southwest bias."

Sean put her hand on Rush's head as she passed by to sit down across from him.

"You want a cup of coffee?" Rush asked.

"Would love one, you dear boy," she said, pouring milk into the bowl.

Rush rose, opened the cabinet, got a cup, and, using his finger to gauge the level of the rising hot coffee, filled it to an inch from the lip. After replacing the pot, he set the cup on the table before Sean and took his seat across from her. She looked into his eyes. If she hadn't known the orbs were painted acrylic, she would have sworn he was studying her.

Rush had lost his eyes in the plane crash that had killed his mother, Eleanor, a flight instructor who was giving her young son lessons when a Beechcraft Baron entered the landing pattern from above and behind the two-seater Cessna and swatted the smaller plane out of the sky. A seasoned pilot, Eleanor had somehow managed to retain enough control so that—even though the small plane, whose back was broken by the collision, fell to earth from an altitude of five hundred feet—she had crash-landed with enough forward speed that Rush wasn't killed. A section of the shattered windshield cut just deep enough into his skull to destroy both of his eyes without damaging his brain. Eleanor wasn't as lucky. Her brain stem had been functional enough to let doctors put her body on life support until Winter, then a deputy U.S. marshal, arrived to hold her just before the machine was switched off. As per her wishes, the doctors had managed to harvest most of her organs, and Sean had seen the collection of letters written by grateful recipients.

Eleanor's heart had gone into an eighteen-year-old

girl. Her liver had been sectioned to save two recipients, both middle-aged men, and her undamaged kidney had been implanted in a woman.

Sean finished her cereal and set down the bowl for Nemo, who rose and lapped the milk slowly. She gazed out the window beside her at the opening in the trees where the logging road entered the woods.

The land was owned by Billy Lyons, a high school friend of Winter's. He was a lawyer who had missed the hunt because he was in the middle of a trial in Memphis. Winter's other regular hunting buddy, Larry Ward, friend since middle school, was the chief financial officer for a large securities firm and had pressing obligations that kept him in London. Sean and Winter had decided to make it a family event and rented the motor home to add a degree of comfort not afforded by the one-room, wood-frame shack the men usually shared. The cabin was fine for a group of men, but between the wood-burning stove, mattresses that looked like they'd been salvaged from the side of the road, and an outhouse fifty feet from the back door, it didn't rise to the level of comfort Sean thought Faith Ann deserved. And Olivia Moment Massey, their child, was at the stage where she walked where she chose to go, wanted to do everything herself, and, when frustrated, was vocal at a disturbing volume. Enough said.

Nemo went to the door and stared at it, whining once—his signal for wanting to be let outdoors.

Sean looked out the window and saw something orange moving up the road through the woods. She smiled when she realized that it was Faith Ann wearing a Day-Glo vest. She was alone and without her backpack or her gun. As Sean stared at the approaching child, she saw crimson lines on her cheek, like war paint made in what appeared to be blood. And she was crying.

Sean ran from the motor home and met Faith Ann before she reached the parking area near the skinning shed. As Sean approached, Faith Ann tilted her head and stopped short.

"He's dead!" Faith Ann yelled.

4

PUTTING ON HIS COAT, RUSH RACED OUT, FOLLOWING Sean and Nemo, his head tilted upward, listening. "What's the deal?" he asked.

"He's dead," Faith Ann said in a strained, trembling voice.

"Who's dead?" Rush asked her.

"Rudolph," Faith Ann said, sniffing a little but smiling proudly. "A mean old twelve-pointer."

"No shit!?" Rush blurted.

"Rush Massey!" Sean exclaimed. "Watch your language."

"A deer has a name?" Rush asked. "Where's Daddy?"

"He's at the food plot," Faith Ann said. "I came back to get the pull-cart thingie to bring Rudolph back here to be skinned out."

"How'd you get the blood on your face?" Sean asked her.

"Your husband did it," Faith Ann said, now exasperated. "First blood. It's this thing you do."

"When you kill your first buck you have to get his blood put on you," Rush explained. "It's a hunting ritual. Sometimes, depending on local customs, you might even have to take a bite of the heart and swallow it."

"Euuuuuwww! I most certainly will not eat any deer heart!" Faith Ann exclaimed.

"I should hope not," Sean said.

"You really killed a deer?" Rush said. "I bet you freaked when you did it."

"It wasn't too bad," Faith Ann said. "A clean kill isn't gross. They get hit by cars, brought down by wild dogs, starve, all kinds of ways to die that are worse."

"I know all that. I can't believe you really killed a deer," Rush said, smiling. "Was it cool?"

"It was totally necessary," Faith Ann said. "You see, Rudolph was attacking a smaller deer to take his does away from him after he found them. Rudolph hurt the little deer's leg and was fixing to kill him. You could just tell. So I just did what had to be done."

"You killed a deer in deer-defense?" Rush said, laughing. "That's got to be the most ridiculous reason for killing a deer in history."

"You didn't see it," Faith Ann said defensively. "He was really big and mean as a snake. The littler deer was brave, but he was going to lose, and they fight to the death, you know," she said importantly.

"Deer don't fight to the death. Only people do that. Are you sure my daddy didn't shoot it?" Rush said. "I bet he did."

"Of course I shot it. He dropped where he stood like he was poleaxed."

"I bet you don't even know what a poleax is," Rush said.

"Duh, it's an axe on a pole," Faith Ann said.

Sean said, "You need me to help you take the cart back?"

"Go back inside. I'll help her," Rush said. "Olivia's awake. I'd rather eat a deer's heart than deal with her."

Faith Ann went to the skinning shed and opened the doors to the storage room. Inside, among the organized clutter, was a two-wheeled cart. She wrestled it out and righted it, opening it to lower the wheels.

Rush lay down in the sling, facing the sky. "Wake me up when we get there," he said.

Laughing, Faith Ann began pulling Rush toward the plot. Nemo ran ten feet ahead of the kids, the ridge of hair on his back standing like a Mohawk.

5

FAITH ANN'S DEER HUNG BY HIS SPREAD BACK LEGS in the open-air shed beside the RV. After Winter had skinned the animal, put the meat in the chiller, and placed the caped head on the concrete floor, Rush suddenly turned. "Somebody's coming," he said. "They took the chain off the gate."

The north gate to the property was seventy-five yards away down a gravel road that curved through the woods. After a few seconds Winter heard a vehicle approaching. He reflexively touched the handgun at his side. Since the front gate was kept locked, whoever was coming in either had a key or knew where the spare key to the padlock was hidden. Billy Lyons had said he wasn't coming down, nor were they expecting any of the other men that sometimes hunted on the four hundred acres. He put the wide-bladed skinning knife down and peeled off the surgical gloves he wore to keep his hands blood-free.

The truck was a silver-gray extended cab Toyota Tundra with large tires and a five-pointed star on the front license plate. The driver cut the motor and climbed out of the cab. There was something familiar about the tall man who walked over to the shed. He wore a short coat that broke above his sidearm, a Colt Python. The letters *TCS* were emblazoned on the brown baseball cap he wore.

"Hello," the man called out as he approached the shed.

An alert Nemo growled and looked up at Winter.

"It's okay, Nemo," Winter said.

"Hello, Winter," the stranger said. "You must be Rush and Faith Ann."

"Who are you?" Faith Ann asked as the tall man came into the shed.

"I'm Brad Barnett," he said. "I'm the sheriff in Tunica County."

"Brad Barnett," Winter said, shaking the sheriff's proffered hand. "Billy's buddy from Ole Miss. I thought you looked familiar. Been a long time." Barnett was six one or so, forty pounds heavier than he had been the last time Winter had seen him, but he looked as fit and quick as he had years before. He had a pleasant, boyish face and an easy smile, his brown eyes radiated intelligence.

"Twenty years, give or take," Brad said. "Who killed the monster?" he asked, bending down and turning the heavy antlers on the animal's head for a better look.

"I killed him," Faith Ann said proudly.

"I don't think I've ever seen a nicer buck taken in these parts," Brad said.

"It was her first one too," Rush said, smiling. "She killed it in deer-defense."

"Deer-defense?" Brad asked.

"He was beating up this other buck," the boy said. "Faith Ann decided the fight wasn't fair, so she rang the bell."

"You wanting to hunt?" Massey said.

"I wish I had time."

Nemo sniffed at Brad's leg, wagging his tail. The sheriff reached down, let the dog sniff the back of his hand, then rubbed the animal behind his ears.

"You smell my dog, Ruger? Last time I saw you, Winter, was homecoming weekend my junior year," Brad said. "You stayed with Billy. He set you up with a blind date he ended up marrying."

"Yeah." Winter smiled. "And Ole Miss lost that game."

"I believe so."

Winter saw Brad's eyes go to his handgun, a custom-made stainless .45 automatic with stag grips.

"Nice-looking piece," Brad said. "Wilson or Kimber?"

"Neither." Massey took out the .45, ejected the loaded magazine into his hand, pocketed it, ejected the shell from its chamber, let the hammer down gently, and handed the weapon over to Brad. "Custom gun maker named Kase Reeder made it."

"Beauty," Brad said, turning the gun to read what was inscribed on the weapon. "Flagstaff, Arizona. I'm not familiar with his work."

"It was a gift from my wife, Sean," Winter said. "Faith Ann's great uncle read about it in a handgun magazine. When Sean asked him what she could get me for my last birthday, he called Reeder and he made it for me. First .45 I've ever carried, but it's the most accurate gun I've ever owned."

Brad whistled and handed the Reeder Rekon Kommander back to Massey, who reloaded it and slipped it back into its holster, snapping the thumb brake closed.

"Billy told me you were the sheriff in Tunica now," Winter said.

"He told me you're off the job," Brad said. "Something about working for a big security company."

"I'm just a consultant on protection programs for their corporate clients."

"Who's mounting the head for you?" Brad asked.

"Calvin Patton," Winter said. "He's at his shop now. That's why I'm hurrying."

"Patton's about the best there is around here," Brad said. He looked at Faith Ann. "You know what kind of mount you want?"

"A left-hand sneak mount," she said. "I'm going to put it over our fireplace."

"Good choice," Brad said.

"Faith Ann always knows what she wants," Winter said.

"That way he'll always look like he's smelling that

other buck's heated-up does just around the corner in the kitchen," Rush said.

"What brings you way down here?" Winter asked Brad.

"Well, fact is, Billy told me you were out here. I called him to find out where you were."

Winter was perplexed. "Why are you looking for me?"

"Well, your name came up and I wondered, if you had some time, maybe you could take a couple of hours and visit Tunica County," Brad said. "I tried to call the number he gave me but there was no answer."

"I don't have my cell on."

"I hate to interrupt your hunt, but I sure could use your help."

The motor home door opened and Sean came out carrying Olivia on her hip. She strode over and stood beside Winter.

"My wife, Sean," Winter said. "Sean, this is Tunica County sheriff Brad Barnett. He's an old friend of Billy's. We spent a wild homecoming weekend together at Ole Miss some years back."

Sean's smile was warm and her eyes sparkled with interest and kindness. "It's a pleasure to meet you," she said. "This is Olivia, our daughter. She's two and very shy."

As if on command, Olivia hid her face in Sean's down vest, then peeked at Brad and smiled.

"Cooww go moo," she said, pointing at the deer.

"Cow," Rush said, laughing.

"What's going on in Tunica County?" Winter asked.

"I'd like to have your input on a case I have."

"What kind of case?" Winter asked.

"Homicide," Brad replied.

Sean Massey's smile remained in place, but her eyes changed.

"Cool," Rush said.

"I was a deputy U.S. marshal," Winter said. "If you need my opinion on how to locate a fugitive, or how to best serve a warrant, I'm your man. Other than that . . ." He shrugged.

"I understand all that. Just a quick look. Three hours, tops."

"I wouldn't be any help with it," Winter said.

"This one looks like a professional killing. It's the first one like it I've run across, and I think I'm in over my head."

"The Mississippi Bureau investigators are your best bet," Winter said.

"I have a nineteen-year-old victim who was shot from almost half a mile away with a high-powered rifle. It will be treated as an accidental shooting because it's hunting season. Other than a polished casing, I've got nothing but some boot prints and tire treads. She's a local girl who finished high school last year. She was a young black girl from a good, hard-working family."

"Maybe she was a target of opportunity."

"It's possible, but the place I'm talking about isn't one anybody would just happen upon."

Sean Massey was silent, thinking. "Rush, Faith Ann," she said. "Come in and wash your hands. Lunch is ready. Sheriff Barnett, will you join us?"

"I'd love to, but I'm sort of in a hurry."

Winter watched the family until the door closed, then turned his now-serious eyes on Brad. "What's the real deal here, Brad?" Winter said. "I know my reputation better than anybody. You have a killing with a rifle, and I'm close by hunting with a rifle? I haven't left this land in two days. And half the people on earth can shoot a rifle better than I do."

"Well, I don't think you were involved, but somebody wanted me to," Brad said, reaching into his pocket and taking out a plastic bag containing a business card. Winter took it and did a double take as he recognized the card.

It read WINTER JAMES MASSEY, DEPUTY U.S. MARSHAL. It was definitely his, with the Charlotte, North Carolina, address and phone numbers.

"That was left at the scene where the shooter set up. Best I can come up with is that he wanted me to think you were there. Anybody else might have believed that was the case, but I know better."

Winter had a hard time forming his thoughts, his eyes locked on the card.

"I can make time," Winter said firmly, handing back the card. Somebody was calling him out.

6

BACK INSIDE THE MOTOR HOME, WINTER WAS WASHing his hands at the bathroom sink when Sean appeared in the doorway behind him. "Your buddy is still sitting in his truck outside," Sean said.

"He's waiting for me," Winter said. He dried his hands and passed by her. Taking off his shirt, he went into the bedroom to change clothes. Sean followed him and eased the door closed. "Wants me to go with him to look at a crime scene."

"So you're going to take a quick trip to Tunica to look at this crime scene."

"Two, three hours. I'll put the head in the Jeep, if you don't mind taking it to Calvin. There's a map in the bedroom. Don't leave the gate unlocked and keep an eye open. Keep the Walther close."

"I always keep the Walther close. So why the concern?" she asked.

"The killer left one of my old marshal cards at the crime scene. That's why Brad's here."

"He doesn't think you . . . ?"

"No, he doesn't think I left it. At least he says he doesn't," Winter told her. "I have to check this out. Best to be very careful until I know what's going on. And get ready to pull out. We're done hunting."

He pulled on a pair of jeans, ran his belt through the loops and slipped it under the magazine pouch and his holster. He stuffed his wallet into his back pocket and put on his chukkas. Sean led him from the room and picked up his jacket.

"Kids, I have to go out for a while with Sheriff Barnett," he said to their inquisitive faces.

He was at the door when Sean said, "Mr. Massey?"

"Yeah?"

"Aren't you forgetting something?" She put her hands on her hips and frowned.

He made a show of patting his pockets while he suppressed a smile. "Wallet. Weapon. I don't think so."

"Winter Massey!" she said, shaking her head. "Think about it."

"She wants her good-bye kissy kiss," Rush said.

"Kiss her good, Winter!" Faith Ann called out.

"Do it, Daddy!" Rush said, puckering clownishly. "Plant one on her she'll remember."

Winter pushed his hair back dramatically, gathered Sean into his arms, leaned her back, and gave her a kiss that drew applause from Faith Ann and Rush. Olivia joined in, clapping and laughing, unaware of what the celebration was all about.

"Cowboy love!" Faith Ann squealed.

7

THE MISSISSIPPI DELTA IS AN ALLUVIAL PLAIN shaped like a spear point, seventy-five miles across at its widest and stretching two hundred and twenty-five miles north from Vicksburg to just south of Memphis, Tennessee. Winter often joked that if it weren't for the trees, you could stand on a kitchen chair and see the levee from the other side of the Delta.

The murder had occurred on Six Oaks, a cotton plantation eight miles from downtown Tunica. There was nothing obvious to distinguish it from most of the working plantations Winter was personally familiar with. Vast fields with the occasional narrow, dead-looking stream, thin ribbons of woodland serving as windbreaks. The cotton had been harvested, and the left-behind wisps of white cotton fiber gave the landscape the appearance of an oceanic thorn field after the stampede of a vast herd of terrified sheep.

The farmhouse was set back a quarter mile from a collection of equipment and storage sheds, on a spacious green meadow surrounded by bleak cotton fields. Six large white oak trees lined the driveway, which curved before a two-story white wooden house with a high-peaked roof covered with slate shingles. The wraparound porch had cypress lattice on the sides, which supported climbing ivy. To the right of the house, separated by an expanse of cobblestone, stood a four-car garage, whose white clapboard exterior mirrored that of the house. The grounds were dotted with mature magnolias and oaks, flowerbeds, azaleas, rosebushes, and boxwoods.

"First, I'll show you the shooter's position," Brad said. He drove past the driveway leading to the house. Fifty yards farther on, he turned down a thinly graveled road that led into the fields toward a tree line.

"We haven't had a hard freeze yet, and I didn't see any fresh deer tracks in the field between the tree and the house that could point to a hunting accident."

Winter nodded. After seeing his business card he had immediately ruled out an accidental shooting.

Brad parked near a downed tree accented with yellow crime-scene tape. "It's difficult to imagine that anybody could make a shot at this distance that *wasn't* an accident," Winter said.

"The right man could do it, given the conditions we had this morning," Brad said.

"You know much about long-range shooting?" Winter asked.

"I know as much as other Marine snipers."

"How accurate is a sniper rifle at this kind of range?"

"Match-grade .308 ammo is accurate at eight hundred to a thousand meters. The brass this guy left was from a .338 Lapua Magnum. Its trajectory is a whole lot flatter and longer than the .308 and can deliver what the shooter can see." Winter saw Brad's eyes lose their focus as he remembered. "It was like an alligator grabbed her head and tore most of it off. I've seen my share of bad death, but this is one I'll remember forever."

"This where you found my card?"

Brad pointed to the trunk. "About here, weighed down with the polished shell casing."

"And the footprints?"

Brad pointed at the ground. "From here . . ." He turned to point through the woods. "Straight back that way a quarter mile to tire tracks."

Winter was looking down at the leaves when he saw something red stuck into the ground through a leaf, something small and perfectly pointed. Kneeling, he lifted the leaf and saw what it was.

"Got an evidence bag?" Winter asked.

"What is it?"

"Looks like the shooter left another calling card."

"That a toothpick?" Brad asked, handing Winter a plastic bag.

"Got a business card with you?"

Winter took a card from Brad, folded it, placed the flats on either side of the point and slid the toothpick out of the ground, dropping it into the bag.

Brad looked at the toothpick, darkened where it had been in the damp dirt.

"He chewed the end," Winter said, smiling. "It isn't a driver's license, but it's better than nothing."

"Son of a bitch. That means it'll have the perp's DNA on it."

Winter put the open bag to his nose and sniffed. "Damn," he said.

Brad leaned over and sniffed it also. "What is that?"

"Oil of clove," Winter said, feeling the way he had felt as a kid when he happened upon a snake he hadn't been prepared to see. *Son of a bitch!*

"You all right?" Brad asked.

"That smell triggered a bad memory." In the realm of understatements, that one took a blue ribbon.

"Judging from the way it knocked the color out of your face, must be a powerful memory attached to that toothpick," Brad said.

"I've run across toothpicks soaked in clove oil before."

"Somebody you chased for the marshals service?"

"The man I'm thinking about is someone I knew in New Orleans a couple of years ago. It's complicated. I'm not going into it right now."

"You're shitting me?"

"There are good reasons not to discuss him just yet."

"What can you tell me? I mean, it's sort of important I know who did this. And you seem to know."

"The guy I have in mind is a professional killer. Don't know about his shooting at this kind of range, though he most likely has the training. But the man I'm thinking about probably didn't do this. It seems more likely somebody wants to make me think that guy was here."

"You don't think he'd kill an innocent girl?"

"There's no telling how many innocent civilians he's killed. No question he would do it, but if he did, somebody would be paying him a lot of money. That or he's working on his own with another purpose."

"What other purpose?"

"Killing me," Winter replied.

• • •

Brad pulled up to the house's garage and the two men climbed out of the Tundra. Through the only open garage door, a dirt-streaked white Lincoln sat with its rear end visible.

"She's home," Brad said, suddenly stern-faced.

"Who?" Winter asked.

"The owner, Leigh Gardner. She's been out of town picking up her daughter, Cynthia, from college. The victim stayed overnight with Hampton, Leigh's son. He's ten. The maid heard the shot, saw her down, and called nine-one-one."

Winter said, "What time did it happen?"

"Call came in at six-thirty-nine this morning. Jesus!" Brad said as they walked toward the house. "Some idiot hosed off the crime scene! Where's the crime-scene tape?"

On the wide wet cobblestone walkway, Winter could see no evidence of bloodstains. Water was pooled in a low spot, and the strong smell of bleach rose from the bricks.

The back door of the house flew open. An attractive rosy-cheeked woman, her blonde hair in a ponytail, slammed the door behind her and strode directly toward them. She was no more than five six and wore jeans, a cotton shirt under a wool cardigan, suede cowboy boots, and a frown.

"Damn," Brad muttered. "By the way, Leigh can come on a little strong."

"Brad, what the blue blazes happened out here! Who in the hell killed Sherry?"

"Hello, Leigh. Leigh Gardner, this is Winter Massey. He's—"

"What are you doing about it?" she snapped at Brad without looking at Winter.

"If you'll calm down, I'll discuss it with you."

Fists on her hips, Leigh Gardner fixed the sheriff with what could only be described as a warrior's glare. "I'm as calm as I'm going to get."

"Who cleared off the crime scene?" he asked her.

"I guess Estelle did," Leigh said.

"It was cordoned off with crime-scene tape. Where is it?"

"You'd have to ask her."

"Tampering with a crime scene is serious."

"We're talking about Estelle. She sees a mess and she cleans it up. Did you tell her not to?"

"Well, no. I didn't think . . ."

"Did you leave someone here to protect it?"

"I left crime-scene tape around it."

"Are you planning to arrest Estelle for cleaning up?"

"Arresting her is hardly the point. It's blatant obstruction of justice and willful destruction of evidence. It was a clearly roped-off crime scene."

"How many crime scenes do you suppose Estelle's been around? If you weren't done out here, you should have stayed until you were. Roy Bishop told me you took off without telling him where you were going."

"If it's any of your business, I went to talk to Winter Massey here who agreed to come out and offer his expertise. He's a highly respected ex–law enforcement officer with a great deal of experience with the type of individuals who would do this sort of thing."

"Well, maybe Mr. Massey ought to be our sheriff. A potted plant could see you're no good at it." She turned her glare on Winter. "So, Mr. Murder Expert, who killed Sherry?"

"That's totally uncalled for," Brad said. "I understand you're upset, but this attitude is counterproductive. He just got here, and we're just starting to gather information to figure this out. If you'll calm down, we can get started."

"Brad Barnett, you're about as useful as a milk bucket under a bull," she said. "Well, quit standing around wasting time. Y'all come on in out of the cold."

8

WINTER AND BRAD FOLLOWED LEIGH GARDNER INside through a mudroom, where he could see down a wide hallway all the way to the front doors at the far end of the house. They turned right adjacent to a utility room, entering into an expansive kitchen with high ceilings. The floor was well-worn wide oak boards. An island was topped with a thick, ancient butcher's block. There were two gas ranges standing side by side and a built-in refrigerator that looked like it had come from a florist shop—its contents on steel wire shelves visible through the glass doors.

At the dining table a young boy with large blue eyes and thick auburn hair sat behind a plate of bacon, grits, and eggs. He wore a black cape with a red lining over his pajamas and he looked up and blinked owlishly when the men walked in. A matronly ebony-skinned woman in a bright white uniform stood at the sink washing dishes. A ceiling fan turned lazily to redistribute the warm air issuing loudly from vents.

A girl with long light-brown hair nodded at the men, tugged back the sleeves of her sweatshirt, and placed the blood-sugar monitor she had just used on the green Formica-topped counter. Her sweatshirt advertised a place called Junior's House of Blues. Her tattered jeans stopped above her bare feet, the toes of which were painted a shade of tangerine.

"Winter Massey, meet Hampton and Cynthia, Leigh's children, and Estelle Johnson, their maid."

"Estelle is our *housekeeper,*" Leigh corrected.

The children merely stared at Winter, but Estelle turned and smiled at him. "Nice to meet you, Mr. Massey," she said.

"Without her the house does not function. Estelle, the sheriff is not pleased that you washed off the walk," Leigh said, crossing her arms.

"Good Lord, Sheriff Brad," Estelle said. "I couldn't leave that for Miss Leigh and Cyn to see. After your people left it was a terrible mess out there. They got most everything up, but . . ." Her lip trembled. "Anyhow, I rolled that plastic line up on a stick and left it in the garage for you." She wiped a tear from her cheek with the back of her hand. "I can't believe that baby's dead. Sherry was a bright, churchgoing child. I've known her since she was born."

"And I know you were upset when I first asked, but

since then have you thought of anybody who would want to hurt her?" Brad asked.

"No, sir. Everybody loved her," Estelle said. "She was an angel. Pure angel. She was going to be a nurse. Got herself a scholarship to Fisk. Only reason she didn't start college was because her mama was down again with the breast cancer."

Estelle turned back to the dishes in the sink.

"Sherry worked for us since she was Hamp's age," Leigh interjected. "She was a serious, sweet girl and the idea that anyone would purposefully kill her is absurd. Some hunter must have shot at a deer and the bullet went astray. A high-powered rifle bullet can travel a couple of miles."

"No," Brad said. "Whoever did it shot from the tree line straight behind the house."

"From way out there?" Leigh asked, pointing out the kitchen window at the trees that were amazingly small in the distance. "Preposterous." She continued, "I've shot rifles myself and those woods are too far away for it to have been done on purpose. There must have been a deer in the field. He missed it and hit Sherry."

"I found the place he fired from," Brad told her. "And he sat there and waited for her to come out of the house."

"A sniper?" Leigh asked, frowning.

Brad nodded.

"There's only one sniper around here that I know of," Leigh said, putting her hand to her mouth in a gesture of surprise, then turning her eyes away. "I didn't mean that. I'm sorry. I'm not myself."

"Mama!" Cyn said.

"There's this one man," Hampton said in a low voice.

"Sherry said he wanted to talk to her. He got mad and grabbed her when she told him to leave her alone."

"Talk about what?" Brad asked.

"Talk doesn't mean *talk*," Cyn said, smiling coyly. "That *talk* means he wanted to—you know."

Hamp continued, "He bugged her. He'd sit in his hoopty and watch her house sometimes. She said he followed her around a lot."

"He ever sit and watch this house?" Brad asked.

Hamp's brow creased in contemplation. "I don't think so. If he did, I never saw him."

"Did you see him last night, Hamp?" Brad asked.

"I saw him last night at the Shell station when we were going to the video store. He waved at Sherry and she told me not to look at him."

"Do you know his name?"

Hamp nodded. "Alfoons."

"Alphonse," Cyn said. "Sherry told me all about him. He totally grossed her out."

"He got thrown out of the Army," Hamp said.

"Why?" Brad asked.

"He told Sherry he punched a white general for disrespecting him. Sherry said he gambles away all of his money and he owes people he doesn't pay back. Sherry said even if he was kind of handsome and dressed up fancy, he was no good."

"Handsome?" Cynthia blurted. "He looks like a bow-legged monkey in a pimp suit. He has creepy eyes and freckles."

"Cyn!" Leigh snapped. "You know better than to say such a thing. If that is what they teach you at LSU, young lady, maybe you'd be better off at the junior college in Senatobia."

"I didn't say it because he's black," Cyn said. "Girls like bad boys, but not stupid, ugly ones."

"Jefferson," Estelle said, without turning around. "That's his name. Alphonse Jefferson. It isn't Christian to talk bad about people, but that is one lazy, liquor-boned, good-for-nothing boy that comes from shiftless people."

"What's liquor-boned?" Hamp asked.

"On account he's mean-tempered when he drinks, which is most of the time. He stays at his grandmother's and hangs out at Bugger's juke joint with other no-accounts. He does look like a organ grinder's monkey in those flashy getups, like Miss Cyn said."

"Don't encourage her, Estelle."

Estelle threw up her wet hands.

Brad opened his murder book and made a note. "I know who he is. We've had him in the jail for drunk and disorderly a couple of times. I'll check his Army records to see about his marksmanship ability."

"Well, there you have it. Pick him up," Leigh said. "Obviously he did it. Put him where he belongs, doing hard labor on Parchman Farm for the rest of his life. Sherry Adams had a productive life ahead of her. She mattered, and if you don't remember anything else, remember that."

"Parchman Farm be the only work he ever did," Estelle threw in. She put the last plate in the rack, dried her hands, and let the water out of the sink.

"I'll check him out, Leigh."

"Good," she said.

"Hamp," Brad asked. "Have you remembered anything else about last night since we talked this morning?"

"Nope," the boy said, absently spoon-stirring the grits on his plate. "I showed Sherry some new tricks I got yesterday."

"Tricks?" Brad asked.

"Magic stuff," Hamp said.

"Hamp is a magician," Estelle said proudly. "He about the best there is around here. He can make about anything disappear."

"And I always get them back," Hamp added.

"The Great Memphister," Estelle said, nodding. "That why he wears that cape he bought at the magic store in Memphis. You wouldn't believe what those little thingamajigs cost."

"It's the Great *Mephisto,*" Hamp corrected.

"He can sure make his mama's money disappear with them tricks he buys," Estelle said, laughing.

"I use my own allowance," he said defensively.

"That's what allowances are for," Leigh said, smiling.

Brad looked through his notebook. "Sherry came yesterday morning just before your mother left for Baton Rouge. At around seven last night, Sherry drove you to town to the video store and y'all got two movies. You both watched them until around midnight. There were no phone calls or visitors during that time. And you didn't see or hear anything out of the ordinary."

"Except for Alphonse Jefferson at the Shell station," Hamp said.

Brad made a notation about the encounter. "The Shell station."

Hamp nodded. "Yay-ah, Mr. Barnett."

"Yes, *Sheriff* Barnett," Leigh chided.

"Yes, Sheriff Barnett," Hamp said.

"Stop playing with your food," Leigh said.

Hamp frowned and put the spoon down on his plate.

"And you were asleep until the gunshot woke you up?" Brad asked.

"Yeah. It was real loud. I heard Estelle screaming and then I came down and she made me get in the utility room while she called nine-one-one. I didn't see Sherry."

"Thanks, Hamp," Brad said, patting the boy's shoulder.

"Leigh, why did you drive to Baton Rouge?" he asked, turning to her.

"To bring Cyn home for Christmas break."

"I mean, why did you drive all the way to Baton Rouge instead of letting her fly home?"

"Good question," Cyn said, frowning.

Leigh looked at Brad like he was an idiot. "Do you have any idea what it costs to fly from Baton Rouge to Memphis? The cotton is already ginned. Brad, have you ever known me to waste money?"

"There's meals and a motel room and time away from the place," he said.

"Motel?" Cyn said, laughing. "Mom spent the night in my room at the dorm and she made ham sandwiches for the trip."

Cyn's cell phone buzzed and she took it out of her pocket and looked at the display. With well-practiced thumbs she typed a message and closed it.

"Not wasting money is why *I* still own Six Oaks and not some damned conglomeration of suit-wearing, citified windbags who don't know a cotton boll from a golf ball," Leigh said flatly.

9

PIERCE MULVANE LEANED BACK IN HIS CHAIR AND gazed affectionately at the framed Walter Anderson watercolors of Gulf Coast wildlife that decorated his office. Anderson's work—sloppy and unfinished looking, in Mulvane's opinion—had appreciated enormously over the past few years. Pierce wouldn't have purchased them himself, and he technically didn't own them, since they had been part of the purchase of the Castle casino. The fixtures, including all existing equipment, had remained with the structure as part of the sale agreement. He didn't know anything about art, but the increased value endeared the paintings to him. He had made a wise choice by talking Klein into buying this marginally profitable, garishly designed casino in north Mississippi, instead of building one on the Gulf Coast.

Mulvane had been employed by Royale Resorts International for twelve years. The Castle had been his idea. He had convinced the owner, Kurt Klein, to purchase the run-down casino to see if the area was viable for a major investment in a future RRI self-contained billion-dollar casino resort—the likes of which had never been seen in Tunica County. After the new resort was built, RRI would sell the existing casino to another group and recoup their investment, plus pocket the profits it had made. Or they might even retain the casino as an operation that catered to low rollers. The Roundtable had only two hundred hotel rooms, four restaurants, five bars, and two acres of gambling floor. The new place, to be built over three thousand acres, would be the grandest operation RRI owned, and Mulvane would manage it.

Pierce's brothers had all followed in their father's footsteps and joined the Boston-based Irish mob. Pierce, more ambitious than the other Mulvanes, had started his career in crime as a bookie, but after three years he had been put in charge of a floating high-stakes poker game. From there Pierce had gone to Atlantic City and worked his way into casino management. After two years rising through the ranks at the Atlantic Ocean Club, he had been hired by Resorts Royale International. He had been running RRI's Atlantic City casino when he suggested to Kurt Klein the concept for the new resort in Tunica County, an area he believed had more growth potential than Las Vegas. Pierce had targeted the Castle, a casino that would have been a gold mine except for the fact that it was being crippled by the skim taken off the top by greedy, silent-partner mobsters. Providentially, and with the help of a phone call to the right people, the mobsters had been caught and RRI had purchased the Castle at fire-sale rates. Due to Pierce's management, an honest count upstairs, effective promotions, and a cosmetic remodeling, the place, renamed the Roundtable, had indeed become a gold mine.

The present Roundtable, originally built with a facade that resembled a medieval castle complete with battlements from which a series of long and colorful banners flew, had become so profitable that Pierce had finally convinced Kurt that the spot was ripe for a major resort operation. Pierce had promised to have the new operation ready to start construction within a year, but he had run into an unforeseen problem. He had explained the dilemma to Kurt Klein, but it was clear that any revision in the schedule would not be tolerated. His boss, a German billionaire businessman unaccustomed to financial disappointment, demanded strict adherence to his instructions.

Pierce left his office and strolled to the elevator where his personal assistant, Patrick "Tug" Murphy, waited. He looked, despite an expensive suit tailored to hide his handgun, like a professional boxer who'd been knocked out and collapsed, the side of his face landing on a pile of sharp rocks. He had not been a prizefighter, but he had been disfigured in a car accident years earlier when an explosion had sent super-heated safety glass into his face. The scars resembled acute acne, mercilessly pitting the skin on his right cheek, the side of his chin, and forehead. As a result, his facial expression gave less information than the backside of a speed limit sign.

"Time for a tour," Pierce said.

"Yes, sir," Tug said, looking down at his watch. Tug was intelligent, had astounding reflexes, no conscience, and executed orders perfectly. Klein's people in New York had recommended Tug. He had only been with Pierce a few months, but Pierce trusted him as much as he did Albert White, his chief of security.

Pierce checked himself out in the wall of mirrors. His crimson hair was perfectly combed, his naturally bushy eyebrows neatly trimmed. He centered the knot of his silk tie perfectly between the stiff collars of his Swiss-made shirt and pulled down the hem of his double-breasted charcoal Armani jacket.

"How do I look?" he asked, knowing it was a rhetorical question.

"Like you stepped out from a page in *GQ*, boss," Tug said.

"Anything else on that incident out at Six Oaks?"

"Nothing yet. Albert's still trying to find out more. It was a young black girl, is all I know."

"If it were Pablo, that wouldn't be the case, would it? He's the best there is, right? Mistaking his target would be impossible," he said sarcastically.

Tug nodded. "Big fuckup for a big professional."

"Then," Pierce said, "it must have been a hunting accident. Still this is definitely not a good thing."

Pierce wasn't yet fifty, and he was at the top of his game. Stepping into the mirrored cab, he was confident that he was going to make the resort happen on schedule. The alternative was unthinkable.

10

"I'M NOT GOING HOME WITHOUT YOU," SEAN SAID with a finality Winter was all too familiar with. She was holding Olivia and standing in the RV's master bedroom while he packed clean clothes into his canvas duffel. "Your problem is you have never learned to say no."

"If it's Styer," Winter said, "I have to stop him. If it isn't, I'd like to know who wants me to think it is. If Brad didn't know who I was, I'd be a suspect under a bright light in some interrogation room."

"Say it is Styer. Maybe if we go home, he'll just leave," she said. "Maybe he's done here and he'll move on."

"And let me go? Not likely."

"But why would he be after you?"

"Who knows? Maybe he's had time to think about what happened in New Orleans and he regrets leaving a loose end. He knows I won't ever forgive him for what he did to Hank and Millie. I'm his enemy. Maybe he figures to end our unfinished business with one of his little games."

"You aren't a killer. Are you prepared to kill him? You know he's trying to kill you, and if anybody can, he can."

"He may figure that killing innocent people is a good way to get me involved. The card and the toothpick mean I'd figure it was him. I have a feeling he'll keep killing until it's time to move on me, while he watches me from close by. It has to end here, and fast."

"You can get those CIA cutouts to deal with him. They would, wouldn't they? They're still looking for him. Let those bastards handle their own kind."

"I won't go that route. Besides, if they tried and missed, I'd be in worse shape than I am now. I've thought this through, Sean."

"How did he know you'd be out here in the middle of nowhere, and now?"

"I don't think he'd harm you or the kids. But he might try something to get me to come after him."

"I thought he underwent some sort of spiritual conversion in New Orleans when he walked away from his contract to kill you."

"So did I. But I think there's only one way to deal with Paulus Styer."

A tear rolled down her cheek, which Winter gently wiped away.

"Massey, nobody ever sees him coming. You aren't forgetting that you didn't."

"I wasn't aware that he even existed then. That isn't the case here. I don't care how well he disguises himself. This time I'll know him when I see him."

"Daddy, gep me op!" Olivia said, reaching out her hands. Sean handed her to Winter and, taking her, he kissed his daughter on her cheek.

"I'll check into a motel in Tunica and call you. Go turn in the RV and take the first flight back home tomorrow. Will you do that so I won't have to worry?"

"I guess falling in love with a man who attracts violence is the downside of our otherwise perfect relationship," she said, hugging him and her daughter. "Good thing the upside makes it all worthwhile."

"I'm sorry, Sean," Winter said. "You don't know how sorry I am."

Sean smiled. "Massey, it isn't like I didn't know what you were when I met you. You'll do what you want to do."

Thirty minutes later Winter put the venison tenderloins and the quarters of deer meat into the camp's cooler, figuring he'd return in a day or two and take it to the processor in Batesville, or let Billy Lyons give it to somebody who would make use of it. Winter threw his duffel into the rear of the rented Jeep, turned the RV around, and Sean followed the RV ten miles to Interstate 55, where they switched vehicles. Sean and Winter honked enthusiastic see-you-soons for the half mile before they arrived at the turnoff to Tunica. Faith Ann and Rush waved and made comical faces from the RV's rear window until it pulled away. And as Sean drove the motor home north toward Memphis, she carried the majority of Winter's heart with her.

11

THE TUNICA COUNTY SHERIFF'S OFFICE WAS LOcated within the jail facility, a building with all the architectural charm of a shoebox, just down the road from a decrepit cotton gin. Winter parked in the lot across from a pole flying the Mississippi State and United States flags, locked the rented Jeep wagon, and strode up the wide concrete walkway to the front doors, opening them for an elderly woman and a small boy wearing a hooded jacket and threadbare shoes. In the reception area, a line of chairs faced a reception nook where two clerks stood behind bulletproof glass. On the far wall was a row of framed black and white portraits of past sheriffs of Tunica County. Several of the early sheriffs looked like hard-faced lawmen from the Old West, with sweeping handlebar mustaches, strong jaws, and serious eyes sheltered by bushy brows. In the more recent photos, they looked less like gunslingers and more like businessmen who had taken the job for a change in routine. Winter wondered if the last photo was of the sheriff who had been arrested by the Feds for corruption.

Speaking through a slot in the window, Winter asked the clerk to let the sheriff know he was there.

After a couple of minutes, an attractive black woman dressed in a gray business suit came out into the reception area smiling at Winter.

"Mr. Massey," she said, holding out her hand, which he shook. "I'm Bettye Barry, the sheriff's assistant."

"Nice to meet you."

"Sheriff Barnett is expecting you. I'll take you back."

Winter crossed through the metal-detector gate and set off the alarm, which the receptionist ignored. They went down a short hall and took a right at the first intersection, pausing at a steel door with a built-in glass panel. Bettye used her card to open the lock and showed him through, then opened the door to the sheriff's office spaces. The reception area was small, but the sheriff's office wasn't.

Inside, Winter spotted Brad Barnett at his desk talking on the phone. As Winter entered, Brad hung up.

"That was the MBI," Brad said.

"They coming in?" Winter asked.

"They aren't overly enthusiastic about it. Said it looked like a county matter—a hunting accident I could solve. They're going to review the evidence at the state lab, the crime-scene pictures, and the autopsy report when it comes back from the ME's office in Jackson. They don't see a likelihood of solving this if it isn't an accident, a jilted boyfriend, or nobody confesses or strikes again. If this is a hate crime they'll get involved, but it's obvious they don't want to jump in on a dead-ender. I think it's more about a dead black girl from a poor family. They assume all county sheriffs here are crooked based on our department's recent history. This guy you think committed the murder, who's he on the run from? The FBI?"

"He's not officially wanted by anyone in this country. If you'll get the toothpick ready to ship, I can check it against a sample of his DNA I have."

"That takes months."

"Get it packed for shipping. I have a friend in the FBI who told me about a technique for getting DNA run in a matter of hours. I'll call her."

"I have someone checking the crime database to see if any toothpicks have shown up in any other killings anywhere. What else can you tell me?"

"We'll see if I need to tell you more. Right now I can't."

"Why not? Is it a government secret?"

"Brad, you don't want to know. If I think you should, I'll tell you."

"I guess I'll have to take your word on it. For the time being, anyway. But I don't like it."

Winter shrugged. "I sent my family home."

"So, you'll help me solve this case?"

Winter nodded. "I'll do everything I can."

"You'll need temporary official standing. Just so happens I have an opening that needs filling in my homicide department."

"You have a homicide department?"

"Of course I do. You think this is some hick sheriff's department?"

Brad reached into his desk, took out a used badge case, and tossed it across the desk to Winter.

"That was Deputy Bratton's. He went to Gulfport after Katrina to help his family and hasn't said if he'll return. Just to cover this legally, we'll get your picture taken in a minute. You'll work directly with me, and you can give orders to anybody in my department as you need to. The Sherry Adams case is your only official responsibility. If that suits you, we can figure out compensation."

"Put me down as an employee, and pay me a buck."

"At least let me cover your expenses."

"Can you recommend a motel?"

"I rattle around in a big old house with four bedrooms. There's just me and my dog, Ruger."

"I don't want to inconvenience anybody."

"You kidding? Guest room is private, has cable TV, clean linens, and a bathroom with big bars of soap."

"That'll do," Winter said.

"What size uniform do you wear?"

Winter's shocked reaction brought laughter from the sheriff. "Just messing with you, Massey. Raise your right hand."

Winter smiled. He had the feeling that the sheriff was like an iceberg—what was below the surface was far more substantial than what wasn't.

12

WHILE BRAD WENT TO GET THE TOOTHPICK READY for shipping, Winter picked up the office phone and dialed a cell number in Washington, D.C. He smiled when a familiar voice answered, "Alexa Keen."

"Alexa, it's Winter."

"Winter. Have you gotten yourself arrested?" she asked.

"What makes you ask that? Oh, the caller ID."

"Tunica County Sheriff's Office."

"Not yet," he said.

"Sean told me you were doing your deer hunt in Como." She laughed. "So how's that family-bonding-over-blood thing going for you?"

"Faith Ann killed her first deer. A major buck too."

"I still think that's a shame, Massey," Alexa said. "Teaching that child to murder poor defenseless animals."

"She'd beg to differ, and obviously you've never been assaulted by a deer. Their little hooves are like razors. Anyway, it's all in the name of game management and a well-rounded education, which was her argument to get me to let her go hunting."

"Cheaper than a shopping trip to Europe, I suppose. She is an extraordinary young lady," Alexa said. "Must be hard on you, being so obviously average and surrounded by extraordinary people. So what are you doing in Tunica? Not gambling, I hope. It's a superhighway to ruin, you know."

Winter told her about the Adams murder, the card, and the used toothpick he'd found. "I need DNA really fast. Awhile back you told me about some new DNA deal that takes hours, not days," he said.

"I did indeed. It's called EDM."

"Wasn't the lab in Nashville?"

"ProCell. I suppose I can have DNA expedited for your sheriff buddy. You get it there ASAP. The procedure they're doing is fast, but results aren't going to be accepted in court. They need three days for accuracy."

"Can I do that without having those results included in any official report along with the tests? I'd cover the costs, of course."

"Sure, but why?"

"No big deal. Just a favor for a friend."

"A favor for a friend is loaning them your car," Alexa said. "Your friends tend to ask you to close the gates to hell."

13

ON THE WAY TO LOOK FOR ALPHONSE JEFFERSON, Brad decided to drop in at the Adamses' home and pay his respects to Sherry's parents. A tall, distinguished-looking black man with graying hair stood alone on the porch of a small home in the predominately black section of Tunica.

Beneath a smoke gray sky, Brad parked on the street and the men got out of the cruiser. They followed behind a fireplug of a woman wearing a black-cloth coat with rabbit fur trim. The hat perched on her head looked like a two-tiered chocolate cake someone had decorated with a trio of long red feathers. Folded potholders protected her bare hands from the heat of the covered casserole dish she carried.

A professionally painted message on the tire cover of the conversion van parked in the Adamses' driveway read LIFE IS GOD'S GIFT TO YOU. HOW YOU LIVE IT IS YOUR GIFT TO GOD.

"Welcome, Sister Bertha," the man on the porch said in a deep melodious voice.

"Brother Adams," the woman said. "Sad day for the world, but it's a day of rejoicing in Heaven, because an angel has arrived at the pearly gates, praise His holy name."

"Go on inside, Sister Bertha," Mr. Adams said, opening the door. "Mother's in here."

After the woman had gone into the house, Brad took the steps and stood before Sherry Adams's father. Winter followed him silently.

"John, my condolences," Brad said, offering his hand, which John Adams took and shook firmly. "We're going to find out who did this."

"Sheriff Barnett," he said, smiling sadly. "Thank you so much for coming by to pay your respects. A little while ago your daddy brought us a beautiful baked ham. Dr. Barnett is a saint of a man."

"John Adams, this is Winter Massey. He's from North Carolina and he's offered to help."

John Adams turned his eyes on Winter and extended a strong hand.

"May the Lord speed and guide you in your work, Mr. Massey," he said. "Thank you for your help."

"I'm sorry for your loss," Winter said.

A familiar, road-film-streaked Lincoln pulled as far into the driveway as possible and stopped, its rear end blocking the sidewalk. The driver's door flew open and Leigh Gardner stepped out, slammed the door behind her, and waited for Estelle to get out before they both walked purposefully to the porch. Estelle nodded at the sheriff and Winter, kissed John Adams's cheek, and went inside. Through the open door Winter saw a large solemn group of people standing around in the living room.

"John," Leigh said, hugging John Adams. "I told Bob Hanson to make sure our Sherry has the best of everything. You and Mary just make the selections and Six Oaks will cover the expenses."

John Adams straightened. "You don't have to do that, Ms. Leigh."

"Don't be difficult, John. I loved Sherry, and I won't take no for an answer."

John nodded solemnly, his eyes filling with tears. "We thank you, Ms. Leigh. Sherry loved y'all too."

Leigh hugged him again and held the embrace for several long seconds. "Sherry was a member of my family too."

"Leigh," Brad said in greeting.

"Sheriff," Leigh said, wiping her eyes with a tissue. "How is your investigation coming?"

"It's going forward," he said.

Leigh studied the sheriff. "I'm going to offer a ten-thousand-dollar reward for the arrest and conviction of the party responsible."

"I think offering a reward is premature, Leigh," Brad said.

"And why is that?" she asked, bristling.

"Because it'll create worthless tips I'll have to run down," Brad said. "Hold off for a couple of days and let us work the case first."

"And do you share Brad's opinion, Mr. Massey?"

"Yes, I do," Winter said.

"John?" Leigh asked Sherry's father. "What do you think?"

Mr. Adams nodded. "The Lord works His will in mysterious ways. If the sheriff says he needs time more than money, I expect I agree with him. The Lord will punish the guilty, and He alone will decide if the man who killed Sherry is going to be delivered into the law's hands, or into His own for judgment. Render unto God that which is God's, and render to Caesar what is Caesar's."

Leigh considered his words and nodded. "Then it's your call," Leigh told Brad. "I'm going to wait until Monday. If you don't find the killer by then, I'm going to give God a hand with Caesar's end."

She turned and went into the house, closing the door behind her.

"John, if you hear anything that I should know, you call me."

"You know I will, Sheriff Barnett. When will Sherry's body be coming home?" he asked.

"Tomorrow," Brad said. "I'll make sure she gets back so you can plan your service for Saturday."

Winter wondered if the Adams family already knew that the casket would have to be closed.

John put a hand on Brad's shoulder, smiled affectionately, and turned his attention to a cluster of women with plates of food coming up the sidewalk toward the house.

14

CYNTHIA GARDNER SPENT TEN MINUTES WITH DR. Barnett, had some blood drawn, and left the doctor's office. She didn't want to go straight back home and sit there with the gloom and doom, but most of her friends were either still at school or townie losers she'd rather not see. She was headed to her car when her cell phone beeped, indicating a new text message.

U meet me big river barn now? J.

Cynthia smiled as she typed a reply.

sure n 20

She climbed in behind the wheel of her Toyota, which her mother hadn't allowed her to have at LSU her freshman year. As she started it, she wondered if this was a good idea. With everything so crazy over Sherry's death, she wasn't sure if meeting the older man was smart. But she wanted to find out what was up, and he was great in the sack. She hadn't enjoyed his energetic charms since that summer, and she was eager to see if he was just as good as she remembered. Older men just knew more about pleasing a woman—it was a shame, but they really did.

Putting the car into gear, Cynthia snapped on her seat belt and flew out of the parking lot. As she drove, she picked up her phone and called her mother.

"Hi, Cyn," her mother said. "What did the doctor say?"

"Everything's totally cool. He said to just keep doing what I'm doing. Listen, I'm going to run to Memphis."

"That's not a good idea," Leigh said. "With everything that's happening. You come home."

"I need to get a dress for Sherry's funeral. It's not like I go to many funerals. I want to look—you know—right."

Her mother sighed. "Simple black dress. Nothing fancy."

"And nothing expensive. I know, Mother. I'll hold it to a buck fifty."

"One hundred max. And straight home."

"I need to go see Grammy too," Cynthia said. "It's been months. I'll stay over tonight." Cyn doubted that her mother could very well deny her a visit with her grandmother, even though the two women hated each other. Truthfully, Cyn didn't care much for the old bat either.

"This is a bad time. Hamp and I will go along."

"God, Mother. Shop with *him* along! Please!"

"You call me and tell me what you are doing. I mean it. My plate is piled to the clouds right now," Leigh said with resignation.

Cynthia hung up, and drove out of town. After a few miles, she turned on a gravel road passing through the opened gate, through a hundred yards of trees, and down a dirt road to the massive equipment barn she'd been to on one other occasion. The building and its graveled parking lot were surrounded by tall hurricane fencing. She recognized the white van parked near the personnel door, to the right of the massive retractable doors through which heavy equipment came and went. She parked, leaving her purse in the car, and patted her hair as she walked to the door.

The interior of the building was half the size of a football field and the roof rose to a peak fifty feet above the packed-earth floor. Scores of bulldozers and other pieces of land-clearing equipment were parked shoulder to shoulder in the interior before her, like soldiers preparing for another assault on the land outside. The last time she'd been there, the recently constructed steel building had been empty and their loud lovemaking had echoed eerily.

It was so cold she could see her breath in the still air that reeked of grease and diesel fuel.

"Jaa-ckeee," she called out, laughing. "I'm hee-ere!"

Cynthia straightened at the sound of someone behind her and turned to the sight of a wholly unattractive stranger with his hands in the pockets of his coat.

"Who are you?" she demanded, remembering that she was trespassing. She didn't even know the name of the company that owned the structure.

"You can call me Pablo," he said, smiling. "Jack's on his way."

"You don't look Mexican to me. What are you, like a night watchman? So where is he?" she asked.

"There's no need to pay anybody to guard this building, is there? I mean, stealing a bulldozer takes real professionals and big trailers," the man said, staring into her eyes.

Something about the man's flat delivery and emotionless eyes filled her with dread.

She froze when he took his hands from his pockets and moved at her with animal swiftness. Pinning her wrists behind her, he met her eyes and smiled. "Jack told me you are one delicious young lady."

Too frightened and shocked to move, she could only close her eyes as his broad and wet tongue ran from her chin up her face to her forehead.

Paulus Styer put the bound and gagged Cynthia facedown on the mattress located in the van outside before he took a tarpaulin and draped it over her still form.

"Cynthia, I have a lot of driving around to do. If you

move a muscle without me telling you to do so, I will throw you into the Mississippi River. I want you to understand that, because I do not make idle threats. Just nod if you understand."

The trembling girl nodded, and Styer took her lover's cloned cell phone and tossed it into a garbage bag.

He moved out to Cynthia's Toyota, drove it over to the far side of the barn near the mechanic station, and covered it completely with an old tarp.

Climbing back into the van, Styer cranked it and drove out of the structure into the stark, flat landscape. Now he could get on with his employer's primary operation, and take the next step in wrapping up his own.

15

PIERCE MULVANE EYED THE ACTION AT THE HIGH-stakes blackjack tables the way a farmer surveys a field for signs of sun damage or pest infestation. A dark-haired, clean-cut young man was winning steadily. He was up over forty-five thousand dollars and, despite the fact that the pit boss had changed dealers on him twice every hour, he showed no signs of a reversing fortune. The kid was cocky, and his success had drawn a crowd. It was both good and bad that people were watching him. It was good because it would encourage them to gamble. It was bad because asking him to leave would attract attention and put a damper on the audience. He'd let the boy win and have Albert White deal with it later.

Pierce thought back to the first cheater he'd caught in Atlantic City, a young man with tattoos covering his arms. The backs of his fingers spelled LOVE on the left hand, and HATE on the right. Using a pair of pruning shears, Pierce had edited the tattoo to read, LOVE HAT. The memory always made him chuckle. He hated cheaters.

After five minutes of watching the young man, Pierce turned and walked slowly through the playing floor, shadowed by Tug Murphy. He paused at one of the craps tables to watch a pig farmer from Arkansas named Jason Parr, whose one-hundred-and-fifty-thousand-dollar line of credit Pierce had personally approved. The year before, he had lost sixty thousand and paid it back within a week. Today Parr was dressed in a T-shirt under a tailored leather jacket, faded blue jeans, and shiny black wing-tips. Pierce watched with an inner glow as the farmer placed stacks of twenty-dollar chips on several numbers. He was chasing his losses, which, according to the floor boss, totaled twelve thousand dollars.

The pig farmer spotted Pierce, waved, and yelled, "Hey there, Mr. Mulvane!"

When the dice stopped rolling on seven and the farmer's chips had been collected, Pierce walked over and rested a hand on Parr's shoulder. "Nice to see you, Mr. Parr," Pierce said, turning on his warmest smile. "So nice to have you with us again. How is everything going?"

"Financially speaking, it's looking grim at the moment, Mr. Mulvane."

"I hope at least your accommodations are satisfactory."

"Room's fit for a king. And I thank you for the bottles of bourbon you sent up."

"Our pleasure. If you need anything, you'll let us know?"

"I sure will. My only question is, what are y'all gonna do with my hog farm?"

The farmer guffawed, and Pierce laughed right along with him.

Pierce stayed long enough to watch the farmer toss back a glass filled with brown liquor and lose another two thousand dollars. He didn't want a pig farm, but if Parr lost enough money, the casino's attorneys would figure out how to liquidate one pretty quickly.

The bottom line was Pierce's responsibility. When all was said and done, gambling was just a business like any other. Pierce Mulvane was just another CEO working long hours to generate profits for a corporation.

The main gaming tables ran the length of the casino center like a narrow island bordered by an ocean of slot machines, row after row like the cash crop they were. Though they were the main source of casino income, they were just machines, and got only a cursory glance from Pierce. Twenty-eight poker tables were surrounded by a low wall, so people could watch games in progress without interrupting them.

As Pierce and Tug rode the private elevator back upstairs, he couldn't shake his curiosity about how the young blackjack player was beating the house. He opened his phone and poked in a number.

"Albert, no-limit blackjack, table four. The man in the yellow V-neck. He's counting, with quite an audience. Let him run his streak. Check the black book and see if he's in it. Handle it with your customary discretion."

Pierce closed the phone. He couldn't allow cheaters to profit and tell their pals that the Roundtable was an easy mark. He knew that White would handle this matter properly. As security director, Albert White received a substantial salary, but the additional enrichment incentives Pierce made available to him here and there ensured results, not to mention the above-and-beyond effort Mulvane expected. And Pierce's above-and-beyond requests often called for tasks he couldn't give to people he didn't trust one hundred and ten percent.

16

THE HOUSE THAT ALPHONSE JEFFERSON HAD LISTED as his address when he'd been arrested three months earlier had long since surrendered to the elements. Several of the paint-starved clapboards were missing and shocks of faded-pink fiberglass shot out from several open spaces like clown hair.

The yard was bare dirt except for scattered clumps of stiff rust-colored weeds, a dead washing machine, a child's bicycle without wheels, a flattened shoe, and an emaciated and shivering pit bull whose head was much wider than his shoulders. The animal, standing in front of a wood-crate shelter with a floral plastic shower liner weighted down by brickbats on top of it, was anchored to a stake by a short section of swing-set chain. The dog growled as though he was saving his barks for more worthy customers than the two strangers he watched approach his master's front door.

Brad stood and loudly rapped on the jamb. The interior door opened a few inches. The unmistakable sounds of a fist-flying talk show boomed from the living room.

"Yeah, what?" a scrappy voice rumbled from inside.

"Mrs. Jefferson, it's Sheriff Barnett. I'm looking for Alphonse," Brad said through an aluminum door whose fabric screening hung like a mainsail from a corner of it. A mangy cat shot out and flew around the corner of the house. The watchdog eyed the fleeing feline without comment.

"What you wants wif my grandbaby?" the old woman asked, her rheumy brown eyes floating in a cocoa lake of skin, her gaze moving between Brad and Winter like a drunk counting fish in an aquarium. "He ain't been here for two, three days. You the sheriff, you say?" she asked, warily.

Brad opened his jacket to show her the badge on his shirt. "Yes, ma'am. Does Alphonse live here?" Brad asked her. "He used this address the last time he was arrested."

"When he want to, he stay here. When he don't, he don't. What you wants him for?"

The old woman reached up to her outraged hair as if to check whether it was still there.

"Does your grandson have a rifle?" Brad asked.

"He a vetrin, so in the Army he might a' did," she said. "He didn't brang one back from thur. It ain't unlegal to have guns when you in the Army, is it?"

"No, ma'am, it isn't. I was just wondering if he has a rifle *now.*"

"Not that I ever seen around here, he don't." She laughed. "If he had one, he sure would of pawnded it."

"Can I come in and look at his room?" Brad asked.

"Not without no warrants you ain't coming in my house. I knows my sivah rights."

"I can get a warrant, Mrs. Jefferson."

"Then why you standing there? Go on and get it." And she slammed the outside door closed, causing the jamb to vibrate.

Winter waited until they were almost back to the cruiser to laugh. Once inside, Brad laughed as well.

"Mrs. Jefferson was downright inhospitable," Brad said.

"Less than cooperative," Winter said. "How soon can you get a warrant?"

"I didn't figure she'd cooperate, so one of my deputies is at the courthouse getting it right now. Watch the front, and I'll cover the back."

Ten minutes later, a beefy young deputy climbed from his still-running cruiser and when Brad came around the house, he handed the sheriff a folded search warrant. Brad and Winter moved swiftly to the porch as the deputy went around to the back.

After Mrs. Jefferson opened the door, Brad handed her the warrant and led Winter inside while she stared down at the folded paper in her hand with no expression on her face.

"You people better not make no mess you don't put

straight. And you don't take nothing neither. I know everything what all's in here."

How anyone had managed to pack so much into a small house without it collapsing was an engineering feat worthy of the ancient Romans. The TV set and two mismatched recliners filled a small nest to the right of the front door. A path of sorts existed between shoulder-high walls of newspapers, old books and magazines, which allowed limited access into the rest of the home-based storage facility.

"Reminds me of a prairie dog town," Brad said in a whisper, referring to several house cats lounging like skeletal panthers on the canyon walls. The first room, which contained a bed, held enough items of clothing and accessories to start a Salvation Army dry-goods distribution center. There were also stacks of electronic appliances, most of which looked like they had been salvaged from the side of the road. A man in his sixties sat up from the bed and blinked at the two men staring into his space.

"Huh?" he asked.

"Sheriff's department," Brad said. "We're executing a search warrant."

He ran his hands over his hair in an attempt at collecting himself. "We ain't hiding nothing," he said in a tone that told Winter the man wasn't at all sure that was the case.

"We're looking for Alphonse's room, Mr. Jefferson," Brad said.

"Next room, but I don't think he's in there."

"Where is he?"

"Sommer else probably."

"Mr. Jefferson," Brad said. "How can you live like this?"

"Axe her," the man said sadly. "City makes her keep the yard up some. You think you can git 'em to come up in here and 'complish the same thang?"

"I expect I could call the fire chief and tell him this is a fire hazard and maybe he can make her clean some of this out," Brad said.

"At be good, if you can."

Alphonse Jefferson's room was by far the least cluttered room in the house. They searched the room, but there was no gun of any kind to be found, only a few pictures of a man at different ages, a wallpapering of nudes torn from magazines, and a framed less-than-honorable discharge sheet from the U.S. Army.

The clothes hanging in the closet were neatly ordered, with each of the articles in its own dry-cleaning bag. The closet floor was covered with pairs of shoes in every imaginable style and color. Chains and other items of ornamental gold-plated jewelry had been laid out on the dresser as if for display.

"No rifles," Winter said after he'd looked under the mattress.

"I doubt he would keep it here," Brad said, moving out of the room toward the kitchen.

A sink hung on the wall in the kitchen beside a rusted refrigerator. Three mismatched chairs surrounded a table piled with food-encrusted dishes. A gas stove, its surface covered with stacked pots and pans, was positioned below partly closed cabinets. On the floor by the back door—beside an overflowing box piled with more dried bits of feline offal than litter—several bags of trash that had been chewed open by tiny teeth waited to be put on the curb.

Winter saw the bags shift slightly—a movement so subtle he almost missed it. Pulling out the Reeder .45, Winter nudged Brad.

"I've seen enough," Brad said, taking out his Python.

Winter and Brad reached down and each took the corner of a trash bag. They jerked the bag up and aimed down at the man curled into a ball on the floor.

"Okay, Alphonse," Brad said, "It's time to take a ride. I want you to stand up slowly. I don't want to shoot you, but if you do anything but get up slowly and come with us, I will."

The young man dressed in a black jogging suit turned his head up slowly, peered at the handguns, and grinned.

17

"I AIN'T DID NOTHIN'," THE SURLY YOUNG MAN SAID when Brad and Winter came into the interrogation room.

"I haven't accused you of anything, Alphonse," Brad said. The file folders under his arm caught Alphonse's attention briefly.

"And you better not. I got my rights, and I know a lawyer. Gone sue you and make me a rich man."

Alphonse Jefferson was taller than his grandmother.

His almond-shaped eyes were an unnaturally light gray, and he had mocha skin with freckles running like a stream of rusty BBs across the bridge of his nose. His lips parted to reveal teeth that were large and even, each one capped with gold-plated snap-ons. His black velvet running suit had burgundy stripes up the pant legs and sleeves of the jacket, which was unzipped to show his hairless chest.

"You can say it. You know." He plucked his lapels. "I look good in black."

"How do you think you'll look in prison dress whites?" Brad asked him.

"Me in prison?" Alphonse barked laughter at the ceiling. "Aw, man. That's all you know? You ain't charging me, then I'm on jus' walk on out of here and get on back to the bid'ness of doing my bid'ness. You dig?"

Brad placed the file on the table in front of him. "I want to ask you a few questions."

"Uh-uh. I'll be talking to you through the Johnny Coc-oh-ran legal firm. Case you missed it, it was him that got O.J. off."

"Johnny's dead. You sure you want to go that route?" Brad asked.

Alphonse placed his hands flat on the table. "I don't gots to answer no questions. 'Bout what?"

"About Sherry Adams."

Alphonse turned his attention from Brad and glared up at Winter, who stood arms crossed with his back against the concrete block wall, looking down at Alphonse.

"What about her?" he asked suspiciously.

"You've been harassing her, Alphonse."

"Who told you that? Them fools are all a bunch of

no-count lying player haters, 'cause I'm a smooth dude. What I said was, 'If she had some of what I got, she would be ruint for everybody else.' You dig?"

"I have your Army records," Brad said, opening a folder and pointing to the faxed pages he'd received before the interview. "They kicked you out for possession of marijuana. At least that was the straw that broke the mule's back. They obviously didn't want you bringing down the average IQ of the armed forces."

"Those fools got they heads up they asses. Always tellin' a brother what to do. Racist haters."

"It looks like you were deficient in every possible area. Your whole short career was a stack of inadequacy, petty criminality, and impulsive behavior. These records say you shot a rifle like a girl. Except all of the girls in the Army could shoot better than you."

"I can shoot a fly off your lily-white butt from far as you can see."

"And you stalk women who see you for the loser you are. Can't let that go, can you?"

"Sherry Adams's full a' herself, prissy ass be-otch. I ain't never laid a hand on her. Ain't no crime wanting to change a girl's mind. She just needs to come around and see what she's missing."

Brad opened the folder and tossed a picture of Sherry Adams's ruined head onto the table so Alphonse could see it. He stared down at it and frowned, looking away. "What that is?"

"That *was* Sherry Adams."

"Naw, it ain't! You lying!"

Winter understood why Alphonse didn't recognize her. The bullet had literally exploded her head, and the result looked like pizza topped with almost human features, torn and splattered on the bricks. Her black hair was reduced to tufts forming a border around the skin that remained.

"Somebody shot her, Alphonse. Maybe somebody that can shoot from as far away as you say you can. Where were you this morning between six and seven?"

"What?!" Alphonse looked down at the picture, lowered his head, and vomited into his lap.

Brad put the picture back into the folder and rolled his eyes at Winter.

Winter shook his head slowly.

"I ain't do that!" Alphonse managed to yell, flecks of bile on his chin. "Lord is my witness, it wasn't me did it. I was sleepin' in my car up by Bugger's place. I ain't never capped nobody. I wouldn't shoot that girl! I liked her."

"I know, Alphonse," Brad said, standing. "You wouldn't know which end of a gun the bullet comes out of. Get out of my building before I lock you up for littering."

Back in the office, Winter said, "Tell me about Leigh Gardner."

"Leigh's family's been in the cotton-farming business here since the county was cleared from cypress swamps. Her grandfather and her father grew their land holdings into the three thousand acres you saw, probably another three in woodland, and some other scattered acreage she leases to other planters. Leigh is strictly a cotton and soybean farmer. She learned from her father, studied agriculture at Mississippi State and she knows her business.

Her old man was a tough-as-nails businessman and an old-school planter. She runs the place the same way."

"Husband?"

"Divorced. She married a jerk named Jacob Gardner whose law practice consisted of spending her money. She kicked him out five years ago. He went over to Oxford and set up a private practice, and got in trouble year after that for misappropriating his clients' funds. Leigh paid back the stolen money to keep him out of jail for the kids' sakes. He was disbarred anyway. He comes around periodically when he needs something and I've heard Leigh gives him an allowance so he doesn't starve. He used to be able to charm the pants off a nun. Now, not so much."

"I think you should investigate him," Winter said.

"What for? The killer was a pro."

"Doesn't take a professional killer to hire one."

"He wouldn't have any reason to have Sherry killed."

"Maybe Sherry wasn't the target."

"Who would be?" Brad asked.

"If anything happened to Leigh Gardner, who would benefit?" Winter asked.

"The kids. Leigh wouldn't leave Jacob a ten-dollar bill."

"Maybe not. But who do you suppose would be their guardian if Leigh Gardner was dead?"

Brad sat up. "The killer shot her babysitter. Leigh wasn't even in the area. What are you thinking?"

"Maybe the killer didn't know that."

18

ALEXA KEEN OPENED HER APARTMENT DOOR AND had to put down her bag of groceries to answer the telephone. It was rare that her phone rang unless it was someone from the Bureau.

"Yes?" she said.

"Alexa?" a familiar voice asked.

"Sean," Alexa said. "Hello."

"How are you, Lex?"

"I'm fine. How are you?"

The silence lasted too long. She put down her shoulder bag, made heavy by the Glock. "Sean, is everything all right?"

"I'm not sure."

"Where are the kids?" she asked.

"In the next room. We're at the Peabody. We've been trying to decide on places to visit, but it's really cold and the kids are ready to go home."

"Winter told me you were going back to North Carolina."

"Then you've talked to him today?"

"He told me about Faith Ann's deer. I guess she's excited."

"And did he mention the other thing?"

"What other thing?"

"The toothpick."

"Yes, he told me about it," Alexa said.

"The DNA results are on their way to the lab for a comparison. If it's Styer's, I'm not sure Winter is up to dealing with him. Lex, he'll kill Winter without thinking."

"Styer?" Alexa heard her voice crack. "Paulus Styer?"

"He didn't tell you he's comparing the DNA to the sample he has for Styer?"

"He left that part out," Alexa said, apprehension and dread mushrooming inside her. Paulus Styer was one frightening son of a bitch, and she'd thought he was gone for good.

"Because he knew you'd go ballistic on him."

Damned right I would have. Good Christ! "Sean, you shouldn't worry. Winter knows what he's doing." Alexa hoped she sounded convinced of her words.

"I'm sorry to pour this out on you. It's just that there's nobody else Winter will listen to. If I told Hank Trammel, you couldn't stop the old buzzard from going there with a tank. And he can barely walk."

"Sean, I'm gonna go down," Alexa said suddenly. "I have some time off coming to me, and if Styer is involved, I want to be there."

"That isn't why I called. I just wanted to talk to somebody who knows Winter and understands the situation. I shouldn't have called you. You don't need to go there."

"Don't be silly. Of course you should have called me. I love that old dog too."

"I know you do." Sean's voice sounded uncharacteristically faint.

"I'm not in the middle of anything at the moment, except writing a procedural manual nobody is going to read. I'll just go down there for a couple of days and watch his back. I won't tell him I know Styer may be involved. He can tell me that when I get there."

"I should argue with you, but I won't. Be careful. He'll kill you, too."

"No, Sean, he won't."

After some small talk, Alexa hung up. She dialed her travel agent's number from memory and made a reservation for the next flight to Memphis.

19

TWENTY-NINE-YEAR-OLD JACK BEALS, A SECURITY officer for the Roundtable, had tailed the kid in the yellow V-neck sweater straight to the Gold Key Motel, a few miles from the casino. The gambler's name was David Scotoni, a single twenty-three-year-old resident of Reno, Nevada, whose ID checked out as legit. Turned out that the reason a man who lived in a town filled with casinos would fly across the country to gamble was predictable—he was known in Reno as a card counter.

Counting cards wasn't illegal, but it gave the player an unfair advantage and was grounds for a casino to invite you to leave and put your mug in the black book system shared by casinos across the country. Scotoni had cashed out his chips to the tune of thirty-five thousand. That was about to be collected and returned to the casino.

Beals waited to call Albert White until Scotoni had gone into his room on the second level.

"Target is in a motel room on the second floor of the Gold Key," Beals told him. "Easy access. I'll come by tonight and deliver it."

White said, "He cashed out for over thirty-five, and he's won in other places. The thirty-five comes back here. The other we cut up as usual."

"Your wish is my command," Beals said, before hanging up. *Whatever he's taken from the others. Not bad money for a day's work.*

He screwed the silencer on the .380. The professional from the outside who Jack had been helping to get the lay of the land, the guy whose name was or wasn't Pablo, had given it to him. Nice fellow, some kind of top-dollar hit man always measuring the world and the people around him like a film director looking for the perfect shot. After putting on a pair of tight leather gloves, Beals climbed from his 1999 Trail Blazer and made sure nobody was watching as he moved up the stairs to Scotoni's room. Stopping outside the door, he took out his badge case and knocked hard on the door three times. A TV set went off and a voice asked tentatively, "Who's there?"

When the young cheater looked out through the peephole, Beals held up a gold five-star badge for the kid to see. "Sheriff's department, Mr. Scotoni," he said. "Open the door, please."

"What's the problem, Officer?" the kid asked without opening the door. Beals felt anger rise from within, his heart beating like a bass drum.

"I'd prefer not to discuss it from out here, sir. We've had a complaint." Beals looked both ways and down at the parking lot. The lot was graveyard still.

When the kid cracked open the door, Beals shouldered it, propelling Scotoni deep into the room. From the floor, a naked Scotoni looked up at the silenced weapon. The towel he'd been wrapped in was beneath him, and when Scotoni reached to gather it back up, Beals put a boot on it. He heard the sound of water running in the bathtub and he had an idea. He'd been thinking the kid would commit suicide by cutting his wrists, but this was even better. Motioning to the bathroom with the gun's barrel, he said, "Dave. You need to take that bath."

20

AFTER FOLLOWING JACK BEALS FROM THE CASINO to a motel where Beals seemed to have some business with the man he himself was following, Paulus Styer turned to look into the rear of the van at the tarp under which lay the bound and drugged Gardner girl.

He turned his attention to the Gold Key—one of several old motels that had been hastily thrown up on a stretch of highway near the original casinos. When larger and finer casinos were built miles away, with newer and fancier motels to accompany them, the Gold Key and its neighbors had been abandoned by the better-heeled clientele, and now subsisted on dregs and scraps from their poorer replacements.

The Gold Key was a long two-story box, whose rooms faced a parking lot on either side. To access the second and third floors, patrons took one of several stairways or the elevator that was located behind the lobby. Time and lack of maintenance had turned the Gold Key into a place where the clientele, even on days when it wasn't bone-chillingly cold, wouldn't pay close attention to the comings and goings of strangers. And most of the clients would be sleeping in after a long night of losing money or turning tricks.

Styer waited until Jack had sneaked up the stairs and shouldered his way inside a room on the second floor. Then he spoke.

"Cynthia dear?"

She was still out.

Styer pocketed his lock-picking tools and patted the survival knife at his side. Then, after checking for witnesses, he climbed from the van, locked it, and walked swiftly but casually toward the stairs.

21

WHEN LEIGH GARDNER WALKED INTO BRAD Barnett's office, the sheriff had just returned from making arrangements for a deputy to deliver the toothpick evidence to the ProCell facility in Nashville via a chartered twin-engine airplane.

"Okay," she said. "What's so all-fired important?"

"Sit down, Leigh," Brad said.

She sat, arms crossed.

"We don't think Sherry was the target," he told her.

"Oh, really. So you believe it was a hunting accident now? I shouldn't be surprised you've changed your mind already. Keeping your crime numbers stacked for a re-election bid?"

"No, it definitely wasn't an accident. I'll let Winter explain the thinking behind it."

Leigh turned in her chair to face Winter. "Okay, Mr. Massey, if Sherry wasn't the intended victim, who the hell was?" she asked.

"I think you were," Winter told her.

"Why would anybody want to shoot at me?"

Winter began, "It makes less sense that anyone who could make that shot would target a babysitter out in the middle of nowhere."

"So you're not pursuing Alphonse Jefferson?"

"We've ruled him out," Brad told her.

Leigh frowned at Brad. "How do you imagine anybody could confuse me—a forty-year-old blonde—with a nineteen-year-old black girl?"

Winter said, "I was looking at the crime-scene pictures and something hit me. At a thousand yards in that early light, a dark-skinned babysitter wearing a hooded car coat and gloves, moving from the house to the garage, would look like a white woman doing the same thing. You're a farmer and I suspect you keep farming hours. If the shooter didn't know you were out of town, and was there to kill you, he might easily assume a woman close to your build heading out to the garage at daybreak would be you."

"Why me?"

"Financial gain, so whoever gains if you were killed is a suspect. Since your kids didn't have it done, we can move to the next most-likely suspect."

"Like who?" she asked. "Nobody would gain anything by my death," Leigh said. Her eyes flickered with some inner thought, some recognition perhaps, but passed quickly. She shrugged. "No. Despite the size of my operation, I am not a wealthy woman. Maybe you should look at the agricultural conglomerates. They're the *only* people who'd profit from my death, since my children would have to sell the place to pay the inheritance taxes."

"What about Jacob?" Brad asked.

She laughed. "Please. If I died, he'd starve to death. He lives with his mother in a two-bedroom apartment in Memphis."

"Brad has to take a serious look at your ex-husband," Winter said.

Leigh stared at Winter for a few long seconds, her expression impossible to read. "Don't be ridiculous," she scoffed. "Alphonse Jefferson is your killer. If that's all?"

"I don't think—" Brad started.

"That's the trouble, you don't think. Anybody wants to shoot me, I'll be the one working my ass off. Good-bye, boys. Six Oaks won't run itself."

Leigh strode out the door without looking back.

"If she was the target, she probably still is," Winter said. "When the shooter finds out he missed her, he might try again. She needs protection."

"Forget it," Brad said. "She's in denial and as stubborn as a mule. But I'll put a car out at the place, double the patrols on the roads out that way."

Winter said, "I think she already suspected Sherry wasn't the target before she came in here. I think she isn't completely certain that her ex isn't responsible."

Brad said, "I can tell you from long experience with Leigh that she isn't going to do anything she doesn't want to do."

"How long ago was it that you two dated?" Winter asked.

Brad's startled look confirmed what Winter had suspected since he first saw Brad and Leigh Gardner interact at Six Oaks.

Bettye stuck her head into the office. "Sheriff, just got a call. There's been a homicide at the Gold Key."

22

THE PARKING LOT AT THE GOLD KEY MOTEL WAS alive with flashing blue lights and several deputies stood on the balcony outside a room with the door open. Traffic on the highway was backed up as people rubbernecked to see what the excitement was about. Here and there, guests gathered in tight clumps.

Winter and Brad took the wide stairs two at a time. The deputies parted to allow Brad and Winter to enter the room. A man's body was sprawled on the floor, a pool of blood under his head, his throat laid open. A second man wearing a V-neck sweater and khakis sat on the edge of the bed, his hands resting in his lap. A deputy in his fifties stood passively with his back to the bureau as Brad and Winter entered.

"What happened here, Roy?" Brad asked the deputy, who handed him a Nevada driver's license with a picture of the young man who sat watching them silently.

"Roy Bishop, this is Winter Massey. He's giving me a hand with the Adams homicide. Roy here is my chief deputy." The chief deputy looked at Winter for a second and nodded.

"Beals?" Brad asked, moving to look at the dead man's familiar features.

"Sure is. Mr. Scotoni here says somebody else came in and killed Beals, who happened to be in the process of drowning him in the tub. Scotoni called nine-one-one, we didn't touch anything."

Scotoni's hair had dried into a grand mess, and his hands were shaking.

Winter looked down at the corpse wearing a flight jacket and winced as he spotted a red toothpick tucked behind the dead man's ear. Brad's eyes followed his.

"Okay, Mr. Scotoni, I need to know exactly what happened," Brad said, sitting on the chair so their eyes were even.

"I was running a hot bath. That guy there came to the door, said he was a deputy sheriff, and showed me his badge. When I opened the door he knocked me down. He had a gun with a silencer on it. He said he was going to take the money I'd won from the casinos."

"He was alone when he came in?"

"Yeah. He was enjoying himself. He was definitely going to kill me. He made me get into the tub and hit me on the back of my head and started holding me underwater. I couldn't really fight back and I was . . . I've never been so scared in my life."

"I didn't see a gun," the deputy said. "I looked under the bed and everywhere else I could without touching anything."

"The other guy must have taken it," Scotoni said. "The one who saved my ass."

"What did this other guy look like?" Brad asked.

"I didn't actually see him. Like I said, that dead guy hit me in the back of my head," he said, turning and pointing at the back of his head. "He had me underwater and I saw the shape of a man in dark clothes come in. He pulled that guy in here and by the time I got out of the tub and came in, the guy that killed him was already gone, so I called nine-one-one."

Winter looked at Brad and nodded slowly.

"Can I get the hell out of here?" Scotoni asked.

"You can leave the room," Brad told him. "You'll have to give a statement at the station."

"Can I take my stuff?"

"We'll release it after we've cleared the scene," Bishop said.

"What about just the money I won?"

"Where is it?" Brad asked.

"In that middle drawer. He never got around to it."

Brad opened the dresser drawer and handed a paper bag heavy with banded stacks of currency to Scotoni.

"Where did you win this?"

"Gold Strike, Horse Shoe, Regency, and the Roundtable."

"Which was the last place?"

"I only played the Roundtable today. The others were over the last two days."

"With all the casinos in Reno and Vegas, why'd you come here?"

"I wanted to see Graceland," Scotoni said, too quickly.

"You an Elvis fan?" Brad asked.

"Sure."

"Young and skinny or old and fat?"

"Sorry?"

" 'Hound Dog' or 'Burning Love' Elvis-era music?" Brad went on.

" 'Burning Love,' " Scotoni said. "I like that one."

"That's old fat Elvis," Brad mused. "Deputy Bishop will take you to the hospital to get you checked out. You'll need another room."

"Does it have to be at this motel?"

"No. Just make sure we know where you are. Don't leave town unless you clear it with me. And if I were you, I'd take that bag to the bank and get a cashier's check," Brad suggested.

"Why? I didn't do anything."

"Large sums of cash can attract attention. I don't want to see you where Beals is," Brad told him firmly. "We'll have someone watch over you until you get to the bank."

"Why?"

"Just in case this dead fellow had friends he was going to share your winnings with. We want you to leave our county a winner," Brad said. "And it would be best all the way around if you didn't ever come back here."

"You don't have to sweat that one," the young man said.

23

AFTER BRAD CLEARED THE ROOM, WINTER SAID, "Close-up skills. These doors lock when they close. Scotoni said Beals closed it when he came in. The guy who came in picked the lock."

"Maybe Beals left it cracked open so a partner could come in behind him," Brad suggested.

"I doubt that. The guy cut Beals's throat. Then he left the toothpick, took the gun, and slipped off without looking for the cash, because either he didn't know about it, or it wasn't part of his plan. He knew Scotoni would call the cops."

"Maybe the toothpick was Beals's," Brad said.

"I think the guy who killed him left it to make an obvious connection between Beals and Sherry Adams." Winter was convinced that Styer had done this and he could read the message loud and clear: *We'll always have New Orleans.*

"Why did the killer want Beals found fast? Usually it's the opposite."

"The killer knew I'd come here, and he wanted to make the connection obvious to me."

"I wish he'd just leave notes," Brad said. "His address and phone number."

"You knew this Beals guy. How?" Winter asked.

"He was a deputy who went to work for the Roundtable casino after I won the election. Most people in the department seemed glad he was gone."

"Why?"

"He was the kind of smartass who sets people against each other for his own entertainment. He made inappropriate comments to female deputies. There were lots of complaints about him. After the election, he told me a casino had offered him a better job and I told him to take the offer. Truth was, I didn't want troublemakers around undermining me."

"Maybe the casino sent Beals to get the money back," Winter suggested.

"Maybe Beals targeted the kid because he won and took it in cash. No legit casino would send Beals here to get their money back. Winners draw in losers. If someone cheats, they call us to arrest them. They ask counters to leave."

"But it's possible that someone at the casino did send him after Scotoni to teach him a lesson."

"Casinos don't operate that way because it would result in the loss of their gaming license and criminal charges. There's too much at stake. Losing future millions over some chump change is stupid."

"It isn't chump change to a guy like Beals," Winter said.

Brad slipped on surgical gloves, knelt, and gently rolled Beals's body sideways. He retrieved a leather badge case from the corpse's back pocket and flipped it open to reveal a Tunica County deputy sheriff badge and the ID. "Bastard kept his star." Beals's coat pockets yielded a large folding knife, a loaded .380 magazine, a cell phone, and three red toothpicks.

"We can see who he's been talking to," Brad said. He looked at the numbers Beals had called. "Last call was made about an hour ago. Just a number, no name listed."

"My question is, if this is Styer's work, how did he pick Beals out, and why Beals?" Winter said, realizing too late that he'd slipped up. "I wonder if my guy has a connection to the Roundtable or to Beals personally."

"Styer is your guy's name?"

"Yes, that's his name. Let's keep it to ourselves."

Winter figured that the casino was the direction Styer wanted him to head in. For the present, like it or not, all he could do was dance to the psychopath's tune.

24

DAYLIGHT WAS FADING WHEN BRAD PARKED IN THE lot outside the Roundtable casino. The facade made the casino look more like a theme park for kids than a gambling hall for adults.

"You don't know what this Styer looks like?" Brad said, shaking his head.

"Paulus Styer never looks the same way twice," Winter said.

"You going to tell me any more about him than his name?"

"He's the most dangerous son of a bitch I've ever encountered."

"That much I sort of picked up on."

"It pretty much sums him up and it's the most important thing to never lose sight of." Winter frowned and looked out at the casino.

Despite the medieval theme, instead of the court jester outfits Brad said the doormen wore under the previous ownership, they now sported tuxedo jackets and red cummerbunds with matching bow ties. The Roundtable's owners had left only as much of the old place's ambience as was financially practical. Winter read a sign in the foyer that said CASH YOUR PAYCHECK HERE AND RECEIVE A $20.00 CREDIT TOWARD ANY GAME! He figured, with a rueful sigh, that it should have read WHY PAY YOUR RENT OR BUY GROCERIES WHEN YOU CAN GIVE US THE MONEY!

The absence of windows, clocks, or any other indicators of time in a casino was a clear sign that the owners didn't want their clients to play according to nature's schedules. Winter remembered that he had once read that the denial of passing time was just one of a hundred tricks casinos employed to keep gamblers seated until their pockets were empty. The use of magnetic cards not only tracked the customers' game preferences, and their wins and losses, but also stored their cash by way of Visa cards, so they had no sense of losing actual money. The more a patron gambled, the more perks they were entitled to receive. The house rigged things so nobody left the place of dream fulfillment empty-handed. Lesser gamblers got cheap liquor, free soft drinks, key chains, and mugs, while the big-fish gamblers were rewarded with free flights in and out, meals, rounds of golf, lodging, companionship, and tickets for big-name performers, all compliments of the house.

A casino's decor, chairs, music, and lighting were all carefully designed to make the customers feel safe and comfortable. Casinos were big supporters of the scientific community, and employed psychologists to increase their edge against the poor schmucks who wandered in through the doors—who were, in the end, hardly more than sheep lining up to be shorn.

Winter mulled all this over as Brad said, "Albert White is head of security, formerly deputy chief of police in West Memphis. His main job is to keep order and running interference for the casino. With the security cameras trained on the lot, and the internal security communication system, we won't have to look for him. Either he or one of his men usually meets me on the way in."

Brad and Winter strolled through the entrance, passing among the legions of comers and goers. Smiles on the faces of the exiting gamers were as scarce as talking monkeys. Just inside, a large man wearing a tentlike suit, carrying a walkie-talkie, and wearing a modified crew cut made his way across the crowded lobby to intercept the two men.

"Sheriff Barnett, can I help you with something?" he asked. His pale blue eyes sparkled. He looked like a bloated razorback that had been dressed up in a cheap suit and taught to walk on his hind legs.

"I hope so," Brad said. "Deputy Massey, this is Albert White, head of casino security."

The man nodded in Winter's direction, the motion compressing his chins. "Chief casino investigator," he corrected, smiling artificially.

"We've got a situation that concerns an employee of this casino."

"Which employee?" His small eyes blinked rapidly

"Jack Beals."

"He's off tonight," White said, nervously, Winter noted. He tapped the radio against his leg. "I can get you his home address and phone number from personnel."

"I already know where he is."

"What sort of situation are we talking about?" White asked, his eyes darting around the entrance area.

"Dead-on-the-floor-in-a-motel-room situation," Brad said.

Winter saw surprise reflected in White's eyes. "How'd he die?"

"Suddenly."

"Heart attack?"

"Loss of blood. Somebody cut his throat from ear to ear," Brad said.

"Who?"

"That's what I'm trying to figure out," Brad said.

White shook his head and frowned. "We need to take this to my office. I can get you next-of-kin information from personnel."

"I'd appreciate it," Brad said. "We probably have it in our files, but yours are going to be more current."

By law a gambling enterprise had to float in a Federal waterway so the gaming wasn't technically on Mississippi soil. So the water it floated on had to be Mississippi River water and the casino had to be floated into place from the river.

So, although the casino's gaming areas floated on massive pontoons to keep the structure suspended in a concrete pond, the room had no more sense of movement than you'd get standing in a chamber in the Great Pyramid. As Winter and Brad followed White through the middle of the casino, Winter scanned the crowd of busy gamblers for a man with any trace of familiarity. Styer would certainly have altered his appearance, but Winter might see something in the way he moved, or recognize his voice if he heard it. The only patron he saw with a toothpick in their mouth was a solidly built woman with fried blonde hair and garish makeup, seated at a slot machine, who would have looked perfectly at home elbowing her way around a roller derby track.

25

ALBERT WHITE LED BRAD AND WINTER TO THE FAR end of the gaming floor and down a long hallway into a small and windowless office.

The only items of furniture in the office were an industrial steel desk, a legal pad, pen, and telephone on its surface, and three matching chairs. This was clearly a generic office, used only when necessary.

"When Beals was killed," Brad said, "he was in the process of committing an armed assault on a patron of this casino. A man who won a great deal of money earlier this evening."

"Armed assault?" White asked.

"He was in a motel room with a silenced handgun, in the process of drowning the young man in a bathtub."

"So this *alleged* patron killed Beals?"

"I'm not alleging anything, Albert. He was here all right. The assault was interrupted by a third party, who cut Jack Beals's throat. Beals used his old departmental badge to gain entry and informed the victim he was acting on behalf of the casino. Beals told him that the casino wanted their money back. By the casino, I assume he meant someone in management, and not the blackjack dealers' union."

"And you know this how?"

"It's what the victim told me."

"How do you know he was telling the truth about anything? If he's committed a homicide, murderers don't always tell the truth." White smiled uneasily.

"Because the victim was semiconscious in the tub when Beals got killed."

White leaned in and told Brad huffily, "We're a legitimate business operation. We do not beat up our customers, and the idea that our management would condone any illegal activity, or order it done, is preposterous. This casino is not owned by the mafia, for Christ's sake. If we discover a customer is not playing fairly, we take their picture, have them sign a statement admitting their guilt—and they view the tapes themselves as a matter of procedure—take down their names and addresses, and tell them never to return. We blacklist them. We have our reputation and our gaming license to think of. I was a law enforcement officer for thirty years. If Beals was dirty, it is a total surprise to me."

"I haven't accused you of anything, Albert," Brad said.

"Was he on duty today?" Winter asked.

"He went off the clock at noon, I believe. I could check that, of course."

"If he hung around after he got off," Brad asked, "would you have him on videotape?"

"Our system is digital, but yes, we would have a record of it. But our employees are not allowed to hang around here after they clock out. They don't gamble here, or in any other casinos, or we fire them."

"If he was here after his shift, how would you know that for sure?"

"We have cameras everywhere and our people would have spotted him if he was in the building."

"So if Beals was eating in one of your restaurants, you would have it on tape?"

"We monitor the entire operation constantly. If I know what time you are interested in, I could locate the corresponding images—although it would be a time-consuming enterprise for our people. But we would be happy to cooperate in any way we can."

"If he targeted the victim during his shift and had robbery in mind, I'd like to know if he had a partner working with him. A partner may have killed Beals, or might tell us who did kill him."

White digested this for several long seconds. "I'll put in a request for my people to go over the captures and see if

Beals turns up while the patron was here. This sort of thing is something we obviously have to discourage."

"You should be able to look at the blackjack player who was assaulted and see who was around him, maybe watching him. Can you do that?"

"I'll see that it's done and you can review the images yourself. If that's all?"

"That'll do," Brad said. "And if you can give me your contact numbers?"

"This has my office and cell," White said as he pulled out a card and handed it to Brad. "I'll show you out," he said, standing. "Can I fax you Jack Beals's next-of-kin information? The personnel office is run by a skeleton crew until eight A.M."

"That would be fine," Brad said.

After they left the casino, Brad said, "You pick up on that?"

"That he looked like he was going to pass a watermelon the entire time we were there? Or the fact that he offered to collect the images of our man at the blackjack table without us mentioning his name or describing what he looked like? I did."

"If he furnishes the images of Scotoni without calling to ask the particulars, we can ask him how he knew who we were talking about, since he shouldn't have been able to read our minds."

"If he asked Beals to talk to Scotoni, it doesn't mean he told him to do what he did to him," Winter said, yawning. "But it could mean that White was working with Beals to rob winners."

"It's late. Let's get some rest and go after this at first

light," Brad said, holding up White's card. "By the way, the last number Beals called . . ."

"Is the cell number on that business card," Winter said.

"We could go back in and ask him about that," Brad said.

"He'd just say he didn't talk to him or that Beals asked his boss a business-related question. He knows Beals called him, and he'll begin to wonder why you didn't ask him. Let him do some worrying. Sometimes it's better just to let things percolate."

26

LOCAL CURRENT EVENTS, MUCH LIKE THE TIME OF day, rarely invaded the Roundtable's upper offices. Gamblers didn't bring the outside world in with them, and the staff was too busy collecting their money to care. Pierce had learned from his secretary when she'd come in that morning that a young woman had been killed at the Gardner cotton plantation. The news had opened the door to troubling questions.

After Pierce had asked Albert White to find out the particulars, White had called his contact in the sheriff's office, a deputy with a gambling problem that had gotten her indebted to the casino for approximately her yearly salary. She told White that a babysitter on the Gardner place named Sherry Adams had been killed by an errant rifle shot. Whatever had happened, it was a very troubling complication in an already complex and delicate maneuver. But he had been told that his involvement was not required. How the death of the young girl fit in, or didn't, was chewing on his guts.

When Tug knocked and opened the door to his office, Pierce Mulvane frowned. He knew by Tug's demeanor that whatever he was about to tell him wasn't going to lift his spirits. After Tug closed the door, Pierce locked his hands behind his neck and leaned back in his chair.

"The sheriff was just here," Tug said. "He met with Albert."

"Yes?" Pierce felt a pang of anticipation in his chest. "What was it about?"

"It was about Jack Beals."

"Yes," Pierce said, closing his eyes. "What about Beals?"

"He got clipped."

"Clipped." A white-hot poker in the eye would have hurt less than those words.

"The sheriff told Albert that Beals was drowning that blackjack-cheating kid out at the Gold Key and somebody killed him while he was doing it. Cut his throat. They're thinking our security tapes might show Beals scoping him out or somebody watching the kid who was working with Beals."

"You know what this means?" Pierce asked, without waiting for an answer. "Police involvement at the worst possible time."

"What do you want to do?"

"This requires more careful consideration than I can

give it at the moment." He shifted uneasily in his chair, tapping a pencil on the desk.

"Barnett thinks the guy who killed him was probably working some strong-arm robbery angle with Beals. Albert told the sheriff he'd check but Beals wasn't here after his shift, which he said was till noon today. He'll rig Beals's time sheets."

"No. Sheriff Barnett is out of his element, but he isn't stupid or lazy. What happens when he interviews the staff? Who knows how many people saw Beals here after noon? Tell Albert to leave the time sheets as they are and say he only thought Beals was on till noon. Albert's got too many people to know who's where and when. I need to know who the cheater's backup was and we need to get to them before the sheriff does. Tell Albert to get on it and brief me before he tells the sheriff anything. Maybe I should put the attorneys between Albert and the sheriff. No big deal. We have plenty of friends who can smooth ruffled feathers."

"I'll handle it."

"Tug, the time for mistakes is over. From here out let's take the word 'fail' out of our collective vocabularies."

Pierce sat back and closed his eyes again. The situation with the Gardners had to be resolved before Kurt Klein arrived. Unless it was handled, Pierce Mulvane would lose everything he had worked so hard for.

He had assumed the professional hired to handle things would do so. Pierce told himself that if he had made a mistake, it had been in trusting Kurt Klein's guy, this mysterious Pablo. Klein had no right to blame Pierce if that Pablo creep had gone crazy and shot some kid. But he knew Klein would never accept the blame for anything that went wrong, even if it was completely his fault. No telling what exorbitant rate this Pablo was getting, and from what Pierce could tell, he was making it up as he went along. Killing babysitters and people on the wrong side, for Christ's sake.

He hadn't expected Pablo would bring the authorities charging into the casino. What he'd expected was a tragic and senseless accident, and a trio of freshly dug graves in the Gardner family plot. Maybe that was still Klein's plan. Maybe the rest was just misdirection.

Pierce made it to the bathroom, knelt at the toilet, and tried to talk himself out of throwing up, like a sick child would. But his reasoning failed.

27

JACK BEALS'S HOUSE WAS TWO MILES FROM THE CITY limits, a small brick ranch house set in a circle of leafless oaks surrounded by soybean fields. The place had a narrow gravel driveway and a neatly kept yard. Winter and Brad climbed out of the Tundra to a stiff northern wind that caused Winter to button his wool jacket against the chill and pull down the bill of his ball cap. The two men slipped on surgical gloves as they approached the front of the house.

The exterior windows were fitted with formidable

burglar bars, and the front door was a steel security model painted stone gray.

"Looks like Beals was paranoid," Brad said, taking an envelope out of his pocket. Opening it, he poured into his hand the ring of keys they'd found in Beals's pocket.

Two dead bolts later, Brad pushed open the front door and they stepped into Jack Beals's living room. Blackout shades made the house as dark as a cave, so using the light from the open front door, Brad found and flipped on the lights.

The living room furniture was spare, but tasteful and expensive. A sleek leather couch and matching side chairs faced each other over a maple coffee table set on a real zebra-skin rug. The light fixture was a sphere crafted of wide ribbons of bird's-eye veneer shaved so thin they were translucent. Two oversized abstract paintings hung on the walls and a freestanding bar near the door to the kitchen was topped with an ice bucket, a pitcher, and several bottles of liquor.

A plasma TV had been positioned on a sleek credenza, which Winter opened. It contained a video/DVD player and stereo setup that shared a pair of surround-sound speakers with the TV. Winter opened the drawers and thumbed through stacks of movies on DVD.

The master bedroom revealed a bed on a platform of polished wood, a large bamboo rug, two matching chests of drawers, and another abstract painting on the wall over the bed. "Not set up for spend-the-night guests either," Winter waxed.

The door to the walk-in closet was open, with the clothes neatly ordered on shelves or hung precisely on rods. A camera case sat on the floor. Inside the case Winter found a video camera.

The bathroom was spotless.

A steel security door with a dead bolt indicated that the room down the hall was probably not a guest room. One of the keys opened it, and Winter found the light switch beside the door. A row of fluorescent fixtures illuminated the room like high noon in Miami. The windows were plated in sheet metal, the floor covered with heavy canvas painted battleship gray.

This room was about as different from those in the rest of the house as a pig and a parrot. In a cabinet, behind sliding sheets of Lexan, a dozen pistols hung by their trigger guards on pegs. Some, like a SIG P-210 and a beautifully engraved Colt National Match 1911 with a four-digit serial number, were expensive. Three tactical shotguns fitted with high-intensity flashlights formed a row on one side. There were two AR-15s, one with a scope.

A pair of electronic earphones hung on another peg.

Two reloading presses were mounted on a sturdy table. Stacked red plastic bins at the rear of the table held cartridge brass in various calibers, bullets, powders, and primers. Hard long gun cases stood together under the table along with three pairs of hunting boots. Targets pinned to the walls held groups of interlocking holes from handgun practice.

An aluminum rifle case leaned against the wall. Winter put it on a table and opened it to find a tactical rifle with a camouflage composite stock and a very substantial scope.

Brad lifted the gun to read the markings on the barrel.

"Dakota T-76 Longbow in .338 Lapua Magnum," Brad

said. He opened the bolt and sniffed the chamber. He smiled. "It's been fired recently. I think we might not be dealing with your Styer after all."

Winter felt momentary relief that Beals might have fired the round that took Sherry Adams's life. But the feeling didn't last but a moment. "Even without my business card, it doesn't wash. He was a very neat young man," Winter said as he took the weapon and looked it over. "Why would he put this one away without cleaning it?"

"It's an expensive rifle," Brad said. "Five to eight grand. Maybe more. The optics could run four or five."

"But there's nothing here that shows he was the kind of marksman who could make a thousand-yard shot. This is the only real sniper rifle he had, and there are no rifle targets here. And," Winter said, "he wouldn't have left the brass behind. Aside from a ballistics match, he was a reloader and a neat freak. Doesn't fit."

Winter opened a side compartment in the gun case, where he found a dozen clove-scented red toothpicks. There were also four loaded rounds and leather shooting gloves.

"So, it still might not be your Styer," Brad insisted, his eyes widening. "Looks like the toothpicks and the gun belong to Beals. He could have intended to leave the toothpick we found behind his ear on Scotoni's corpse."

"This is a setup," Winter said firmly.

"You think Styer set Beals up? Think he knew Beals well enough to know about this room? Came here and planted the weapon after he killed him? Happened to have had a key to the house and this room?"

"Maybe or maybe not. I could get past the locks in a couple of minutes."

"You said Styer always works up close."

"Only with his primary targets, and I'm sure he was trained in long-range marksmanship," Winter said as he studied the handgun targets pinned on the walls. He noticed by the holes in the corners that one of them had been unpinned and pinned numerous times, and the others hadn't. He moved closer and pulled out the push-pins holding the top of the target, letting it fall so it was held to the wall by only the bottom pins. It revealed a metal front to a safe imbedded between the studs.

"Check the keys," Winter said. "There should be one that fits this."

One key slid into the lock and turned easily. Winter opened the door and took a deep breath.

"Christ," Brad said. "We need one of those bill-counting machines."

A dozen DVD cases sat on top of several neat stacks of currency. Each was carefully labeled with a date.

"Looks like we need some boxes," Winter said.

28

AFTER LEAVING THE MAJORITY OF THE EVIDENCE they'd gathered from Jack Beals's house in the sheriff's vault, the two tired men picked up fast food hamburgers and went to Brad's house to eat and get Winter settled.

Winter had checked out the DVDs so he could watch them away from the prying eyes of the other deputies. Where Styer was involved, the less that people knew, the better.

Brad lived in a two-story brick house on a tree-lined street near downtown with a muscular—and suspicious—Labrador and pit bull mix named Ruger. Brad showed Winter to a guest bedroom on the second floor. A few minutes later, the two men were sitting downstairs in Brad's den wolfing down the hamburgers they'd brought home. Ruger sat beside Brad's recliner, his dark eyes glued to the new guy seated in the recliner opposite his master.

"Ruger's a handsome dog," Winter said. "Bet he keeps strangers out."

"He's actually a she," Brad said. "She's just big boned. Aren't you, baby?"

Despite Brad's continuing admonitions, Ruger growled at their guest from time to time. Deer heads mounted on the walls stared out through glassy eyes and stuffed ducks on plaques flew imaginary circles around the furniture. Framed family pictures included one of a younger Brad Barnett in Marine fatigues. In the snapshot, he was holding a scoped rifle in the crook of his arm.

"I guess you're wondering what the friction between me and Leigh is about?"

"None of my business," Winter said. "But she does remind me of this girl I knew in grade school. Alice Murphy went out of her way to make my life hell. Whenever she saw me, she'd either stick out her tongue, rub my hair the wrong way, or pinch me. At a class reunion years later she told me she'd had a horrible crush on me in the third grade, and when I ignored her, she gave me a hard time to get my attention. Didn't seem like that to me at the time, of course. I mean, she terrorized me."

Brad smiled. "I went with Leigh from the sixth grade through high school," he said. "She was something back then. A finer, better looking, and sweeter girl never drew a breath. All the way up until I joined the Marines. I wasn't ready to go to college, and she was, and there was no war on then.

"Leigh's mother died from a heart attack a few weeks after I entered boot camp. No warning. She just closed her eyes while sitting in her chair watching some TV sitcom. Leigh and her father didn't even notice until the show was over. They thought she'd fallen asleep. That's the way to go out."

"I like to imagine I could die in my sleep," Winter said.

"During my four years in the corps, we drifted apart. Each time I came home, our thing was more strained and since we weren't together like before, our differences were more obvious to us. And I picked up drinking in the corps out of boredom. Leigh rarely drank and she had no patience for a drunk. We didn't fit the way we had before and I wasn't the same person I was when I left. She couldn't cope. In my defense, I was a cocky jerk with a beer in one hand and a large chip on my shoulder. I was TPP positive then."

"TPP?"

"Tested pumpkin positive. Means if you'd shined a light in my ear my face would have lit up like a jack-o-lantern."

Winter laughed, and Ruger growled at him for it.

"When I got back we had one last weekend in a

Memphis motel to try and rekindle something. Playing couple was great at first, but we ended up fighting, said terrible things to each other. She left, and I got drunk. I met a woman in a club and she came back to the motel with me. Nothing happened—at least I don't think it did—because I passed out in a state of undress. Leigh had a change of heart, drove back, and the gal opened the room door wearing her panties and bra. I was out in bed, and Leigh didn't ever want to speak to me again, and so for a long time, she didn't."

"Man, oh man," Winter said, shaking his head slowly, picturing Leigh standing there looking at the unsteady and scantily clad woman at the door, not to mention a naked Brad passed out across the mattress. "I can imagine that might've been hard to explain away."

"Before I got out, she ran off and married Jacob Gardner, one of those handsome guys who says all the right things to everybody, but once the newness wears off you can see he's an egotistical, insincere rooster. His family had an old name and not much money left, though nobody knew it until everything collapsed after he married Leigh. He's the kind of guy who always has a new set of best friends, and he climbs socially, or he did as long as there were fresh rungs available. She got pregnant, they got married, and she played mother hen and ran the place with her father while old Jake played golf and dabbled in dabbling."

"You never tried to patch it up after Memphis?"

"The ice never thawed and I went to Ole Miss. Once Leigh decides something, that's it in stone. My father's reputation here gave me an initial edge with voters because he brought about half the population of Tunica

County into the world. All I need to stay in office is to have his patients vote for me." Brad smiled and patted his dog. "I expect the people around here vote for him, not me. I'm trying to change that."

They talked on, about their friends in common, their law enforcement experiences, farming, and county politics. Winter told Brad about how he'd met Faith Ann and explained how she had become like a daughter to him and Sean. After that, he excused himself and called Sean's cell phone.

"Hey, cowboy," Sean answered. "Where you staying?"

"Call me Deputy Massey . . . again. I'm staying with my new boss, the sheriff. Where are you guys?"

"Have you leveled with him about Styer?"

"I haven't decided how much to tell him. I think I'll wait for the DNA comparison."

"Tell him, Winter. Don't let him be vulnerable because he doesn't know what he's dealing with."

"Maybe it's time."

"Yeah. Just in case, he should know. Faith Ann wants to visit Graceland, so I thought we'd stay a couple of days."

"I'd rather y'all would go on home. I'd feel . . ."

"I thought we'd eat at that rib place you told me about."

"Rendezvous. Yeah. It's close to the Peabody."

"Any objections to our staying over? He won't bother us. Besides, he's there, right?"

"You're right, Sean. But I'll be worried and if I'm worried . . ."

"Okay. We'll leave tomorrow morning at eight," Sean said. She was the strongest woman Winter had ever known, but she also knew when to give in. It was one of the things he loved most about her.

"Styer won't go after you guys at home."

Winter spoke briefly and wistfully to Rush, Faith Ann, and Olivia before he hung up and returned to the den.

"I think it's time you knew who I think we're probably dealing with," Winter said quietly. "How much do you know about me, what I've been involved with in the past?"

Brad fed Ruger what was left of his burger as he spoke. "I've heard some things. The Tampa courtroom shootings. I know there was some kind of big incident outside New Orleans a few years back with Sam Manelli's gang, and another one there a little over two years ago. And I know there was an incident in South Carolina involving the trial of Colonel Bryce, some rogue military intelligence officers, and the kidnapping of a judge's daughter and her child."

Winter nodded and said, "Brad, what I am going to tell you has to remain between the two of us. If you tell anybody I told you what I'm going to tell you, I'll deny it."

"I'm listening."

"Styer is a professional assassin from the Eastern Bloc who used to trade in seemingly impossible-to-kill targets, first for the KGB's elite Special Situations Unit, and after the wall came down, for a private murder-for-hire organization. When I sent your toothpick to the lab, I also sent them Styer's DNA. I got it from a scented toothpick he left in a rental car in New Orleans. I'm having that sample compared to your toothpick, and if it matches, we're going from bad to worse real fast. I've gotten what little I know about this guy from people who know things I don't. They talked to me because they hoped I might somehow lead them to him."

Brad crossed his legs at the ankles.

"Paulus Styer was born in East Germany and sent to the Soviet Union where he was groomed to be a weapon of selective destruction. He became a world-class professional assassin—a human chameleon who vanished two years ago after failing to kill me."

"You were his target?"

"He was told I was his target. The CIA used a hit on me to get Styer in the field so they could take him out when he made his move on me. They underestimated Styer and sent a single professional to kill him, but Styer found out the hit was a ploy and escaped. Faith Ann's uncle, my friend Hank Trammel, is a cripple, and his wife, Millie, was killed. Faith Ann saw Styer run them over with an SUV merely to manipulate me into a death game. He has a compulsion to show his victims, just before he kills them, how amazingly talented he is. I guess since he can't show the world his genius, he plays to an audience of two—himself and his target."

"He tried to kill you and failed?"

"He easily could have, but he decided not to. Look, nothing he does is without purpose. Maybe he killed Sherry Adams for another reason, but he definitely used that murder as bait to get me here. It's all a game with him. He isn't part of the same reality normal people share."

"Seems really farfetched," Brad said. "He knew I'd go right to you?"

"He is a grand master of manipulation."

"Can you take him?"

"Only if the playing field is slanted in my favor. Styer is way out of my class. In a toe-to-toe gunfight, I'd have an even chance. But outside that scenario, my odds crash."

"Could you . . . I don't know . . . contact the CIA for help getting him?"

Winter sat back and shook his head. "Asking the part of the CIA I'm talking about for help is the last thing we want to do. Be like asking a pack of starving wolves to guard your henhouse."

29

AFTER BEING KEPT BLINDFOLDED, GAGGED, AND tied up on the mattress in the back of her abductor's van for what seemed like hours, Cynthia Gardner found herself fully awake and completely alone.

The guy had to be some kind of serial killer or rapist or something.

Although she couldn't see anything, she knew that he had taken her back to the equipment shed. When he jerked the tarp off her body, she smelled the diesel and the cool earth floor of the barn.

"We're going to be here for a while. I'll let you eat and use the portable toilet, but remember my warning. You'll be spending the night here. You have any problem with that?"

Cynthia shook her head. As soon as her mother figured out she wasn't at her grandmother's she would be FTFT—freaking the fuck totally. But if he had let her live this long, she hoped the bastard was going to ransom her, and her mother would pay, and maybe he'd let her go home. She couldn't believe Jack would get her kidnapped, but he was certainly a man who liked money. It worried her, though, that the man hadn't bothered to hide his face from her. That could mean he was going to kill her, but it might also mean he was from out of the area and figured she couldn't identify him because they wouldn't catch him. Jack was smart and he probably didn't figure she'd know he was involved. He would probably think she was that dumb, the smug bastard.

She wondered if the man was serious about killing her if she tried to escape. Probably not, but doing what he said made sense. No sense pushing him.

He untied her hands and feet and led her to the toilet. She reached up to free the gag and he slapped her so hard she almost fell. Stunned, tears blurred her vision.

"Nothing you have to say is of any interest to me," he told her sternly. "Do your business."

Nodding, she turned with her back to the seat and looked pointedly at him, waiting for him to close the door, but he just held it open and stared back at her. Her bladder was bursting, so she bit her lip, looked at the floor, and slowly undid her jeans.

After she finished, he led her back to the van and retied her. She felt a sharp pain in the back of her arm and realized, when he pulled back, that he was holding a syringe. She protested in a low growl, but the sensation of floating in space killed the sound. She closed her eyes. Oblivion seemed like a good idea.

30

AFTER MEETING WITH THE SHERIFF AND HIS DEPUTY, Albert White spent several hours guzzling coffee while reviewing the camera captures of David Scotoni seated at the blackjack table, and that of the surrounding tables. Nothing he saw indicated that Scotoni was being monitored by anybody who might be the mysterious Pablo. Of course, he erased the eight-minute section of the tape that slowed Mulvane watching Scotoni from every camera that had recorded it.

Albert figured Pablo killed Beals, probably because Jack was nosy, or knew something that the guy thought threatened his future. Professionals hate curiosity—and witnesses. And they could be paranoid.

Several of the cameras covering the parking area caught Scotoni coming from his rental car and returning to it seven hours later. Albert erased the images of Beals following Scotoni to his car, getting into his Blazer, and trailing Scotoni. No cars seemed to have followed Beals from the lot. With selective edits he could leave footage of Scotoni leaving without a tail. He would have given the sheriff the footage of Beals, which could only make the case against Beals stronger—but Mulvane had decided he would tell the sheriff that Beals had indeed been in the casino while Scotoni was gambling—and had left an hour before the young cheater did, even if it gave Barnett a reason to dig deeper. That was better than being caught in a lie. But Albert wasn't going to give Barnett the keys to his own cell if he could help it.

Legally speaking, whatever Beals had told the kid was hearsay, and what could they prove? Barnett was just a small town sheriff, and he had a department packed with dim bulbs, drinking coffee and making their assholes' wages aside from what they could make on the sly. Without Beals to testify about Albert's partnership in picking off a lucky shit-heel here and there, this would probably go away. Anyway, Albert knew that nothing connected the two of them to each other.

Sheriff Barnett had less in common with his two more immediate predecessors than a rooster had with a python. Barnett never came into any of the casinos unless an investigation led him there, and he had enough of his own money to make him risky to try to bribe. Plus he was a straight arrow.

White had never before seen the new deputy who accompanied the sheriff. There was something about the name, Massey, that seemed vaguely familiar, and he had been trying to make the connection by not trying hard to do so. A psychologist once told him that thinking on anything too hard often drove the information deeper into the recesses of your mind.

He made a still print of the deputy, wrote *Massey?* on the bottom border, and filed it in the cabinet. The casino kept files on any and all politicians and law enforcement officers they came in contact with. He could make inquiries later.

What made Albert White so valuable to the casino was his commitment to protect the casino's profits to the best of his ability. He knew how to keep his mouth shut and he made sure he had the *right* people on his staff. Albert collected intelligence, fed it into the computers for cross-referencing and storage, and evaluated it for threats. After many years in law enforcement, he had discovered that the real secret of being successful lay in knowing not just what criminals were thinking, but how law enforcement officers thought and acted. It was all about staying on top of things, and following your instincts. For now, at least, this was familiar territory.

31

WINTER HAD BEEN UP SINCE FOUR THAT MORNING, so after eating he had gone upstairs for a shower and a few hours of shuteye. Lying in Brad Barnett's guest bed, staring up into the darkness, he realized that despite his burning desire to pay the monster back for what he had done to Millie and Hank Trammel, the last person on earth he wanted to come face-to-face with was Paulus Styer. Styer was more single-purpose machine than human being, and he killed with less thought than a smoker gave to crushing out a cigarette.

There was no doubt in his mind that Leigh Gardner had been the sniper's target. But why would Styer be targeting a lady farmer in Mississippi? Could Styer be so desperate for work that he would take on what had to be a low-paying assignment?

Winter closed his eyes and yawned. If Styer had left the toothpick and the card, he had fired the rifle, because according to everything Winter had learned about him, he killed alone. He didn't share the thing that made him tick—his ego wouldn't allow it.

The targets had something in common, and he had to figure out their connection. Later. Now, he would sleep.

32

FRIDAY

AT FIVE A.M., A STEAMING MUG OF COFFEE BESIDE him, Winter sat at the kitchen table and picked up the stack of Beals's DVDs he'd taken from the wall safe. Each of the jewel cases was labeled with a date, spanning the past two and a half years. Brad had placed a small TV set with a DVD player built into it on the table, and Winter opened the tray to feed it the first DVD. Brad had spent two hours at his office to tie up loose ends, since he knew his day would be taken up with the homicides.

For an hour Winter watched a series of sometimes shaky videos of people taken from inside a car, or through windows, exteriors and interiors of houses, close-ups of furniture in various anonymous rooms.

He looked beside him at the stack of DVDs waiting to be viewed and frowned. He decided to start with the tapes dated from the past few months and work his way to the present. After all, if any of this was going to be helpful—like spotting a partner, or if by some miracle Beals had photographed Styer and had been killed for that—it would probably have been filmed recently.

Flipping over the stack, Winter opened the last DVD Beals had made and inserted the disk dated six weeks earlier. After he watched it, he called Brad into the kitchen.

Ten minutes later, Winter and Brad stared at the screen. On it, a white pickup truck pulled up and parked in a nondescript lot. The doors opened and Leigh and Hamp Gardner got out as the camera zoomed to follow them into a grocery store. Hamp said something to Leigh and she laughed and popped him on the shoulder.

"Jesus Christ," Brad said. "Beals was following them."

"So I thought."

As Winter spoke, the camera held its focus on the doors and Jack Beals exited the store carrying two plastic bags of groceries in one hand, reading a gun magazine as he walked to his Blazer. Winter didn't think Beals was aware that he was being filmed—or that he knew he had walked past the Gardners.

"Wait a minute. If it isn't Beals taking the shots, he did have a partner," Brad said excitedly.

"Nope," Winter said. "Nothing to say so on the DVDs. I'd bet Jack took the others, but I think Styer shot this one."

The camera stayed on the Blazer until Beals drove away. On the dashboard the camera operator had placed a postcard with the image facing out.

"What's that on the card?" Brad asked.

"A ferry," Winter said.

"The Mississippi River," Brad said. "That's the New Orleans skyline."

Winter nodded. "Canal Street Ferry. It's a card from Styer to me. The ferry has meaning for him and me."

Brad said, "Maybe it's someone else who's been in New Orleans. After Katrina, this place was thick with refugees. Some stayed. Some of them were very bad people."

The rearview had been turned away in order not to capture the shooter's reflection. They watched as the photographer trailed Beals home, took a long shot of Beals's house as he drove slowly by. There followed a few seconds of close-ups of Beals's front door, and then five minutes of the interior of Beals's home, including the gunroom.

"Was Styer following Leigh or Beals? Is that how he spotted Leigh? Maybe the killer, your Styer maybe, got the tag number on the Gardners' truck or something and that was why he targeted them. Jesus, what the hell is this about?" Brad said, shaking his head as if to clear it.

"It was definitely a leer from Styer," Winter said. "Only he knows what this is all about. He's screwing with my head. But he's also giving us something to work with."

"Knowing it would confuse you? Us?"

"It's just part of the game," Winter said, sighing.

"Which part?" Brad asked.

"His favorite part. The smoke and mirrors."

33

AFTER VIEWING ENOUGH OF THE OTHER DVDS TO make sure they were worthless to their immediate investigation, Brad had returned to his office to count the cash they'd found in Beals's safe.

They hadn't found anything in Beals's house to explain the money in his wall safe. His computer, located in a drawer in the bedroom, contained nothing out of the ordinary. There were no password-protected files. They had his financial information and bank records, and copies of his IRS filings for the past five years. The computer tech said that Beals visited sites for dating, several for gun lovers and shooting aficionados, several militia groups in the western United States, and hard-core bondage pornography.

Styer had somehow known enough about Beals to cast him as the perfect patsy. Had they met on a web site? Maybe Styer hoped they would search through the computer to find all his posts and responses, but they had neither the time nor the manpower to do that yet. And

Winter doubted they could spot Styer in them. It was certain that Styer had removed any evidence of his connection to Beals when he left the rifle and the DVD he'd made. And while the fingerprint evidence wouldn't be processed for a few hours, Winter knew Styer wouldn't have left any. The techs had said that all of the prints looked, at first viewing, to belong to Jack Beals.

The one shot of the Gardners was all the footage there was of the family. After going over the videos that Beals had made, the only differences between them seemed to be the subjects leaving the Roundtable. Winter figured he had been selecting robbery victims, but who he had actually robbed, if he had done so, was not going to be easy to pick out. Brad would have to send fliers to sheriffs' and police departments asking for possible victims of strong-arm robberies who had gambled at the Roundtable.

It was after seven when the doorbell rang and Brad went to the door. While Ruger barked from the backyard, Winter could hear Brad's voice but not the person he was talking to. He heard Brad say, "Come in." Seconds later, Brad came into the kitchen and said, "Winter, this FBI agent says she knows you."

When Alexa Keen entered, Winter grinned, jumped up, and embraced her. "What are you doing here?"

"Would you believe me if I said I was just in the neighborhood?"

"Why didn't you tell me you were coming?"

"I knew you'd tell me not to," she said.

While Winter shook his head, his cell rang. He opened the phone and saw ProCell Labs on the ID.

"Massey," he answered. *Talk about timing.*

"Mr. Massey, John Jolly at ProCell. I just finished those

prelims. Now, once again, the test is not yet proven so it isn't acceptable for legal purposes."

"I don't care about that. Do *you* think it's accurate?"

"So far accuracy of the results is moving in the right direction, but in lay terms it's because we're doing a fast cook, forcing things. Not square pegs in round holes, exactly . . . We have it down to about a twenty percent negative error read after the other testing is completed for comparison accuracy, and I'd say we're closing the gap."

"What do they say?"

"Your sample matches the one Sheriff Barnett sent."

"So it's eighty percent."

"No. There is no difference between the two. I'd say it is one hundred percent."

Winter hung up, and looked from Brad to Alexa. "That was ProCell. It's a match."

He noticed that Alexa was staring at him. Knowing her as he did, it was obvious that she was pissed off.

"So," she said. "It's Paulus Styer?"

"Yes," Winter admitted.

"That's interesting," she said simply. "Do go on."

"Styer shot Sherry Adams, and he killed a man named Jack Beals," Winter said.

Winter shrugged and felt his face flushing like a kid caught shoplifting candy. "I should have told you."

"Yes, you should have." Alexa put her hand on Winter's forearm. "Well, now we know for sure what we're up against."

The call wouldn't change anything. Maybe having Alexa there would help, if only because she fully understood Styer's game.

Winter and Brad filled Alexa in on the investigation

while the trio had a breakfast of cold cereal. When the front doorbell rang, Brad answered it and returned with Leigh Gardner.

"Just coffee for me, Brad. And thank you for asking," she said, taking a seat at the table across from Winter.

"Morning, Ms. Gardner," Winter said.

"Call me Leigh and I'll call you Winter."

She smiled at Alexa and offered her hand.

"This is Alexa Keen," Winter said. "She's an old friend of mine. She's also an FBI agent."

Leigh raised her eyebrows. "The FBI is interested in Sherry Adams's murder?"

"No. I'm strictly here as a friend of Winter's and to help if I can," Alexa said. "Unofficially."

"I don't believe I've ever met an FBI agent before. Nice to meet you. Do I call you Agent Keen?"

"I answer to Alexa."

"Coffee," Brad said, placing a cup before Leigh.

She frowned, lifted the mug, and sipped gingerly. "Not bad brew, Brad. For a man." Her fingers were shaking as she set the cup down.

"I'm glad you think I can do *something,*" Brad said. "Is everything all right?"

"Well, Sherry is dead, so no."

"Sorry," Brad said, nodding.

Leigh looked down and back up at Brad. "That and Cyn didn't come home last night. I'm sure she's fine. This isn't unusual for my daughter. She does as she pleases. She went to Memphis yesterday and I wanted to go along. I should have insisted, but I had a lot on my mind. I got a text message from her late last night saying she'd run into a friend from school. She was supposed to be staying at her grandmother's, but I just got Adelle's machine. I've been trying to call her this morning and she sent a text, she always does when she knows I'm angry. It said, 'Get over it. GOD!' She's fine . . ." Her words trailed off.

Brad patted her shoulder but she drew back. "Can I do anything?"

"No. She'll come home dragging her tail and I'll yell at her. She's just like her father in some ways."

Winter saw the look of concern on Alexa's face.

"This thing with Sherry. It's got all of us crazy. It's Cyn's way of trying to hold on to normalcy and dealing with grief. Except for my father, nobody close to her has ever died," Leigh went on.

"I can start running her down," Brad said. "Get the Memphis PD to locate her."

"No, it's fine. I'll deal with it," Leigh said, straightening. "You know as well as I do that this is just like her. There's something I wanted to tell you."

Brad nodded.

She picked up her coffee but didn't drink from the cup. "I've been thinking about what you said about me being the target, and all I could think of is that if I had been killed, my children would not be able to continue my operation. And since their father has proved beyond any shadow of a doubt that he couldn't boil water in hell on their behalf, they would have to sell the land to ensure their futures. Jacob would not receive anything if I died, and I can't imagine he could have hired a professional killer."

"Okay," Brad said. "But he would be their guardian."

"I have made arrangements for my attorney to handle

my estate, and to handle my children's financial interests if I die."

"Jacob would fight that, and he is their father," Brad said.

"This is very personal," she said crisply, finally taking a sip. "If Jacob fights my will, my attorney has certain papers that prove he is as crooked as a wisteria trunk." She patted the side of her cheek and frowned.

"That's fairly common knowledge," Brad said.

"Anyway, although I certainly don't believe Jacob hired a hit man, I may have some idea why someone shot Sherry. A few years ago I once again paid off a collection of Jacob's debts, and I made him sign over some land he inherited from his father. I paid him three times what it was worth because it was the only collateral he had. Six hundred and thirty-six acres of bottomland that isn't good for a damn thing except duck hunting, which is what Jacob's father and then Jacob used it for. I made him a loan secured with that property and when he didn't repay me or make any attempt to do so, I foreclosed on it, figuring I'd leave it to the children, since it was the only way to ensure he would leave any legacy, even if I paid for it."

She took another sip of her coffee. "A few months ago Jacob mentioned that he wanted to buy it back from me. I told him to go piss up a pole. Since then, he has become more and more insistent, whining that it was his sole inheritance from his father, and he wanted it back. His father actually left him a small fortune that he went through in a matter of months. When I pressed him, he said he wanted to duck hunt on it and I said he could shoot ducks there until there wasn't one left on the face of the earth, but I'd never sell it to him under any circumstances."

"You don't think it's sentimental?" Winter asked.

"Jacob is as sentimental as a hungry possum. I told him that he'd had ample opportunity to pay me off, and didn't, and if his children wanted to sell it to him after I was gone, fine. But I said as long as I had air in my lungs, I was keeping it."

"And he dropped it?" Brad asked.

"No. He didn't. Last night he told me that some corporation was interested in buying it for four hundred thousand with a plan to turn it into a duck-hunting club along with the land around it, saying I could use the profit to make things right with Sherry's family."

"So," Winter said, "do you think it's possible Jacob hired someone to kill you?"

A look of concern crossed her features. "It's more likely the potential buyer would. Mr. Massey, did you know Tunica before the gambling joints came here?"

"I know it was the poorest county in the state."

"It's the richest now," Brad added.

Leigh continued, "Which made it the poorest county in the country. You know what's happened around here since those casinos came in? We've gotten the absolute dregs of humanity, political corruption, crooked cops and highway patrolmen. The last sheriff and deputies were caught protecting drug dealers—and there's been all sorts of rumors about people not getting the money they won and being threatened by employees of the casinos when they made waves. In exchange we get cheap license plates, new schools, low taxes, paved roads, and a fancy golf course for visitors. It's been a deal with the devil."

"Do you think mobsters are interested in your land?" Winter asked.

"That land is worth zip."

"Is it near the other casinos?" Winter asked.

"Not at all," she said. "Way south of them. The *improvements* they've made for the casinos have caused even more flooding down there than there was before. But Jacob Gardner would sell the gold out of our children's teeth and blow the money before their gums quit bleeding."

"I'll check it out," Brad said. "Where is Jacob now?"

"He stayed at my house last night. He'll sleep until sometime this afternoon."

"More coffee, Leigh?" Brad asked.

"Can't do it. I have to stay busy, and I've got plenty of work to do." Leigh stood and started for the front of the house. "By the way, some press people have been on the road this morning filming the house. And one of your prowl cars is obviously tailing me."

Brad shook his head. "I meant to tell you. We thought it was a good idea to have deputies watching you and the kids until we get this solved. I'm sorry for any inconvenience, but it's something Winter and I felt was necessary."

"You decided to have me followed without telling me," Leigh said, frowning.

"You can't be too careful. I think it's absolutely necessary, since we have no idea who we're dealing with," Alexa lied.

"Then you can tell them to follow closer, because I'm afraid if they miss a light and run through it someone might be killed," Leigh said.

"Not much I can do about the press," Brad said. "As long as they don't trespass."

" 'Not much I can do' seems to be your mantra," she said. "Finish your Wheaties. I'll show myself out."

After Leigh left, Brad said, "Cyn's always doing this."

"But with everything that's happened . . ." Alexa said.

"Cyn is . . . well, she more or less has to be the center of attention," Brad said. "I'll put through a description of her car, and make sure the Memphis police get it. Leigh is right. She's done this 'meeting a friend' thing since she was fifteen or so."

Winter could see that Brad was troubled, and offered the only reassurance he could think of. "Well, she did send that text message, at least."

34

ALEXA VOLUNTEERED TO GO TO THE COURTHOUSE to check the records on the parcels surrounding Leigh's land while Brad and Winter drove out to Six Oaks to interview Jacob Gardner.

Estelle opened the door and looked out, smiling broadly. "Brad Barnett again! I remember back to a time when every time I opened this door you was standing right where you standing now."

"Any word from Cynthia?" Brad asked Estelle.

"Lordy. That child! All the advantages she has and she shows her butt like she do. She is unresponsible and always has been. I told her a million times that proper young girls don't chase after boys like she do, but do she listen? No." Estelle shook her head sadly. "People gone think she a loose woman who don't have a heart, the way she torture her mama. Miss Leigh ain't home."

"We're here to see Jacob."

"Come on in. He's layin' up in the guest room bed like he the king of the world. He wakes up, he gone commence to ringing that little bell." Estelle stepped aside. "Like having a invalid in the house."

"Thanks, Estelle. I know the way," Brad said, stepping into the entrance, Winter shadowing him up the wide stairway.

Without knocking, Brad opened the door to the guest bedroom. The interior was made cave dark by thick curtains. As Brad flipped on the light, Winter was treated to the sight of Jacob Gardner lying on his back with his mouth open, the bed linen twisted around his feet like a binding. His comb-over stuck straight up, flying from his head like a flag. On the nightstand sat an almost empty bottle of Glen Salen and a glass partly filled with light brown water.

"Rise and shine, Jacob!" Brad hollered.

Like a doll, Jacob's eyes rolled open, and he stared up at the ceiling for a solid three count. He then sat bolt upright and looked at Brad and then Winter before gathering the sheets to cover himself. He tamped down his brown hair and blinked rapidly.

"What the hell are you doing barging in here?" Jacob asked.

"Investigating a murder," Brad said.

"In my room?" Jacob said.

"At the moment, yes," Brad replied, opening the curtains to let in daylight. He sat in a chair beside the bed and indicated that Winter should take the fabric-covered chaise lounge. "We need to ask you some questions."

"How about you do it after I get showered and dressed?"

"How about we do it now," Brad countered. "That way you can go back to sleep when we leave."

"Christ," Jacob said, lying back down and rubbing his eyes. "My head is killing me."

"If it does, I guess I'll have three deaths to investigate."

"So ask your questions," Jacob said, looking over at Winter.

"Sherry was killed accidentally," Brad said.

"Damned poachers," Jacob said. "Shooting wild. Jesus, it's terrible. How the hell are you going to catch the bastard?"

"No, the shooter was a professional killer. I have reason to believe that Leigh was his actual target, and Sherry looked enough like her in the hooded coat for him to assume she was Leigh. He obviously didn't know Leigh was out of town."

"How the hell can you know that? You caught the bastard?"

"Not yet," Brad said. "But we're closing in on him."

"It sounds like wishful thinking," Jacob said. "Why do you think anybody would try to kill my wife?"

"Ex-wife," Brad corrected.

Jacob rubbed his bloodshot eyes. "What would be the motive?"

"Money."

"In case you don't know it, only the kids would gain from her death. Maybe they're behind it. I'd look close at Hamp. He'd kill to have the money to buy a genuine beaver fur top hat."

"Nonetheless, I can't rule you out," Brad said.

Jacob looked at Brad like he was an idiot. "Me? And how would I profit from Leigh's death? Leigh has it fixed so if she dies, I'm left twisting in the wind. Not that I don't deserve it. I've made some mistakes. My life is an open book, Barnett. Her death would be a lose/lose situation for me. And when Sherry was shot I was in bed in Memphis with a former Miss Tennessee, whose number I will happily furnish." He grinned.

"The bottomland Leigh bought from you comes to mind as a motive."

Jacob frowned, but his eyes reflected the fires of concern. "She owns it outright, in case she didn't tell you *that* when she told you about *it*."

"Why do you want it?"

"It's been in my family since eighteen ninety."

"It's still in your family."

"Well, not exactly. I mean, yes, it is. But a man who doesn't own land is a second-class citizen. And in case it has escaped your astute powers of deduction, if I wanted to piss in a pot, I'd have to borrow one from my ex-wife. And odds are my bladder would explode while I was waiting for her to mull it over."

"I can't figure out how a man without means can afford to buy worthless land for hundreds of thousands over value. Leigh would expect hard cash," Brad pressed.

"I can use the land as collateral," Jacob said quickly.

"No offense, but based on your track record, you'd

probably lose it to the bank or whoever loaned you the money. I understand a corporation wanted it for a duck club," Brad said.

"She did tell you about it. Well, one has expressed interest, and mentioned a figure," Jacob said. "And maybe I could sell to said corporation for even more than I offered her. Did you think of that?"

Brad said angrily, "You should tell one story and stick to it so you won't have to try to keep the lies straight."

"Gamblers might just want to shoot ducks, or hogs, or frigging bison. They'll pay for the pleasure same as they pay for sex." Jacob smiled as though he'd just made a closing argument that had the judge and the jury nodding.

"I see," Brad said. "You have big plans, as usual."

"I can't believe you think I'd kill Leigh," Jacob said. "You're wasting my time. Of all the things I might be, I am not a killer. Like I said, I was in Memphis yesterday morning."

Brad shook his head. "I didn't say you fired the shot, Jacob."

"Mr. Gardner," Winter said, "do you gamble?"

Jacob shook his head.

Winter said, "See, if you owed money to someone, you might not be aware of that person's plan to kill your ex-wife in order to get his hands on her land. That someone might figure if she dies you inherit enough to cover the loan. If you told someone that, you don't have clear title, but you would if Leigh wasn't around . . ."

"No," Jacob said. "That's not possible. I don't owe anybody money. I don't gamble anymore."

"I've heard you don't gamble any less," Brad said.

"I have a law background and I know how things work," Jacob said.

"If you are being threatened," Winter said, "we can help. Whoever did this failed, but they may try again."

"If they harm Leigh, and I find out you've lied to us about anything, I will see that you pay," Brad said.

"Your affection for my ex radiates from you like sunshine, as always. That's what this is really about. You're white knighting to impress her by trying to make me look bad. Don't threaten me, Barnett. You're a sheriff, not a judge and jury."

"Fine," Brad said. "And I'm glad you aren't worried about your daughter being out of pocket."

"Out of pocket? Please. Cyn's been sexually active since she discovered she was cute. If she isn't at my mother's, she's shacked up with some boy."

"Your mother isn't answering her phone," Brad said.

"She turns off the ringer."

"Leigh has left messages."

"My mother hates Leigh. If Cynthia wasn't there, she'd call. Mama loves Cynthia."

"Let me know when you hear from her so *we* can stop worrying."

Jacob Gardner's eyes relaxed and he smiled. "If that's all," Jacob said, lying down, "Cyn's an adult. Cut the light off and get the hell out of my room."

"Tell you what. If we talk about this again, it'll be in *my* room."

Brad walked to the door, which Winter had opened.

"By the way," Jacob said. "I didn't take Leigh away from you. You threw her to me."

35

AS BRAD AND WINTER ENTERED THE MAIN DRAG near the courthouse, the radio came to life.

"Sheriff, what's your twenty?" Chief Deputy Roy Bishop's voice crackled.

"I'm almost at the courthouse."

"Me too," Bishop said.

"I see you," Brad said.

A cruiser flashed its lights ahead and pulled over on the opposite side of the wide street. Roy Bishop got out and hurried over as Brad rolled down the window. "What's up, Roy?"

"The damned press is driving me crazy. We have to tell them something soon."

"Soon," Brad told him. "Tell them we're getting close on the Adams murder, and as soon as we have things sorted out, we'll let them know. You met Winter last night."

"I did." Roy reached over Brad to shake Winter's hand. "Bettye said you were some kind of specialist. Welcome aboard."

"Winter's a retired U.S. marshal. Grew up in Cleveland, Mississippi. He's agreed to help us with the Adams homicide and Beals. As a personal favor."

The chief deputy gave Winter a quizzical look. "Wait a

damn minute," he said, his face reddening. "You're *that* Winter Massey? I mean, Jesus Christ! You're that U.S. marshal. Hell, I thought you would be taller."

"So did my mother," Winter said.

"We don't get many murders around here," Roy said. "Now we get two in one day. Jack Beals was a first-class prick, but he didn't deserve to die like that. Hey, is this something bigger than it looks?"

"Looks plenty big to me as it is," Winter said.

"Where's David Scotoni?" Brad asked.

"At the Best Western with Walters watching him. He wants to get the hell out of Dodge."

"No problem," Brad said. "He's told us everything he knows. Get his phone numbers and escort him to the state line."

"Sure thing," Roy said, straightening as a speeding Lincoln Navigator flew past, then made a sweeping U-turn. "Damn," Brad said. "Go on, Roy. If you need me, use the cell. I don't want to use the radio with the press all over the place."

Winter saw a red-faced man in a suit who looked like a newscaster get out of the Navigator and race toward the truck. The man maneuvered around Bishop and looked into the cab.

"Brad," he said.

"Ed," Brad said. "I want you to meet Winter Massey. Winter, this is our prosecuting attorney, Ed Moore."

Moore nodded at Winter. "I had a call from the head of MBI. They want in on these killings now. They said you're blocking them so they want me to make the request. I wanted to clear it with you as a courtesy before I did it."

"Don't need them," Brad said. "This is proceeding nicely."

"Two homicides, Brad. Why wouldn't you need them, for Christ's sake?"

"That's why I asked Massey in. He's a specialist in this sort of thing and has no dog in the fight. Lab assistance is all I need from the MBI for now."

"Captain Mackey was very insistent," Moore said.

"He said I'm in over my head, right? They only want in on the Beals killing because it's tied to a casino employee, and they want to clear it up however they can. We're already on top of it and it's staying that way."

"Damn it, Bradley. If it concerns the casinos . . ." Moore said nervously.

"Relax, Ed. It concerns an ex-deputy dead guy who worked security at a casino. If you want, you can tell them it was an armed robbery gone bad. We both know that MBI will only come in and make us look bad if they can, to make sure the casino doesn't get any negative publicity. They're always working in the casinos' best interests."

"That's not something I know at all," Moore said defensively.

"Know this. If the MBI comes in, I'll request the FBI come in and we'll have us a sharp-elbow sideshow and I can guarantee you that the casinos will get more negative press than they can deal with."

"Wait a minute," Ed said. "That's not something we want. That sounds like a threat."

"I can make that a promise if you'd feel more comfortable with that. The FBI isn't coming in unless I request their assistance," Brad said. "MBI is not going to use my department to wipe the casino's butt, and they aren't going to bury anything as long as I'm in this office. If someone from the casino operation is responsible for a murder, that's just going to be a shit-hits-the-fan deal. Early next week we'll reevaluate where we are and if I need MBI, I'll pull them in."

Moore said, "Your office doesn't exactly have a sterling reputation around the state. People see the MBI as better suited, less able to . . ."

"You say 'be bought off,' and I'll climb out and beat your ass right here in the street. I whipped your ass in the fifth grade and I can do it again."

"I've known you all my life, Brad. You don't have to say shit like that to me." Moore smiled. "This is still our county. It's your call."

"I know it."

Using the back of his fingers, Ed Moore slapped Brad's shoulder through the window.

He turned and took a few steps before turning around and coming back. "And, Brad. You didn't beat my ass in the fifth grade. I slipped and fell."

Brad pushed open the door, and Ed made a show of hurrying toward the Navigator. His laughter echoed richly in through the window as Brad rolled it up.

"In the fifth grade I whipped old Ed like a redheaded stepchild," Brad said, winking at Winter. "He's been in denial ever since."

36

THE LAND-TRANSACTION RECORDS FOR THE COUNTY were kept in the basement of city hall. A clerk who looked like a Jessica Tandy impersonator located the plot and its corresponding numbers on a county map and wrote them down. Armed with the scrap of paper, Alexa placed the book the clerk had pointed out on the table, opened it and ran her fingers down the columns, looking for the numbers for the southwest corner of the county.

She found the entry where Jacob Gardner had transferred title of the plot to Leigh nine years before. Checking the adjoining plots, she quickly discovered that a corporation named RRI Limited had systematically purchased the surrounding land over the past eighteen months.

Alexa decided the best way to check out this RRI corporation was to see whether the kind of people who would resort to violence might be connected to it. She dialed an extension at FBI headquarters and asked for Louis Sykes with the Organized Crime division.

"Louis, it's Alexa. I need a favor."

"Name it," he said. "Anything but my peanut butter cookie recipe."

"Can you check your files for a corporation named RRI Limited? All I have is the name on some land transfers."

"Sure."

"I'll be waiting for your call."

Alexa put the books back and went outside, where Winter and Brad had just parked. After Winter got out and opened the back door, she climbed into the backseat of Brad's truck.

"A company named RRI Limited has been buying up the land around Leigh's parcel."

"It could be a hunting deal like Jacob told us," Brad said. "But I wouldn't believe Jacob if he said tornados scatter dirt. Who'd kill to put together a duck-hunting club?"

"Twenty-nine hundred acres so far," Alexa said. "I assume that since RRI now owns all of the surrounding land, they'd want Leigh's. I'm having OC look to see if there are any red flags associated with their name. Then we can look them up on the Internet and I've got friends who can get us the pertinent information."

"I bet Jacob is aware of RRI's purchase, and thinks he'll make serious bucks on the deal," Winter said. "If RRI can't do whatever they have planned with their land unless they have hers, that's a motive."

"If anything happens to Leigh, the kids inherit the land," Brad said, "but it would be tied up in probate for a long time."

"Unless a judge sped that up for the right person or group," Alexa said.

Winter said, "We could check to see if there are plans to improve the roads, deal with utility upgrades, power, sewage, water pipes, that sort of thing."

"I haven't heard anything," Brad said. "Anybody starts pulling permits from the county, people talk. Maybe they're waiting until they have the land sewed up to start that process."

Alexa said, "I don't know, Leigh, but I got the impression that something was eating at her."

"Like her babysitter getting her head blown off?" Winter said. "Her daughter going AWOL?"

"Just a feeling I've got. You know her, Brad. Do you think Leigh is telling us everything? Is it possible that she knows more about the land than she's letting on?"

"I've known Leigh most of my life. She's a tough cookie and she pinches a dollar until Washington pees his pants, but if you're insinuating . . ."

"I'm not casting aspersions on her character," Alexa said. "But I've got a sense there's things she isn't telling us. I could be wrong."

"My mother had this old adage. 'Have more than you show, pay as you go, and tell less than you know,' " Winter said.

"That sounds like it was written about Leigh," Brad said.

"What do you guys say to having a look at this land?" Alexa said. "I'd like to see what three thousand acres of worthless land looks like."

37

PAULUS STYER PULLED THE VAN BACK INTO THE equipment barn. He found Cynthia asleep in the mummy bag in her tarp-covered car, still knocked out from her last injection. A corpse would take less of his valuable time, but he had decided to keep her alive for the time being. If he changed his mind, there would be plenty of time to finish her before he had her mother and brother in the same place, and then he could stage all three of their accidental deaths. His instructions were clear, but how he accomplished the task was up to him. It was nice to be in a position of trust, though he had more than earned it over the years.

He watched the girl's eyes slowly open and he saw the fear gathering in them, so he quickly took out the syringe and, leaning over, gave her another injection. This time she would not be asleep as long as she had been before, but he was going to move her closer to his base of operations, and somebody might come along to check on the equipment.

After she closed her eyes, Styer lifted her and carried her to the waiting van. As he laid her inside, he was sure he heard something and went to the open door. Looking out, he saw a truck pull into the fields from the woods. He pressed the switch to close the massive overhead doors, cursing the slowness of the winch that growled as it dropped the steel door from the ceiling. He ran to the van and took out his pistol, waiting as the door finally closed and went quiet.

He moved to the personnel door, cracked it open, and watched as the sheriff's truck moved slowly toward the building. He didn't see how they could have tracked him, but they must have seen the big door closing.

Angry that he had left the gate open, he cursed the fact that Massey and the sheriff were taking all the fun out of his operation. But Styer was prey with teeth. He smiled as he thought, *What is, is.*

38

IT TOOK TWENTY MINUTES OF DRIVING ACROSS THE bleak landscape on blacktop county roads, plus a trip down a rutted thinly graveled trail, before they arrived at the site, a vast flat field nestled against the levee. Under the smoke-gray sky, it looked like a black and white photograph of a WWI battlefield. Stagnant water stood in a series of shallow ponds inhabited by hundreds of ducks. For half a mile to the north and south, trees had been cut to the ground. Scattered piles of tortured tree limbs and other organic debris lay where hardwoods had been pushed or broken down as if by artillery shells. At the southern end of the scalped land stood an enormous, newly constructed metal building. It stood alone on a graveled lot surrounded by a tall hurricane fence topped with barbed wire.

"This is recent," Brad said.

"Equipment came over from that building to do the clearing," Winter said, tracing the dozer tread tracks with his eyes to the fenced-in structure. "Whose is it?"

"That's just outside the county line. I recall something about the Corps of Engineers putting in an equipment facility to support their dredging activities, but we don't really patrol this corner unless we're called because it's all private land."

Alexa wondered aloud, "Would the Corps of Engineers have done that for a company?"

"I don't know," Brad said. "They've worked all the way around Leigh's parcel, and can't go onto hers until that acquisition is final. But as soon as they know it's a done deal, whoever it is can begin doing whatever the hell they have in mind."

Alexa's cell phone rang and she looked at the ID. "It's Louis Sykes from OC." She opened it. "Louis, that was fast."

She listened for almost two minutes without interrupting, thanked him, and hung up.

She said, "RRI stands for Royale Resorts International. They own casino resorts all over the world. Most are high-end all-inclusive resorts with a couple of exceptions, most notable being the Columns Casino in Atlantic City and the Roundtable."

"I guess the connection between the Roundtable and the Gardners is solid enough now," Winter said.

"Sure looks that way," Brad said, as he drove toward the barn.

Alexa asked, "If they were going to put in a casino, they could cut a channel in the levee and replace it once the casino gaming structure is in place. That is how it's done, isn't it?"

"They could put fifty casinos on this place," Brad said.

"Or one extremely large gambling resort," Winter said. "It'd cost hundreds of millions of dollars."

The personnel door next to a large equipment door swung closed. "You see that?" Winter asked.

"Sure did," Brad said. "Someone's in there."

"Let's go talk to them," Winter said.

"And say what?" Alexa asked. "I don't think we should let them know we're interested in this land."

"You're right," Winter said. "We'll just say we're looking for a duck-hunting site."

As they approached, it was easy to see from the truck that the gate wasn't locked. The logging chain and padlock were hanging from the chain links, and the gate hadn't quite closed the last time someone had come through it. Winter opened the gate and they drove into the lot. Brad parked near the door and they climbed out. While Alexa and Brad stood on either side of him, Winter made a fist and pounded on the corrugated steel personnel door, which was locked.

"Hello in there!" he shouted.

"Who is it?" a muted voice called from inside.

"Deputy Sheriff Massey," Winter called out.

"Sheriff Barnett," Brad yelled.

Alexa was silent.

"What y'all wants?" The voice was that of an elderly black man.

"Open the door and we'll talk," Brad said.

"Y'all ain't supposed to be here unless Mr. Todd says so. I been instructed not to open the door for nobody what ain't been announced 'forehand. That's the rules and I don't wants to get fired."

"Who owns this building?" Brad said.

"I don't know all that," the man answered. "You the sheriff. Don't you know it?"

"Open the door," Brad said.

"Push your warrants beneath the door," the voice called back. "I can't open unless Mr. Todd says to. Ain't you the sheriff over in Tunica County?"

"I am," Brad called out.

"Well, no disrespecting untended, suh, but this here ain't Tunica County. I have to ask y'all to leave. If you want, I'll call Mr. Todd and he can come out and you can talk to hum. He could be here in about a hour or two. He in Memphis."

Brad was thinking. He looked at Winter, who shrugged in defeat.

"That's all right. We were just checking out a call about a rabid fox. You seen any foxes wandering around foaming at the mouth?"

The man inside was silent for a few long seconds.

"I got me a rifle and if I sees hum I know what to do with it."

"Okay. Sorry we bothered you," Brad said.

The trio walked back to Brad's truck, got in, and drove slowly back out of the gate.

"Rabid fox," Alexa said, laughing.

"We've had them," Brad said defensively.

When they had reached the road in the woods, Winter looked back just in time to see the personnel door close.

39

ALBERT WHITE ARRIVED OUTSIDE THE TUNICA County Airport and parked as close as he could get to the main doors. He climbed out and went around to the passenger's door. Seconds later, a man with short blond hair, an overcoat, and sunglasses strolled out of the terminal carrying a suitcase and a hanging suit bag. The man moved like a professional athlete.

"I thought Tug Murphy was meeting me," he said, smiling like a salesman offering up his private stash of brilliant white teeth.

"I'm Albert White, director of casino security. Tug was out of pocket, so I came. He should be waiting for us when we get back."

"I was messing with you, Albert. Part of my job is to know what everybody at the casino looks like. Nice to meet you."

He slipped off his sunglasses and shook White's hand firmly.

"Welcome, Mr. Finch," Albert said.

Finch looked directly into White's eyes as if he was reading a sign hanging on the inside back wall of his skull.

White opened the rear door to allow the man to put his baggage inside the compartment. Usually RRI employees arrived in chartered aircraft, landing and pulling into a hangar to keep nosy people from seeing who was arriving or departing. This man was at the main terminal, and no commuter or commercial flights had landed within the last hour. A man who worked security at the airport took money from the Roundtable to steer arriving passengers their way. White had spoken to him and after giving the man Finch's description, he'd told White that Finch had walked into the terminal from the parking lot to wait near the doors as though he'd just flown in. Very odd. White figured he'd been around scouting before he officially appeared. Supposedly he was good, and Kurt Klein could afford the best of everything.

"I hope your flight was okay, Mr. Finch," White said.

"My flight was fine, Albert. Call me Steffan," the man said, nodding. His accent sounded British, but White knew from his research that Finch was South African, and he'd spent years living and working in England with the SAS.

"Let's be off," Finch said, checking his watch, a matte black chronometer.

"So Tug is a recent hire, I understand."

"That wasn't in your files?"

Finch smiled. "Tug isn't his real name, is it?"

White shook his head. "A nickname he had legally changed to his Christian name."

"The nickname Tug," Finch said. "What does that signify?"

"He told me that when he was a kid, he used to pull on his old man's pant leg to get his attention. His dad called him Tug."

"Oh," Finch said. "I hoped it would be more interesting."

Albert White put the SUV in gear and rolled off into the bright Delta day.

Finch turned on the radio, which Tug must have set to NPR, and tuned in a classic country music station. While White concentrated on his driving, George Jones told the SUV's occupants about a relationship he had a few regrets about.

40

ALTHOUGH HE'D HAD A WARNING FROM SECURITY, Pierce Mulvane didn't look up when Jacob Gardner entered his office accompanied by a security guard. Pierce calmly finished reading the floor reports from the past twenty-four hours. Despite the fact that the numbers were very good, he held a frown on his face. Finally he looked up, feigning surprise at finding that someone had come into his office while he was engrossed in his business.

Mulvane dismissed the guard with a wave of his hand, waiting until he was gone to speak.

Jacob Gardner wore the sincere smile of a desperate used car salesman and did his best to appear relaxed, but Pierce could smell the anxiety radiating from him, just as strong as the stale odor of booze that wafted from his pores.

"How've you been, Mr. Mulvane?" Jacob asked.

"I guess if you didn't have good news for me you would not be here," Pierce said. "So I assume your ex-wife has accepted my generous offer."

"Well, I was inches from getting this resolved, but there was an incident at her place yesterday, so there wasn't any time for a business discussion. Unfortunate set of circumstances."

Pierce said, "The hunting misadventure involving the young girl. I heard about it. Very unfortunate, but just as well it wasn't your daughter or your ex."

"Leigh's pretty damned upset, as you can imagine. She was very fond of that girl. We might have to conclude this after the funeral," Jacob added.

"When is the funeral?"

"Saturday, I think. I'm sure we can negotiate a deal before Monday, Tuesday latest."

Pierce took out his pen and opened it. "I'm sorry, but this matter has to be concluded before Monday, or it will be out of my hands. This is what I am going to do. I want you to pass on an offer that should negate the need to haggle further. This is going to be the absolute top dollar we will pay and our absolute final offer. We have the political clout to have the land condemned and if I have to wait that long, your ex will be paid a sum for the land based on what we paid for the adjoining properties, which wasn't very much."

Jacob had his hands clenched together in his lap, waiting for the number. *Not just yet,* Pierce thought.

"If memory serves," he said, "we have your checks totaling three hundred and twenty-one thousand dollars. One ten you lost here and the rest was consolidated from certain other casinos and individuals with the help of the list you furnished us."

"Yes."

Pierce stared at Jacob. "A substantial amount, secured by a piece of land you claimed to own at the time you agreed to these actions."

Jacob's fevered eyes darted around the room as he nodded.

"The last figure we discussed for the parcel was nine hundred thousand, which you told me you passed on to Ms. Gardner. My question is how this woman, an astute businesswoman, can refuse such an offer. You did present her with our offer, didn't you? Nine hundred thousand dollars?"

Jacob Gardner's eyes fell to his lap. "Well, I actually . . ."

"I thought as much. How could I be so stupid to believe anything an attorney—especially a disbarred one—says? What figure did you offer her?"

"Well, I had to cover my losses here in the deal."

"I told you months ago we'd work that out. And each time we have discussed it, we've had to track you down. Each time I pressed you and like a wet eel you slipped away." Pierce felt his anger rising and clenched his teeth.

This was worse than he'd imagined. He should have figured Jacob would try to screw her as he had them.

"I am a patient man, Gardner. Truly I am, but there are people upstairs putting pressure on me who are not nearly as indulgent as I am. I have depended on my powers of persuasion as well as your intelligence, but obviously I badly misjudged you. Even for a degenerate gambler who lives by feeding off the labors of his ex-wife, you set a new record for sleaziness, dishonesty, and selfishness."

"I know," Jacob blurted. "I'm not a well man, mentally or physically. I might have cancer. They're running some tests."

"I can check that," Pierce said, adding a note of warning.

"I'm going to have testing done," Gardner mumbled. "I have some troubling symptoms."

"Here's what I'm going to do," Pierce said, making notes on a piece of stationery. "I will pay Ms. Gardner two point five million dollars for the land. In the interest of rewarding you for brokering the deal, I will not merely cancel your debt to the casino, but I will give you an additional five hundred thousand dollars in cash, which is a net to you of eight hundred and twenty-one thousand. And we will all live long and healthy lives—assuming you *don't* have cancer, naturally."

Jacob Gardner straightened suddenly and his lips turned up at the corners. "Okay. I mean, man alive. That's a very, very generous offer."

"Now, use all of your persuasive powers to make sure she accepts it."

"See, I haven't told her who wanted the land because I know her and I thought that if she sees the intended use for the land, she'll want more. It has taken a great deal of finesse."

"Explain to Ms. Gardner that she must take this, or I will pursue alternatives that will be far less financially rewarding. We do not want further unpleasantness, but if there is any, it's going to be unpleasant for you. That's all I intend to say on the matter."

Jacob stood.

"And, Gardner." Mulvane held out his open hand. "The recorder?"

Meekly, Gardner took a tape recorder from his pocket and placed it in Mulvane's hand.

"I just wanted to make sure I had it so I'd remember the meeting, the specifics of your offer."

"Yes." Pierce snapped the recorder off, took out the cassette, and tossed it into an open drawer before throwing the empty device back to Gardner, who managed to catch it clumsily.

"We have to trust each other. Not to do so is courting disaster."

"I understand, Mr. Mulvane."

"I certainly hope so," Mulvane said, cranking up his smile. "This works as planned. If you screw this one up, nobody on earth can help you."

41

AS JACOB GARDNER RODE DOWN IN THE SMALLER private elevator, he blamed his hangover for the fact that he was sweating, his hands were trembling, and he felt oddly disconnected from reality. The tape recorder had been a risky move, but he had wanted to have evidence of Mulvane taking credit for the girl's murder on tape to give him an edge, if necessary. Mulvane hadn't admitted to the killing, but it didn't mean he didn't have it done. It was good that he hadn't taken the recorder personally, though.

It infuriated Jacob that his spoiled bitch of an ex-wife would get any of the money. It was all rightfully his since she had stolen the land from him when he was down-and-out, but at the moment he could see no choice. Despite Mulvane's Monday deadline, he probably still had time to try to figure out something. Without buying the land, there was no way Mulvane could get his hands on it unless Jacob got the kids to agree to sell it. If Leigh were out of the picture, getting the children to agree would be simple, if he could get power of attorney. With every foot the elevator descended, Jacob was more certain that Leigh was the only obstacle to his financial well-being.

He knew Mulvane had sent the shooter, who had delivered the message that it was a simple matter to kill whomever they chose, whenever they liked. Lucky thing for Leigh that it was the black gal that was targeted, but too bad for him. With enough cash Jacob could start over, buy a successful business, and live like a king without a worry in the world. He couldn't do that on the pittance Mulvane had offered him—not by a long shot.

As Jacob exited the elevator he almost ran into Albert White and another man who fit the image of what Jacob imagined professional killers looked like. He wondered if that was the man who'd shot Sherry Adams.

Just after Jacob got into his Cadillac, his cell phone buzzed. Checking the ID, he answered it.

"So what the hell are you pulling now, Cyn?"

"Listen carefully, Mr. Gardner. I won't repeat myself." The unfamiliar voice sounded almost mechanical. "I have your daughter. She is fine and will stay that way unless Mrs. Gardner holds on to that land. Make that sale happen. Let's keep this just between the two of us. Any cops get involved . . . well, you know what."

The phone went dead.

42

ALEXA'S CELL PHONE RANG, AND WHEN SHE LOOKED at the readout her heart almost stopped. The display read H. HATCHER. Waving to Winter, she stepped into the sheriff's conference room to take the call. Assistant FBI Director Hayden Hatcher, who ran the Counterterrorism Division, was calling from his office.

"Alexa Keen," she said.

"Alexa, Hayden Hatcher. I hope I'm not catching you at a bad time."

"Not at all, sir. Can I help you with something?"

She pictured the sandy-haired Hatcher, a Bureau golden boy in his late thirties, a few inches over six feet tall, trim as a boxer, and handsome in a corn-fed Midwestern kind of way. He had worked his way up from the Omaha field office due to successful outcomes, an appealing personality, a head for political gamesmanship, and—most of all—a talent for clasping the right coattails. He had been promoted after 9/11 to the growing anti-terrorism arena—the department with the biggest budget, which was therefore where the sex appeal stayed these days. His and Alexa's offices were on opposite sides of the building, and their paths seldom crossed.

"I understand you have made inquiries into RRI. May I ask what this request for intelligence relates to?"

"A casino operation in Mississippi. The Roundtable. I made an inquiry to assist an investigation by Tunica County, Mississippi, authorities." Alexa couldn't imagine why casinos would be of interest to Hatcher, unless they were somehow being used to funnel money to terrorist cells, which seemed unlikely.

"I see. And how is it that the Tunica County authorities went through you? The sheriff called you for it?" he asked.

"Yes." Alexa felt a heat deep in her stomach and managed to keep her voice neutral. "Actually, one of his deputies asked on his behalf."

"I assume this somehow involves an abduction, if you were called?"

"No, sir. A murder. The sheriff suspects there may be a connection to the casino because the victim worked for casino security."

"And do you mind telling me why a deputy sheriff contacted you to make the request?"

"He called me because we've known each other since we were teenagers. And we worked together on a case."

"Who is this deputy?"

The heat in her stomach suddenly felt like a forest fire. "Massey." She suspected that the deputy director already knew that Winter had made the request, which seemed impossible.

"You worked with Winter Massey on the kidnapping of Judge Fondren's daughter and grandson in Charlotte." His lack of hesitation signaled that, sure enough, Hatcher had already known. "Naturally I'm familiar with the case and with Winter Massey. I wasn't aware that he was a deputy sheriff in Tunica County."

"He's working with the sheriff there as a personal favor. Does his inquiry intersect with another investigation under way that involves Counterterrorism?"

"No, I was just curious when I heard about your inquiry. Usually when Massey appears on our radar screen, unpleasant complications arise from his activities. I'm just wondering if the Bureau should become involved in supplying information to him. I'm calling to make an informal inquiry to get clarification on the nature of the request."

"Does this threaten any CT investigation?" she asked pointedly.

"Not directly."

"The director has asked us to cooperate with local and regional law enforcement. I was involved with NOPD last year under that policy, and it seems to me that this falls under that heading," she said.

"Still, you aren't the proper channel for requests like this one. Since you asked OC, I wondered about a suspected connection to organized crime. Often our cases do intersect."

"They don't suspect the casino of being involved with organized crime or terrorists, as far as I know. They just wanted to know if there was anything that pointed to one."

"I just don't want to get caught by surprise if any complications arise that could impact the Bureau. Due to their nature, and the money involved, casinos tend to have open case files, and maybe what Massey learns in his investigation could be helpful to us. A two-way street is always preferable to a dead end. You get the picture. You're a team player. If you tread on anything, I'm sure someone will let you know. Massey can be trouble. I'd hate for you to be embarrassed if something goes off on this one."

"I've known Winter Massey for over twenty years. He is a capable man who acts in both a legal and deliberate manner. If anything happened to me, I'd want him finding out what happened. He's the sort of person you want to work with, given a choice."

"Very good," Hayden Hatcher said. "Carry on. We should have lunch when you get back."

"Absolutely," she said.

He hung up.

Alexa knew that unless a company or an individual was flagged by Counterterrorism, there was no reason for Organized Crime to notify Hatcher. The Bureau was eighty percent politics and, like all intelligence organizations, it was a paranoid monster that lumbered about blindly, its feet entangled in red tape and its hands bound by sibling rivalry. Sharing information between departments usually took a request from one to the other.

Alexa Keen didn't trust many people in the Bureau, and she especially didn't trust Hayden Hatcher because his loyalty depended on the direction of the political winds. She trusted Winter Massey without reservation, and she knew that getting in his way was a very bad idea.

43

AFTER HANGING UP, HAYDEN HATCHER LIFTED HIS encrypted phone and dialed a number he had committed to memory.

"Yes?" the familiar voice said.

"It's Hatcher. It appears we have another scented red toothpick left at the scene of a killing south of Memphis," Hayden said. "This one is being handled by Bradley Barnett, the sheriff in Tunica County, Mississippi."

"Who was the target?"

"A young black girl. Nineteen years of age. Shot from long distance with a rifle. Not like the others, is it? You said any reports of red, clove-flavored toothpicks at murder scenes. This makes four in fifteen months."

"How did this one come in?"

"Through Alexa Keen, she's in—"

"I know who she is," the voice said. "You found out how?"

"Well, it was picked up via an *overheard* conversation." He wouldn't admit over the phone that she was under continuing internal surveillance ordered by Hayden at the behest of his benefactor. "She got a request for expedited DNA on the toothpick from a friend of hers. Are you familiar with Winter Massey? It seems he had a sample to compare it to."

The only sound coming over the line was that of breathing.

"So the toothpick is connected to the man you're looking for? The East German?" Hayden asked.

"We'll deal with this. If anything else pops up, you will let me know immediately." It wasn't a question. The line clicked as the man hung up.

Hayden placed the phone in its receiver and rocked back in his chair.

He was excited. Pleasing his benefactor was the key to his amazing run of successful operations against terrorist cells inside the United States, its territories, and, most recently, Canada. His man had alerted Hayden to a Hamas cell that was bootlegging low-tax cigarettes from North Carolina to New York and other cities, and then to a group of amateur Canadian terrorists plotting to blow up targets across Canada, take over parliament and—as absurd as it sounded—behead the Canadian prime minister. Hayden had, as instructed, given the intelligence to the Canadian authorities, who had in turn given him personal credit for his assistance. It was this voice in the darkness that had put Hayden Hatcher this close to the throne.

Whoever this murderous East German toothpick dropper was, he was someone the shadow man's group had been after for a long time—and he was someone his secretive friend clearly wanted very badly. Hayden certainly hoped they got him. And if all worked out as planned, he was confident that someday, as the man had insinuated on many occasions, Hayden Hatcher would be the director of the FBI.

44

SHORTLY AFTER ONE P.M., BRAD STEPPED TO THE podium in the sheriff's department briefing room and was instantly bathed in the floodlights used by the TV news crews that represented the Memphis, Tennessee, and Jackson, Mississippi, affiliate stations. Roy Bishop stood to one side.

"I'm Brad Barnett, sheriff of Tunica County, and I'm going to make a statement. Yesterday morning, Sherry Adams, a nineteen-year-old resident of Tunica, Mississippi, was killed as she walked from a county residence to her car. Yesterday afternoon, Jack Beals, a resident of Tunica County, was killed in a room at the Gold Key Motel, while he was in the commission of an armed assault and attempted robbery. We believe that whoever killed Mr. Beals may have seen the attack in progress and acted in the urgency of the moment to rescue the man Mr. Beals was assaulting. We urge anyone who has any information on this incident to contact our office. At this time we have no suspect in that crime.

"Upon investigating these two deaths, we came upon what appears to be conclusive evidence that it was in fact Mr. Beals who fired the shot that killed Sherry Adams. We have recovered from Mr. Beals's residence what we believe to be the murder weapon, along with other evidence, and are continuing to investigate these cases. As of yet we do not have a motive in the Adams murder, and it appears that it may have been a random act of violence."

"Was it a hate crime?" a reporter yelled out.

Hands went up and almost every newsperson shouted a question.

"Since these are ongoing investigations, I will not answer any questions beyond what I have already told you. As there are new developments, and as we have verified them, my office will release that information."

Brad left the room with his chief deputy following him. The reporters shouted questions behind them, but the sheriff neither responded nor slowed. Winter and Alexa, who had waited in the hallway, followed Brad to his office.

The press conference was part of Winter's plan to get the media off the streets and away from the investigation. He hoped the press would report the few details they'd gathered, file their stories, and, without more information immediately forthcoming, lose interest by rapid degrees. And he hoped Albert White would sweat some and maybe do something dumb. The murder of a poor black girl in a rural Mississippi county—one that had been solved—was, when it came to the bottomless stomach of Americans for graphic violence, less filling than an airline snack.

45

"HERE'S WHAT IS GOING TO HAPPEN," THE MAN who'd kidnapped Cynthia told her when she came around. She was tied up and blindfolded but no longer in the barn. The place smelled of disinfectant and she was sure she'd been dressed in new clothes. They felt cheap and stiff and smelled like they had never been washed.

"Please, my stomach hurts really bad. Like worse than cramps. It's what happens if I don't get my insulin. I feel like I'm starving."

"But you aren't going to starve," he said.

"It feels like I am. Even if I eat, it won't help."

"How about candy?" the man asked her.

"Sugar would make it much worse. I feel so sick. Please let me have a shot."

"Well, that's interesting. You feel like you are starving, but when you eat you won't feel any different for it, even though you'd be full?"

"Yes. It's diabetes. If I don't get a shot, soon, I'll have other symptoms."

"Like what?"

"I've never gone without insulin since I was diagnosed, so I'm not really sure what all can happen. When I realize I'm really thirsty, I check my blood sugar and give myself a shot. If it's, like, under two hundred fifty I'm feeling tired or my stomach hurts. If it goes to, like, three hundred fifty, I could go into a coma and have to be on an IV. I could die. So I need to do a check with my testing monitor. Look, I have two loaded syringes in my purse. You do have my purse, don't you? My kit's in there."

"It's in the van," he said.

"Could you go and get it?"

"No."

"Why not?"

"I abducted you. This is not a hospital, and I'm not a physician. If you die from insulin shock, you die."

"But I need it," she told him. "I'm serious."

"You can go a long time without a shot without dying."

"I'm not sure how long that is," she said, frightened.

"Well, I'll tell you what I will do. I have a sandwich you can have that may be staler than you're accustomed to. I will give you plenty of water, and I will let you pee. I will only get your purse when I don't have anything else that I have to do. If you give me any trouble, or try to escape, my associate outside this room will cut your nipples off. If you try a second time, I will cut your throat. Do you understand me?"

She still didn't know who this man was or how he fit in with Jack. Her father—even given the bastard he was—would not allow anything to happen to her. It had occurred to her that her father might be involved in this to get money out of her mother. The thought pained her, but she couldn't dismiss it. But she didn't believe he could allow this man to hurt her. But maybe Jacob wasn't in charge. At this point, very little would surprise her.

She felt the shooting pains of hunger worsen, a bad sign. She couldn't just die like this.

She just couldn't.

So she nodded.

"I understand," she told the man who'd kidnapped her. "If you have time later on."

"That's better. I'll see what I can do." The man gave her a big smile, and she suddenly felt very cold.

46

THE PRIVATE JETS CARRYING THE ADVANCE SHADOW team members—a cell comprised of dark ops specialists from four different cities—all arrived at the Memphis airport within the same forty-minute window. They had been dispatched as soon as word that Paulus Styer was in Tunica had been received by their organization. Once they were on the ground, the group was driven to Millington Naval Station, where two Yukons, already loaded with their equipment, had arrived in a C-130 cargo plane from North Carolina. The Millington gate guards had been instructed by their base commander to ignore the arriving team members and to wave their matching Yukons through when they exited the base.

The men in the cell knew each other well because they had worked numerous missions together, but they knew each other only by the names they had been assigned. They were ex-military Special Forces members who had died in combat or in training accidents. Their given names, along with their histories, had been buried with the bodies—or parts thereof—supplied by the shadow cell to fill their coffins.

The search for Paulus Styer, who was called Cold Wind by the CIA, had been going on for over ten years, and had cost six of the shadow team's elite professionals and millions of dollars. The team members knew that Paulus Styer was a continuing top priority, and that the men who ended him would be generously rewarded. Even as the shadows traveled toward Tunica, Mississippi, other units were moving to join them.

47

STANDING AT ATTENTION IN THE VAST HOSPITALity suite, windows at his back, Pierce Mulvane watched as workers finished assembling an architectural model of the River Royale resort. The model, made in Los Angeles by a company that built scale models for use in movies, had cost a great deal of money, but it would all be expensed. Press releases would show dignitaries standing behind the model, and pictures of it would be used to illustrate brochures and vacation articles. The model would then be moved downstairs in the lobby and placed on a table for public viewing while the actual complex was completed.

The River Royale, situated far south of the other casinos in Tunica County, would eventually cover over three thousand acres. The model depicted indoor tennis courts, swimming pools, fountains, two eighteen-hole golf courses, a spa, the casino itself, designed to replicate a palace in Monaco, a seven-hundred-room hotel, five mini-villas, a concert hall, a four-screen movie theater, a promenade with high-end specialty shops, heliport, and eight restaurants. The closest competing casino would be fifteen miles away, as if any casino could compete with a world-class, one-stop destination where gaming was the core profit generator, though it appeared to be only one more method of entertainment for the guests.

Pierce looked at the model, and although it wasn't physically apparent, a large section in the center of the project stood out—the parcel that Kurt Klein didn't yet own. Looking at it, Pierce felt another wave of nausea rise within him.

The workers finished their task and left without saying anything. Pierce had hardly noticed until he turned to find Tug Murphy waiting for him.

"Yes, Tug?"

"Klein's guy, Steffan Finch, wants to see you."

"Again? I shouldn't keep him waiting . . . long, I suppose."

"It's a beautiful resort," Tug said, nodding in the direction of the model.

Pierce rubbed his hands together briskly. "We have a great deal to accomplish and not much time to do it in. I wonder if Albert knows more about this Beals thing than he's said."

"That could be," Tug said.

"I wish I knew everything that's going on. Maybe it's best I don't. Given the circumstances, deniability may be my best friend," Pierce said as he lifted a tiny golf cart and moved it from the cart path to a fairway. He thought, *Maybe Herr Klein has done me a huge favor by being so damned secretive.*

Across the desk from Pierce Mulvane, Steffan Finch sat, his sunglasses still on. Beside him, a visibly nervous Albert White sat twiddling his thumbs.

Finch said, "Instead of waiting until Tuesday, Herr Klein will be arriving tomorrow from Atlantic City. I have some good men coming in with Herr Klein to handle his personal security needs."

"I told Mr. Finch that if he needs anything from us, I will arrange it," Albert White said.

"Quite a bit of bother over this Beals fellow," Finch said. "When I spoke to Herr Klein earlier, I mentioned its being on the news, and he indicated I should place myself at your disposal in case this threatens to expand into something larger."

"Yes," Pierce said. "If it does, we'll make sure you are kept apprised."

Albert said, "It was a very unfortunate thing. Beals seemed to be completely trustworthy. It appears, however, that he was up to something on his own."

"His connection to this casino should be of no concern," Pierce said. "Isn't that right, Albert?"

"No way this can come back on the casino," Albert said, straightening his tie and shooting Pierce a nervous glance. "I can assure you he wasn't acting on our behalf."

"Herr Klein is always concerned about blowback, and my job is to address his concerns. These are very important people who can't afford to be associated with any hint of scandal. So tell me what you know about Beals's escapade. Herr Klein says that you are to level with me."

Pierce said, "Well, I mentioned to Albert that I wished I could discover how a certain young man was managing to cheat this house. Albert asked Jack Beals to talk to the young man to find out how he was cheating. I have no idea who killed Beals. He was making himself useful to a certain someone whom Kurt sent to help with a land complication, and perhaps that man may have decided to take matters into his own hands for some reason not known to us. I mean, Kurt—"

"You're mistaken," Finch said, interrupting. "Have you seen anyone sent here by Herr Klein? Did Beals tell either of you that he had been helpful to anyone who was dealing with any problems for Herr Klein?"

"Of course not," Pierce said quickly. "You?" he asked White.

"I've seen nobody. I just told Beals—as Mr. Mulvane told me to—that when someone approached him and used the name Pablo that he should do whatever this person asked him to, and that Pablo would compensate him directly. Jack never told me he had been approached, but I had also told him never to mention it again," Albert said, smiling uncomfortably. "That's all I know, and I only know that much inside this room, between us. Mr. Mulvane told me to find someone that could be trusted, and I picked Beals since he has always performed with professionalism. And, as a lifelong resident of Tunica County, he could furnish information on the Gardners. Is it possible this Pablo killed him so he wouldn't have to pay him? Or to keep him quiet? I mean, with Beals dead, nobody else has even seen Pablo—if he actually ever arrived."

"I see," Finch said. "Beals was someone you could depend on. Isn't it possible that this cheater had someone watching his back who was in the room when Beals went inside?"

"I didn't know he killed that girl," Albert said. "Out on the Gardner plantation."

"The girl yesterday?" Mulvane said, turning his eyes to exchange glances with White, who nodded.

White said, "The sheriff said so on the news a little while ago. They searched Beals's house, according to my source at the department, and found the rifle used to kill the girl, and close to two hundred grand."

"Where did Beals get that kind of money?" Mulvane asked immediately. "We don't pay him anywhere near that much."

"He might have inherited it, sold something, saved it up, I guess," White said. "Maybe Pablo paid him that money for helping him."

"But you can't be sure it wasn't stolen from us," Pierce said. "I mean, if he was embezzling, that makes him appear more criminal and less like he could have been acting on our behalf, like he told that gambler. Right, Albert?"

"He was never alone with large sums of cash. None of my people are." White seemed confident.

"Nobody pays that kind of money to a helper, not even a full partner," Finch said.

Mulvane opened his hands expansively. Albert was being slow on the uptake. "Well, obviously he was stealing from us, which means he didn't get paid to kill anybody, or anything that would need further looking into. We were victims too. Exactly how much money was found?"

"One hundred and eighty thousand, two hundred twenty dollars," Albert said. "And he had an arsenal in that house. Like thirty guns."

"Well," Finch said, clapping his hands together. "I see we're on the same page here. I'll tell Herr Klein all of this when I see him. No sense bothering the man with details, is there? He's not really interested in details, just the overall picture."

"Of course not," Pierce said. "Not at all."

48

THE BLUE & WHITE RESTAURANT, PAINTED ROYAL blue and white, was located on Highway 61. The Tunica County institution looked like a large roadside restaurant and gas station. Years before it had been a popular truck stop, but all that remained of that was the original cafe structure, the gas pumps long since removed. There was an L-shaped dining room, tables, and a series of booths against the open kitchen.

Brad waved at or made small talk with several diners before joining Winter and Alexa Keen at a corner table.

Brad said as he slid in, "I went over our missing-person files, and some of the people were supposedly headed here, or had called someone from here to say they'd won big. So it's safe to assume Beals was using his casino job to target people like Scotoni. People he checked out. Maybe he killed them and disposed of their bodies. According to the IRS, four of the missing people paid taxes on winnings at the Roundtable."

Winter said, "Beals was a security guard, so he would have needed a partner with access to information on the targets. He filmed them leaving, so I think he was off duty when they took their winnings out."

"Could Styer have been his partner?" Alexa asked.

"I doubt it," Winter said. "Robbery would be lower than bottom-feeding for him. Styer killed Beals, but Beals's robbery operation wasn't their connection. I think the Roundtable is connected to Styer's presence, and the land Leigh owns has to be why Sherry is dead. Maybe Beals knew about Styer. It's quite possible the casino wanted Beals killed, so Styer did it, tying Sherry's murder to Beals so the trail ends there."

"He knows you'll know it's him, but you won't be able to tie him in officially," Alexa said.

"The casino may have had Sherry killed as a message," Brad said.

"Far as the FBI knows, the Roundtable is clean," Alexa said.

"Doesn't mean they're clean," Winter said.

Brad said, "Albert White knew we were talking about Scotoni and we never used his name. Not proof we can use. White left his job in West Memphis and took the casino position when RRI bought it. Beals went to work there three years ago."

"Circumstantial at best," Winter said. "Could be White and Beals were in cahoots, but it still isn't enough for a search warrant on White's place. What do we know about RRI?"

"RRI is owned by a German industrial family named Klein," Alexa said. "Kurt Klein is the present CEO of Klein Industries, which owns RRI. Klein is a billionaire industrialist. RRI is his hobby."

Winter looked around the room.

"A big-deal German would have access to Styer's services. He may have brought in Styer to clear the way for the land acquisition. Maybe the purpose of killing Sherry was to put pressure on Jacob. And he killed Beals because Beals could identify him," Alexa speculated.

Winter said, "Only thing I know is that whatever Styer's up to, he's not finished yet."

"How can you be sure?" Brad asked.

"Because he hasn't yet made an appearance before Winter," Alexa said. "And that's his bow before the curtain falls."

The trio had finished eating when a slightly stooped white-haired man wearing a wide-brimmed felt hat and a bulky wool coat over a cardigan walked in, looked at their table, and made a beeline for it. A second man, about the same age but twenty pounds heavier, came in behind him.

"Looks like we're about to have company," Winter said. "Based on the pictures in your den, I'd say this is the famous Dr. Barnett."

Brad turned and raised his chin in salute to his father, who was greeting diners as he made his way toward them. "The other man is his best friend, Woody Seiders. They grew up together. Woody is a fixture and a hell of a handyman. He oversees Daddy's rental properties, keeps my yard straight, and plays nickel-dime poker with Dad and their buddies every other Monday night."

Woody smiled and waved at Brad as the two men approached.

Brad stood and pulled out a chair beside him, which the doctor lowered himself into. Woody took a chair from a vacant table and sat at the corner to Dr. Barnett's left.

"Alexa, Winter, this is my father, William Barnett, and Woody Seiders. Dad, Woody, meet Alexa Keen and Winter Massey."

"Call me Will," he said, shaking hands with Alexa and Winter. His handshake was firm, his hand warm, the skin loose, bones close to the surface. His bright gray eyes locked on Alexa's. "My, what a delightful dinner companion you gentlemen have. Ms. Keen, you bring sunshine into an otherwise dreary evening. Is there a Mr. Keen?"

"Alexa," she said, smiling.

"Cut the crap, Dad. You're about forty years too late for her," Brad said, shaking his head.

Woody guffawed. "Doc's just window-shopping these days. Sex at his age would be like playing the drums with cooked spaghetti."

"Nonsense. Some younger women appreciate the added value and benefits offered by a mature gentleman. Especially when he's a Harvard-trained physician who isn't going to live forever or leave his considerable estate, which includes an above-average coin collection, to his surviving son."

"Where's my shovel? It's knee-deep in here," Woody said.

Alexa smiled. "Most women do appreciate a mature gentleman," she said. "It's nice to meet a handsome man who is also a physician," she went on. "Not even counting a coin collection."

"General practitioner for forty-four years," William said.

"Alexa is with the FBI. Winter is . . ."

"Been helping you find Sherry's killer," William said. "I know all about him, and he did a great job wrapping it up. Little of consequence, or without, escapes my network of ever-faithful patients. Speaking of which, I saw Cynthia yesterday afternoon at the office."

"She came to see you for. . . . ?" Brad asked.

"That's about six miles into none of your business, Bradley. Beautiful child, Cynthia. So, Agent Keen, before my son interrupted, you were about to tell me about your present marital prospects."

"I didn't have any before tonight," she said, smiling.

"You were once married, I bet," William said.

She shook her head. "Not yet, Will."

"Well now, my dear, that has to be a situation of your own choosing."

"Just haven't found the right gentleman," she said teasingly.

"I don't suppose my son mentioned that I am an accomplished ballroom dancer."

"Mostly he accomplishes flattening toes," Woody said.

"Daddy," Brad said, "Alexa's young enough to be your daughter."

"I often wish I'd had a daughter," William said, frowning at his son.

49

PAULUS STYER SAT IN THE VAN IN THE PARKING LOT of the Blue & White and watched Massey, Barnett, and the unidentified woman wrapped up in conversation. He could safely go in. Winter was the only one in the group who had ever seen or spoken to him and after the work he'd had done on his features, the disguise he wore, and the stolen accented voice, Winter couldn't possibly recognize him. But Massey was remarkably intuitive, and it was smart not to give him anything until the time was right. While he would not recognize Styer, he might remember seeing him in the disguise later. He couldn't afford to lose a vital identity at this point. And they would be meeting face-to-face before long.

Styer had become familiar with Dr. Barnett when he was setting up the game, along with the old coot, Woody, who was often in his company. Because William was the sheriff's father, and might prove useful to the situation, Styer had spoken with them that morning at breakfast. In the guise of a visitor considering a move to the area, Styer asked the men question after question, even joining their table at the doctor's invitation. Dr. Barnett had been friendly, his companion less so.

Tonight, he had not been able to hear their conversation, but it shouldn't matter since they were following a trail of his design.

Styer looked across the highway at a Yukon that had parked in a lot facing the restaurant shortly after the trio arrived. The occupants hadn't gotten out, and smoke trailing from the tailpipe was the only indication that it was inhabited. He wondered why anybody would be following Massey or the sheriff, unless it was someone from the casino. He considered the thought, that the woman with them might have a protective detail, then realized with a jolt that she matched the description he had of Alexa Keen, Massey's FBI pal, an abduction specialist. So she was involved now, which meant they knew about Cynthia. *Good luck, bitch.*

He started the SUV and backed out slowly. He drove a hundred yards and parked in a hardware store's lot, waiting to see where the Yukon went when the dinner party split up.

50

CYNTHIA WAS LYING ON THE CARPETED FLOOR OF A closet. Thanks to a noose around her neck that was tied behind her back to her feet, she would strangle if she moved. Straightening out was impossible, and even if she could, the pain in her stomach made her want to double up. Her pants were cold and damp from urine, and she needed a shot badly. She had no idea how long she could go without one. Nobody had ever told her that.

The man had been gone a very long time. Hours earlier, he'd given her an injection of only half the amount of insulin the needle held. She had begged for more, but the cruel asshole had told her that he couldn't waste the little insulin she had in case "it" took longer than he thought it would, saying calmly, "Trust me, I won't let you die. I need you alive."

Cynthia sobbed quietly, trying to calm herself. She was sure that her mother would have people looking for her by now, and she prayed they would somehow be able to find her. One thing was certain: she was going to make sure Jack Beals paid dearly for this.

She desperately needed to pee again, so she let it go in the quiet darkness.

51

ALEXA PLACED HER BAG ON THE BED IN THE GUEST bedroom located next to Winter's. When she came downstairs, Ruger, who had been in the backyard when they arrived, ran to her and jumped up on her, trying to lick her face with a broad and dripping tongue.

Brad grabbed Ruger's collar and pulled her back. "She and my father have a lot in common," Brad said. "They are both enamored with the FBI. Stay down, Ruger."

"She doesn't care for me," Winter said.

"Ruger doesn't know you like I do," Alexa said, kneeling to put her face on the dog's level. "Pretty girl. Ruger, be nice to Winter. He is a friend to man, woman, and beast alike. With the exception of deer."

Ruger looked at Winter as if she knew what Alexa had said, and her wide tongue bobbed.

"Get anyone a beer?" Brad asked.

"None for me," Alexa said.

"Thanks anyway," Winter said. "I need to get some rest."

The ringing doorbell sent a barking Ruger bounding to the back door. Brad walked through the kitchen, leaving Winter and Alexa standing in the den. Winter heard a familiar voice and the door closing.

After thirty seconds, Leigh Gardner came in, followed by Brad and a joyful Ruger.

"Leigh has something she wants to tell us."

"Brad, do you have any bourbon?"

"I didn't know you drank," Brad said.

"I could use a stiff drink if it's all the same to you," she said, collapsing in an armchair. "Just ice."

"Have you heard from Cynthia?" Alexa asked before Winter could.

"Her father spoke to her an hour ago. She's fine. She stayed overnight with a girlfriend she knows from LSU. I'm furious, but at least she's all right. He told her how worried we all were and she called me silly. Jacob says she's trying to keep from thinking about Sherry and she said she's going to her grandmother's to spend the night. Probably for advanced bitch lessons. Like she isn't going to get one from me when she gets home. I've half a mind to go up there and drag her home."

"At least she's safe," Alexa said.

Leigh nodded and smiled. "That's some consolation. Do you have children?"

"No," Alexa said. "I don't."

"Count your blessings," Leigh said flatly.

Brad opened a cabinet and took out a bottle of Maker's Mark, found a short glass, dropped two cubes of ice from the freezer in, and poured it half full. He crossed the room and handed it to Leigh.

Leigh drained half the glass before she said anything further.

"The main reason I'm here is because of the conversation I had with Jacob this evening. I find myself in need of advice from . . . I suppose all of you," she said. She drained the glass and set it on a coaster on the coffee table.

"Whatever we can do," Winter said.

"I told you Jacob's been after me to sell him the bottomland. He brought me an astounding offer. He said that a company needs the land for some project and they won't take no for an answer."

"How much did they offer?" Winter asked.

"Two million dollars. Well, two and a half. Jacob said they might go higher, but that there's a risk if I try to hold out. It seems they have been offering big money from the start, which Jacob failed to mention. Of course, he made it sound like it was all for the children." She massaged her right temple and closed her eyes.

"We've been looking into the land," Brad said. "That fits with what we found out."

Leigh raised a brow. "He owes a lot of money to whomever is behind this interest in it. It seems they have been exerting increasing pressure on him to make sure it happens. Now it has to go forward immediately for some reason Jacob swears he doesn't know. I'm here because it's very possible, based on what Jacob did tell me, that Sherry may have been shot to make him level with me. What kind of people would murder an innocent child to make a point?"

Alexa and Winter exchanged looks.

"Does Jacob know you came here?" Brad asked.

"I said I was going to the Adams's house, and I am, after I leave here."

Winter said, "A corporation called RRI owns the adjoining land. They also own the Roundtable casino."

"And Jack Beals worked for the Roundtable," Leigh said.

Brad said, "They intend to build a three-thousand-acre resort, and your parcel is right in the middle of it."

Leigh raised her brows. "Resort? No, he said he didn't know what they wanted it for. He did mention a man named Mulvane. At first I told him I had to think it over. He told me that it was their final offer, and that I couldn't take any time because I'd already held the deal up, which made the people very angry." Leigh put her elbows on her knees and placed her forehead in her hands. "Evidently he's told me one thing and them another while he tried to figure out a way to get more money. He's lied to me for months and months, but that's just Jacob's nature. And Sherry's dead because of it."

"What did you tell him?"

She sat up. "He was really afraid, Brad. He told me . . ." She stopped and looked at her hands. "He said I could either take the offer, or next time, instead of a servant, it might be me, Cyn, or Hamp lying dead in the yard."

"That bastard!" Brad said. "It's your fault even though he kept you in the dark. I bet he's been playing them and they're onto him."

Leigh shook her head. "He said if I'd have sold it to him, earlier, Sherry would still be alive. He acted like it was my fault, that I made some kind of selfish choice and that was why she was dead."

Leigh started crying, and Brad sat on the edge of her chair and put an arm around her. She rested her head against him for a split second before straightening. "God," she asked, "could it be true?"

"It isn't your fault, Leigh," Brad said.

"I know it isn't *my* fault," she said. "Could he be telling the truth? Is this a case of 'sell to us, or your children will die next'? I'm doing it. What else can I do? People will always gamble, and at least I'll have a legacy for my children and they will never *have* to farm like I did. It won't bring Sherry back, but I can use the money to help them out."

"We can see them punished for killing Sherry," Alexa said. She looked at Winter and he frowned. Tying anyone at the Roundtable to Sherry's death was a real long shot. Styer was the link, but proving that connection might be close to impossible.

"If you, or someone else, could get Mulvane to admit to ordering the killing," Winter said. "He's the casino manager."

"You mean carry a recorder and ask this Mulvane to admit ordering a murder?" Leigh smirked. "Just tell me what to do. I want those people to pay for what that Beals bastard did to Sherry."

"It might be dangerous," Brad said. "Pinning Mulvane will be tricky."

Leigh looked at Brad, her eyes dancing. "You can arrest him after I sell him the land. Let the bastard pay twice, so at the least, the money will do some good."

Winter asked, "How did you leave it with Jacob?"

"I told him that if I had no choice, if our children were in danger, I would sell it. I said to tell them to write the check and give me the papers to sign."

"And what did he say?"

"He said he'd tell them and took off. What can we do now?"

"We have to develop a plan," Alexa said. "And a good one if we're going to take them down."

And at that, for the first time since Winter had met her, Leigh Gardner smiled.

52

PIERCE MULVANE WAS SITTING AT HIS DESK, WATCHing Jacob Gardner on his flat-screen monitor. Two minutes earlier, Albert White had alerted him to the lawyer's presence in the lobby, and Pierce had been following Gardner's progress—going camera to camera—from the time he'd entered the casino. He had dispatched Tug to intercept him downstairs and bring him up. Pierce noted how the degenerate slowed as he passed by each of the craps tables until Tug showed him into the elevator. In the hallway, Tug would frisk Gardner, looking for hidden recorders, wires, or other devices he might be planning to use to get a record of Mulvane incriminating himself. Pierce switched off the monitor and gathered his thoughts during the thirty seconds it took the pair to arrive at the door.

"Great news!" Gardner boasted. He swaggered to a chair facing the desk and sat, leaning back and crossing his legs. "She's going to sell it, Pierce. She agreed. Her exact words were, and I quote: 'Tell them to prepare the papers. The sooner, the better.' "

"It's *Mr.* Mulvane, Gardner."

Gardner shifted in the chair uncomfortably. "Mr. Mulvane. Sorry, I didn't mean any disrespect."

"You told her what, exactly? What was it that swayed your ex-wife?" Pierce asked.

"The money, of course. So much money."

"You didn't tell her that I threatened you in any way?"

"No, of course I didn't. She's a greedy bitch. Two and a half million is a big score. I said that if she didn't sell, you could afford to go somewhere else."

"She doesn't think Mr. Beals killed that girl to frighten her and force her to sell?"

"No. Why would she?"

"So she doesn't know that Jack Beals worked here?"

"Everybody with a TV set knows he worked for your casino. But I never told her it was you making the offer. She doesn't care."

Pierce felt a growing hollowness in his stomach. "I have a problem. This man, Beals, was a killer and employed by this casino. Why he targeted your wife's babysitter we may never know. The dilemma now is that certain people might see this unfortunate connection between our desire for the land, the fact that a man working for us killed someone on the plantation owned by someone who owned the land we needed, and the fact that they sold it to us the next day. As an attorney, you have to understand that I can't afford to have some overly zealous law enforcement persons thinking our company's desire to own that property might be in any way connected to a homicide. I can't risk our one-point-five-billion-dollar investment."

At the word *billion* Pierce saw Jacob's fevered eyes light up, as he knew they would. Pierce mentioned the figure because he wanted Jacob to understand how very little a life was worth against that kind of investment. "Perhaps you can see my concerns more clearly than most. Your ex-wife cannot bring this offer to anyone's attention."

"I never thought for a minute you had anything to do with the murder," Gardner said. "I never said there could be a connection of any kind. She is only interested in the money. Believe me, I know her like the back of my hand."

"But you see my problem," Pierce said. "The timing of it all. I'm a legitimate businessman working for a very influential man who is worth billions, with worldwide and varied business interests. That is all I've said to you, correct?"

Pierce could see Gardner's eyes darting nervously, avoiding his own.

"There must be some way we can do this so there is no illusion of impropriety or pressure," Pierce went on. "Any ideas?"

"What if she transfers the land to me," Gardner said. "And I could sell it to you and pay her with the money you pay me. Although she might get hinky about trusting me. Our divorce made her pretty bitter."

"Does your ex gamble?" Pierce asked.

"She's a farmer, Mr. Mulvane. She gambles every day. But she'd never enter a casino," Jacob said. "Just getting her to agree without triggering her greed reflexes and have her asking for a lease and profit-sharing deal is a miracle."

Pierce said, "We'll do it. I'll sweat the details."

Gardner stood. "That is acceptable. Completely. Sorry this has taken so long, Mr. Mulvane. We'll get this done."

"Please. It's Pierce to associates."

53

HANDS BEHIND HIS HEAD, WINTER FINISHED HIS crunches. He hadn't gone for a run since he'd arrived in Mississippi, and he wouldn't get back to his schedule until after this was over.

Alexa seemed off her game to Winter, but he knew she'd worked a difficult abduction case in New Orleans—right as Katrina had hit—and that it had taken a heavy emotional toll on her. She was as tough as she was intelligent, but he often wondered if perhaps she wasn't too sensitive for what she did. She took her job seriously, and when she succeeded, she merely met her own expectations, but when she failed—and failure was a constant occurrence in her work—she blamed herself.

Winter knew that Alexa had seen a psychiatrist after that case, but he doubted she had given the doctor much to work with. Alexa didn't trust people easily. Alexa's reputation in law enforcement circles was second only to

Winter Massey's, quite a coincidence considering their twenty-year relationship, and their common geographical backgrounds—or given their strong personalities, perhaps not quite so remarkable.

The sound of Alexa's door closing was followed by a light rapping on his door.

"Come in, Lex," he said, standing up and grabbing a towel to wipe the perspiration from his face.

The door opened and Alexa came into his room. "You aren't sleeping?"

"I was working out," he said. "You?"

"Nah. I was thinking about Leigh Gardner." She closed the door gently, and sat on the end of his bed. "You talk to Sean tonight?"

"She took the kids home this morning. I didn't think she'd go until this was wound up. I guess she figured since you're here, she could do what I wanted her to do," he said.

"You think?"

"Lex. I assume that she called you and told you about Styer's DNA. That's why you came down here, right?"

"*You* should have leveled with me, Massey." She was quietly angry. "As soon as you suspected Styer was here, you should have gotten the hell out and let the people handle it who are equipped to do so. This is, if not out of your league, spitting distance from it. You have a family to consider."

"Styer somehow put this deal together to get me involved. I assume he plans to kill me, and if that's true, then no matter where I go, he'll just change locations. At least this way, my family isn't in danger of being used against me. But now you're in danger. I wish you'd have stayed out."

"I was on my way before Sean called."

"You're the world's crummiest liar, Lex. I want you to promise me that you won't try to take him on. No matter what happens, if you find yourself standing between him and the door, let him go through it. Even if I'm down."

"You know I can't promise you any such thing," Alexa said. "If I can stop him, I'll have to do it. He's a man of considerable ability, but he isn't bulletproof. You thought he had Cyn, didn't you?"

"He's certainly capable of that. She would have been a great card to play. But I believe he's working with the casino, and he'd know that taking Cyn could have had an adverse effect on the land acquisition."

Winter was quiet for a few seconds before he told Alexa what had been troubling him for some time now.

"A year ago I was in Rogers, Arkansas, consulting with Wal-Mart's security director about executive protection in other parts of the world. After I got to the airport, a man I'd never seen before sat down beside me. He started a conversation about Wal-Mart before he told me that if he was Paulus Styer, I'd be dead. He told me he was delivering a message for the people who wanted to find Styer. He told me that Styer killed the Russian KGB colonel who trained Styer, a man who was a father figure to him—the man who had betrayed him. Styer was no longer connected to any organization and was without the restraints that brings."

"Why did the colonel betray Styer?"

"The CIA cut him a deal for Styer's head because he

made them look bad by killing people they were protecting."

"Anyway, this colonel was paranoid and he knew Styer better than anybody. He was heavily guarded. One night he goes to bed with a young woman. There are guards just outside the room. In the morning they open the bathroom door to find the colonel has been skinned alive. The woman was in bed asleep. Styer left behind a single red toothpick soaked in clove oil. He is still being paid to kill, but nobody knows who's paying him. I'm wondering if Styer found out about that cutout I met in Arkansas. Why else would he have shown up? The way we left it . . ."

"You said, if you left him alone, he'd do the same."

"I made a deal with the devil, and based on what I know about him, he'd have kept it. At least I always believed he would. If I'd wanted to track him, it would have been all but impossible for me."

"You saying he's an honorable man?"

"No. Well, yes, I guess I am. Maybe I misread him, but I thought there was a glimmer of some kind of honor or decency in him. That maybe leaving me alone was a way to atone for what he'd done to Hank and Millie Trammel. But maybe he always planned to come after me, and this was his opportunity."

Alexa said, "Hatcher's call is still bugging me. There's no way he should have known about my request for intel on RRI. I called Louis, and Louis called me back. He told me that there was no active file on RRI. If so, why did Hatcher call me? And I'm sure he already knew you were here."

"You think he's been listening in?"

"If that's the case, I'm worried on lots of levels."

Winter said, "J. Edgar is alive and kicking."

"You should worry about Brad," she said. "He's way out of his element here. No matter what you've told him about Styer, he has no frame of reference for a man like that."

Winter shrugged. "All I know is this is my opportunity to stop Styer."

Alexa shook her head slowly.

"We should get some rest," Winter told Alexa.

"Massey, just do your ripping-shit-apart thing. I got your back," Alexa said, slapping his foot playfully.

You always have, he thought, smiling.

54

LATER THAT NIGHT, AFTER FOLLOWING THE YUKON to the sheriff's house and seeing that it had parked a block away, Styer shut off the van and got ready to approach the house on foot. In the driveway, parked near the sheriff's truck, were a Jeep and the Dodge the woman—Alexa Keen—had been driving—both rentals with Tennessee plates. Massey and Keen formed a nice round variable to roll around in his mind.

A single light burned in a downstairs corner room in the rear, most likely the master bedroom where the sheriff would be sleeping. He based his assumption on the fact that the window in the room beside that one was smaller, so it had to be a bathroom. Massey and Keen would be upstairs in guest bedrooms, probably sleeping peacefully.

Styer figured the watchers there expected him to make a run at Massey, and that Massey had enlisted their help, and who could blame him? They never learned, always merely reacting to whatever he did. Creativity in cutouts was seriously lacking. They were bulls in a china shop. If he took out their team—and here they were, sitting around with their thumbs up their butts and asking for it—the hunters he couldn't see would be even more infuriated than they were now. It was very tempting. Of course, that move would change it into a different game altogether, because there'd be cutouts everywhere, but then again, that might add some sport.

He took out his Ruger MK II pistol, a Luger-shaped semiautomatic in .22 LR with a built-in suppressor that was seamlessly connected. The small gun was reliable, easy to conceal, and accurate for close work. The suppressor made the shots as quiet as cat farts.

"Time to go to work," Styer said to himself.

55

WINTER WAS DREAMING THAT HE WAS WITH HANK Trammel and Faith Ann Porter in New Orleans when something awakened him. Lying there in the darkness gathering his wits, he wondered what it was that had interrupted his dream. The travel clock beside the bed clicked away each second. He knew he was in Brad's guest bed, and he reached beside him for his Reeder .45, but his hand found only flat sheet where he'd left the cocked-and-locked weapon.

"Well, well," the eerie voice said. "We meet again."

In the darkened room, Winter could make out the shape of a man standing beside the bed.

"Your friends are dead, and it's all your fault. If you had kept our bargain, they wouldn't be."

A sudden flash from the gun's barrel illuminated the room and Winter yelled out. Sitting up, he grabbed his handgun.

The light came on and Alexa rushed in, sweeping her Glock around to cover the room. "What happened?" she asked, looking at him and the gun in his hand, which was aimed at the wall beside the bed. Styer's presence had been one frightening dream wrapped in another.

"Nightmare," he said, his voice cracking. The clock read five-thirty.

Alexa dropped the Glock to her side and frowned at him. "Want to talk about it?" she asked.

"No, Lex," he replied. "Sorry I woke you."

She looked at him with tired eyes and said, "Maybe you should keep that gun a little farther away when you sleep. Just a suggestion, since I'm on the other side of the wall." She flipped off the light and closed the door.

Winter lay back, resting his head on the pillow, which was damp from perspiration. He lifted his head and flipped the pillow over to the dry side.

He was shaken by the dream, and doubted finding sleep again would be possible. There was no question in Winter's mind that Styer was responsible for both killings, and since the casino had the only motive in both, someone there had to be involved. Winter figured he'd turn the casino upside down and see what hit the ground.

56

THE TWO TEAMS OF CUTOUTS FOLLOWING MASSEY split up after the trio had settled into Barnett's house for the evening. The second team would rest until daybreak, then relieve the overnight team, and eight additional team members would be arriving the following day. While one of the two men put Global Positioning System locators on the Jeep and the Tundra and took up a position behind the house, the other remained in the Yukon watching the front of the house for lights. Massey's history with their organization had taught them that you couldn't take him for granted. The ex-deputy U.S. marshal was a legend with the group, having taken out several of them a few years before—a feat unparalleled in the organization's shadowy fifty year history. Five members of the team remained in Tunica, and several cleaners were on call, if and when that became necessary.

Traffic in the sheriff's neighborhood was extremely light. Of the six or seven cars and trucks that passed on the street after eleven o'clock, only one was a police cruiser, and the sole officer occupant didn't even slow as he passed the SUV. The Yukon carried Mississippi plates, a move designed to make the vehicle fit in. If the plates were run, they would be traced to a corporation set up for regional dark operations. If, by some miracle, cutouts were taken into custody, they would be out before they were booked and within hours, there would be no record of the arrest.

As each vehicle passed the Yukon, the watcher there would open his laptop and type in the plate. None of them raised any flags in the computer, which had immediate access to governmental mainframes.

Around three in the morning, the watcher in the Yukon radioed his partner. When he received no response, he climbed from the SUV, tacking a silenced Heckler & Koch Mark 23 under his jacket and putting on night vision goggles. Slipping into the cover of bushes, he moved toward the place the second watcher was supposed to be.

As he approached the neighboring yard where his teammate had set up his surveillance, he spotted the man's shape, sitting in the grass with his ankles crossed, his back against a tree. The older cutout appeared to be asleep, and the watcher approached stealthily from behind. Suppressing a chuckle, he reached around and clasped his hand over his partner's mouth. As soon as he touched the still man, he jerked his hand back. Looking at his hand in the moonlight, he saw that his gloved fingers were covered with warm blood. Pulling his pistol and kneeling beside the man, he saw that his partner's head was exploded on the left side. Something heavy dropped to the ground behind him, and as he turned, he felt a spray of cold liquid, smelled it for what it was, and covered his mouth too late to stop the chloroform from taking him down.

57

THE CUTOUT AWOKE AND COULDN'T FEEL HIS hands or feet. Opening his eyes with difficulty, he saw that he was in a kitchen chair—not trussed, but still totally powerless. The light from the open door of a closet illuminated his surroundings—an empty house that was, based on the new Sheetrock and plastic-covered floor, being renovated. Daylight was gathering outside, and he could make out the shapes of trees through the filmy windows. Across the room, a man dressed entirely in black and wearing a watch cap leaned against bare wood studs, studying him. The man didn't look like the descriptions they had of Paulus Styer, but a convincing disguise was part and parcel to Styer's method.

"Welcome," the abductor said. "Does your head hurt? Chloroform in the face delivered from a bulb is so much neater and faster than pouring it on a cloth."

The cutout didn't answer.

"I guess not. Anyway, I gave you a shot that has your body paralyzed. It's a variation of Special K, the animal tranquilizer developed for brain surgery when they want to make sure the patient remains perfectly still but can communicate. The effects will last for a few hours. You can still feel, think, and talk, but you can't move away from pain. The drug affects only the motor responses, but not the nerve endings in your skin. Don't you love medical research?"

The cutout watched his enemy, more furious than frightened.

"Do you know who I am?" the shadowy figure asked.

"Cold Wind."

"I haven't been called that for several years," Styer said, grimacing. "We can dispense with the small talk. Who is the woman with Massey?"

"Her name is Alexa Keen. She's an FBI agent."

"Why is she here?" Styer asked, letting the cutout see his hand and the knife it held. "Is she investigating an abduction?"

"What abduction?"

"A young girl."

"We'd have picked that up. She's here to assist Massey because you're here. That's all I know."

"How many of your kind are here, besides you two?"

"Just the two of us."

"We both know you are lying. There are at least two more of you here, many more than that within fifty miles of us. No way your handlers would hold back after all the failed, under-gunned attempts to take me."

The cutout knew that they had been close to catching Styer on three occasions. There was the team member Styer had taken out in New Orleans, another member Styer had left crucified in Seattle, and one he'd tortured to death and left in a car trunk at the airport in Mexico City.

"You can join us," the cutout told him. "Control told us to tell you that if we caught up with you."

Styer walked over casually, tapping the blade of a survival knife against his thigh. "If you failed to kill me, you mean?"

"Our orders are to give you an opportunity if possible. He thinks you could be a valuable addition to our cell."

"I could be useful," Styer said. "But even if it's true, sooner or later a new control could decide my skills are less valuable than repaying me for leaving egg on the group's collective face. I don't trust anybody in a control position. Should I? Would I be able to trust him? Or your friends now that I've killed your partner?"

The cutout nodded. "You wouldn't be the first transplant we have. My partner was collateral damage."

"But I am an old man in our specialized business. My years of usefulness would be few."

"They don't confide in me beyond need to know. I'm just a watcher."

"And not a very good one, based on how easy it was to take you. How did you people know I was here?"

"I don't know," the man said truthfully. "I suppose NSA picked the intel out of a conversation over the wires."

"A key in on the toothpick thing, no doubt. I have certainly developed an affection for the taste of clove. So Keen and Massey talked about me over the wires?"

The cutout lowered his gaze. All he could do was move his head. "Just get it over with," he said.

"What's your hurry? Valhalla is open twenty-four/seven." Styer reached up and drew his blade down the cutout's forearm. Blood rushed from the wound, which, due to the sharpness of the instrument, merely felt like a dull pressure. Pain was something the cutout was conditioned to ignore—to a point, at least. But, as if Styer were reading his mind, he reached behind the chair and lifted a bottle of bleach.

"I can't just take your word for it. I know you understand that. We can't just take each other's word, can we?" Styer said, looking out at the coming dawn. "We have time to talk. I want to see how much I can learn from you first. You'd do the same for me, I am sure."

Styer tugged the cutout's left nipple out and used the blade to excise it. The sensation was similar to having a concentrated jet of cold air aimed at the spot. He would not tell Styer anything useful, because he didn't know anything that could be useful. Styer probably knew that already. The cutout could take a great deal of pain, and Styer was sadistic, which meant this was going to last a very long time.

58

SATURDAY

WINTER CLIMBED OUT OF BED AND WAS GETTING dressed when he heard Brad open the back door. Seconds later he heard Ruger's steady barking from the backyard. He slipped his gun rig on over his wool vest and went downstairs, where Brad stood at the back door in sweatpants and a T-shirt looking out through the screen. He whistled several times in rapid succession.

"Ruger after a rabbit?" Winter asked.

"I don't know," Brad said. "She's going to wake up the neighborhood. This isn't like her. She always comes when I call her." He whistled again.

"Come back from the door," Winter said, drawing his Reeder and moving to a window in the den for a better view. In the wash from the porch light, Winter could see the dog standing at the picket fence, looking out at something from between the slats.

"Get a gun," Winter said. "Cover me from here."

Winter took his high-intensity flashlight from the vest

pocket. Hurrying to the front door, he opened it as silently as possible and moved around the house, his trigger finger flat against the receiver, aiming the .45 as he went. When he got to the fence he turned the flashlight on, aiming the light spot and the gun at a figure seated at the base of a tree with his back resting against it. Winter slipped through the gate, keeping the shape illuminated.

The seated man wore all black, assault boots, and a knit wool balaclava with eye and mouth holes in it. His gloved left hand held a pair of night vision goggles, and in the dew-coated grass next to his right hand lay a silenced HK SOCOM Mark 23 with a noise suppressor. Much of the left side of his head was missing, and a red toothpick had been jammed between his front teeth.

Using his flashlight, Winter quickly scanned the neighboring yard. Thankfully there were no lights on in that house.

Winter clicked on the thumb safety of his cocked .45 and waved Brad out before he moved over to the body for a closer look.

He heard Brad and Alexa talking as they approached the fence, Brad commanding the dog to stop barking. Lights from a car pulling into the driveway washed the garage and trees in Brad's backyard. Winter prayed it wasn't the cops.

"What is it?" Alexa asked.

"Looks like a dead body," Brad replied. "That'll be my father coming for breakfast before he does his early rounds at the hospital."

"What are you kids doing?" Winter heard Dr. Barnett ask as he approached the fence.

"Stay back, Daddy," Brad said.

Dr. Barnett ignored his son's warning.

Brad opened the gate for the others to enter the yard where Winter was using the harsh light to study the dead man.

"I'll call the police," Brad said.

Ruger whined.

"You *are* the police," Dr. Barnett said. "Quiet now, girl."

"This is a city matter," Brad replied.

"Hold up," Winter told him. "We need to think this through."

"Who is he?" Brad asked. "Is it . . . ?"

Winter looked up at the three faces. "It isn't him. But he did this." He pointed at the toothpick.

Dr. Barnett came through the gate, knelt beside the corpse, felt the wrist for a pulse, and lifted the head for a look at the wound while Winter held his light for him. "This neighborhood is going to hell."

"Excuse my father's humor," Brad said.

Winter checked the dead man's pockets. He removed a folding knife with a four-inch blade and three extra magazines for the HK. The corpse had an earpiece connected to a radio unit secured inside a jacket pocket. A green light on the radio showed that it was on. Winter turned it off. Reaching around behind the man, Winter worked a wallet out of his back pocket and opened it. "New York driver's license. Andrew Mark. Manhattan address. Credit cards. Several hundred dollars in cash. Business card says he is an importer. Twenty-nine years old. Picture of two small children and a woman." There was also an automotive key in the wallet.

After laying out the items, Winter removed the right

glove and inspected the corpse's heavily callused hand and the chronometer on his wrist.

"That handgun silenced? He some kind of hit man?" Dr. Barnett asked.

"Something like that. Brad, we need to take a quick walk around," Winter said.

"Where?" Brad asked.

Winter used a handkerchief to wipe his prints off the items and put them back where he'd found them. He stood, snapped off the light, and holstered his .45. "This guy had someone at the other end of the radio. Since he's been here like this for hours, I doubt his backup made out any better than he did."

"You going to call the cops?" Dr. Barnett asked.

"I don't think we should rush into anything just yet," Winter said. "He's not going anywhere. Let's see if we can find the vehicle this spare key unlocks."

"When I lived here, we almost never found dead professional killers in our yards," Dr. Barnett said.

59

WINTER FOUND AN ABANDONED AND LOCKED GMC Yukon a block away, and opened it using the spare car key from the dead man's wallet.

Based on the thermos and the two cups abandoned on

the console, there had been a team using the vehicle. The dead man's partner wouldn't have abandoned the vehicle, so Winter figured a second body could be close by. There was a laptop on the floorboard. Winter opened it and the small screen showed a map grid with three closely spaced dots representing three of the four vehicles in Brad's driveway. In the backseat, he spotted a small receiver with digital recording capability for audio transmissions. He erased the contents. He'd look in the vehicles later for corresponding microphones.

In the back, two Pelican equipment cases held an HK semiautomatic shotgun and a pair of MP5SDs, military-issue fully automatic 9mm machine guns with noise suppressors and rubber baffles. Armed with subsonic rounds, they were as silent as suppression sciences allowed. Neither had been manufactured with serial numbers. There were enough loaded magazines to supply an Army platoon patrolling downtown Baghdad.

"Brad, we need to go back."

"He *was* a hit man."

"This was a two-man team."

"Where's the other one?"

"If he's lucky, he's dead. If not, Styer has him."

"What the hell's going on?"

"Can you trust your father to keep his mouth shut?"

"Can you tell us why he should?"

Winter nodded.

"He can keep a secret."

"Good. If these people don't know he knows, he'll be safe."

"What about us?"

"We'll have to wait and see," Winter said.

• • •

After Winter and Brad took a quick look around for the second cutout's corpse, and were satisfied he wasn't close by, Dr. Barnett joined the trio in the gazebo fifty feet from the corpse to talk.

"Our dead friend's ID isn't legit. The calluses on his hands aren't from unpacking boxes of plastic flyswatters from China. The weapons and equipment in the truck point to him being the worst kind of professional."

"Hit man," Dr. Barnett said.

"The dead guy over there was a cutout. You familiar with the term?"

"I am," Dr. Barnett said. "Men, usually killers or intelligence gatherers, with false identities who work for the government running about the world engaging in dark ops and wet work. Very scary individuals who are immune to the legalities and societal conventions the rest of us are compelled to follow. They can do whatever they want and nobody can do anything to them, because our government goes all out to cover up whatever they do. They're like guided bolts of lightning."

Alexa looked at William Barnett, puzzled.

"Between medical journals, I read the occasional spy novel. Clancy, LeCarre, and Ian Fleming. Am I close?"

"Yes," Winter said.

"They were here to kill us?" Brad asked.

"If they were after us, we wouldn't still be here. Best I can figure, they were hoping we'd turn over a rock with Styer under it, so they could kill him."

Winter went on. "I think it's most likely that Styer followed us here, spotted this team, killed one, and took the other off so he could gather information. He knows this will distract us. The cutouts are after him, but I think he likes that because he loves to show off."

Dr. Barnett said, "Sounds invincible."

Alexa said, "He has some weaknesses. Most importantly for us, he is a narcissistic psychopath without any control to rein him in. The cutouts will get him eventually, and he knows that on some level."

Quickly, Winter recounted the story of Styer's game in New Orleans. Brad and Dr. Barnett were clearly amazed. It was a perfect illustration of Styer's talents.

"So do you try to find the other cutout before Styer kills him?" Dr. Barnett asked.

"We won't find him alive. As soon as we report the body to the police, their team will move in to clean this up. In the meantime, since the corpse is in your neighbor's yard, we'll get a lot of attention from the cops, and we'll be slowed down."

Alexa said, "Winter is right about these people. They don't like Winter because he outgunned one of their teams and blackmailed them into a truce. We're all vulnerable."

"Look at what happened in Roswell, New Mexico," Dr. Barnett said.

"So what do we do?" Brad asked Winter.

Winter said, "First off, Dr. Barnett, can you go back to your normal life and just forget this happened?"

Dr. Barnett stepped down onto the grass. "Not a problem. Just let me know if you need anything. And look after Brad. He doesn't get this spy stuff like I do."

The trio watched the doctor until he walked around the corner.

Winter told Brad, "The rest of the team that's in the area will assume Styer got these two, and if they don't know we've caught on to their presence, they should just keep monitoring us. Our vehicles are almost certainly wired, so we'll let the bugs stay in place."

"Brad, can you go along with this?" Alexa asked.

"Tell me what to do."

60

PAULUS STYER STOOD UNDER THE SHOWERHEAD, letting the cold water wash a red river of blood down the drain. He was satisfied that the cutouts had been only monitoring Massey, the sheriff, and the FBI agent, figuring Styer would show up. That much they had certainly been right about. He smiled at the fact—which he had proved many times before—that the organized opposition was made up of lesser men. They had been on his trail for years and he had effortlessly stayed well ahead of them, leading them around by their noses and kicking them in their collective ass. Now he had killed two more of them. He hoped to kill a lot more before this, his last game played strictly for sport, was over and it was time to tally it all up.

He turned off the water and dried his false face off carefully, running the towel over his body and combing his wet hair. He checked the seams and was satisfied that they were hidden. Using the towel might dislodge the latex panel at his hairline. He studied his features in the mirror and went into the next room to get dressed so he could get on with the business of killing Winter Massey and the Gardners. He also needed to check in on Cynthia and call her daddy again.

61

THE FIRST LIGHT FROM THE SUN ILLUMINATED THE vast Delta with a warm orange glow as they rolled across the barren landscape at sixty miles per hour. Brad was behind the wheel of an old station wagon that had been his mother's, and Winter drove the Yukon. Six miles from Brad's door, surrounded by cotton fields bisected here and there by long straight lines of leafless trees, twin hills made of soil stood just off the road. The dirt in the county-owned dumpsite was used for construction projects. Driving down a narrow dirt road, the vehicles entered a sixty-foot-wide valley crisscrossed with deep impressions left from dump-truck tires. The dirt would block the Yukon from the prying eyes of all living things except the birds, and perhaps some poor fool walking across the fields to collect scraps of cotton that were now being blown horizontal by a stiff northeastern wind. It was unlikely that anybody would stumble across the vehicle and, if they did, there was little chance they'd break in and steal the weapons with a corpse sitting inside keeping watch.

Winter left the SUV without looking again at the body that sat belted in the passenger seat. He climbed into the Buick wagon to join Brad, who drove out fast. They were a mile from town when Winter saw an oncoming SUV and slumped down in the seat so he wouldn't be seen.

"Keep driving," he told Brad.

"What are you doing?" Brad asked.

"An SUV at our twelve o'clock."

"I see it." Brad pulled at the brim of his ball cap before the SUV passed, heading in the opposite direction at a high rate of speed.

"Talk about close shaves," Brad said, exhaling loudly. "Five minutes off and they'd have found us dumping their pal."

"Too close for my taste," Winter said, meaning it.

They entered a long curve and the SUV was out of sight.

"There were at least three men in that truck," Brad said. "How many more you think there are?"

"Fewer than there will be pretty soon. They take losses very badly. They'll swarm in now."

Brad opened the glove box, found a sealed pack of Kool cigarettes, and opened it. After he put one between his lips, he lit it with the car's lighter and dropped his window a good six inches.

"I didn't know you smoked," Winter said.

"I don't," Brad said, inhaling deeply. "Want one?"

62

THE GRIME-ENCRUSTED EIGHTEEN-WHEELER, WHICH had been parked at a rest area just across the Mississippi state line for ten hours, made the trip to Tunica in twenty-three minutes. Despite the well-worn exterior, the working parts—the brakes, suspension, tires, and the motor—were painstakingly maintained. The electronics and the communication system, most of it hidden from prying eyes, were highly advanced. The transmissions it sent and received were encrypted and routed through the network of NSA satellites encircling the globe like buzzards.

The truck's two-man crew, both professional cleaners with twenty years of experience between them, had spent the idle hours watching movies in the cabin. The well-stocked selection of DVDs was all action movies. These men enjoyed critiquing films on subjects they knew best. They agreed that the action choreography between the two criminals in *The Way of the Gun* was perfection, and not something such criminals would have developed without the sort of training the cleaners themselves had received. Obviously the authors of the script had consulted with a talented professional with advanced training.

When the emergency broadcast came in, the men were watching *The Departed.* Herf, the designated driver, climbed into the rig's driver's seat and rolled out south while his partner, Watts, watched the rest of the movie. As he climbed through the gears, Herf took an amphetamine and vitamin cocktail packet from a secret compartment in the dashboard and poured the pills into his mouth, washing them down with an energy drink. One of the pep pills was uncoated for immediate impact and the other was a time-release capsule buffered with a mild sedative to prevent speed nervousness.

When he pulled off the county road and drove between two massive piles of dirt, he waved at the waiting three-man watch team, drove past the Yukons, then pushed a button and released a ramp that extended itself hydraulically and dropped gently to the ground.

Watts, freshly dressed in a disposable jumpsuit, a particle mask, and surgeon's gloves, climbed down and ran around to get behind the wheel of one of the Yukons, which he drove into the trailer. As soon as he returned to the truck, Herf closed the rear. After Watts climbed back up into the rig, carrying the jumpsuit in a garbage bag, Herf expertly turned the truck around and headed east toward the interstate.

"One cold one in the Yukon," Watts said. "It's Duncan."

"How'd he buy it?"

"Edge to the throat."

"What about his partner, Rowe?" Herf asked.

"Missing and presumed captured," Watts said.

"Missing and presumed Styered," Herf said flatly.

"Makes you glad to be on the truck this time," Watts

said. "Cold Wind is a rough job. I'd love to land that bastard. What's the bonus on him now?"

"One point five, last I heard. We're to drop off this load and be back in position ASAP."

"I knew the team should have been larger from the get-go," Watts said.

"This might be one long weekend," Herf said. He used the GPS to plot the fastest route to the naval air base north of Memphis, where a C-130 would be waiting to take the Yukon and its cold-meat cargo to a backwater base in Texas where the equipment would be salvaged, the Yukon would be crushed into a block of steel, and their dead comrade would be unceremoniously cremated.

"The way of the gun," Watts said to himself.

63

WALKING INTO THE HOUSE, WINTER AND BRAD found Alexa breaking eggs into a skillet.

She pointed to a note on the kitchen counter that said, *Didn't find any bugs, but there might be a window vibration reader.*

"Smells good," Winter said after reading the sheet and handing it to Brad. Alexa had the radio blaring rock music from the late '60s.

"Be ready in three shakes of Ruger's tail," she said

cheerily. She looked at him inquiringly. "Woody called looking for your father."

Winter scribbled on the paper, *Dropped off and others passed us as we were coming back. No problem.*

They ate while making small talk about the Delta and the weather. Afterward, Winter cleared the dishes and washed them in the sink.

"What's on the schedule today?" Alexa asked.

"Sherry's funeral," Brad said.

"Think Jacob Gardner will be there?" Winter asked.

"I wouldn't be surprised. He'll be sticking close enough to count Leigh's heartbeats until the deal is done," Brad offered. "That cash'll hold him like a gut pile holds bottle flies."

"You'll be done there by what time?" Alexa asked.

"Funeral's at one. Say two-thirty. I'll leave after the graveside service. City cops are handling the traffic."

"Lex and I will be there, too, with the family. I think this morning we ought to go talk to that casino manager and stir the pot," Winter said. "Press him about Beals, see how he reacts."

"He may be totally out of the land loop," Alexa said. "His Bureau files are squeaky clean."

"And so are RRI's," Winter said. "Maybe their files are all clean, but that doesn't mean the individuals are. If the land deal isn't done, their other land is worthless."

"They could build around it," Brad said.

"Probably," Alexa said, "but that would be a pain in the ass and a complication down the road. Especially if Ms. Gardner left it as is, or worse, made it into a trailer park. Think of the view from the hotel rooms."

Brad smiled. "Under normal circumstances she would

do just that. She's that ornery. But you're right, they are better off acquiring it. If by some miracle we get Mulvane or whoever is behind this for the murder of Sherry Adams, the owner can just say he didn't know the details. Hell, according to Alexa, he doesn't even live in this country. One thing for sure," Brad continued, "having an FBI agent along while we're asking questions might be a sobering experience for whoever is behind this mess. Mulvane may control the MBI in this, but the FBI is a different matter."

"I don't think we should show them an FBI badge just yet," Winter said. "Best to keep you in reserve."

"Whatever you think, Winter," Alexa said.

"I need to think about it some more," Winter said. "I'm still trying to work out some plan other than using Leigh if we can help it. The risk is too great."

"Well, as a last resort there's always the trusty bull-in-the-china-shop approach," Alexa said.

64

AT EIGHT-THIRTY A.M. BRAD PULLED INTO THE Roundtable's parking lot. "Alexa, you going to wait out here?" Winter asked.

"Drop me here and park closer. I want to go in and

look around while nobody knows who I am. Ring me when you're ready to leave. Is there a metal detector?"

"This is Mississippi, Alexa," Winter said. "Everybody is packing heat."

As Alexa made it to the front doors, a large rosy-cheeked man with bright red hair and bushy brows held the door open for her. He was dressed in a leather sports coat over a T-shirt. His new-looking jeans broke on fancy cowboy boots.

"Hope you brought money and luck with you," he said cheerily.

"I sure did," she replied.

The man walked in after her, drawing even as they entered the expansive foyer. "Normally, I'm surrounded by pigs," he said.

"Normally, so am I," she said.

"Jason Parr," the man said, offering her his hand, which was dry and callused. "I raise hogs all year until my vacation rolls around, and then I come here to Tunica and roll dice. I sure could use some luck, if you've got any to spare. As of last night, I'm down to my last two thousand hogs."

"You're playing craps?" Alexa asked. She was amazed that the place could be so busy so early.

" 'Playing' isn't the first word that springs to mind."

"I'm sorry. Maybe your luck will change."

"You ever played craps, Miss . . . ?"

"Alexa Keen," she said. "No, Mr. Parr. I never have."

"Well," the smiling pig farmer said, "it's about time you did. It's a fascinating game."

"I don't know anything about gambling," she said, giving him a once-over. "I just wanted to look around."

"All you have to do is throw dice. I'll do the rest. If I win, I'll give you ten percent of whatever I get. And I'll cover one hundred percent of the losses. It's what they call a win/win situation, Mrs. Keen."

"I'm not married. Call me Alexa. I can only play until I get a call from my boyfriend. Then I have to leave."

"Okay, then, Alexa. Let's you and me put a choke hold on the cashiers' cage while you're on the playground."

Alexa saw Winter and Brad enter the casino and spotted a large man in a loose-cut suit holding a walkie-talkie and following them. He was built like a pineapple and his face was red from exertion. When he shouted, Winter and Brad turned at the sound of his voice. Based on Brad's description, Alexa figured he was Albert White, the head of casino security.

65

AS WINTER AND BRAD ENTERED THE CASINO, ALEXA walked ahead of them, beside a beefy red-haired man who talked with his hands waving in the air. Alexa was smiling at him, probably using him as cover.

"Sheriff," a voice behind them called out. "Hold up!"

Brad and Winter turned and waited for Albert White. Winter hadn't seen Albert outside, but there he was coming up behind them, his face as red as if he'd been running a city block after a bus.

Winter turned and saw Alexa walking away, the man's arm making dice-shaking motions. Alexa put her hand behind her back and waggled her fingers to say good-bye.

"What brings you fellows back out?" Albert asked, smiling tentatively as he mopped his brow with a handkerchief.

"We need to talk to Mr. Mulvane," Brad said.

"Mr. Mulvane is a very busy man," White said. "You should have called first. He has a guest arriving shortly and he's tied up with last-minute details."

"A VIP?" Brad asked, smiling. "A whale?"

"Yes. Exactly. In half an hour or less," White said.

"Now is good," Winter said.

White turned angry eyes on Winter and frowned. "I was talking to the sheriff."

Brad said, "It's official county business."

"Let me call him and see if he has a minute," White said, lifting his cell phone.

"We'll need more like ten minutes," Brad said.

White clipped his radio to his belt, and took out his cell phone to make a call. "Mr. Mulvane, sorry to disturb you, but Sheriff Barnett and a deputy are down in the lobby. They want to talk to you for a few minutes." White listened to whatever Mulvane was saying for several seconds, nodding.

"I explained that to them. Yes, sir, I'll escort them upstairs," White said, closing the phone.

"After you," Brad said.

Albert White led them through the casino. As they

walked, Winter scanned the crowd scattered around the playing floor on either side of the wide aisle.

Albert White's size made the private elevator ride to the executive office suites a close affair.

Albert led them into a mirrored foyer and down the hall to a door marked GENERAL MANAGER. An attractive young woman with dirty blonde hair, a pink ribbon lapel pin, and a wide smile sat at the desk in the reception area. The nameplate on her desk read JANICE PRITCHETT, EXECUTIVE ASSISTANT.

"Mr. Mulvane is expecting you," she chirped.

Albert led them to the hand-carved door and knocked firmly.

"Enter!" a booming voice called from inside.

As Brad and Massey came in, Pierce stood and rushed to greet them, wearing an expression Winter had seen car salesmen put on as they came out from their showrooms to welcome potential customers.

"An unexpected pleasure," Mulvane said jovially. "I am so sorry I can only give you a few minutes. Any moment now I have a VIP arriving that I have to welcome personally. Sheriff Barnett, it's a pleasure to see you again."

"This is Deputy Winter Massey," Brad said.

"Please have a seat." After they sat, Mulvane went around the desk and made a show of gathering the papers and files into one stack, which he dropped into a desk drawer. Winter suspected the papers had been placed there in the minutes before they arrived.

"The work is never done," Mulvane said, shrugging. "What can I do for you?"

"It seems clear," Brad said, "that Jack Beals killed Sherry Adams."

"That was the young girl's name?" Pierce said, looking at Albert White.

"Yes," White said.

"Tragic," Pierce said, losing the smile and furrowing his brow sympathetically. "Such a terrible waste of life."

Brad said, "What we can't figure out is why Beals did it. What could possibly have put him on the Gardner plantation, and what was his motive for killing a young girl?"

"You don't presume to imagine I could know what was in a killer's mind. I'm not a psychiatrist . . . or a psychic," Mulvane said.

"Are you familiar with the Gardners, Mr. Mulvane?" Winter asked. "Jacob. Leigh is his ex-wife who owns Six Oaks."

"I'm not a local," Mulvane said. "We have hundreds of locals who gamble in our establishment. The name does seem familiar. Do you know them, Albert?"

"I am familiar with Jacob Gardner. He is here on occasion. You may have met him. He is very friendly. Outgoing, I'd say."

"Does he ever win?" Brad asked.

"I'm not sure," Albert said, shrugging. "You'd have to ask him."

"Naturally, Sheriff, we do not discuss our customers or their personal affairs," Mulvane said. "Our clients expect a level of discretion."

"Mr. Mulvane, you're obviously a very busy man who doesn't seem to have any idea what is going on. Maybe we should go back and talk to Jacob Gardner," Winter said. "He told us that he knows you."

Mulvane shrugged.

"I'm sure Gardner can clear it up for us," Winter said.

Pierce's smile was eroding. "Maybe that would be your best course," he said weakly.

"See, we've been wondering if the death of Sherry Adams could possibly have something to do with a piece of land that Leigh Gardner owns. We had the impression that you are interested in acquiring her acreage," Winter said.

Mulvane said, "Why would I know anything about her land?"

"Because it's surrounded by land that your parent corporation RRI has been buying over the past few months to build a major resort. Jacob told Leigh you made her an offer through him," Winter said.

When Winter said the word *resort*, Mulvane's face twitched.

"We're not saying the two things are connected," Brad said. "We're just looking at everything that comes to our attention as we investigate."

"You can see where the timing of the killing, Beals's connection to your casino, his own death, and the land you need so desperately . . ." Winter let the last word hang in the air between them.

A ringing phone saved Mulvane for the moment. He grabbed his cell out of his pocket and answered it, raising a finger to put Winter on hold. "Yes, Tug? Seven minutes." He closed the phone. "Gentlemen," he said. "My guest is arriving. If we need to continue this, it will have to be at a later time. Look, I can't discuss RRI business in progress with anyone outside the organization. The land you mentioned . . . well, it's a delicate negotiation, and since you know about it, fine." He opened his hands as he stood. "We have been trying to acquire it from Mr. Gardner for a long while. We discovered that Mr. Gardner does not in fact own it, so we asked him to tender a very, very generous offer to his ex-wife. As far as I know, this has no connection to anything else that has happened. Our project will bring hundreds of jobs and hundreds of millions of dollars in tax monies into the state. The project represents an operation unparalleled in this county. Which I hope will stay between us until it is announced."

"Leigh Gardner may or may not sell her land to you," Winter said. "She is upset that she received your offer from her ex-husband along with what may have been an implied threat that something bad could happen if she didn't take the offer. Something along the lines of what happened to Sherry Adams."

"I resent your insinuations," Mulvane said. "When we discovered that Jacob Gardner didn't own or in any way control the land in question, which he told us he did, it put us in an awkward position. He assured us he could make the deal happen and would represent Ms. Gardner. That is why we have been going through Gardner. If we can't reach an agreement on the land from Mrs. Gardner, we can have it condemned by the state and buy it anyway—probably for much less than our offer. But the idea that we would resort to threats or violence is preposterous."

"Jacob led his ex-wife to believe that she or one of her children could suffer a similar fate as Sherry Adams," Brad said. "This is a very serious accusation. And one of your employees did kill Sherry."

"I never said any such thing to Jacob Gardner!" Mulvane stammered. "The man is a liar and a fool."

"By the way," Brad said, "I understand you believe

Beals stole the money we found at his place from your casino? Any idea how much?"

"Ballpark," Albert White said, "we're compiling the exact figure, but it looks to be two hundred thousand dollars and change. How much did you find?"

"Albert, you know that's confidential," Brad said. "I'll be looking forward to seeing your figures."

Winter said, "We have evidence that Jack Beals was robbing, maybe even killing, winning customers, and we think he was picking them carefully so he wouldn't get caught. We believe he may have had a partner here in the casino with access to information on the victims. We were sure the money we found hidden in Beals's house was from that enterprise. But you say it was stolen from this casino, so we'll be interested in your evidence, since it contradicts ours."

Mulvane's face had lost any semblance of its former cheeriness. White seemed at a loss for words as well.

"Maybe we should be talking to the director of RRI," Winter said. "We have his name and address. Thank you for your time, Mr. Mulvane. We know the way out."

The men stood to leave, and Pierce took a deep breath and followed them to the elevator. "I'll ride down with you," he said.

Winter and Brad stared at Mulvane in total silence after the door closed. Albert White had to take the stairs down since the elevator was too small for the four of them.

"Has it ever been brought to your attention that people who win here sometimes don't always get to keep their winnings?" Winter asked.

"Of course not," Pierce said, punching the button

for the first floor three times even though the cab was moving.

"Well, Beals told David Scotoni that the casino sent him to retrieve the money he'd won at your tables. Scotoni is the guy who was being drowned by Beals just before Beals was killed. You know, Mr. Mulvane, you strike me as a man who's living in a world filled with unfortunate coincidences. I know this place is a fantasy world without clocks or invasions of reality from outside, but beyond these walls, actual consequences await everyone."

When the elevator stopped and the door opened, Brad stepped out and walked off a few paces. Massey blocked Mulvane's exit, smiling at him.

Mulvane straightened and looked Winter in the eyes. "Are you threatening me?"

"Yes," Massey said in a low voice. "That is exactly what I am doing. You may have some other people fooled, but I have you pegged. And I know that some others in here have dirty hands too."

"How dare you," Mulvane said.

"I'll make this real simple," Winter said. "Anybody threatens or tries to harm Leigh Gardner or her kids, I'll assume it was you. And I generally act on my assumptions."

"Who the hell do you think you are?" Mulvane said, baring his teeth. "I can have your badge."

"You think I need a badge? You should check me out," Winter said. "James Winter Massey. People who know anything about me will assure you that I am a man of my word. And I am giving you my word. So if the threat fits, wear it."

66

WINTER STEPPED OUT AND PIERCE MULVANE brushed past him to hurry into the casino, followed by a red-faced Albert White, who had just burst through the stairway door.

"What did you say to Mulvane just now?" Brad asked.

"Not much. I think I got through to him. If he and White haven't checked me out, they will now. Having a reputation like mine is sometimes a good thing. Hopefully their sources are good, and they'll get rattled, which is something those fellows aren't accustomed to. Mulvane will stew some and then he'll make a move."

"Well, now I'm a little confused. See, I thought we had a plan that involved wiring Leigh and catching Mulvane forcing the sale. The thing we discussed with Alexa—Federal charges of extortion, uttering threats, maybe murdering Sherry Adams?"

"I changed that plan," Winter said.

"So I noticed. Why?"

"Mulvane's smart and he's never going to say anything incriminating to Leigh. And wiring her would put Leigh in more danger. I'm convinced that he's done some stupid and criminal crap, and I want him to know that the only way out is through me. It could get intense."

"This hasn't been intense?" Brad asked, incredulous.

"Yes, it's been that, but all of it could pale in comparison to the next day or two. Styer hasn't left the area, and maybe this will spur Mulvane or White to sic him on me."

"You seem sure of that," Brad said.

"Yeah," Winter said. "Trust me on this stuff. I know how to fuel a fire."

67

ASIDE FROM PLAYING BOARD GAMES, ALEXA HAD never rolled a pair of dice. Right now, she felt as clueless about the goings-on at the craps table as a dog would be about open-heart surgery.

"Here's the deal," Jason told her. "You have to place a bet to get a turn at throwing the dice, so I'll make the bets. You just concentrate on rolling the dice when it's your turn."

"Okay," she said.

Jason Parr put several stacks of chips in the racks before him on the table's ledge, and with each roll, he reached over and placed them on various marked areas. When it was his turn to throw the dice, he was up thousands of dollars, which he attributed to Alexa's presence. After he rolled eight times in a row, he kept tossing chips down and when he rolled his point, he won big. He rolled three more times, making his point each time. When he rolled boxcars—double sixes—on the fourth point roll, he placed bets for Alexa as the croupier pushed the dice to her using his L-shaped stick.

"Just throw them hard enough so they hit the back of the table," he told her. "And don't change hands with them once you pick them up off the table. You might arrange them on the felt and throw them thinking you can control them, but you can't."

"So it's a crapshoot?" she asked, smiling.

"Sure as shootin' is," he said, laughing.

Alexa rolled a nine. Unbelievably, she rolled ten times after that, hitting a nine on the last one. Each roll brought about a flurry of activity from the players, and she watched without any understanding of why the chips were going down and being taken up again. Nobody seemed all that concerned when she crapped out.

"Dang," Jason said, looking at the long lines of black and yellow chips he had stacked in rows in the racks before him. "Alexa, you've put me ahead for the trip. I'm in the black. We're gonna clean the house out. I got the feeling in my bones."

"How much are those black and yellow chips worth?" Alexa asked.

"Five," Parr said.

"Five dollars?" Alexa asked.

"Five hundred," he replied.

Alexa's cell phone rang.

She flipped it open.

"We're leaving," Winter said into her ear.

"Yes, dear," she replied. "Two minutes."

"Aw, don't tell me," Jason said.

"I have to go in two minutes."

"Hey, will y'all let this little gal roll one last time?" he asked the other players.

Everybody at the table clapped their agreement.

Alexa rolled a six.

She watched as Jason Parr took everything he had in the chip racks and placed it in tall stacks around the board. "What are you doing?" she asked in horror.

"Gamblin'!" he said, smiling.

"But . . ."

"Get it, girl!" someone yelled.

"Roll them bones!" a woman in her sixties, who was wearing a red cowgirl suit, exclaimed.

"Roll," Jason said.

"Hit that six!" someone yelled. Alexa noticed a red-haired man who looked like an evangelist walking through the casino with Albert White. He stopped behind the croupier, and stared down at the chips on the table. His smile was crooked.

"Mr. Mulvane!" Jason hollered. "Read it and weep!"

Alexa felt sick to her stomach. After rolling a four, a five, a four, an eight, and a three, Alexa rolled a six. While everybody around the table was screaming and celebrating—except the evangelist-looking man, who was smiling insincerely—Alexa moved away unnoticed, making a beeline for the front door.

68

WINTER AND BRAD EXITED THE CASINO JUST AS A limousine, its windows covered by dark film, rolled to a stop under the portico. An enthusiastic Pierce Mulvane rushed up, flanked by Albert White and the blonde secretary, who was holding an opened notebook, pen poised, awaiting dictation. A man in sunglasses with slicked-back brown hair and a deeply scarred face stood off to the side, scanning the crowd.

Two bellboys, each pushing a bag carrier, appeared and took up positions on the street side of the Lincoln. People on their way in and out of the casino stopped to gawk.

Albert White took out his cell phone, looked at the display and took the call, turning his wide back to the group.

Winter watched as the passenger door opened and two bull-necked security types got out and stood behind the limousine driver, who had opened the passenger door closest to the curb. A third security man, wearing an unbuttoned cashmere overcoat over a turtleneck sweater and gray woolen slacks, stepped out and scanned the area, his eyes hidden behind sunglasses. No doubt he was armed, the coat open to allow him immediate access to a weapon. He leaned back into the car and gave an all clear.

The main occupant, a man with short silver hair, gold-rimmed eyeglasses, and manicured nails that shone in the daylight like abalone, climbed out and the driver shut the door behind him. He smiled as Mulvane approached with his hand out. Winter was too far away to hear what was said, but close enough to read Pierce's lips. As they shook hands, Pierce said, "Welcome to the Roundtable, Herr Klein. This is a great pleasure for us all."

Klein? Now this is an interesting development, Winter thought. He looked from Mulvane to Albert White to the man with the deep facial scars, whom Winter caught staring in his direction. Although Winter had never seen the man before, he seemed to be familiar with Massey, probably thanks to Albert White. Big surprise. The scarred man was about Winter's height and built like a middleweight. Winter figured he was with casino security. Unlike the men protecting the head of RRI, scar-face looked just like the sort of hard-edged muscle who might break legs when he was asked to, and would probably enjoy the work. Winter paid close attention to Klein's and Mulvane's security people, because he had a distinct feeling he would see them again soon. Unfortunately, he was rarely wrong about that feeling.

69

ALEXA WAS HEADED TO THE FAR EDGE OF THE casino parking lot when she heard someone yelling her name.

"Alexa! Alexa!"

She turned to see a panting Jason Parr running toward her, waving frantically. Alexa stopped and waited for him to catch up, breathless.

"Jason."

"You . . . you . . . left before . . . you got . . . your cut."

"Don't be silly. I had a blast. You don't owe me anything."

"Man, I ain't had a run like that since my second wife caught me with my secretary and got her hands on my forty-four Bulldog."

"Sorry to hear it."

"Well, my wife got me good."

"She shot you?"

"Be better if she had. She gave me a divorce so I could marry my secretary. Talk about revenge." Jason took an envelope from his coat pocket and offered it to her. "This is roughly ten points. I didn't have time to do a count because you run off on me. They're counting it up now."

"I have to go," Alexa said. "And I can't take that."

She saw Brad's truck heading toward her.

"Sure you can," Jason said. "We had a deal and I always honor my word."

Brad pulled up. Winter was in the rear passenger seat.

"Good luck," Alexa said to Jason.

"You come back anytime I'm here and gamble with me. Same deal. I'll be here till Sunday."

"I think this is my last time," she said.

Alexa didn't know Jason Parr was going to hug her, but he lifted her off her feet and turned them both three hundred and sixty degrees before putting her down.

"Now I'll be lucky all day. I can feel it."

Alexa said good-bye, opened the truck door and climbed inside, closing the door behind her. Jason was already running back to the casino.

"I think your new pal really likes you," Winter said.

"He only likes my luck," she said. "Who was the VIP in the limo?"

"That was Klein, the owner," Winter said.

Alexa asked, "Mulvane was the carrottop fancy pants with fat Albert?"

"By the way, Winter changed your plan," Brad told her.

"I'm not surprised," she said. "I wasn't in love with it."

70

BACK AT THE SHERIFF'S OFFICE, ALEXA WENT ON THE Internet to research the Klein family and its businesses.

"Kurt Klein is the head of a family-owned industrial manufacturing conglomerate with roots that go back two hundred years," Alexa said. "RRI is a very small piece of their holdings. Most of the RRI properties are large self-contained resorts located in Europe, the Caribbean, Las Vegas, and around the world. The Klein corporation isn't publicly traded so there are no published financial figures. Maybe Klein isn't aware of what is going on. If we assume he knows about the land and the murder, why would he be here before it was resolved?"

"If he isn't aware, it could give us some leverage. Sometimes people are insulated, and they just say they want something to happen and other people make sure it does," Winter said.

Alexa said, "And sometimes men with a great deal of money and influence aren't what they seem, but what they choose to project. We just don't know enough about Klein. I suspect the CIA would have a better idea about him than the FBI. I doubt Klein's family businesses could have survived World War Two without some unpleasant alliances."

"You think Leigh is in any danger now that you told Mulvane we were aware of the implied threat? He'd be crazy to let anything happen to her, right?"

Winter shrugged. "You'd think so."

"I can have more of my people cover her," Brad said.

"I can stay with her. Nobody knows me," Alexa said. "I could just be a friend of hers visiting for support during a difficult time."

"A larger official presence couldn't hurt," Winter told Brad.

71

RAYMOND GEE HAD BOUGHT THE THREE-BEDROOM house as an investment, and he made his son, Alan, work on it like a slave all that summer, only paying him twenty bucks a day for ten hours or more of hard labor. All that was left was to sand and paint the Sheetrock, which would take another couple of weeks. The central heating was hooked up, as was the plumbing. Raymond Gee owned seven rental houses and was always telling his son that by the time he retired, the houses would be paid for and the rent checks they generated, after legitimate expenses, would pay him more than he made as a salesman at Gates Tires in Batesville.

Since Alan had a key, he and his best friend, Buddy

Graham, had been hanging out in the house's basement. They would smoke cigarettes, drink a beer or two, and party with Amy Buckley when she could sneak out and come there with them. While she was only fourteen to their sixteen, she was built like an eighteen-year-old, and she loved to get high. In exchange for a few hits on a pipe and their sworn promises not to ever tell anybody, she would take off her shirt and let the boys look at her breasts as long as they didn't touch them. She enjoyed watching them masturbate to the sight of her boobs. Although this had only happened twice in two months, they were getting worried. The house would soon be ready to rent and, once it was, they'd be without a clubhouse for their tit-peeking jerk-off sessions.

The boys knew that the neighbors were accustomed to Alan working inside the house, and since he parked his Ford Fiesta there all the time, they paid no particular attention to when the young boy's car arrived or left the property. They were smart enough not to let other kids hang out or party in the house, as it would certainly have resulted in Raymond finding out and putting an end to the clubhouse, not to mention Amy's intoxicating generosity.

When Alan put his key into the lock and turned it, there was no resistance.

"Damn, it isn't locked," Alan said, locking and unlocking the dead bolt twice, testing it. "If I forgot, and any tools got ripped off, my dad's going to freak out."

"Maybe your dad was here and he didn't lock it. Sounds like there's water running," Buddy said. "Is the shower on?"

"Maybe a pipe busted," Alan said. "Shit!" Alan rushed to the bathroom door. "My dad's gonna freak out."

When Alan opened the door and saw what was in the bathtub, he screamed, slammed the door, and ran from the house, Buddy hot on his heels.

72

AFTER PICKING UP HER BAG FROM BRAD'S HOUSE, Alexa trailed Brad's truck out to the Gardner plantation. They passed a cruiser parked on the road going in. As they were pulling up, Jacob darted from the house and stopped beside his car, fumbling with the keys. He froze when Brad and Winter climbed from the truck and Alexa got out of her car.

"Come inside," Brad told him. "We need to talk."

"I have to go pick up Cynthia at my mother's house in Memphis," Jacob said, his hands visibly shaking. "So she can make the funeral. So the harassment will have to wait a couple of hours." One side of his shirttail was out and his eyes looked feverish.

"When did you last talk to your daughter?" Alexa asked.

"Lady, if it's any of your business, just a few minutes ago," he snapped.

"Now is the only other time you are going to get," Brad said. "You leave here now and you're on your own."

"What are you talking about?" Jacob asked him.

"This is Alexa Keen with the FBI," Brad said, indicating Alexa. "She may be the only thing standing between you and Mulvane."

"I don't know what you're talking about," Jacob said.

"Your call," Alexa said. "But you should know that Mulvane knows that Leigh told us everything. I expect that puts you in a bad place."

"Mulvane never said that he was involved in anything like that. I never told Leigh that. And, anyway, if that is true, you think you can protect me from him? Like it's just him we're talking about. None of you know what you're messing with. There is a billion dollars in play here."

"Be that as it may, we're the only shot you have, Mr. Gardner," Alexa told him.

"So am I under arrest?" Jacob asked.

"No," Alexa said.

Brad added, "But you know he killed Sherry for a lot less, and how good his hired killer is. He knows you're a threat."

Jacob took off his coat and threw it into the car. He looked at each of them, seemed to weigh a thought—it was easy to imagine what it was—then jumped into his Cadillac and roared off down the driveway. When it turned onto the farm road, the heavy car fishtailed, squealing the tires.

"He'll be back," Alexa said.

"I don't know," Brad said. "He isn't exactly known for intelligent moves."

"We need him," Winter said, flatly.

As they were heading to the porch, Hamp ran out of the house, his face bright red.

"What's the matter, Hamp?" Brad asked, grabbing him.

"Daddy!" Hamp yelled, stamping his foot. "He hit Mama!"

Brad left Hamp and ran into the house. Leigh was in the den seated on the raised stone hearth. She was trembling. There was a red spot below her left eye, and she had a split lip. Estelle came in and handed Leigh a plastic bag filled with ice to hold against her cheek.

"Damn his hide," Brad snarled, his arm around Leigh's shoulders. "What happened?"

Leigh turned her eyes to Hamp. "I'm fine," she replied.

"I heard him hit her from the kitchen," Estelle volunteered.

"Estelle, take Hampton to the kitchen," Leigh said firmly.

"Arrest him, Brad," Hamp hissed. "Lock that asshole up."

"Hampton!" Leigh snapped. "He's your father."

"Not anymore he isn't. I hate his guts."

"We'll discuss this later, after you've calmed down," Leigh said. "Let me talk to Brad."

Estelle and Hamp left the room reluctantly. Alexa and Winter took seats across from the fireplace.

"What happened, Leigh?" Brad asked.

"This is terrible. I don't know what to do—how to tell you."

"Take your time," Brad said.

"Cynthia . . . Jacob said Cyn called from his mother's. Jacob said Cyn wasn't coming to the funeral, so I picked up the phone to call her, and he stopped me and told me that I had to sign papers on the land."

Leigh waited a few seconds before she said, "I told him I would sell the land, but I wouldn't do so unless I could meet with the buyer and negotiate a better deal. Like we discussed, so I could get it on tape. I didn't tell him that. I told him the land was obviously worth more than they offered, and I wanted to negotiate personally. I told him to tell the buyer to take it or leave it. He freaked out. He was yelling that these people weren't screwing around, that they'd kill all of us. He said this was the final offer and that if we were dead, it would make it more convenient for this person."

"Did he mention a name?" Alexa asked.

"Mulvane. Pierce Mulvane. He said the casino had to have the land and the casino owners weren't going to take no for an answer. He said they had over a billion dollars on the line, and life was cheap against that kind of investment. He said they'd kill him first, or all of us at the same time. I've never seen him so scared. I told him I was going to make sure our children got the maximum benefit possible."

"And that was when he hit you?" Brad asked.

Leigh started crying. "He told me he'd lied, that they took Cynthia. That she wasn't in Memphis at all and that she was fine, and she'd be released after the land deal was finished, but we'd never see her again if it didn't go through."

"You think he was in on it?" Brad asked.

"No. Maybe. I don't know. He said he didn't know who had her, that he'd spoken to some man twice who had her phone. I said I would call Mr. Mulvane and get her freed." Tears streamed down her cheeks. "God, I think he's telling the truth. And she needs her insulin. They might hurt her. You have to do something."

"Leigh, Alexa is going to stay with you," Winter said firmly. "We'll figure this out and get her back."

He nodded to Brad, and the two men left the room in a hurry.

Alexa said, "Leigh, Winter threatened them and I don't think they'd dare harm Cynthia. But if you decide you want me to do so, I'll bring in my FBI Immediate Response Team. Though I have to tell you that I can't guarantee it won't do more harm than good at this point. We need to talk to Jacob and make sure that he told you the truth. She'll be fine."

"But you aren't sure," Leigh said.

"No, I can't be one hundred percent, but this is my field of expertise. Mulvane is in a very difficult position because he knows we know about the land. If he's behind this, he'll make sure she's all right."

"Jacob won't cooperate," Leigh said. "There's no telling what he'll say or do."

Alexa heard the sound of Brad's siren wailing in the distance.

"They'll catch up to him," she said.

73

CYNTHIA LAY NAKED ON HER SIDE ON THE ICE-COLD tile floor of a fancy bathroom. Her abductor sat on the toilet contemplating her, an empty insulin syringe in his hand.

He said, "Did that help? I'm new at this diabetes thing."

"You need to give me more," she said weakly, covering herself as best she could with her hands. "Let me measure my blood sugar." Her vision was still blurred, but maybe clearing. There was a bottle of water on the floor beside her and she managed to keep herself covered until she took a long drink. He didn't seem interested in her sexually. Maybe it would be better if he were. She had decided that, in exchange for a shot to make her feel better, she could let him screw her. It was no big deal. She'd had sex with a few men she wasn't attracted to when they had something she wanted.

"The water in the tub is warm," he told her. "Get in. You smell like piss and bile."

"My clothes?" she asked.

"They're in the washing machine. I have to wash them before you put them on. I have a nice warm robe for you when you get out of the bath."

"Of course I ruined my clothes. What did you expect?"

"I'm no expert, but if I gave you more insulin, I suspect you'd be a lot more trouble."

"Please," Cyn said. "I won't try to escape."

"But you might, Ms. Gardner. I know a great deal about you. More than I care to, in fact."

"My mother will pay you whatever you want."

The man said, "All I want at this moment is for you to get into the bath."

Standing, the man helped Cynthia up. Her knees buckled, but she stepped into the warm bath and sat. The man recaptured his former position on the closed toilet and watched her as she bathed, but the ugly bastard didn't seem to want to do more than that.

And she made sure he saw plenty. She knew that men went stupid when she showed them even less of her body than he was seeing.

"You know," she said, mentally bracing herself, "this doesn't have to be so unpleasant. I mean, if you wanted to, like, have sex with me, I wouldn't say you couldn't. We couldn't," she said, smiling.

The man smiled back. "You want to trade sex for your freedom?" And then he laughed loudly. "I don't think so."

Angry at the rebuff, she thought, *He's gay.*

74

JACOB'S CADILLAC HAD LEFT THE ROAD, SHOT straight across a cotton field for fifty yards, and ended up nose-deep into a tree. Brad left the road and drove to the scene, cutting the siren when he stopped, but leaving his blue lights flashing. As Winter climbed out, the cold wind was like a slap in his face.

The car's front end was bent around the tree's trunk, like a man in the water holding on to a pier leg for dear life. The front windshield looked like a blanket made from thousands of beads. Jacob lay in the dead leaves twenty feet in front of the car in his sock feet.

"He's dead," Winter said as they walked up on the body.

Brad whistled. "He was still doing a good fifty when he hit the tree. Looks like he never even braked. Didn't have his seat belt on. Wasn't for his clothes, I wouldn't recognize him."

Winter stared down at the body. Half of Jacob's head was smashed and pushed against his shoulder. His brains were out, leaving an open and empty white bowl connected to his neck. Winter figured they were both thinking the same thing: Cornered and desperate, Jacob Gardner had taken a coward's way out of his wreck of a life.

While Brad called for the coroner and a backup unit, Winter went to the driver's side and looked into the Caddy. The driver's side window glass was scattered in the interior, but the passenger's side window was intact, and splattered with blood and bits of brain matter. And the blood droplets each formed lightning bolts, as if Jacob's blood had already been running down the surfaces when the sudden impact had caused a violent change of direction.

"It wasn't suicide," Winter said. "Somebody shot him in the head."

In the distance a siren announced a cruiser approaching from the plantation.

A cloud passed between the wreck and the sun, and the birds scattered in the woods chirped like gossips.

75

TEARFULLY, LEIGH LISTENED TO THE NEWS OF Jacob's death, nodding as Brad filled her in. It was impossible to tell if she was particularly upset by the news, since she was already overwhelmed with worry for Cynthia. Afterward, she went into the kitchen to tell Hamp about his father.

When Leigh left the room, Winter, Alexa, and Brad were left alone with their thoughts.

"We shouldn't have let him go. We could have helped," Alexa said. "If he'd just listened to us."

"Nobody could ever help Jacob Gardner," Brad said. "He spent his life building fires for other people to put out. And he never told the truth unless he thought it was a lie. We have to concentrate on Cynthia."

Winter figured that even a disaster of a man like Jacob Gardner deserved a better end than the one he got. Jacob's death was no great loss to society, but it was a sin that Hamp's last memory of his father would be of him punching his mother in the face and roaring off, with Hamp wishing him dead. He would always feel a sense of guilt over it, and nothing anybody said or did could change that. As a young man, Winter had often wished his own father dead, before he actually died from an esophageal hemorrhage in his rented room while the drunk barfly he was sleeping with was passed out ten feet away. No matter how much he had despised James Massey, he always carried a sense of guilt for hating him.

"Jacob got three calls from Cyn's phone since she's been gone," Brad told Alexa, handing her Jacob's cell phone so she could see for herself.

"And one is a text message." She handed the phone to Winter so he could read it.

"It's from Styer," Winter said.

"How do you know?" Alexa asked.

"He signed it. The message he sent is 'PS I said no cops. No FBI grab experts!' "

"PS where there's no reason for a postscript. PS for Paulus Styer," she said. "And 'n.o. cops.' "

Winter said, "The word 'no' has periods after the 'n' and the 'o.' That took effort and it was done on purpose."

"New Orleans," Alexa said.

"It's a relief," Winter said.

"Why is that a relief?" Brad said. "The man is a psychopath."

Winter said, "Styer plans, and if he took her it's part of his overall scheme. He has either already killed her, or he won't unless and until it suits his purpose. If he hasn't killed her, Mulvane should have called him off by now, and we'll get her back. Styer figured I'd see the text message and know it was him."

"With Jacob gone, Mulvane's rid of his most immediate threat—a witness. The question is, what is his next move?" Brad asked Winter.

"Mulvane has to get the land deal done fast. If he hasn't leveled with Klein and has to have the land—or this casino resort is dead in the water—then Sherry's death and Cynthia's grab make more sense."

Leigh walked in, her face, except for the bruise, blanched. "I told Hamp his father was killed in a wreck. I didn't mention murder."

"Leigh, do you have extended family?" Winter asked. "Uncles, aunts, cousins?"

"On my father's side. I have an uncle and an aunt in Nashville. Another aunt in Miami. Six cousins."

"Are you close?" Winter asked.

"It's one of those bad blood situations. They're embittered over the fact that my father ended up with the plantation because he was the only one in the bunch who worked the land. They were already off spending my grandfather's money long before he died. My grandfather left the land to Daddy and a lump sum to each for the accident of their births. That was over forty years ago, and they still think they got screwed."

"If they owned it, would they sell the plantation for a large profit if anything happened to you and the children?" Winter asked, knowing the answer.

"In a New York minute," she said. She gave him a curious look. "But the children would inherit everything."

Winter nodded. "Temporarily. And if something happened to them?"

"My aunts and uncle wouldn't be knowingly involved in a plot to kill us. They aren't the sort of people who would do that."

"We're talking millions of dollars, Leigh," Brad said. "The plantation alone is worth several million. Not to mention the woodland and the land Mulvane wants."

"Do you think Mulvane has already talked to them?" Leigh asked.

Alexa said, "He couldn't very well tell them what he was thinking. But I bet he's aware they'd sell. He could tell them he'd offered you the deal and you accepted. They aren't farmers. They feel they're owed. Most people would cash out under those circumstances."

"It would be just like Jacob to have told Mulvane about them," Leigh said.

"I'm working on the best way to handle it," Winter said. "I'm leaning toward going over Mulvane's head."

Winter hoped that Mulvane would want to call Styer off, but Winter had a feeling that Styer's game was only going to be a part of Mulvane's plan as long as it served his own.

76

PIERCE MULVANE TAPPED AT THE DOOR TO VIP suite 825. Kurt Klein's security man, Finch, answered the door. Behind him the elderly German, wearing a silk robe and slippers, stood waiting in the sunken living room. "Come in, Pierce."

Finch closed the door. "Please raise your hands, Mr. Mulvane."

"Do you think Pierce means to do me harm, Steffan?"

"Sorry, sir," Finch said. "There are security procedure's in place for a reason. Would you like me to suspend them?"

"I can't tell you not to do your job," Klein said, shrugging.

Finch searched Mulvane by moving his hands up and down his frame, then gently but firmly into Pierce's genitals as well as the crack between his buttocks. After Finch moved back, satisfied, Mulvane's boxer shorts remained inside the crevasse.

"No problem," Pierce said, as cheerily as he could. "We must all follow rules."

"Without following rules, we are no better than animals," Kurt agreed, with barely a trace of his native German accent. The son of a prominent industrialist,

Kurt had graduated from Harvard with an international law degree. During WWII, the Klein factories had made vehicles and military equipment for the German army. After a few years in jail after the war, Kurt's father had gone right back to it, manufacturing toasters, stoves, train cars, buses, and treaded earth-moving equipment instead of Tiger tanks. Kurt had taken over the Klein businesses some thirty years earlier, and had expanded and diversified until the family name was once again synonymous with goods made from German steel that performed as they were supposed to.

Kurt Klein's easy smile was as disarming as the eyes of a baby seal. But beneath the polished exterior and gentle demeanor, he was as ruthless as a WWII SS Special Action Unit commander.

"I hope your accommodations are suitable," Pierce said.

"Quite so, Pierce, my old friend. It is a pleasure for me to be here in your *temporary* palace," he said, emphasizing the adjective. "This little Disney World."

" 'Temporary' is the right word," Pierce said.

"Steffan, you may leave us," Kurt said.

Finch walked to the kitchen and waited with his back to the cabinet, watching, but out of earshot.

"Please, sit," Kurt said after he had taken a place on the sleek leather sofa.

Pierce sat and crossed his legs to reflect a casualness he didn't feel.

"Fill me in on the River Royale."

"Well, Herr Klein, I regret that I have some unpleasant news on that front. Well, not unpleasant, because it is going to be handled, but I seek your advice on a matter or two. You have experience with such complexities. I know this is a small venture for you."

"Every one of my businesses is as important to me as any other." Klein's soft eyes hardened and the smile changed into one that filled Pierce's veins with ice water. "I'm listening. Please make this *business* discussion as quickly to the point as possible. This is supposed to be an inspection trip for me. No sugar coating, Pierce."

"Your man Pablo, the one who was to help with the land acquisition, made a snafu," Pierce said.

"What sort of snafu?"

"It appears he killed the wrong person. The local authorities have gotten involved and now they suspect the murder is connected to the land acquisition. The sheriff and a deputy are investigating. The deputy is new, and evidently has been involved with several violent situations. He has killed several people. His name is Winter Massey."

"Finch!" Kurt yelled, keeping his eyes fixed on Pierce.

Pierce jumped involuntarily at the sudden bark, spilling the Gardner files onto the carpet, but not daring to pick them back up.

"Finch!"

Finch moved into the room, gun in hand, with amazing speed. He stopped behind Pierce like a malevolent shadow. Pierce could see Finch in the mirror across the room, and that the gun was being aimed at the back of his head.

"Sir?" Finch said.

"You swept these rooms?"

"Yes."

"This *idiot* has taken a very simple assignment and

turned it into toxic waste." Klein's ability to mask his fury was slipping. He grabbed a heavy ashtray from the coffee table and for a second, Pierce was sure he was going to throw it at him. Instead he put it down again, took out a cigarette case and a gold Dunhill lighter from the pocket of his robe, and lit a cigarette.

"Sir," Pierce said. "I didn't have any part in the mistake. I'm sure—"

"Shut up!" Kurt snapped. "Why is this Winter Massey person here? Steffan, do you have any idea who he is talking about?"

"I've never met him, but I know him by his reputation. He was a United States marshal. From the little I do know about him, he is a formidable individual. He's killed some very capable people."

Pierce nodded and looked at his hands, which were tightly gripping his knees. "He's retired. I don't have any idea how he ended up in this, but he is here and he is involved."

Kurt said, "We may have some repairs to make. I will talk to Pablo and see how he explains the snafu. Then, together, we will all figure out the best path to take. Have you spoken with him?"

"No," Pierce said. "I've never met him. As instructed, I gave him someone local who could be trusted, to assist him as requested, but I am pretty sure he killed him. Jack Beals, the man Albert assigned to work with him, was the only one who ever met him."

"Maybe this Massey killed your Beals?" Kurt relaxed, sat back against the back of the sofa, and took a long drag from the cigarette before expelling a cloud of thin white smoke.

"This will all work out," Pierce said.

"I hope so," Kurt said. "Steffan, you will handle it. Use that man . . . Tug, isn't it?"

"Yes. Tug Murphy."

"Where did you get this Murphy?"

"He came to me highly recommended by friends of mine in Boston. He can be absolutely trusted."

Finch nodded. "I checked him out. He has a solid background with the Irish mob. Follows orders and knows how to keep his mouth shut."

"What does Albert White know?"

"A little. I asked him for someone we could trust totally for a special job, and he recommended Beals immediately. He said he had used him for delicate matters in the past. Beals was an ex–deputy sheriff. Local, but he had a history with White. Beals's father was a contractor for the Dixie mob."

"What does White know about our prior discussions?" Kurt asked.

"As far as he knows, I am acting alone, doing what I think needs to be done for the project," Pierce said.

"Where do you stand at this moment with Mrs. Gardner?"

Pierce said, "I have a two-and-a-half-million-dollar offer before her. I am hoping she accepts it. That would make the other thing unnecessary and expedite groundbreaking. The sheriff and Massey are snooping around, and Massey threatened me, but there is no proof of anything they can use against us. They won't keep her from selling. In fact, it would be best to openly buy from her since they are nosing around."

"I agree," Kurt said, inhaling smoke from his cigarette.

"We negotiate. But if we don't succeed in negotiating by Sunday, we go with the relatives. If we get behind schedule on the project, it will cost me hundreds of thousands of dollars a day. You should remember that you talked me into this investment. You made me assurances on start and completion dates, and I have based everything on your timetable."

"Which was given to me by the construction companies, based on other things."

"I don't care about their dates or contingencies or problems. You gave me dates. You made the decision on how to handle the Gardner situation, and I said okay, do it. I am in this here and now because of you. If we succeed, you will be running the finest resort in this country. On the other hand, people who fail me, do so only once."

Mulvane wanted to scream. He looked at his image in the mirror and saw that he was smiling like an idiot. How it was that a man so close to ruin could be smiling was something he couldn't fathom. But try as he might, he couldn't change his expression.

77

WINTER HAD JUST HUNG UP HIS PHONE WHEN BRAD came into the Gardners' kitchen. "We've got a body."

Winter jumped into the car as Brad was starting the

engine. He reversed fast, spun the wheel, jammed the vehicle into drive, and punched down on the accelerator. "I think it may be the missing cutout. Chief of police called me a few minutes ago from the scene. Couple of kids found a dead man in a house being renovated near my place."

Winter said, "The more pandemonium Styer creates, the better it suits him."

The house was three blocks from Brad's home, which would have made bringing the cutout to it a simple matter for Styer. Police cars, a sheriff's department cruiser and an EMS bus were parked outside, and the neighboring properties held a growing audience of townspeople.

Two teenage boys sat on the front steps with William Barnett's friend Woody Seiders. One of them, a redhead, looked at Winter and Brad with unfocused blue eyes. His thin trembling fingers clenched around his knees like roots.

"Hello," Woody said. "Your father's inside playing coroner."

"Alan?" Brad said. "Are you all right, son?"

The redhead tried to smile.

"Sheriff Barnett. It's really horrible," the dark-haired boy said. "There's a dead guy in the bathtub."

"You found him, Buddy?" Brad asked.

"I didn't look in," Buddy said. "Alan opened the bathroom door, started screaming, and we both ran like hell. He said the guy was all cut up. I'm glad I didn't look."

"Whose house is this?" Brad asked.

"My dad's," Alan said softly. "We're fixing it up to rent."

Brad patted the boy's back sympathetically, then led Winter through the front door into a room crowded with uniformed cops, Roy Bishop, and several EMS personnel. Winter smiled when he saw Dr. Barnett come into the living room from down the hallway. "Hey, Bradley, Deputy Massey," he said.

"Daddy, what are you doing here?"

"I'm filling in because Phil had to take a body to Jackson."

"Where's Chief Boddington?"

"He's back there making calls. You should see this." He crooked his finger and Winter and Brad followed him to the closed door.

Speaking in a low voice, Dr. Barnett said, "Before you go in there, I want to tell you I haven't seen anything like this since medical school. Brad, the man in that bathroom suffered. Someone skinned him alive, and used bleach as he went. He finally died from blood loss when the killer cut his femoral artery."

"Any red toothpicks?" Winter asked, knowing there would be.

Dr. Barnett nodded. "Stuck in his right eye. I left it there. You want to look in there, Winter?"

"No."

A thin man dressed in a blue uniform came out of a bedroom, snapping his cell phone closed.

"Bradley," he said, grimacing. "You see the shit in there?"

"Nope," Brad said. "No reason unless you want me to."

"Yeah. Well, I'm wondering if the bastard that did this might be the same asshole that killed Jack Beals. Or the dead guy might be the one who killed Beals and somebody's paid him back. I'm wondering if that fellow who was in that motel room might know who did it. Hell, maybe he did it. Was both knife work, wasn't it?"

"Cut throat. He's gone back home to Nevada. A couple hours ago one of my guys put him on a plane. He's been under surveillance by my people since we found Beals," Brad said. "He didn't see who killed Beals. He didn't do it."

"Doc, could this have been done before Beals died? Maybe Beals did this one too?"

"No," Dr. Barnett said. "This one was killed a few hours ago."

"I'm wondering if all these murders are part of some kind of organized crime war that's spilled out down here. I'm calling in the MBI to deal with this. I sure as hell don't have this kind of shit going on around here very often, so I need some help."

"I think that's a smart move," Brad said.

"The dead guy have identification?" Winter asked.

"A wallet. I bagged it," Boddington said, studying Winter for the first time.

"Massey," Winter said.

"He's my newest deputy," Brad told the chief.

Boddington nodded. "Nice to meet you."

"Once you run the ID, maybe you'll get a hit and some answers," Winter said.

"Call me if I can help," Brad said.

As they were getting into Brad's truck, he asked, "Styer does this kind of shit all the time? Goes from one gruesome murder to the next like a wild dog?"

Winter nodded. "It's all he knows. He'll stop as soon as he's dead."

"We have to put an end to this. Good Christ. He's killed five people in three days."

"That's easier said than done," Winter said. "The cutouts are the best hope to nail him, but so far they can't get close to him without dying."

"Maybe you should get in touch with them. They have to want him stopped worse than we do. Especially now."

"They want him, but to get him they might sacrifice us."

"What do we do next?"

"Put some pressure on Kurt Klein."

"What kind of pressure?"

Winter looked at his watch. "The legally binding, wrath of God kind. And we are going to pull the trigger right after Sherry Adams's funeral."

78

THE ADVENT CHURCH OF THE HOLY SPIRIT WAS AN old structure made from ancient brick with a galvanized steeple perched on its sagging roof like a dunce cap. Sunlight poured in through colored plastic replicas of stained-glass windows. Threadbare carpet ran between the worn pine pews, and water-stained ceilings peaked fifteen feet above the center aisle. A huge cross, made from six-by-six beams, was suspended above a simple plywood pulpit by plastic-coated steel cables. Mourners stood two deep against the plaster walls.

Winter and Alexa stood in the rear.

Leigh, Estelle, and Hampton sat just behind the Adams family as one person after another spoke, extolling Sherry Adams's attributes. It was a dignified affair, with only muted crying supplying background static for the service. The minister spoke with raw emotion in his voice about God's mysterious selection of his angels from the earth's best and brightest.

Leigh's makeup covered her bruise, but the swollen and split lip was apparent underneath her bright red lipstick. As the choir sang "Swing Low, Sweet Chariot" and six pallbearers rolled the bronze casket's gurney to the back of the church, Winter stood in the yard and caught a glimpse of Alphonse Jefferson standing on the corner wearing a lime green suit, a matching fedora held to his chest as a show of respect.

Since word travels at the speed of light in small communities, people attending Sherry's funeral were aware that Jacob Gardner had died in a car accident, and most of them took a few seconds to offer Leigh their condolences. Winter doubted that any of them would miss Leigh's ex, but they obviously felt genuine grief for Leigh and her children. It was apparent that despite her no-nonsense exterior, the people there knew Mrs. Gardner had a good heart.

Leigh told the people who asked after Cynthia that her daughter was too distressed to leave the house.

After a lot of discussion, Alexa and Winter had convinced Leigh that the odds were Cynthia would not be harmed for two reasons: the purpose for having her as a captive was over, and killing her was not a priority for Styer. In a couple of hours, Mulvane's best interests would be in freeing her.

79

PAULUS STYER HAD FIGURED CORRECTLY THAT DUR-ing the Adams funeral, the Gardner home would be lightly guarded, if at all. He had come in on turn roads from a county road and parked two miles away, and he hadn't seen one patrol car during his trip out from the casino. Like worker bees, they had followed the queen, leaving the hive unguarded. Carrying a knapsack, Paulus made his way from the thin tree line that ran like a fence east and west of the house, across two hundred yards of cotton stalks.

At the back of the house, he paused only long enough to pick the dead bolt. The grandfather clock in the hallway filled the house's silence with its metallic ticks.

He found the door leading to the basement and crept downstairs, carrying the rucksack in his right hand. After surveying the moldy basement, used to house the heating and air-conditioning systems and littered with stored boxes, old bicycles, and other junk, he made his way to the oil tank that fed the furnace. He found a small box labeled X-MAS and dumped the contents into a larger box. As he knelt behind the heater, it suddenly came noisily to life, the fan sounding like a jet revving for takeoff.

He carefully wedged the box containing the device into the cobwebby space between the brick wall and the unit. Smiling, he removed a cell phone from the satchel and put it in his pocket. When the time was right, he would press the send button on the phone, which was programmed to dial up another unit that would set off the detonator. The amount of Semtex inside the package would reduce the Gardner home to a smoking crater. *Hello. Good-bye.*

He looked at his watch, imagined the funeral party at the graveyard, and stood. He decided to take a quick tour of the interior to familiarize himself with the layout. Just in case things didn't work out as he planned, he would be very open to alternative endings for Massey and the others.

He thought about looking around for another vial of insulin for Cynthia, but decided she had about enough to get through the rest of her life.

80

PIERCE MULVANE MADE HIS EARLY AFTERNOON IN-spection trek through the casino as usual, but for once what was happening in the casino held little interest for him. Tug had been busy over the past days taking care of business, so he had been around less and less as things needed his specialized attention. Pierce stayed in close telephone contact, believing that Tug, more than Albert White, was the person he could most fully trust. Tug was Irish, and Mulvane's cousin, a gangster with a large hard-core crew, had vouched for Murphy.

Pierce was confident again that Klein's displeasure at the setback was temporary. Pierce had put the Roundtable in the black a full year ahead of the most liberal projections, and it was more profitable, based on percentage of return on dollars invested, than any casino RRI operated. He was certain that Kurt would remember the pluses, and after the land was secured, everything would be as it was before.

Pierce was passing the craps pit when he spotted the familiar face of pig farmer Jason Parr standing near the table. He had the unfocused look of a man who had just lost his last nickel. Pierce felt a warm glow, assuming the casino had acquired a sizable chunk of Parr's assets. He always marveled at how people never seemed to understand that gambling, aside from the occasional hit here and there, was financially suicidal.

"Mr. Parr," Pierce said as he approached, his face a blank canvas. "How is everything?"

"Gotta say, this week I've been on my backside more than a two-dollar whore in a lumber camp on payday," Parr said with a weak grin.

"And are you up or down?"

"Well, I lost my lucky charm, so I stopped to catch my breath. At present I'm up one fifty. I'm thinking about quitting, and calling it a trip. Get back to my wife and the other pigs tomorrow afternoon."

Pierce laughed, despite the fact that chuckling at this yokel's pathetic joke was the last thing he wanted to be doing. "One hundred and fifty dollars is hardly going to cover your gas back, Jason. We will fill your tank for you, of course."

"I figure I'm down a half million over the past ten years. That, my old son, is a lot of bacon up the chimney. Right this minute, I'm standing here thinking my gambling days are over for a while."

"Quitting while you are ahead is very smart, Jason. As your friend, I suggest you take your winnings and go home. You should have a check cut."

"Well, that would be fine, but I kind of like having the green in hand when I get home. Gets me a little piece of the pie," he said, elbowing Pierce in the arm. "My fifth wife won't do no work to speak of, and she ain't usually big on getting in the bed except at night to sleep. But if I cover the danged sheets an inch deep in hundreds, you can't keep her out of it."

Pierce looked with disgust at Parr's expansive stomach and his pendulous breasts. It made him want to go straight to the fitness center and spend the rest of the day in the sauna.

81

ALEXA WAS IN THE GUEST BATHROOM WASHING HER face when her cell phone rang. She went into the bedroom, took it out of her purse, and saw on the readout that it was Assistant FBI Director Hayden Hatcher.

"Keen," she answered.

"Hatcher here," Hayden Hatcher said. "I went by your office yesterday afternoon and found out that you were on personal leave until next week."

"That's right, sir. I'm taking care of a few personal matters."

"Might I ask where you are?"

"Tunica, Mississippi." Alexa was certain he had known where she was before he asked, and she knew he had the means to easily discover that she'd flown to Memphis the day before.

"Is there anything about your trip that might be of interest to us?" he asked.

Alexa was not going to lie to a superior officer. "There have been two additional murders in Tunica that may be connected to a piece of land a casino wants for an expanded operation. The sheriff is presently investigating. It is possible that the family who owns the land where the first murder took place, as well as the land the casino needs, may be in continuing danger. I'm here merely to give moral support to the family. That's all I know at the present."

Hatcher asked, "Would that casino be the Roundtable?"

"Yes, sir, it would."

"Do you suspect anyone associated with that casino or RRI of being involved in any of the three murders?"

"There's no direct evidence, just circumstances that point in that direction. It appears as though the local casino manager might be involved."

"So he is probably acting on his own volition. The owner of RRI, Kurt Klein, is an influential individual. Are you familiar with his name?"

"I am."

"According to our information, Mr. Klein is in Tunica, staying at the Roundtable casino. This is very delicate, Alexa. Kurt Klein is a good friend of our state department. The Klein family, and their friends, are very influential and are often quite helpful to our interests around the world."

"There is no evidence that Klein is involved, or knows anything about what has been going on here."

"If any Federal statutes have been violated by people working for the casino, it will have to be handled very carefully. Would you be more comfortable if I sent some agents to protect the Gardner family?"

"No, sir. I don't believe that is necessary at the present." Alexa knew that she had not mentioned the Gardners by name. "It seems unlikely this man would dare harm them, since Winter Massey told him he suspected him of involvement."

"I know this is not an official FBI matter at the present, but I expect you to keep me posted on this, Agent Keen. I cannot overstress the fact that you are not, under any circumstances, to take any unauthorized action against or involving Mr. Klein. Is that perfectly clear?"

"It is clear."

"You are a valuable asset to the Bureau," Hatcher said. "Let's keep it that way. Does the sheriff have a case against this manager?"

"Not at the present. Jacob Gardner, the landowner's ex-husband, had information crucial to that investigation, but unfortunately he was killed before the sheriff could convince him to cooperate."

"I'll alert the Memphis field office that if you need help, they will offer any necessary assistance. I want you to explain to Mr. Massey that we are watching over his shoulder. I think it would be wise if you make certain this doesn't become an international incident."

"I understand."

"I know you have a good relationship with the director, and I want you to know that I have spoken with him about this. He told me that he has faith in your loyalty to the Bureau, and in your ability to handle yourself appropriately."

Alexa hung up and reached to pick up her coat from the bed. She felt a bulge in the pocket and pulled out a thick wad of cash held together with a rubber band. Thumbing the edge, she saw that the folded currency was comprised entirely of one-hundred-dollar bills. It took her a few seconds to realize that Jason Parr must have put it there when he'd hugged her in the casino parking lot. There were several thousand dollars in the bundle, and there was no way she could keep it.

Alexa left the room to go downstairs and tell Winter about Hatcher's call.

82

WHEN BRAD ARRIVED, WINTER AND ALEXA WENT out to talk to him.

"My father found an entry wound in the left side of Jacob's head. He excised the section of scalp," Brad said.

"Alexa spoke to her boss," Winter told Brad.

"Well, he is and he isn't my boss," Alexa said. "He is a deputy FBI director, but not for my branch. He's counter-terrorism."

She filled Brad in on her conversation with Hatcher.

"So," Brad said, "what does that mean? Klein is important to our nation's counterterrorism efforts?"

"Klein has serious sway," Alexa said. "We go after him, and hell will look like heaven."

"This is a little unsettling," Brad said. "So if he's in on this, I can't arrest him?"

"You can do what you please, but they won't hold

Klein accountable," Alexa said. "And certain people could make sure you regret arresting him, if you do."

"It's like that sometimes," Winter said. "Nothing to do about it. But we don't know that Klein's aware of what Mulvane's been up to. Men like Klein are accustomed to saying they want something to happen while men like Mulvane make sure it does."

"So you're telling me that nobody pays for killing Sherry Adams?"

"No," Winter said, looking out at the spot where the young woman had fallen on the cold hard stones. "Somebody is definitely going to pay for that."

83

THE OVERCAST SKY AND A STEADY DRIZZLE MADE the afternoon air seem much colder than thirty-four degrees. According to the weather reports, the temperature was going to drop overnight into the mid-twenties as an arctic blast came through the Delta. Winter and Brad stood together on the porch, the cup of coffee in Winter's hand going cold as the men watched the gravel road.

"This is a good plan, right?" Brad asked.

"It should take Leigh and Hamp out of their sights and get Cynthia back," Winter said.

"Should?" Brad asked, shaking his head slowly. "I should move Hamp and Leigh to a safer location."

"There is no safer location at the moment. Moving them before I put this under Klein's nose is a lot riskier than holding them here. Trust me."

Brad looked at his watch. "He should be here by now."

"He'll be here soon," Winter said.

Brad's radio sprang to life. "Unit Four to T.C. One, there's a black Lexus a half mile out. One occupant."

"Plate?"

"Vanity Tennessee LAW-ONE. We're behind him. You want us to pull him?"

"Negative," Brad said, smiling at Winter. "We're expecting him. Let him come in."

"Sheriff." The deputy laughed. "It looks like he's dancing."

Winter unzipped his jacket, took off his glove, and slipped it into his pocket. Reflexively he touched the Reeder to make sure it was secure in its holster, and that all four of the loaded eight-round magazines were secure in the twin holders.

A few seconds later the Lexus flew into view as it roared up the long gravel drive.

"I just hope he isn't, you know . . ." Brad said.

"It's early for that," Winter said.

The sedan stopped, and when the door flew open, something by ZZ Top spewed out from the interior at an incredible volume. After a few seconds, a man with a flowing blond ponytail, a long beard, and dressed in a topcoat, English riding boots, and a wide-brimmed hat leapt from the car and began to dance in the rain with what could only be described as a blending of the Frug, the Jerk, and the Boogaloo. When the song ended, the man reached in, cut the car motor, brought out a valise, and slammed the door.

"Gentlemen, your law dog has arrived to save the day," he said, taking the porch steps two at a time.

Winter expected the rib-squeezing hug he got from his friend Billy Lyons, but not the kiss the attorney planted on his cheek. Releasing Winter, Billy turned to Brad and opened his arms.

Brad held out his palms defensively. "Don't you come a step closer, Billy Lyons. You want to kiss my cheek, fine, but let me drop my pants first."

"Well, here I am," Billy said. "This sort of top-secret, faxed-map, come-to-Papa-right-now crap is why I get three bills an hour."

"Don't friends get a discount?" Brad asked.

"That's with the discount, Bradley."

Billy was hanging up his coat and hat on hooks in the foyer when he saw Alexa standing in the doorway of the den.

"Hello, Billy Lyons," Alexa said.

"Well, hello, Alexa Keen," he said jovially. "I didn't know you were here."

"Nice to see you, Billy," she said. "Been a long time."

"Are you still working for the man?"

"Yes," she said.

Alexa had never cared much for Billy Lyons, but she was glad to see him now. It wasn't that he was a show-off. He had developed his eccentricities early on to entertain his contemporaries and to separate himself from the crowd—especially his legal competition later in life. Alexa still held a slight grudge against him because he had once made people laugh by mocking her when she was a fifteen-year-old, mixed-race outcast who'd been shunned by both races in their high school. Billy had been close with Winter until she came along, and he had resented and not understood her friendship with Winter. That, as much as anything, had kept Billy and Alexa from becoming friends. But he was a friend of Winter's, and she knew he had been a good and loyal one at that, and he was about to help them out in a big way.

Alexa stepped back as Winter led Billy into the den, where Leigh was staring at a picture of her children with a faraway look in her eyes. "Billy Lyons, this is Leigh Gardner," Winter said.

"Nice to meet you, Leigh. Winter told me about your situation on the telephone," Billy said, sitting in an armchair. "I've got most of it already prepared for your approval."

Billy Lyons opened his briefcase and took out a laptop. After reading the document aloud, he listened to what Leigh had to say and added her suggestions to the legal document. He hooked up to Leigh's computer, printed the document and Leigh signed it, as Alexa and Winter acted as witnesses. Using Leigh's scanner and her Internet connection, he sent copies of the signed document to his office and to a judge pal in Jackson, Mississippi, storing a digital copy in his Yahoo e-mail folder.

"Now all I have to do is pop in at the courthouse on my way out of town and file this to make it official," he said, slipping the original pages into his inside coat pocket before putting the coat on.

84

AFTER BILLY FILED THE PAPERS AT THE COURT-house, Winter had him drop him off at his Jeep. A white SUV—which Winter assumed was carrying cutouts—tailed him from town out to the Roundtable. Winter figured Tunica County was filled with cutouts.

He parked in the Roundtable's lot. After putting on a ball cap and shades he walked to the entrance, joining the arriving gamblers. With any luck, he would get inside before he was spotted by security. Winter wanted to get to Kurt Klein before Mulvane or White got between them.

Winter walked onto the gaming floor and, unbelievably, spotted Kurt Klein seated at a three-card poker table next to the security man Winter had seen arriving with the wealthy silver-haired industrialist. While Klein gambled, the security man sat with a glass of water in his left hand.

Winter put his sunglasses into his pocket, walked straight up to the table, and took a seat beside Kurt Klein. The security man looked across Klein to stare at Winter.

"My name is Winter Massey," he said.

Casually, Klein said, "I'm Kurt Klein. Nice to meet you."

Klein placed a bet, looked at Winter for the first time,

and smiled. He slid a stack of chips from his pile to rest in front of Winter. "Something to keep your hands busy?"

Winter pushed them back. "I'm not much with cards."

The security man beside Klein nodded almost imperceptibly.

"This is Steffan Finch," Klein said. "He works for me."

Winter looked around and saw the two other security men who had arrived with Klein move forward, their hands behind their backs.

"I'm not armed," Winter said, slowly drawing back his jacket so Finch could see the empty high-rise holster on his belt.

Kurt Klein won with a pair of kings. The dealer had jack high.

"Do you believe in luck?" he asked Winter.

"Sometimes luck is better than skill," he answered. "It's just not very dependable."

"I never depend on luck," Kurt Klein said, raking in the chips he'd won. "I bet you are more skilled than lucky yourself."

Winter shrugged. "I'm careful when I can be."

"So, Mr. Massey," Kurt said. "Are you here because you want to test your luck?" He placed four chips in front of Winter. "Play a hand with me."

Winter placed the chips Klein had given him into the bet box, and Klein made a large bet. They watched the dealer toss out the cards.

"I guess I'm all in," Winter said.

Klein chuckled. "That appears to be the case."

Winter had nothing, Klein had a pair, and the dealer a king high hand.

The dealer stacked black and yellow chips in front of Klein.

"Luck doesn't seem to be on your side," Klein said.

"Not with cards. Is there a place we can talk in private?"

"Let's go upstairs," Klein said, tipping the dealer a pair of black and yellow chips. A man dressed in an official Roundtable jacket and red tie picked up Klein's winnings, stacked them onto a tray, and walked off.

"Accompany me to the elevator," Kurt Klein said, standing. Winter stood and walked beside Klein.

Finch led the way, the two arm-breakers trailing behind him.

85

"SO," LEIGH SAID, "IF THIS SPECIFIC INDIVIDUAL didn't have Cynthia, what would you be doing differently?"

"Every case is different," Alexa said.

Leigh's voice cracked with emotion as she spoke. "You must think I'm a terrible mother. Sherry just murdered and I let my daughter leave the house alone."

"Beating yourself up is a normal reaction, but you didn't know what was going on then," Alexa told her. "She's going to be fine."

"I always let her do what she wants to do. I can't believe I was so stupid."

"She'll be fine."

"Is that your personal or professional opinion?"

"Both."

"I know what you people think. If she's dead, she's dead. If she isn't, she probably won't be killed."

"I didn't say that," Alexa said.

"Winter believes it. You're saying you don't think that's the case?"

"Winter knows this man who has your daughter as well as anyone does."

"The man is a professional murderer."

"Yes, he is. But he doesn't kill unless it works to his advantage. We should talk about something else."

Leigh looked at the fire in the hearth. "How in God's name can I talk about anything else? I can't think of anything but Cynthia."

"Please, try."

"You and Winter both grew up in Cleveland."

"We met in high school."

"You were good friends?"

"We were best friends. I've never had a friend that came close to him."

"Not more than friends?"

"Never lovers, if that's what you mean. I was an outsider—a misfit. My parents were drug addicts. My sister and I were split up in foster care. Winter came along at a crucial time in my life, and he reached out to me. He saved my life. He lost friends over it and didn't care at all. We had a lot in common. He married my best friend and roommate from college." Alexa laughed. "I was his best man and her maid of honor."

"Brad says he is very good at what he does."

"He's awesome at what he does. His instincts are truly amazing. He is one of the few people on earth I trust completely." Leigh nodded, and there was a silence, after which Alexa said, "I understand you and Brad went together."

Leigh's eyes lit up. "We were engaged. We almost got married."

"Tell me about it."

Fifteen minutes later, as Leigh was smiling at Alexa with tears in her eyes, Brad came into the room.

"We were talking about high school," Alexa said, grinning at Leigh, who blushed.

"That was a long time ago," he said. "Winter called. He's gone to talk to Klein at the casino. He's taking a copy of the papers Billy filed."

"Alone?" Alexa said.

"Yeah. He had Billy drop him off at his Jeep."

Alexa swore under her breath. "Leigh, can I take your truck?"

"Sure. Key's hanging by the back door."

Alexa got into Leigh's truck and struck out for the casino, passing three parked cruisers whose deputies, armed with AR-15s and shotguns, were guarding the road leading into the plantation.

Alexa couldn't believe Brad had let Winter go out to the casino without backup of any kind. Mulvane could react violently if he thought Winter was going to bring his sinister actions to his boss's attention. And if Klein was protected by his own security and the U.S. government, he could probably do whatever he pleased without worrying about repercussions or legal accountability. She knew Winter was not intimidated by these facts, at least not the way she would be. But frightened or not, she wasn't about to let anything happen to Massey if she could help it.

It was dusk when Alexa pulled into a space in front of the Roundtable. Putting the purse's strap over her shoulder, she strode toward the front doors. Walking purposefully through the casino, she caught sight of Winter, Klein, and three security people heading for the elevators. Moving quickly, she tried to intercept the group so Winter would see her, but they turned the corner before she caught up, and she didn't think running or waving her arms in the air was a good idea. She saw Winter, under no apparent duress, step into an elevator cab with Klein. Klein dismissed the other two men, allowing only his personal security man to accompany them.

Alexa had some time to kill and remembered something she needed to take care of. She went to the hotel lobby and stopped at the house phones.

"Can you please connect me to Jason Parr's room?" she asked the operator.

There was a momentary pause as the operator looked up the room number and handed her the receiver. It rang four times, after which the gambling pig farmer answered. "Parr here."

"This is your old gambling partner."

"Alexa?" he said, suddenly excited. "That really you?"

"Yes," she said.

"I'm really glad you came by. After the dust settled I found out I shorted you by about nine grand," he said. "I didn't know how I'd ever find you."

"Can you come down? I really can't accept it."

"I can't at the moment. Could you come up? I'm on the eighth floor in suite eight-twenty-two. Unless you feel weird about coming to a stranger's room . . ."

"Of course not. I'll be right up."

86

CYNTHIA GARDNER WAS DRESSED IN CLEAN CLOTHES, still bound, and lying on a king-sized bed, watching mesmerized as the man who'd kidnapped her peeled away in ragged pieces what she had believed until that instant was the actual skin on his very unattractive face. As he scrubbed the adhesive from his cheeks, he became another person entirely. He wasn't bad looking, but he wasn't male model material either. And thanks to the tight spandex underwear he had on, she could see that he was built like a gymnast. Sure, he was sort of old, but every muscle was as perfectly defined as anybody her age.

"Where'd you learn to do that?" she asked him.

"In school," he said, frowning thoughtfully in the mirror at the sight of his irritated skin.

"Makeup one-oh-one?" she asked.

"Are you feeling one hundred percent yet?" he wanted to know.

"Yes. Thanks for the shot." *Asshole. I could have died. I almost did, I bet.*

"Now you are completely out of insulin. So the timing was perfect. By the time you need another shot, you'll be at home, safe and sound. You have some at home?"

"Yes, I do. You know, I really thought you were going to let me die," she told him.

"Don't be silly, Cynthia," He turned to look at her, smiling. "Do I look like a murderer to you?"

"I'm not really sure what a murderer looks like."

He said, "Let's hope you don't ever find that out."

"So how long till I go home?"

"Tonight. Around nine."

As Cynthia watched, the man reached into a cardboard box, lifted out a mannequin's head, and placed it on the dressing table. All she could make out from the backside was a hairpiece. After applying adhesive from a bottle to a section of latex he'd removed from the head, he pasted the section on his own forehead, patting it down in places.

"So how long does this usually take you?"

"Takes as long as it takes. It's the painting of the latex skin that takes the longest, and I do that first. This one took longer because of the amount of texture in the panels. It has to be accurate to hold up under close scrutiny. But it's more than looking right. You have to have the subject's movements down, and the voice pitch and patterns have to be perfect."

"So who are you going to be when you finish?" she asked him.

"Well, little sister," he said in a totally different voice, "just watch and you will see."

87

WINTER WAS IMPRESSED WITH THE SCALE MODEL of the resort in the large conference room on the executive floor. He and Klein were alone, his security man having thoroughly searched Massey.

"This is going to be the finest gaming resort ever built in the United States," Kurt said, sweeping his hand over the model. "It will cost over a billion dollars. Mulvane brought the idea of this location to me, and after a lot of relentless persuasion, and seeing what he did with this casino, its potential became obvious. I would not be investing in it unless I was sure it would be profitable. I do not take chances when it comes to risking such sums."

"I heard that when you borrow ten grand from a bank, repaying is your worry. But when you borrow millions, your repaying is the bank's worry."

Kurt smiled in agreement.

Winter picked up a small human figure from the model, then another, and another until he had five of them in his hands.

Winter said, "It appears that five people have been killed because of this *investment*."

"You think so?" Klein said, seeming surprised. "I find that hard to believe. Are you sure?"

Winter reached out and laid the figures down, side by side, one at a time. "Sherry Adams, Jack Beals, Jacob Gardner . . ." He placed the other two male figures next to those. "I don't know these men's names, but them too."

Kurt Klein crossed his arms and rested the fingers of his right hand under his chin.

"There is also the matter of Cynthia Gardner, who has been kidnapped by the person who killed these people."

"The Gardner girl was kidnapped?" Klein said. The surprise in his eyes seemed genuine.

"It hasn't been publicized and possibly won't have to be, if she finds her way home."

Winter didn't know whether or not Klein knew about the deaths, or if he did, whether he cared one way or the other. Klein wasn't the sort of man who gave anything away unless he chose to. At his level, like any major commanding officer far from the front, the realities of life or death struggles on the battlefield were just numbers, the bodies left in the ruins a million miles away.

"All of this has been the work of a top-notch professional killer," Winter said.

"Does this killer have a name?"

"Paulus Styer," Winter said, watching Klein's face for a reaction, which came in the form of a brief tightening of his smile.

"And why is he killing and kidnapping people?" Kurt Klein asked.

"I think it has to do with a piece of land located within this model." He gestured to a part of the model. "Six hundred and thirty-six acres owned by Leigh Gardner."

"I think you must be mistaken. I have been assured that all of the land necessary for the project has already been secured. Are you saying that I have been deceived in this matter?"

"I hope so. That would mean that you would pay a fair price for the land and also tell me that you weren't part of a plan to have the Gardners killed so the land could be purchased from their relatives who might have been in line to inherit it."

"I am fairly ruthless in the practice of business, but I do not hire killers, Mr. Massey."

"It's irrelevant now. Mrs. Gardner has fixed things so that if anything happens to her or her children, none of her relatives will inherit her holdings. In fact, if anything happens to any of the Gardners, it will be years, if ever, before anything is built on that parcel. That includes Cynthia Gardner. I think it would be mutually beneficial for you to pay Mrs. Gardner a fair price and sign the papers, which is as it should have been from the beginning—a perfectly clean and legal business matter."

"Let's move this discussion to my suite," Klein said, nodding. "It will be more comfortable." He picked up the five tiny figures and slipped them into his pocket before heading for the doorway.

Winter accepted a bottle of water from Steffan Finch, taking a seat across the coffee table from his host. He removed the copy of the legal document from his inside jacket pocket and slid it to Kurt Klein, who put on reading glasses, opened it, and read through the pages in silence.

"So in the event of her and her children's deaths, Mrs. Gardner has willed her estate to the parents of Sherry

Adams, who would be the young girl who was killed by this assassin you mentioned?"

"Yes," Winter said. "They are corecipients along with their church congregation, the Advent Church of the Holy Spirit. I should mention that the group is unrepentantly anti-gaming. They will also be given a document that states Leigh Gardner's strong suspicions that Sherry Adams was murdered in order to secure the land for a casino resort. And they all loved Sherry Adams."

"If that document isn't based on provable facts, it would be slander."

"Unless it is merely her opinion, which it is, as it is mine and the sheriff's, along with others I'll leave unnamed."

"And you suspect Pierce Mulvane ordered these killings?"

Winter explained what led him to that conclusion as Klein listened patiently without interrupting.

"And after this land is transferred—if I do not already own it, as I have been led to believe by Mulvane—what else do you want from me?"

"I'd like for Mr. Mulvane to call off Styer and secure Cynthia Gardner's safe release."

"Anything else?"

"I'd like to know how to find Styer."

"The professional killer you believe he hired."

Winter nodded. "Truth is, I had the feeling when I mentioned the name in the conference room, you recognized it."

Klein shrugged. "In the world of international business I hear many things about many people." Klein smiled, looking suddenly weary. "If Mulvane did hire this man to do what you said, he will be held accountable, and he will see that this Styer releases the girl unharmed. Would that be satisfactory?"

"It would."

"And what do you think is a fair price for the Gardner land?"

"Five million dollars, at this point."

"So can we do this tonight?" Kurt asked. "I can draw a check, or give her bearer bonds. You may use my phone and call her."

"I will ask her," Winter said.

Winter stepped across the room and dialed Brad Barnett. He asked to speak to Leigh, and ran through Klein's proposal with her, hung up, and returned.

"She agrees. Either a cashier's check or bearer bonds, and have your attorney bring the transfer papers. Her attorney will be here, along with Sheriff Barnett and myself. We'll have security in place for her protection. Nothing personal."

"Done. And I insist on your security measures." Kurt Klein stood, extended his hand, and the two men shook.

"And Mulvane?" Winter said.

"If he has done what you say, I will know soon, and my people will hand him over to the sheriff, accompanied by a signed confession."

"He may not want to sign one," Winter said.

Kurt Klein smiled, showing his slightly yellowed teeth. "If he is guilty of what you say, Mr. Massey, I am certain he will sign it. On that you have my word, and if you know me, you know my word is good. And if he knows anything about Paulus Styer, he will share that with you, and you may do with that information what you like."

"Then we'll be here at nine sharp."

As Klein showed Winter to the door, he said, "Mr. Massey, the thing to keep in mind is that I will not tolerate any threat to my family's financial well-being."

88

ALEXA TOOK JASON PARR'S CASH OUT OF HER PURSE in the elevator riding up to the eighth floor. She looked in at her Glock and her badge case and frowned. Most women her age had never touched a gun, much less fired one. How many of them carried one in their purse ten hours a day as they might a tube of lipstick? But since she spent most of her time behind a desk, the gun in her purse was hardly more than a little extra ballast, which she was quite accustomed to by now.

The wide polished oak doors opening into the suites were hand-carved. According to the signs, there were twenty-five suites on the eighth floor, reserved for high rollers. Eight-twenty-two was down the hall on the right. She did a double take as she passed 825, which had double doors inside a foyer protected by closed wrought-iron gates.

Alexa stopped at 822 and tapped gently. "Come in,

Alexa!" she heard Jason Parr yell through the heavy wood.

From deep in the suite, Jason called, "I'll be right with you, I was just getting out of the shower when you called. Make yourself at home while I get dressed."

"Okay, Jason," she yelled back as she walked into the living room. "I can only stay a minute." No expense had been spared in furnishing the living room. Instead of a medieval theme, modern furniture was placed on an oriental carpet, which made a horseshoe around a marble fireplace. The curtains were open, revealing large sealed windows, the Delta growing dark outside. To her left was an open kitchen with light marble floors, stainless appliances, pickled wood cabinets, and granite countertops.

"I could grow accustomed to this," she called out.

"We sure ain't in Kansas anymore," he hollered back. "I'm almost presentable."

"I brought your money back. I can't keep it. I appreciate the gesture though."

"Whatever you say. Just put it on the coffee table, would you?"

Alexa walked into the room and stopped at the large coffee table. She was about to put the cash on the table when she saw, evenly spaced out in the center of the slab of frosted glass, four red toothpicks. She picked one up and smelled it.

Realization gave way to a thick disorienting fear. She let the currency in her hand fall to the table as she reached into her purse for the Glock. She knew—as she sensed a figure rushing up from behind her—that she'd never get it out in time.

She turned, registered that the man coming at her was narrower than Jason Parr, and felt a stream of cold liquid hit her face—searing her eyes. Even so, she almost got the Glock out.

89

AFTER MASSEY LEFT, KURT KLEIN SAT IN SILENCE for several minutes, thinking over his options. All things considered, five million was a bargain. Even if it were not, purchasing the land from Mrs. Gardner was the only move he could make without changing the location and starting over, which was not an option. Time was money, and every hour of delay would be financially painful, because his family's entire empire depended on the continuing trust of a trio of international financiers. These men, who didn't know better, believed Klein sold them points in RRI's profits as a personal favor. If they lived, they might find out that Klein had oversold future profits to nine investors at an inflation of almost three hundred percent. However, Klein counted on the fact that for a fee, Paulus Styer would whittle down the money men, and the percentages, to something he could live with.

Klein was in financial straits because of unfortunate choices he'd made regarding the futures of new markets and acquisitions that had unexpectedly tanked. His financial balance sheets were fiction, and if the River Royale resort didn't open on schedule, everything could collapse like a house of cards. He was a man on the edge.

Styer was the only problem that had not yet been solved. Kurt would call him off, pay him a nice bonus, and send him home until he required his services again—and he was going to need to call on him in the near future.

Kurt placed the five tiny figures from the scale model on the table before him. He lit a cigarette and studied them before separating the two mystery men from the three deaths he was aware of. He had to talk to Styer and get some assurances.

He reached into his pocket and squeezed the key fob he kept close. Seconds after being summoned electronically, Finch walked into the room.

"Steffan, I need my laptop."

Finch strode to the master bedroom and returned with the laptop, opened it on the table before Kurt, and stepped out to allow his boss some privacy.

Kurt watched the AirPort symbol darken as it found the hotel's wireless router and connected to the Internet. Kurt went to his private encrypted site before typing the hyperlink to the page he had used to communicate with Styer for the past few years, and keyed:

> New developments require an immediate halt to your assignment. I am purchasing some land at nine P.M. tonight. I understand you may have some company. Do remember that young ladies should be home before ten P.M. Please acknowledge receipt of this message.

After he closed the link, he typed an e-mail to the GM of RRI in Manhattan, which read:

> Harvey,
>
> RRI paying 5 million US dollars for parcel C tonight. Have that amount in bearer bonds delivered immediately. Alert Jerry Cunningham to come at once with papers for the transaction.
>
> Kurt

He sent the e-mail. Klein smiled. Even though the relief he felt at that moment would be temporary, any break in the chaos of commerce was welcome.

90

WINTER CLIMBED INTO HIS JEEP, SLID HIS REEDER .45 from under the seat, holstered it, and drove toward the plantation at seventy miles an hour, checking his rearview mirror every few seconds for a tail. He was now certain of several things. When Kurt Klein had immediately agreed to pay the five million, Winter knew that Klein had not only been informed of the land situation all along, but he believed Klein himself had put Styer in play to make it happen.

Klein would have to call Styer off the family and go through with the purchase, but Winter figured that would have little, if any, effect on Paulus Styer's intention to kill him.

Winter approached the roadblock at Leigh's driveway, slowed and rolled down the window so the deputy could see him.

"How's it going?" Roy Bishop said, slinging the AR-15 onto his wide shoulder.

"Never better," Winter said. "Any traffic?"

"Nope. Cold and quiet. Had a Memphis TV crew come up, asking to see Ms. Gardner, but I shooed them off. The sheriff is expecting you." Winter rolled the window back up and drove toward the house.

91

WHEN ALEXA WOKE UP, SHE WAS GROGGY AND lying in an extremely large bathtub, enclosed by marble on three sides. The frosted glass sliding doors were closed. Her wrists were handcuffed behind her. She was wearing only her bra and panties, her suit and blouse on hangers suspended from one of six showerheads above her. Her ankles were joined with cable ties, and a strip of duct tape covered her mouth.

Classical music played from hidden speakers. Her head

ached, and she remembered the stream of chloroform hitting her face.

Had Styer partnered with Jason Parr, who had masqueraded as a pig farmer? They could have seen her get out of Brad's truck. If Parr hadn't won, and put the money in her jacket, she never would have come back. Winter had told her that nothing was beyond Styer's diabolical planning ability. She cursed her naivete, squirming against the cold marble.

She managed to scoot forward, lie on her back, and open the doors using the bottoms of her feet. The heavy doors slid aside effortlessly and Alexa maneuvered into a sitting position. She yelped involuntarily at what she saw. Wearing a tightly stretched T-shirt, starched jeans, and cowboy boots, Jason Parr sat on the floor in a corner of the bathroom, staring out through wide-open but dry and frosted eyes. In death, he looked subtly different than she remembered. His mouth was open and his swollen blackened tongue protruded from his lips like a half-inflated balloon. Around his neck was the red silk tie that had been used to throttle him. The tie looked like the same one that the bellboys, clerks, dealers, and probably room service personnel at the casino wore as part of their uniform. The real Jason Parr looked as though he had been dead for a couple of days, which meant that the man she had gambled with was Paulus Styer.

She saw shadows under the door, and watched as the gold-plated lever dropped from the nine to the six o'clock position and was cracked open. There was a gentle rapping followed by a voice she knew but couldn't quite place. "Ms. Keen. Are you in there?"

She felt momentary relief at hearing the familiar

voice. That was replaced by horror as the man entered the room, and looked down at the corpse in the corner. "Oh, damn, you're in quite a predicament," he said in a honey-smooth Southern-edged accent.

When the man turned his gaze on her and smiled, she realized it was Styer in another nearly perfect disguise. Although the similarities to the man Styer was impersonating were more than superficial, his smile was an insincere imitation of the original owner's.

"I see you've found me," he said, switching to Jason Parr's voice, indicating the body. "You're an honest gal, but not a very careful one."

Alexa glared at her abductor as she realized what he could do with his current disguise. Paulus Styer had found the perfect Trojan horse.

92

BRAD MET WINTER IN THE GARDNERS' FOYER, AND after following him to the master bedroom where a still-dressed Leigh was stretched out on the bed, he filled them in on his meeting with Klein. He didn't tell them he suspected that Klein had been behind the plan to kill the Gardners, as the injustice would gnaw at them. The important thing was that the Gardners were no longer in danger and Cyn would soon be safe at home.

"He's paying five million, in cash? Just like that?" Brad asked.

Winter nodded. "I think he would have probably paid more, Leigh. But it's what you thought was fair and it is an amount he can live with."

"What about Mulvane?" Brad said. "Does he know what he's done?"

"He seemed convinced," Winter said. "Hard to tell with a man likc Klein. He gave me the impression that he has suspected some subterfuge on Mulvane's part all along. After the deal is done, we'll take the bonds, put them in Brad's evidence safe, and you can move them to your bank when it opens."

"I don't care about the bonds," Leigh said.

Winter asked, "Where's Alexa? I want to tell her."

"You didn't see her? She took off to watch your back when I told her you went to the Roundtable."

"No," Winter said.

He opened his cell phone and dialed Alexa, his fingers trembling involuntarily. After three rings she answered.

"Yes?" she said.

"Lex!?"

"What's up?"

"Where are you? Brad told me you followed me."

"I saw you leaving the casino and as I was getting ready to follow you, I got a call from Deputy Director Hatcher. He insisted that I meet with some field agents from the Memphis office. No biggie. I'm driving to the FO now."

"Okay. We're doing the deal tonight at nine."

"So you don't need me right now?"

"No. I guess not. You scared the hell out of me is all. I was about to call in the cavalry."

"I'll be back from Memphis as soon as I can get away," she said. "I want to be there when Cyn calls or shows up. You stay sharp, you hear?"

"There's no danger. Klein will make sure Mulvane doesn't pull anything." Winter closed the phone and slipped it into his pocket.

"Can you imagine Mulvane's face if a dozen armed deputies had thundered into the casino hollering out Alexa's name?" Brad said.

"The only thing I know is that nothing is going to happen to Alexa on my watch. Anybody does anything to her, and it's scorched earth time."

93

STYER TOOK THE PHONE FROM ALEXA'S EAR, CLOSED it, and removed the earpiece he'd used to listen in on her call. She was in an armchair, where Styer had placed her after carrying her from the bathtub, still bound. Paulus put the second phone into his pocket where she could see it. She had cooperated because Styer told her he had planted a bomb containing three kilos of Semtex in the Gardner house. The detonator was rigged to his cell phone. All he needed to do, if she tried anything rash, was to hit the SEND key. She had taken his word, seeing in her mind the faces of everyone inside the house. She knew he would not hesitate to kill them.

"So Cynthia's alive?" she asked.

"She is indeed. You'll see her very soon."

She watched him, still so convinced by the disguise that to hear his Eastern European–accented English flowing from the familiar lips was as unnerving as having a dog talk to you.

"Why Winter?" she asked.

"I don't understand your question," Styer said.

"Why all this to kill Winter?" she asked. "What did he do to you?"

Styer sat in the chair across from her, crossed his leg, and studied her without answering.

"I understand you were supposed to kill him in New Orleans. Why did you lie—say you weren't?"

Styer said, "He both knows and talks too much. He talks about me to the CIA and the FBI. I saw a photo of him meeting with the new leader of the shadow group that is seeking to kill me. I explicitly forbade him from looking for me as the condition for allowing him to rejoin his family and take care of the orphaned Porter girl. He chose to ignore that. Did he imagine I wouldn't know everything? I thought he was smarter than that."

"I know for a fact that he hasn't been looking for you. A man he presumed was from the CIA spoke to him about you, in the guise of warning him."

"I saw a picture of him meeting with a cell leader."

"Somebody made sure you got it then. If they told anybody he was looking for you, if there was a picture of that meeting, it means they took it to spread the word, figuring you'd come after him so they could nail you. Doesn't that make more sense?"

"Winter lied to you," Styer said, rubbing his chin gently so as not to disturb the synthetic skin or the makeup that covered it. "He wants revenge for those old people in New Orleans."

"You mean Millie and Hank Trammel?"

"That wasn't personal. I explained that to him. In this line of work, there is often collateral damage."

"The Trammels were like family to Winter. I don't expect you to understand that. But it's more than that, isn't it?"

"I'm sorry?"

"You're a killer. He isn't."

"Don't be so naive. Do you know how many men and women he has killed?"

"He only kills when there's no alternative. His life is filled with people who love him. You don't have any idea what that is like. Despite all of your expertise, you're never going to be more than a heartless calculating predator."

Styer smiled warmly. "Alexa. We are all only animals of varying intelligence. Our thoughts are no more than chemical reactions. Our movements are just electrical responses to stimuli. Like all living things, we are born, we live our lives, and we die and rot right off our skeletons. Family is accidental and random, based on sexual desire and fertility. Friendships are merely selfish associations. We join together as animals to feel safer, to pool emotions others have convinced us are necessary to feel better about ourselves. He has to kill me, as I have to kill him. As long as I live, he will not be able to feel the world is more than chaos, that there is a god, that anything matters. Conversely, as long as he lives, I will have to look over my shoulder, and I can't allow that. I gave him a chance to live, but he can't forget about me and what I did to those old people."

"How did you know he'd be here?" Alexa asked.

"I keep close tabs on him."

"You don't know everything."

"What don't I know?" Styer asked.

"You'll see," she said.

"Tell me," Styer said, taking a knife out of the pocket of his cardigan, and opening it so she could see the short serrated blade. "I'd like to know what the great FBI agent Alexa Keen could possibly know that I don't."

Styer stopped smiling and stood, casually holding the knife down by his leg.

"Oh, there's one thing I should tell you," Alexa said, taking a deep breath.

Her scream was the loudest, most powerful sound she had ever made, and completely took Styer by surprise.

He lunged at her.

94

KURT KLEIN TRIED TO RELAX, BUT EVERY FEW MINutes he checked the computer for Styer's reply, softly cursing the empty screen. He was accustomed to business-borne intrigue and suspense, but so much was hanging on this deal that he was screaming inside.

Kurt winced when the phone rang. Finch answered it and spoke softly into the receiver before placing his hand over the instrument and walking over. "Sir, a Senator Raffleman wishes to speak to you."

Kurt took the phone and waited until Finch had left the room. "Klein here."

A woman said, "Just a second, please."

After a click, Bert Raffleman's voice came on. "Kurt, how are you?"

"I am fine, Senator."

"And Freida?"

"She's in Paris spending money. And how is Cindy?"

"Doing the same here in Washington, of course. Any word on when you're going to hold that press conference on your resort?"

"Absolutely. I will be scheduling it tomorrow, and the invitations will be going out Monday. Can't do it unless you'll be here to take credit, since you have been so instrumental in paving the way for it." *Not to mention the nine hundred thousand dollars I paid you and your crooked, blood-sucking pals, you slow-talking, two-faced ass.*

"Well, it's not every day we get an investment like yours down there. Going to be a big boost to the economy. I can't wait to get on one of those golf courses you'll be building. And Cindy is excited about the spa. Not that she needs any help in the beauty department. Just let me know when and I'll be there. You know I wouldn't let you down. That's what friends are for," Raffleman drawled.

After he hung up, Kurt glanced at the computer screen and saw that Styer had answered his e-mail. Sitting forward on the edge of the couch to see better, he put on his glasses and read the response.

> Uncle,
>
> Message understood. Good news on land. Girl will be home by ten tonight. Will be away from computer from here out. Wire money if satisfied. I have personal business to attend to before leaving.

Kurt closed the connection and sat back, thinking. Styer knew he had been called off the Gardner family. The part that was of concern was the "personal business" reference.

He removed his glasses and rubbed his eyes. Massey's name had been vaguely familiar to him even before Mulvane mentioned it. Kurt had learned from his source in D.C. that Winter James Massey, while he was a deputy U.S. marshal, had crossed swords with a rogue group of shadows, killing several of them in a series of firefights.

He knew that when Yuri Chenchenko had betrayed Styer, he had sent him to kill an ex–federal marshal. That contract had been a ruse, designed to put Styer in a position to be killed by the CIA-sponsored shadow men. Since Massey knew Styer by name, and knew he was in Tunica, the only explanation was that Massey was Styer's target, and that had to be the personal business Styer mentioned.

It all made sense. Styer had pushed Klein for the assignment in Tunica after Klein had asked Styer to recommend a lesser talent for the job. Styer, claiming he needed an easy assignment to stay sharp, had asked Kurt to let him solve the Gardner problem. For the past eight months Styer had lived here among the natives, doing research and crafting a plan that would make the land deal happen by the drop-dead date Kurt had given him. That date was at hand, and, however it had happened, the land was as good as Kurt's.

Styer could not kill Massey. Not here or now. He stared out the window unseeingly as something came to him. The only people who could possibly take Styer out were the shadows—the cutouts who'd been Styer's main adversaries before the Berlin Wall fell. They had wanted Styer dead for years, and had made a very expensive deal with Yuri to get their hands on him. If the two unidentified men Massey had told him were dead were cutouts, they would have been expecting to find Styer, and now that he had killed two of them, they would be looking even harder for him.

Kurt had an idea and a new direction for his thoughts.

95

PIERCE MULVANE HAD BEEN RELIEVED WHEN KURT Klein had summoned him with the news that the Gardner land transaction would be done that evening by nine. On Monday the crews would come in from their hotel rooms in Memphis, and in two weeks the ground would be raised several feet, and a trench would be dug to the base of the levee. Soon, a temporary hole would be cut in the levee to connect to the river so the actual casino could be floated there in sections from the fabrication yards. Using the Mississippi River as a highway, they would put the casino together section by section in the concrete pond. The levee would be put back as it had been by the corps, the trench filled in by private contractors, and the casino's foundation would forever float in a few inches of water.

Klein had invited him to have a celebratory dinner in his suite after the papers were signed. Mulvane picked up his receiver and pressed the intercom button. "Send Tug in."

Tug Murphy came through the door seconds later, closed it behind him, and stood in front of the desk, hands behind his back. "Yes, sir?"

"Sit," Pierce said, smiling. "Take a load off."

Tug took a seat and sat with his back straight, folding his hands on his knee.

"I've been asked to have a celebratory dinner with Herr Klein tonight," Pierce said, suppressing the glee he felt. "The Gardner land deal is in place, and I believe he wants to make my position with River Royale official. The Germans are big on formality."

Tug nodded once.

"As a reward, he asked me to give you and Albert the night off," Pierce said.

Tug's expression became worried.

"You should be honored that he's so thoughtful. Not that you don't deserve that and a nice bonus—which will be forthcoming—but that he has thought enough of your efforts to make the gesture."

"A few minutes ago his man, Finch, said he wanted to go get some local color," Tug said. "He said we—him and Albert and me—ought to go to a restaurant that had good local food, and hit the blues bar. He said Mr. Klein wanted to treat us to a big night out. He said maybe there'd be some female company later on. It felt kind of . . . I don't know . . . weird to take us out on the spur of the moment. He's usually such a planner. I told him I had some things I had to see to, and he sort of insisted. He said the two men who worked with him might want to come with us, if that was all right."

"I see," Pierce said, thinking through what Tug had said from several angles.

"What seems weirdest is that Klein would have all three of his bodyguards out as well, leaving him unprotected," Tug said. "Even stranger is that he would send Albert and me along too."

Pierce thought it was possible that Klein felt secure enough now that the land deal was done that he didn't feel he needed protection. But Tug's troubled expression concerned him.

"If Finch wants to see the sights, seeing he's a foreigner and all . . . And naturally they want someone to show them around. What time did Finch say he wants to go out?"

"Around eight-thirty."

"I give you my approval," he said with a big smile. "Go and have fun. I'll tell you all about it when you come back. One thing . . ."

"Yes?" Tug asked.

"When we move out there to the new resort, you're going to be getting a big raise and expanded duties."

96

KURT KLEIN SHOULD HAVE FELT AN INNER PEACE, since he had made one of the most difficult decisions of his life. Once he had decided that Styer had to be sacrificed, he knew how to accomplish the task. Kurt had used Paulus Styer's skills for more than a decade, and so he was very familiar with Styer's methods. Styer would have infiltrated the casino in disguise in order to blend into his larger theater of operations. Klein had monitored the employees closest to Mulvane carefully, and only one employee had come in after Styer was given the nod to deal with the Gardners. That hire was a man Mulvane had asked for, but a man Mulvane didn't know very well. He was a man recommended as being capable of performing difficult assignments, who could also be trusted to take secrets to the grave. Although Klein had never met Paulus Styer face-to-face, he was certain Styer had met him.

When Steffan Finch came into the suite, Kurt Klein closed the computer, lit a Dunhill, and nodded for Finch to speak.

"White is on, but Murphy says he has personal business he has to attend to. He says he can meet us at the blues club later. Do you want me to force the issue?"

Kurt thoughtfully expelled a stream of smoke. "He said 'personal business'? Are you sure that is what he said?"

"His exact words."

"Don't press it," Kurt told him, comforted by hearing the expression Styer had used in his message. "I've got that covered."

"If you're sure."

"Absolutely," Kurt said, nodding. "That will be all."

After Finch left him, Kurt crushed out his cigarette, opened the computer, and typed his contact in D.C. a short message. After he had finished, he felt no relief at all. He knew that in business a man had to do things he didn't want to do for the greater good. He trusted that Finch and his associates would be capable of performing the future business-related jobs that he had earmarked for Styer. He reviewed the note he had typed out and nodded.

> Confidential:
>
> FYI—it may be of interest to your shadow friends now operating in the South that Cold Wind is disguised as Tug Murphy, Roundtable's GM, Pierce Mulvane's personal assistant.
>
> Payment will include a double amount as bonus and will be credited to your account when Cold Wind stops blowing.

Klein parked the cursor on the SEND button and, inhaling slowly, pressed it with his trembling finger. He knew that his name would not be passed along as the source of the information, and he didn't think it intelligent to tell anyone that he had been employing Styer. He doubted the shadows would botch things again. But if they somehow did, there was no way Styer would put together that Kurt had figured out who he was.

97

ALEXA WATCHED STYER CLIPPING HIS FINGERNAILS over an ashtray. The tape on her mouth prevented her from saying anything.

"Now," Styer told Alexa as he dropped a final clipping into the glass bowl. "If you want to save the Gardners, and I assume you do, you and I are going to walk out of this casino together. While Mrs. Gardner and Massey and others, I presume, are conducting their business here with Mr. Klein, we will go to the Gardners' home. I will collect the explosives I put there during the funeral of the unfortunate young lady with the ruined cranium. After that, I will leave Massey a note and you and I will take a ride in the country. Winter will come alone to rescue you, and he and I will have our reckoning. It will be a fair fight and I will kill him. If you try anything now, I will explode the device, and whoever is in the house will be vaporized. Do you understand?"

Alexa nodded.

"If you scream, I will set off the device, stroll up to Massey and Mrs. Gardner, which we both know I can do, and kill them inside this establishment. On all of this, and I mean every bit of it, you have my word. Please tell me you understand."

Alexa nodded again.

"Oh, and there's one other thing you should see. Just in case you don't grasp the entire situation."

Styer stood and went into the bedroom. When he came back, he was not alone. Cynthia Gardner's eyes were wild, her hands behind her back, her mouth covered with tape. Around her waist was a belt containing a brick of explosives with a detonator and a receiver attached to it. Styer pushed her roughly onto the couch and she blinked rapidly, looking from Alexa to Styer, confusion and fear clouding her features.

Styer came around the table and jerked the tape from Alexa's mouth. "Alexa, do you know Cynthia Gardner? I told you she was all right. Cynthia, meet FBI Agent Alexa

Keen. She's an abduction specialist who has found you against all odds."

Cynthia turned toward Alexa, alert and terrified.

"So you didn't know I had her?" Styer said. "You being the world's leading abduction expert?"

Styer picked up Alexa's purse, took out her Glock, removed the magazine, jacked the receiver, and caught the round in the air. He slowly thumbed each of the rounds from the magazine into the bowl along with his nail clippings. That done, he slammed the empty magazine into the gun's handle, tossed the other loaded magazines on the couch, and put the Glock back into her purse.

"I won't hesitate to kill her. You believe me, I hope. Cyn's explosive is rigged to the same signal and will go off in sync with the one in her home. Double jeopardy, you see. I think I've covered all my bases."

Lifting his cell phone, he checked the readout, and put it into his left hand, thumb on the SEND button. "One queer move and I'll press it."

"Okay," Alexa said.

"I know you may think I'm bluffing so I want to show you something." He reached into his jacket pocket and showed her a Polaroid of him holding a bomb made of eight blocks of explosive in the foyer of the Gardner house.

"I'm pretty photogenic, don't you think?" he said.

"Jesus," Alexa said.

"Do as I say and you will live. I want your word."

"It's your game," Alexa said.

Styer cut the cable ties on Alexa's ankles and unlocked her handcuffs. She sat up, rubbing her wrists slowly.

Cynthia was sobbing hysterically.

"It's okay, Cynthia. He won't do anything if we do as he says."

"Now, Cynthia," Styer said. "You are going to make a call. If you say exactly what I tell you, you'll be fine. If you screw this up, you are going to be very dead."

Cynthia nodded slowly as she locked eyes with Alexa. "Cynthia, do exactly what he says," Alexa told the girl.

98

PIERCE MULVANE HAD EXPLAINED TO HIS WIFE THAT with Kurt Klein visiting he wasn't going to make it home tomorrow for his usual Sunday visit with her and the kids. He listened patiently to her long litany of complaints, all the while going over the stack of gamblers' complaints passed up to him from his managers. Most of the complaints were no more important to him than the tripe his wife came up with about him missing his son's soccer finals, or his daughter's hidden candy stashes, or his wife's inability to find decent shoes in her size that were the right color. Why they couldn't live in Vegas, where they had everything, was simply beyond her. He promised her that when River Royale was up and running, the shops would stock her sizes and colors, and she'd never have to mention Las Vegas again—and neither would anybody else.

By the time he finally told her he would get up on Wednesday to spend the night, he had initialed the customers' gripe reports and placed them into a stack for further consideration, probably around the time the temperature of hell finally dropped below thirty-two degrees.

Pierce's phone buzzed.

"Yeah," he said.

"Pierce," Kurt Klein said. "Am I interrupting anything?"

"Absolutely not. I was just finishing up some paperwork. What can I do for you?"

"One of my security men was in the model room a few minutes ago and he reported to me that he caught a man with a camera who claims to be from one of the newspapers in Memphis, taking pictures of the resort model."

"That room was locked," Pierce said.

"Maybe one of your people let him in. My man does not think he is who he says he is, and he may be with a competitor. They found some interesting items in his room—number seven ten. I am going to go down myself in a minute. Meet me there?"

"I'll be right there as soon as I call Tug. He's very good at this sort of thing. Don't you think you should stay clear of it?"

"Good thinking. But use Steffan's people, no need to hassle Tug. Meet me up here after you have a look and we will decide what action is required."

Pierce hung up. If pictures of the resort were released before the official press conference, it would greatly lessen the impact of the announcement. When over a billion dollars was on the line, care had to be taken.

Pierce tried to call Tug anyway, but there was no answer. He went to the elevator and got off on the seventh floor. One of Klein's beefy security men waited in the hall beside the door. As Pierce drew close, the man gave him a troubled smile. "Sorry to bother you, Mr. Mulvane," he said, opening the door. "I think you will find this very disturbing."

Pierce went through the door into the short hallway and the security man came in behind him. The first thing he noticed were the leather suitcases beside a laundry cart. A sheet of plastic covered the floor and there was more covering the furniture. He wondered what the guest was up to that had made protective covering necessary. When he realized that the suitcases were just like his, the bathroom door opened, and Finch stepped out wearing a raincoat. Even as the guard muscled Pierce farther into the room and onto the plastic, Pierce had no idea why Finch was aiming a gun at him.

99

ALBERT WHITE TOOK OFF HIS TIE AND PUT IT IN the drawer along with his .38. He took the two speed loaders from his jacket pocket and tossed them in before closing and locking the drawer. In the five years since his wife left him for his second cousin, a roofer, he had rarely spent any of his off time—and there was less and less of that—with other people. He didn't much care for company. Now he was going to spend the evening with a South African jerk-off and two of his pals. The prospect made him bone-tired. Why the old Kraut hadn't just given him a cash bonus was beyond him. He was going to sit in a restaurant for a couple of hours, eat a thick steak. Then instead of lying down, which is what he'd want to do, he would have to go out carousing with the sons of bitches. And he'd bet ten dollars against a donut they'd want free trim at casino expense.

He looked at his watch and frowned. Why was it that time passed so quickly when something unpleasant was coming at you, and so slowly when there was something tasty ahead? Well, if things worked out as planned, he'd be getting a nice bump from a real estate deal he'd been working on. He thought about Jack Beals. Although White had never cared for him, he had been useful. He may have been a preening smart-ass, but he would do anything for money, and he and White had made a few hundred grand by taking winnings from people who walked away with money they didn't deserve. White knew the cash that had been found in Beals's house was from their little sideline venture.

Albert had his money well hidden, and once in a while he would take it out of the vents and count it. Since he didn't go on vacations or buy expensive toys, he had more than he needed. When he wanted sex, Albert had a colored gal who would come over and set him right as rain for a fifty-dollar bill.

Albert was saving for retirement. He had bought a small house on a lake in Florida, and when he walked out in five years, six months, two days, and fourteen hours, he would have enough to pad his retirement from the force in West Memphis, his social security, the bundle he'd saved from the years of collecting money to look the other way in West Memphis, Arkansas, and the liberated winnings he and Beals had put together. Nine hundred thousand dollars, but he planned to have well over a million before walking away into the glorious sunrise.

Albert's thoughts were interrupted by a rapping on his office door. Finch opened it. "You ready, big buddy?"

"Yeah," Albert said. "Where's your two guys at?"

"Waiting outside in the limo," Finch said, smiling. "We're going first-class all the way, big fellow. We go eat at that steak house you were bragging about, have a few drinks with Tug at that blues club outside town, and then we get some girls and have our ashes hauled. You up for all that?"

"I reckon I am," Albert said.

"Then let's have a run at it."

Albert nodded, took a look at the locked drawer, and followed Finch down the hall toward what he was sure was going to be a pure pain-in-the-ass experience.

100

ALEXA DRESSED IN THE LIVING ROOM WHILE STYER and Cynthia looked on.

"You are a very attractive woman," he said.

She buttoned her blouse.

"I find women of small stature attractive."

"Girls who look boyish."

"I didn't say that," he said, frowning. Styer's eyes hardened for a few seconds, then softened.

"You don't have to. Maybe psychotic young men like Jack Beals are more your speed. I'll just use my imagination."

"Jack . . . ?" Cynthia said, startled. "He's dead?"

"Males have never held any sexual fascination for me. Jack had a high opinion of his mediocre talents with a gun. He never allowed his targets to face him on even ground. He was a thief and a coward, who used a badge to get close."

"Why did you kill him?"

"*You* killed Jack?" Cynthia asked, her lip trembling.

Alexa didn't know that Cynthia knew Beals. She would have loved to ask her how she knew him.

Styer shrugged. "The young man was supposed to be helping me, but I discovered that he was trying to figure out what I was up to so he could tell certain people with interests contrary to those of my employer. All of this intrigue over the land, and so much duplicity swirling around. As it happened, his body was a convenient sign holder for Massey." He smiled.

"Did you kill Sherry Adams just to draw Winter in?"

"File that under killing two birds with one bullet. Now, Cynthia, put on your parka. If you so much as look the wrong way, your fashion accessory will spread your lovely body, and unfortunately ours, too, all over the landscape. You get that?"

Cynthia nodded mutely.

Styer made Alexa's skin crawl. She was fairly sure, despite his assurances, that he didn't intend to leave her alive after she'd served his purpose. Time was running out, and she had to start looking for a weakness to exploit.

Alexa put on her coat and slipped her purse on her shoulder. After Styer fixed the do-not-disturb sign on the door, she walked beside him down the hall toward the elevators. His left hand, hidden in his coat pocket, held his cell phone. The valise in his right hand contained God knew what.

They didn't speak as they rode down to the casino, now crowded with Saturday night gamers. The gamblers ranged from fat to fit, rich to poor, and their clothes reflected a wide range of fashion and functionality—from gowns to jeans and halter tops, Armani to hunter's camouflage jackets and matching ball caps. The air was thick with cigarette smoke and the insipid sounds of ringing bells, as the wheels of a thousand slot machines spun in place.

Alexa kept her eyes on the floor in front of her, thinking in ten directions at once. "We'll take your vehicle," Styer said. "Wouldn't be good if Massey saw it sitting here, what with you supposed to be in Memphis meeting with those FBI agents."

As they exited the casino, Alexa spotted Albert White climbing into a limousine. He stooped to get his considerable bulk into the Cadillac, reminding Alexa of a fat groundhog slipping into a narrow opening in a wall.

At Leigh's pickup, Alexa unlocked the door and handed Styer the keys. He aimed Cynthia into the rear seat and placed the valise on the floorboard beside her feet. He watched as Alexa opened her door and climbed into the cab. She started the engine and backed out carefully.

"So what's in the valise?" she asked.

"Maybe I'll let you look if you behave yourself. Aren't you going to try and use psychology on me? It's a long drive out to the plantation, and I like entertainment where I can find it."

She shook her head.

"Well, then, what's your listening pleasure?" he asked, turning on the radio.

101

ALBERT WHITE SQUEEZED PAST FINCH'S PALS IN THE jump seat and crabbed back to the rear bench, lowering his bulk to the cushioned leather. The other two men, whose names he hadn't bothered to learn, were large and serious individuals who didn't look like they were going to enjoy this any more than he was. Only Steffan Finch was smiling, and as soon as the car rolled away, he opened the bar on the side bench and started fixing a drink, dropping ice cubes into a crystal highball glass, then pouring in scotch from a decanter.

"You know how to get to the steak house?" Albert

called to the driver as they stopped at the entrance to the casinos, facing the highway.

The driver shook his head.

"You shouldn't be driving for the casino until you know the area," he said, annoyed. "Take a left."

The driver looked into the rearview and lit a cigarette, illuminating his features for a couple of seconds. He didn't look familiar to Albert—at least the back of his head didn't, but the cap made it hard to tell.

One of the two large men coughed.

"Put out that cigarette," Albert commanded.

Instead of tossing out the cigarette, the driver took a deep drag from it and turned right onto the road, pushing down the accelerator.

"Fuck's sake," Albert mumbled. "I guess he doesn't want to keep his job. Well, then close the glass."

The driver slid up the glass partition.

"And turn around, damn it!" Albert said, his anger rising.

The man who had coughed leaned to the side, reached down under his leg, and took out a pistol tipped with a thick black silencer. Resting the gun on his knee, he aimed the automatic directly at Albert's chest. Albert froze.

"Albert," Finch said, tasting the scotch. "This is very good, by the way. Would you like some?"

"No," Albert heard himself say. "I quit drinking ten years ago."

"Never too late to go back," Finch said, bringing smiles to the two goons' faces. "Unless it turns out that way. It's entirely up to you."

Albert said, "This isn't funny. Don't aim that thing at me."

"No, it isn't, is it? Not funny at all. Here's the deal. We're going to make a stop a few miles from here. You are going to make a tape for Herr Klein. On this tape you will tell the story of how you hired Jack Beals to kill Leigh Gardner so her ex-husband could sign over the land Mr. Mulvane so desperately needed. He had already purchased the land from Jacob Gardner when he found out that Gardner did not own it, his ex-wife did. When Mulvane discovered that she would never sell it as long as Jacob needed her to do so, he became desperate because he had intended to take the land from Gardner by force and say he paid a million dollars for it in order to cover the embezzling he has been doing for a long while. Beals killed the wrong person and panicked. Mulvane had Tug Murphy, or yourself, if you'd like to go to prison, kill Beals and Jacob Gardner to keep them quiet. You, being a decent man, couldn't live with this sin on your head, so you're making the tape to incriminate Mulvane and Tug Murphy. Then you leave town, or die by your own hand. I don't care which, though you might. I think that's about it."

"That's crazy," Albert said. "Who's going to believe that?"

"Some of it is true enough." Finch took a small recorder from his coat pocket. "People will believe it because it explains everything nicely, and people like for things to make sense. And Herr Klein will make sure they do. He is investing over a billion dollars locally, and you are a fat, stupid, crooked ex-cop who works for a casino. The alternative is that Herr Klein will have Tug make the tape and blame you, which seems just as logical to me. All the denials you can muster won't help you. One way or the other, Mulvane is going to take the rap. So is it going to be you or Tug in a cell with Mulvane?"

"I have a lot of money," Albert said. "Let me go and it's yours. Half a million dollars. Cash."

"No, you don't have that kind of money. Does old Albert here have any money, Gregory?"

The man who wasn't aiming at Albert said, "We visited your home to look around and we found your twenty grand."

"It's nine hundred grand," Albert growled.

"Nine or five, we only found twenty grand. Isn't that right, Carl?" Steffan said.

The man with the gun nodded. "That's right, Steffan."

"Better for us. People will believe you took twenty from Mulvane for dirty favors," Finch said. "Any more than that just complicates things. And Beals got what the cops found in his place for getting rid of troublesome individuals for you. It all works in more than one way."

Sweat oozed from every pore in Albert's large body.

"So," Finch said holding out the recorder. "You choose. You have thirty seconds to begin your confession."

Albert took the recorder and, shifting uncomfortably, promptly emptied his bowels.

"Nice," Finch said. "Carl, roll down some windows."

102

WINTER SAT WATCHING HAMP PLAY A VIDEO GAME. To everyone's great relief, Cyn had just sent a text message saying she would be home by ten P.M.

Seated on the floor with his legs crossed, the controller in his small hands, Hamp worked his fingers expertly, his eyes glued to the screen where muscular figures dressed in tight outfits traded punches and kicked at each other.

"Which one are you?" Winter asked.

"The white one," Hamp replied. "The good wizard."

Winter's cell phone rang and he opened it, stood, and walked out of the room so he wouldn't disturb Hamp.

"Yeah," he said.

"Yeah, what?" Sean's voice said.

"Yeah, hello, my dear."

"What are you doing?" she asked.

"I was sitting in a room with a child that reminds me of my son."

"How's it coming?"

"We're winding down. We have a meeting in a little while to transfer some land that has already cost three lives."

"Three?"

"Yeah. I'll tell you later."

"What about you-know-who?"

"He who must not be named?" Winter said, infusing the joke with a joviality he didn't feel.

"Yes."

"Nothing but tracks," he said truthfully.

"You're being careful?"

"Of course I am. How's Trammel doing?"

"Hank's really proud of Faith Ann's deer. He is getting the pictures blown up for the wall. Is Alexa with you?"

"Not at the moment. She had to go handle some Bureau politics."

"The FBI getting involved?"

"No. It's still a local matter."

"I wish you were here," Sean said. "I wish you were here in our bed with me. I could use some of that special Massey attention."

"I'll bring you a few pounds of that when I get this done. Word of honor."

"Should I worry?"

"No, you definitely should not."

Winter heard Olivia crying in the background.

"I have to go. Sleeping Beauty is awake. Call me in the morning?"

"Of course I will."

"Massey, you know what?"

"No, what?" he asked, smiling.

"When you get back, I'm going to show you what."

"I love you, Sean," he said. "Tell the gang I said I love them."

"Even Hank?"

"Don't tell *him*."

Winter closed the phone after Sean broke the connection. He formed a picture in his mind of Hank and Millie Trammel and felt his eyes narrow into slits, as he pictured them run down and shattered in that rain-soaked New Orleans street.

Winter looked over his shoulder and what he saw stopped him cold. There through the partly opened kitchen door Winter was treated to a view of Brad and Leigh. They were embracing, her head against his chest. As he watched, Leigh leaned back, looked up, and instead of stepping back, as Winter expected, the two looked into each other's eyes and put their lips together.

When their kiss finally ended, they tightened their embrace, and when Leigh opened her eyes, they met Winter's and enlarged in the same sort of embarrassment that one might expect from a teenager caught singing to her reflection in a mirror. He wondered, as he turned away, if she'd seen the same expression on his face.

103

AS SOON AS ROY BISHOP AND ANOTHER DEPUTY arrived to stay at the house with Estelle and Hampton, Winter, Leigh, and Brad prepared to leave. Four other armed deputies would caravan to the casino and wait until Leigh's business was concluded, then stick with them until the papers were signed. Billy Lyons was going to meet them at the casino at nine o'clock to make sure the documents were legally binding and correctly signed.

Before the trio filed out of the house, Leigh embraced her son and told him to mind Estelle and the deputies. He agreed easily. All Hampton and Estelle knew was that Leigh was going with Winter and Brad to a business meeting.

Brad drove them in Winter's Jeep since it was being monitored. They'd decided they wanted the cutouts to know if Styer made an attempt on Winter.

The drive to the casino was uneventful. Winter wondered if Brad knew he'd seen the couple kissing in the kitchen. He supposed Leigh might have said something to him, although he didn't act any differently than before.

Winter couldn't help but wonder if this trouble had broken down the icy wall between them. As far as Winter could tell, the years they were apart had been unnecessary, due to their youth and misunderstanding. He supposed that Leigh's stubbornness had played a big part in their lengthy split. It was Winter's experience that successful relationships depended on open communication, mutual respect, and forgiveness, but he figured they understood that now.

At the casino, the cruisers parked and the deputies stepped out to their assigned posts, where they would await further orders. Billy Lyons waited under the portico, briefcase in hand.

Leigh's cell phone rang and she looked at the caller ID. "It's Cyn!"

She flipped open the phone. "Cyn, where are you?"

She listened for a few seconds.

"That's great. We'll see you later at the house and you can tell us all about it." She hung up and smiled.

"She's being dropped off at a public place as soon as the deal is done," Leigh said. She wiped a tear from her eye. "She's fine."

"Did she say where she was?" Brad asked. "Who had her?"

"No," Leigh said. "But she said she's fine. She sounded fine. She said to call her phone as soon as the papers are signed."

"Let's get this over with," Winter said, relieved.

After the deputies were in position, Brad cut the motor and said, "Showtime."

They walked toward the casino, Winter's and Brad's eyes scanning the crowd like two cowboys headed toward the only saloon in a lawless cow town.

104

ALEXA SAT IN THE EXTENDED CAB OF LEIGH'S PICKUP parked in a dark pecan orchard a mile from Six Oaks, waiting for whatever Styer was waiting for.

"Can we go home now?" Cynthia asked. "I told Mama what you said to."

"Sit quiet and let the adults talk. We'll be going in

shortly," Styer said. He continued thoughtfully, "I should have been an athlete. My father was a gymnast, a gold medalist for East Germany. My mother was a chess player, a grand master who was a cryptologist for Stasi. When I was eight, I had an IQ of over one hundred and sixty, amazing physical strength and agility."

Styer smiled, his eyes far away. "My parents were good Germans. Hitler and his generals were giants, conquering an entire continent one country at a time. Few complained while they were winning because their stomachs were full and they could feel proud again."

"Good Germans," Alexa said, not knowing what else to say.

"My parents let the KGB take me from them when I was nine. I remember them telling me how wonderful it was that I would be trained as so few were. How fortunate I was to have been born so special that such very important men and women would prove my greatness to the world. They were so proud." There was a distinct note of bitterness in the last words.

"When they came for me to take me to the school, it was winter. I recall how the exhaust pipe smoked in the dark, how the snow crunched beneath my shoes. I was taken by plane to a base at the foot of the Ural Mountains, and out from there, by military helicopter."

"What kind of academy was it?" Alexa asked, curious.

"It was a school for assassins, but of course I didn't know that at first."

Styer stopped talking when three sets of headlights came into view. "There they are. Massey and the others. Jeep and two cruisers. Let me remind you, Alexa, before you try to turn on the lights, that I have the cell phone in my hand."

"I know that."

After the caravan was out of sight, Styer set down the binoculars. "Where was I?"

"You were talking about your parents."

"Last year I dropped in for a visit with them. Not a word had they had from me in twenty-nine years, and they begged me to stay. But we were no more than strangers. My mother said she was sorry she ever let them take me, but had no choice. She and my father were just being good Germans who showed their appreciation by giving their beloved only son to the state. I became no more than an instrument for others to use to their own ends, instead of something else like a doctor, a musician, even an Olympic gold medalist." Styer smiled strangely. "You can't imagine all those nights I cried silently in my bed so no one could sense my weakness and use it against me."

"I know there must be something of the boy you were deep down inside you," Alexa said. "None of this is necessary. If you leave, Winter won't be a threat. His children need him. His wife needs him."

Styer put the truck in gear, then turned it off and looked at her. "It will be less suspicious if you will drive again from here, Alexa. Cyn, no warning looks or I will kill the deputy and cut your throat. Come around, Alexa, and I will slide over."

Alexa got out and climbed back into the cab to find that Styer had adjusted the seat forward for her. She cranked the truck, deciding to keep him talking if she could. She wanted to reach the little boy who had once loved his parents.

"Do you keep in touch with your parents?"

"That's hardly possible, darlin'," Styer said in the voice of the man he was now impersonating. "They died in an accidental fire while I was visiting with them. Of course, being an only son, I stayed in Berlin long enough to make the funeral arrangements."

105

A MAN DRESSED IN A CASINO EMPLOYEE'S ATTIRE waited at the elevators, smiling at their approach. "Mr. Klein and his attorney are expecting you."

His name tag said he was Alex Coyle, the concierge. After they got into the car, he signaled to a young bellboy who was standing beside the desk. The youth came over and got into the elevator, taking a key from the concierge. He put the key in the lock, pressed the button for the eighth floor, and watched the panel with a customer-service smile plastered on his face.

"Hello, Mr. Green," Winter said to the boy whose name tag read, JOHNNY GREEN.

He nodded. "I'm supposed to show y'all up."

"Nice night," Leigh said.

"I guess so," Johnny said. "In here you wouldn't know if it was night or day. Is it freezing over yet?"

"It's getting colder by the minute," Billy Lyons said as the elevator stopped.

Johnny Green escorted them down the hall to suite 825, and rapped on the partly open door with gloved fingers.

"Enter!" Kurt Klein's unmistakable voice cried out.

Billy Lyons reached into his pants pocket, withdrew a money clip, and peeled off a twenty, which he handed to the bellboy.

"Thank you," Johnny Green said, putting the bill into his pocket without inspecting it. He held the door open until they were inside and closed it gently behind them.

"Never would have found the eighth floor on our own," Winter said, ribbing his friend.

"What I'm charging for this," Billy said, "I can afford to be generous."

106

THE LIMOUSINE FLOATED ALONG NEARLY DESERTED county roads, while Albert recorded the confession Finch had demanded.

"That was almost perfect," Finch said, after listening to

the second version. "Concise and covers all of the major points."

Despite the fear that he was about to be killed, Albert was furious that Klein was going to cover his ass using Albert's dead body.

Albert knew where they were going before they turned off the paved road, through the woods to where the landscape opened up like a battlefield. The limousine rolled among great tortured clumps of gathered tree limbs toward the lone equipment-storage structure, which was visible against the levee that ran north to south like a great wall.

The limo driver got out and opened the gates, then drove into the parking lot surrounding the structure, leaving the gates standing open.

"You don't have to kill me," Albert said weakly.

"In fact, I do," Finch told him. "Those are my orders. How I accomplish the task is up to you. I can torture you and roll your fat carcass into a hole and let you smother as we push dirt over you, or I can put you to sleep painlessly. I don't dislike you, Albert. There's nothing personal in this. I believe the mitigating factor is that you and Jack Beals robbed and murdered customers of Herr Klein's casino for profit. Pretty shortsighted—liquidating future customers—don't you think?"

Albert didn't know how they knew about his side enterprise, but seeing that they had found his stash, and knew about Beals's stash, there was no sense denying it.

"How much did Mulvane take?"

"He wasn't in on it."

"Was Murphy involved?"

Albert shook his head.

"Just you two?"

Albert nodded. He was thinking about the gun locked up in his desk, and wishing Tug had come along. With Tug, there would be hope. Without him, there was none.

The limo stopped ten feet from the door. The driver and the two thugs climbed out. The driver used a key to open the personnel door and stepped inside to turn on the lights. Meanwhile, Finch aimed his weapon at Albert. "After you, Albert."

Albert rolled from the seat and crabbed out of the vehicle, hardly aware of the icy drizzle that stung his cheeks like BBs. When he took a step, he slipped in a slick patch in front of the door and his feet flew out from under him. At the sight of Albert flat on his back and flailing in pain, Finch and the thugs laughed—cruel children delighted by the struggles of a flipped-over turtle. With one of the big men pulling on either of his arms, Albert scrambled to his feet, his pants clinging wetly to his soiled buttocks.

107

TUG HAD FOLLOWED THE LIMOUSINE, AND PARKED White's SUV at the edge of the woods. On foot, he trailed the five men into the enormous barn filled with massive earth-moving equipment. The tires on some of the pieces were taller than he was. Only the closest rows of overhead warehouse lights were on, and the men were clustered below a steel support beam in front of the manager's trailer.

After slipping into the rows of equipment, Tug watched as the driver placed a cinder block and a wooden crate side by side below the beam. The larger of the thugs went into the office trailer and returned with a looped yellow nylon rope, which he threw over the beam. The driver tied a slipknot in one end and, after taking out the slack, the noose dangled five feet over the crate.

"You're planning to hang me?" Albert asked in a horrified voice. "Not that!"

"Do as we say," Finch told Albert. "There are propane torches in here, if you'd like to go that route."

"Get up on the crate, fatso," the largest thug demanded. "There's also dynamite in the explosives shed. We could shove a stick up your ass and light it." The men all laughed, no doubt delighted by the prospect.

"We could roast your little pig balls," the driver said, snickering.

Tug moved closer each time the men said something, using their noise to cover his stealthy movements.

Resigned, legs shaking, Albert climbed onto the cinder block and stepped onto the crate, which shifted under his considerable weight. While the smaller of the thugs kept his gun aimed at Albert's groin, Finch climbed up onto the block and placed the noose around Albert's neck. The driver pulled the far end tight and tied it to a steel water pipe.

Albert began begging for his life, steam issuing from his mouth in the cold building.

"Please . . . please . . . don't do me like this, Mr. Finch," he said.

"Mr. Finch . . . please!" the driver called out. The four men, standing in a loose line with their backs to the equipment, were laughing and jeering.

Tug Murphy was in position, his shotgun loaded to its steel gills with five rounds of double-ought. It would be enough. He had left his coat outside so he would have immediate access to the USP45 in his shoulder holster, along with the six loaded magazines suspended under his right armpit.

"Please!" Albert screamed. "Please let me have me a few last words!"

Tug stopped behind a bulldozer that stood between him and the men. He crept around the massive steel treads and in behind the lowered blade. Tug put the shotgun against his shoulder, took a deep breath, let it out slowly, and straightened, now square to the men as the gun cleared the top of the steel blade. While only his head and shoulders were exposed, the men between him and the wall had no cover at all, and not one of Klein's henchmen had a gun in their hand at the moment.

The limousine driver saw Tug rise into view, but the barrel aimed at him froze him in mid-laugh. When Tug squeezed the trigger, the driver's head literally vanished. As his corpse collapsed, his hat spun away like a Frisbee.

Tug aimed the next shot at Finch's legs, but because Finch was already moving, the buckshot only took his right knee off. The South African fell hard on his left side and went for his gun, but Tug swung the barrel to one of the others who had drawn steel and was raising the muzzle of his handgun. Tug blew a hole in that man's chest, a few inches below his neck.

There was a dull clap as Finch's gun barked, but the bulldozer blade deflected the round. Tug's third blast hit Finch in the right shoulder, rendering his hand inoperable as the gun locked in his grip fell heavily to the dirt.

Tug heard a report and felt a slap to his right shoulder. He turned to see Albert kick out at the last standing shooter, striking him in his back before he could fire again. It didn't keep the man from firing at Tug, but it spoiled his aim. As Albert shifted his balance to kick out again, the crate fell on its side, the noose abruptly ending his fall. It took longer than it should have for Tug to point the gun, but the back-kicked man was squatting now to get a more solid shooting stance. He took the buckshot square in his stomach and fell behind the overturned crate. Tug pointed the shotgun at the crate and fired again, the buckshot piercing its wood slat walls to find the man behind it.

Having counted his shots, Tug was peeling a shell from the bandolier as he made his way around the blade. Albert grunted and clawed desperately at the noose and began spinning and kicking, moving in a jerky circle. In the time it took to get a shell in the tube, jack it into the gun's receiver, and aim at the swaying rope, Albert's tongue was already sticking straight out between his teeth.

The lead pellets cut the ski rope and Albert fell, flattening the crate.

As Tug rushed past Finch, he kicked his Browning away. He set the shotgun down and loosened the slipknot. Albert gagged and choked, but he picked up one of the shoes he'd kicked off and hummed it at Finch.

Albert couldn't talk, but he grunted pitifully, pointed a fat finger at Finch, and made a throat-slashing motion.

"Good idea," Tug said, plucking out a foam earplug. He stood, took out his folding knife, and went over to Finch, who looked at him with furious eyes. "Go ahead, wanker. You don't know what you're in for," he said.

"I know what you're in for," Tug said.

Finch smiled. "They know you're . . ." Tug grabbed Finch's ear, and as he was drawing the serrated edge hard through Finch's throat, the man said something that sounded like "Paulazar." Whatever it was, he wouldn't be saying it again, because Tug severed Finch's windpipe as he drew the blade through his neck, with no concern for the warm spray that hit his face. When Tug stood and looked at Albert, he saw figures moving behind him and several bright muzzle flashes. The kneeling Albert White jerked like he'd grabbed a live wire. His shirt sprouted red blossoms as more red spray filled the still air.

Tug felt dull punches all over his body. He threw himself behind the manager's shack as the dirt where he had stood was still being churned. Bullets pinged the pieces of equipment as, with great effort, Tug pulled out his pistol and fired several rounds toward the figures dressed in black who'd come through the same door he had. He heard a loud grunt and smiled bitterly. At least he'd hit one of them, but they had to be SWAT because they were in black assault suits with body armor, so the hit wouldn't do more than knock the breath out of him. He had seen at least four shapes, though it was likely there were twice that many.

"You think you're going to arrest me?"

A man laughed. "We aren't the arresting type. Here's the offer. Come out and we'll hold fire."

"Go fuck yourself with a stick," Tug barked, spitting blood. If they weren't cops, were they Finch's backup? Christ, what had the man expected he might run into? He could hear more men running into the building and dispersing. In a few seconds they would kill him where he lay mortally wounded.

He looked from the door to the explosives safe facing him. Sitting up, he crawled over, aimed, and used two bullets to blow off the hasp holding the large padlock. Painfully, he pulled the door open and scooted inside the dark cold space.

"You aren't getting out!" the voice yelled.

Tug set the handgun down and used the flashlight from his pocket to look at the stacked crates of TNT. He figured there were several hundred pounds of explosives in the small shack. He was losing focus as the blood ran in gushes from a dozen holes in his body. The bullet-struck organs were closing down, and coupled with blood loss, it made it difficult to remember why he was there. He stared at the boxes in the circle of light from the flashlight he had dropped, reached for one of the small cardboard boxes on the shelves beside him, and put it on the floor against the carton of dynamite closest to him.

"Hey!" he yelled, coughing. "Come on in. I've got something for you!"

He heard men talking outside the structure and, opening the box, he looked at the cylinders stacked inside.

"Ten seconds to come out or we start filling that shed with holes," a voice replied. "Ten, nine, eight, seven . . ."

Tug used his remaining strength to stick the muzzle of the HK down against the blasting caps and tighten his grip.

"Three, two . . ."

His hand trembling, Tug felt the trigger giving.

"One!" the voice outside yelled.

Smiling, Tug Murphy closed his eyes and squeezed.

108

KURT KLEIN STOOD IN THE LIVING ROOM BESIDE A tall balding man wearing an expensive-looking suit, horn-rimmed eyeglasses, and a yellow and blue paisley silk bow tie. The man smiled when he saw Billy Lyons.

"Billy?" he said, crossing to shake hands. "I didn't know you were representing Mrs. Gardner."

Shaking the man's hand vigorously, Billy said, "Jerry, I can't believe after all these years with me thinking you knew everything, you're admitting there's something you don't know."

Jerry laughed and turned to Leigh.

"Jerry Cunningham, may I introduce my client, Leigh Gardner."

"A pleasure to meet you, Mrs. Gardner. My condolences," he said, taking her offered hand in his.

"For whom?" she asked.

Jerry's smile faltered. "Your ex-husband. I understood he was killed."

"He and Sherry Adams, who worked for me. Nice to meet you, Mr. Cunningham."

Winter was looking at Klein when Leigh spoke. He saw the industrialist's eyes turn away, but the German's smile stayed perfectly focused.

"And these gentlemen are Winter Massey, who I've known longer than I like to admit, and Bradley Barnett, the sheriff around here. Him, I've only known since Ole Miss. We were fraternity brothers," Billy said jovially.

Jerry shook each of their hands as they were introduced. "And this is my client, Kurt Klein," he said, stepping back as Kurt approached, hand outstretched.

"Mrs. Gardner. So nice to finally meet you." He took her hand, held it for a second, and said, "My condolences in the matter of both of your recent tragic losses."

Winter half expected her to say something like, "You've done enough already," but she chose to let it go. What she said was, "Thank you," and she smiled as she said it.

Kurt indicated that they should take seats in front of the roaring fireplace, which was a natural gas fire licking steel logs that appeared to be real.

"These are the bearer bonds," Kurt said, pointing at an envelope on the table. "Ten instruments each worth five hundred thousand U.S. dollars."

Billy took the bonds out, inspected them, and nodded his approval.

Signing the papers took two minutes. Once notarized and signed by Leigh, along with Winter and Brad, who served as witnesses, they stood and prepared to leave.

Leigh handed Brad the envelope. "If you'll see this is put in a safe place."

"Safest place there is," Brad said.

As they were leaving, Kurt said, "Mr. Massey, might I have a word with you in private?"

Winter followed Kurt across the living room to the windows.

"About that other matter. We have discovered by interviewing Albert White that Mulvane did hire Beals to shoot Mrs. Gardner and to kill her children, which luckily he never had a chance to do. He also had a man named Tug Murphy, his private security agent, kill Beals and Jacob Gardner. I could not hold Mulvane, and he was seen leaving with two suitcases an hour ago in the company of Mr. Murphy."

There was a bright flash on the horizon. Winter assumed it was lightning, since a cold front was moving in.

"Albert White told my man Finch that Tug Murphy shot Mr. Gardner as he was driving. Perhaps you should have someone with the necessary forensic knowledge check that out. I don't believe Mr. White lied, since he admitted his own involvement in the matter."

"And where is Mr. White now?"

"We had no authority to hold him, and he left after making a full taped confession. I was told that he seemed genuinely remorseful. He shouldn't be hard for the authorities to find. His recorded confession will be delivered to the sheriff's office in the morning."

Winter stared into Kurt's eyes for several seconds and said, "I'm glad your man was able to obtain a confession."

"He is very good at these things," Kurt said, smiling. "I won't keep you."

I won't hold my breath until Mulvane, White, and Murphy turn up. He shook Kurt Klein's hand and said, "Glad it all fell into place so perfectly. I expected no less from you."

In the hallway outside Klein's suite, Leigh called Cyn's number, and she answered, "Mama?"

Winter and Brad stood next to Leigh, Winter's head against Leigh's so he could hear.

"Okay, darling," Leigh said. "The papers are signed. Tell the people who have you I want to speak to them."

There was a pause and a man's voice came on. "Okay?"

"I signed the papers. Let my daughter go."

"I know you did. I'll let her out in five minutes."

"Where?"

"A public place. She'll call you when I'm gone."

"If you aren't telling the truth, I can cancel the deal."

Winter nodded.

"If she doesn't call me back in six minutes, I'll do what I said. And if you harmed her . . ."

"Nobody's done shit to your brat," he said. "And, lady, you're welcome to her."

They were outside the casino six minutes later when Cyn called.

"He let me out at the Blue & White," Cynthia said. "Dr. Barnett is here."

"Let me speak to him," Leigh said. "Your father is with her at the Blue & White," she told Brad.

Brad took the phone from her.

"Dad? Is Cyn all right?"

"She's fine. A little shook up. She told me she was kidnapped?"

"She was. Does she need to go to the hospital?"

"I don't think so. She says she just wants to go home."

"Take her home. We're on our way."

109

A MINUTE AFTER CYNTHIA BROKE OFF THE CALL TO her mother, Alexa drove within sight of the Gardner house, stopping at the end of the driveway near the waiting cruiser. The deputy got out, and pulling up his hood against the rain and wind, stood by the truck as she lowered her window. The deputy recognized her and gave a friendly nod to the killer. He looked in the backseat at Cynthia.

"Welcome back, Miss Gardner," he said cheerily. "Y'all go on up to the house. Deputy Chief Bishop and Clarke are up there. I'll call them so they don't shoot at you. I guess I can call and cancel the BOLO."

Alexa looked at Styer, who nodded and patted the seat

using the cell phone. "You best get back in your car and stay dry," Styer said.

"I will, sir. Y'all be safe."

Alexa pulled away slowly, closing the window.

"I think that went well," Styer said. "When we get to the house, I'm going to cuff you."

Alexa's heart fell.

They pulled onto the circular front driveway as Alexa saw a single bright flash. She waited for the thunder to follow, but the storm was still too far off.

"I've given your request some thought," Styer said. "About allowing Massey to live."

"And?" Alexa asked.

"I can't do it," he said. "You already knew that, didn't you?"

Alexa nodded. "And you lied when you said you never lie, didn't you?"

"I only lie when it suits my purpose. I have to tie up the deputies in the house. Don't make me kill them, because I will. Winter will come after he is done at the casino, and he and I will conclude our business."

"He'll kill you," Alexa said.

"I promise I'll be really careful."

Styer laughed, but she didn't. Alexa figured that he had to have made the mask he was wearing over his own features by casting it on the owner's face, which meant he had most likely killed the subject before replicating his features. She gritted her teeth hard.

Alexa parked behind a cruiser as freezing rain pelted the hood of the truck. She believed Styer planned to kill her, the deputies, and everybody else, but she didn't think he would as long as he needed them. Leigh might call, and if nobody answered, Winter would know it was because Styer was there.

Styer got out and came around. As promised, he cuffed Alexa's hands behind her back before helping Cynthia from the extended cab. With rain pouring down on them, the three started toward the porch.

"Easy, girls," Styer hissed.

110

BRAD WAS PUTTING THE ENVELOPE CONTAINING the bonds in the evidence vault when Brad's deputy, who was posted at the Gardner's driveway, called to say that Cyn had arrived at the plantation with Agent Keen and Dr. Barnett. Brad asked him how the girl looked and the deputy said she looked the same as usual to him.

"Thank God," Leigh said with a shaky sigh.

As they were leaving the building, Brad's phone rang. "Sheriff Watson from next door," Brad said, reading the caller ID. He listened for a few seconds, said, "I'm on my way," and hung up. "There was a big explosion on six twelve. Seems it came from the levee right there at the county line. Sheriff Watson's on his way out there with firefighters and units."

"That's out at the equipment barn by RRI's land?" Winter asked.

Brad nodded.

Winter said, "I think I saw that explosion when we were in Klein's suite."

"I need to check it out," Brad said. "I can have somebody take you home."

"I'll go with you," Leigh said.

"If it's going to take a while, Winter can drive you home and I'll get a ride," Brad said. "I know you want to see Cyn and I'm sure she wants to see you."

"I think Cyn's in good hands," Leigh said, smiling and slapping his shoulder playfully from the backseat.

111

AS SOON AS THEY DROVE OUT OF TUNICA COUNTY, they ran into a line of vehicles behind a highway patrol cruiser with flashing blue lights. Using the shoulder of the road, Winter pulled even with the cop. A patrolman wearing a Smokey the Bear hat with a plastic cover and a reflective vest over his raincoat was waving cars through, and he gave Winter an irritated glare. Brad climbed out and spoke to the patrolman, who nodded and waved Winter through.

At the gravel road ahead on the right, a sheriff's department car illuminated the roadside. A female deputy looked in at Brad using her flashlight.

"Sheriff's expecting me," Brad said.

"He's on up this road at an equipment shed, Sheriff Barnett," the deputy said.

"What's the deal?" Winter asked.

"Explosion. Big hole in the building, and what's left of a limousine. Just park out of the way of the fire trucks. I'll radio Sheriff Watson you're coming in."

As he drove in, Winter slowed and looked at the SUVs parked beside the graveled road at the mouth of the woods. A deputy was using his flashlight to peer into the last one, a Toyota Highlander with Tunica County tags. The other two parked behind it—a Yukon and a Trailblazer—had Tennessee plates and dark film on the windows.

Winter drove out into the open landscape. The fenced lot around the barn was alive with the flashing lights of cruisers, EMT buses, pickup trucks, and three fire trucks. Winter pulled through the open gates and parked. A dozen deputies were walking around the lot, shining flashlights on the ground to search for evidence.

There was indeed a hole in the barn, although the word *hole* didn't begin to describe the opening in the shed, which was large enough to push an eighteen-wheeler rig through sideways. The aluminum roof that remained was blackened and peeled sharply back, and a fan-shaped blast crater extended out from it for fifty feet. The limousine, only distinguishable as such by its length, looked like a giant had picked it up, plucked off the tires, twisted it like a pretzel, and drop-kicked it through the hurricane fence. A section of the fence was down, and the poles that had held it up were bent over or snapped off.

"Stay here," Brad told Leigh.

"Don't worry," she said, looking off to her right where her parcel was located. "I'm as close as I want to be."

Winter followed Brad to the sheriff standing at the mouth of the hole, using a powerful battery-operated searchlight to peer into the building. Winter could see other moving light beams scattered around inside the structure. The sheriff saw Brad and handed the light to the deputy beside him.

"Brad," Watson said.

"Sheriff Watson," Brad said. "You know who was in there?"

" 'Was' is the operational word," he said. "I don't know who they were, but they ain't nothing at all now. I'll get some dogs here from Jackson to help find the pieces. Doesn't look like there are any survivors. They found a pair of boots with the feet still in 'em, some meat and scraps and cloth so far. Hopefully we can find some wallets or something. Whatever they were doing went wrong. I don't imagine they knew what hit 'em. Looks like they must have had a few hundred pounds of dynamite in there that went up."

"Sheriff!" a deputy hollered as he ran up, holding something pinched between his gloved fingers like it smelled bad. "It's a gun with a silencer on it. Was back over there by the bottom of the fence."

"Sure is," Sheriff Watson said. "That ain't any construction equipment I know about."

"Destruction equipment's more like it," the deputy added.

Winter looked at the remains of an MP5SD with a blasted away stock and a bent suppresser. "Have you run the plate on that limo and the other SUVs?"

"I did," Sheriff Watson said. "Limo belongs to an RRI corporation. You know of it?"

Brad looked at Winter, and Winter nodded his agreement that he should tell the sheriff. "The Roundtable casino is owned by RRI. They own all that land they've been clearing there in my county."

"They own this land and the building too," Watson said. "Why you suppose they had a machine gun?"

"I couldn't tell you," Brad said. "It's a foreign corporation."

"Foreign? Maybe it's some terror mess going on and they were making those fertilizer bombs to attack Memphis with. I'm going to let the ATF figure it out. I called them soon as we rolled up."

"Maybe you should call Homeland Security," Winter said. "Give them those vehicle tag numbers."

"First I'm going to search those vehicles," Watson said. "Might get some idea of what they were doing here."

"You could," Winter said. "but they could be booby-trapped or some damned thing. If it's a terror cell, the Feds will want to get right on it."

"You run the other plates?" Brad asked.

Watson took out a notebook and opened it, using a penlight to read what he'd written. "The Toyota is registered to an Albert W. White, lives in your county."

"He's the security chief at the Roundtable," Winter said.

"You know him?" Watson asked Winter.

"We know him," Brad said. "He was assistant chief of police in West Memphis. Been with the casino since RRI bought it."

"He clean?" Watson asked.

"Seemed all right."

"The other two go to a Trinity Corporation. You know, I believe I'll call the FBI, right now. They want to call in Homeland Security, they can do it," Watson said. "Shit, we can't do much. No fire, no bodies, no electricity. And we got this freezing rain that's going to get a lot worse pretty quick. Who would you suggest I talk to at the casino about this?"

"The manager is Pierce Mulvane," Brad said.

"You should ask for a man named Kurt Klein," Winter said. "He's the owner and maybe he can help you figure out who was here and why. Be a good start."

"I'll do that," Watson said. He made a note and closed the pad. "The number we had for a contact for RRI is connected to an answering machine."

"Well, looks like you've got this under control. If I can help you out, let me know," Brad said.

"Your casino or not, this is my mess," Watson said. "I wish to God it wasn't."

As Winter and Brad were walking back to the Jeep, Brad said, "You think the cutouts got Styer?"

"Looks like it. I think they followed White here. Maybe Styer was with him or they found out he was meeting Styer. Styer could have come out in the stretch. If they did get him, he got them back. Soon a lot of men in suits are going to swarm this place, and that could be pretty unpleasant. I think we should get clear."

At least I can stop looking over my shoulder for a while, Winter thought.

112

THE FREEZING RAIN DROPLETS PECKED AT ALEXA'S face as she walked toward the front porch, hands cuffed at her back, a silenced gun pressed into her spine. Styer was walking behind her, Cynthia on her left. "You try and warn them, I'll have to kill them."

A backlit figure appeared at the window, vanished, and the door opened. Roy Bishop and a young deputy sheriff were visible just inside.

"Hello, Cyn," Jeff said.

"Where is young Hampton?" Styer asked in character. Alexa knew they would be fooled by the purloined voice.

"Asleep," Roy said, smiling and extending his hand to shake Styer's. "Good to see you . . ." He stopped and a cloud passed quickly behind his eyes as he realized something was wrong.

Alexa didn't feel the gun leave her back or see Styer's hand come up until she heard the pops, which sounded like finger snaps from the .22, spaced impossibly close together. Both men collapsed, shot at close range through their foreheads.

Cynthia yelped.

Styer shoved Alexa hard from behind, and as she flew through the open front door, she tripped on Chief

Deputy Bishop's body and crashed to the wooden floor. Cynthia went past her, landing on her right side.

Without her arms free to slow her fall, Alexa's torso and the side of her face struck the floor hard. She waited, sure Styer would shoot her, too, but he grabbed her by her coat collar and dragged her a few feet into the house before dropping her.

Kneeling beside her, Styer said, "I think my disguise fooled them."

"Dear God, please. You said you wouldn't hurt them," Alexa begged.

"They didn't feel anything. What kind of man do you think I am?"

Cynthia whimpered loudly, but Styer aimed the gun at her and she quieted.

As Styer moved over her, Alexa's last conscious thoughts concerned Hamp and Estelle.

113

WINTER GOT THE CASINO'S MAIN NUMBER FROM information and asked the hotel operator to ring suite 825 for him.

After several rings, Kurt Klein's voice came on. "Yes," he answered pleasantly. He had no idea who was calling, because there was no caller ID on hotel phones.

"It's Winter Massey."

There was a short pause before Klein said, "Yes, what can I do for you?"

"There was the flash of an explosion when we were there. You and I were chatting, remember?"

"Yes? And . . . ?"

"At the time I thought it was lightning, a transformer blowing or something, but it was actually dynamite and a lot of it. It came from an equipment storage building of yours across the Tunica County line, near the river. The place is crawling with cops, fire trucks, and EMS. Albert White's SUV was there, along with what's left of a limousine you own."

"Okay, Mr. Massey, and I'm wondering why this is of interest to me?"

Winter knew by his voice that it was very much of interest to him, and he was sure Klein knew who had been out there and why.

"I just called to tell you that the sheriff of that county is going to call you very soon, as will the FBI and ATF. At least one of the people out there had a machine gun, an MP5SD, which if you look it up on the Internet under Heckler & Koch, you will understand the significance of. I do not want to know who was carrying that particular military-use-only weapon. Whoever it was out there is now scattered all over the landscape. I kind of thought you might want to make some inquiries of your own."

Winter snapped the phone closed.

"You think he knew anything about it?" Brad asked.

"I doubt the old bastard is going to get any sleep tonight."

"Did you notice that there were none of Klein's security men at the meeting tonight?" Brad asked.

"Why would Mr. Klein need security people?" Leigh asked.

"He might need to hire some new ones," Winter said.

"Well, it's too late to eat," Leigh said.

"You have to be tired," Brad said.

"Not too tired to cook you fellows a nice thick steak. Let's stop at the grocery and pick up a few, and we'll go to the house. I bet your deputies could eat a hot meal about now."

114

STYER PUT A KNEE IN CYNTHIA'S BACK AND TAPED her mouth shut. Then he removed the explosives belt she had been wearing and laid it aside. "Remember the bomb downstairs, Cynthia," he whispered tenderly as he secured her hands and lashed her ankles with tape.

He surveyed the blood rapidly pooling under Alexa's head and listened for any sounds of people coming to investigate the noise made by bodies hitting the floor. After a few seconds, with only the sound of the grandfather clock ticking, he heard something in the back of the house—a motor perhaps. Moving slowly down the hall he went into the kitchen, which was filled with the smell of coffee. On the table he spotted a copy of a tabloid lying open, a cup of coffee beside it. It was still hot and freshly poured.

He moved to the closed door of the utility room and realized the sound was a clothes dryer running. Someone was doing the laundry. He heard the lid of a washing machine close, the unmistakable sound of the dial being twisted and pulled, and the water running into the tub.

Crossing the hall, Styer moved back into the kitchen and sat down at the table to wait, placing the gun in his lap.

The door opened and the maid came out and turned into the kitchen, her arms holding a basket filled with folded towels. When she saw Styer, she smiled, glad to see him. Most of the locals knew the physician. "You pour you some coffee, Doc, and let me go fold these towels up. Been a busy and tragic time around here lately. I'm way behind. I didn't know you was coming out. Take your hat and that wet coat off and stay awhile."

"I'll be here just a little while," he said.

The maid's expression changed slowly, and she tilted her head. He knew he had been pressed to make a quick study of this subject. His disguise depended on people not knowing the man more than superficially or getting a good look, and it hadn't fooled that chief deputy either. The woman's eyes narrowed slightly and Styer saw that despite the wide-brimmed hat pulled low, the accent and pitch of the voice, and the resemblance, she knew.

When the gun came up, she just stood wide-eyed—the proverbial deer frozen in the headlights.

"If you want to live," he said in his own voice, "tell me where the boy is."

"Gone," she said, turning her eyes to the counter, where the block held a selection of knives. He knew she was trying to decide if she could get to them before he could shoot her.

"I don't want to hurt him," he said. "Word of honor."

The big woman hurled the basket at him. For her size, she was amazingly agile, but of course she couldn't outrun a bullet.

115

THE SLEET HAD BECOME A CHILLED RAIN THAT coated the tree limbs, roads, and wires with ice. Brad said that if it stopped soon, like the forecasters said it would, the damage wouldn't amount to much more than a few snapped limbs and fender benders.

Winter used the few minutes Leigh was spending inside the grocery store to search the interior of the Jeep. He found an audio transmitter the size of a coat button attached to the backside of the rearview mirror, rolled down the window, and tossed it out across the parking lot, certain that the listeners were busy figuring what to do about their dead team members.

While they waited, Winter shared his theory about what had happened at the barn. "Styer was probably in charge of getting White to do a taped confession and the cutouts figured out who Styer was and followed him there. I expect the explosives were set off during the shoot-out."

"Could Styer have been disguised well enough to be one of Klein's guys?"

"A cakewalk for him."

"It's just hard to imagine," Brad said. "At least they let Cyn go beforehand. Sure solved your problem."

He dialed Alexa, got her voicemail, and left the message. "Lex, we're heading to the Gardner house. See you when you get there." He closed the phone. "I know she's there. She probably can't hear it ringing through her purse."

Through the window Winter saw Leigh checking out and chattering happily with the young cashier.

"She's something," Brad said.

"Yep," Winter agreed. He thought it was amazing that, after all she'd been through, she could be thinking about feeding a bunch of people. She was something, all right. Delta women were a breed apart.

"You know, don't you?" Brad asked him meaningfully.

"Yeah."

"I think everything is going to work out now. She's the girl I fell in love with. I hate that she went through all this grief, but I think it's going to be Brad and Leigh again, like it should have been."

"Does Cynthia have any idea?"

Brad stared at Winter. "All this just happened."

"Well," Winter started, "it's none of my business, but I have eyes. Somebody else must have noticed. It's fairly obvious."

"What's that?"

"Cynthia's got your eyes and your smile. I understand why you and Leigh didn't want to tell her, but doesn't you guys being patched up mean you can tell her now? Or will she keep thinking Jacob is her father?" He saw Brad's eyes change and his face slacken, and only then did he realize that the poor guy had had no clue about his daughter. Winter felt that old hollow, what-the-hell-have-I-done feeling, and he knew he couldn't make it right. "Listen, Brad, maybe . . ."

Staring out at Leigh, Brad opened the door to the Jeep and strode to the store without seeming to notice the icy rain. He stood outside and waited for Leigh to approach. Her smile vanished when she stepped out and he started talking to her. He saw her chin drop before rising again, and she nodded. Winter didn't have to hear what they were saying to understand that Leigh had just confirmed what Winter had assumed Brad knew all along. He knew that Cynthia was why Leigh had married Jacob Gardner so suddenly after she turned her back on Brad.

Winter cursed himself for screwing with something he had no business getting involved with.

116

ALEXA'S HEAD THROBBED WHERE STYER HAD pistol-whipped her unconscious. She opened her eyes to find herself lying on her stomach on the polished wooden floor of Hamp's bedroom. In the dim light from a TV set with the sound turned off, she could see the figures of Hamp and Cyn lying on two beds whose heads met at a corner desk, a flat L-shaped piece of furniture with a writing surface and bookshelves that rose to the ceiling. The Gardner children faced her with their hands behind them and ankles secured. Hamp's were tied with thin cord. Like her, their mouths were taped shut. At least Styer hadn't killed them, but why had he not finished her off?

Hamp lifted his head, and his eyes opened wider in alarm. Alexa nodded at him, and he lowered his head. Alexa saw that Cyn was crying, tears glistening on the bridge of her nose, her body shaking. When Alexa tried bringing her cuffed hands under her body, the pressure on her neck made her realize that Styer had looped a cord around her neck and tied the other end to the cuff chain. Her ankles were bound with thin nylon cord, probably cut from the Venetian blinds in the room.

She pressed her face against the polished oak floorboards. If she could catch the sticky edge of the tape on the floor, she could use pressure and movement to peel it off her cheek. That way she could at least comfort the children.

She knew Winter, Leigh, and Brad would walk in soon and Styer would have the drop on them. She had seen him shoot two men with no more effort or hesitation than a horse flicked his tail to shoo a fly. She knew she was no match for Styer, but she had to become one, no matter what. She concentrated her energy on the tape. The headache slowly drifted away as she told herself, *Don't rush and don't make noise.*

117

WHEN BRAD AND LEIGH FINISHED TALKING OUT-side the grocery store, they hugged for a long time, and Winter saw Leigh wipe tears from her eyes. The sleet was coating the windshield, being cleared by the wipers. If the sight of the sheriff and the plantation owner embracing outside the grocery was shocking, you couldn't tell from the woman who walked past them and nonchalantly said hello. They returned the greeting while they were still hugging each other, and Leigh laughed after the woman went inside. After Brad took the grocery bags, they ran to the Jeep and jumped inside.

"I guess I should be mad at you," Leigh said to Winter.

"I thought I was the only one who knew how much Cyn resembled Brad."

"I've got a daughter," Brad said wonderingly, smiling at Leigh in the backseat. They clasped hands momentarily.

"I was sitting here thinking I'd screwed up," Winter said.

"It's fine," Leigh said. "Better than fine."

"Better than fine," Brad repeated.

"I've always wondered if I would ever be able to tell Brad," she said. "Now, I just have to tell Cyn. I've had some strange conversations with my daughter, but this one is going to take the cake."

"How do you think she'll react?" Brad asked almost sheepishly.

"I think she'll be pleased after it sinks in. She's always liked you."

With a wave of panic, something occurred to Winter that should have hit him much earlier. The deputy said Alexa was with Dr. Barnett and Cynthia. He didn't know how they all three had ended up together at the plantation. Thinking about it now, he realized how odd that was.

118

STYER FELT THE DOCTOR'S CELL PHONE IN HIS pocket vibrating, and took it out and read the display. He decided he had to answer it, because this time it was the sheriff. He tested his voice, decided it was right, and pressed the green button.

"What?" he answered.

"I'm with Leigh and Winter," Brad said. "We're heading out to Leigh's. Daddy, I didn't ask before, but how did Alexa wind up with you and Cynthia?"

"Right after I talked to you, Alexa, who was heading out here, saw us getting into my car at the Blue & White and she stopped. She offered to drive Cyn home. I hitched a ride, thinking I should stay with Cynthia. Like I said, Cyn was upset and . . ."

"Winter wants to talk to Alexa. She close by?"

"She's upstairs with Cynthia. I think Cyn's taking a bath."

"We're still a few minutes out. Leigh picked up some steaks. You hungry?"

"I could eat," Styer said.

"By the way, do you know if Woody let Ruger out?"

"Yes," Styer said. "Woody told me he was going by to 'walk him.' "

Styer hung up and smiled. The rain was really coming

down now. He inclined his head and listened for any sound from the boy's bedroom directly above the kitchen. He wondered if Alexa was still out cold. He had thumped her pretty good. He hadn't needed to kill her, but she would die anyway in short order. While he'd been talking to Barnett, he'd heard Gardner and Massey talking in the background. Leigh Gardner and Winter Massey. Styer smiled. Life was good. Life was very, very good to those who deserved it.

All he had to do was add the explosive from Cyn's belt to the bomb that he had placed in the basement and, after Massey and the sheriff and the woman were down, he'd get clear and set it off. The explosion would bring the deputy from the road, but Styer would deal with him and be long gone before anybody suspected it was a bomb and not a natural gas explosion.

Afterward, he would change into the benign salesman he had ID for and fly to New York, and from there he'd make his way to his apartment in Paris for a well-deserved rest.

After no more than a minute in the basement, Styer went back up into the kitchen, set down his Ruger, covered it with the maid's tabloid, and took off the doctor's wide-brimmed Stetson.

Opening his valise, Styer lifted out the cell-phone remote trigger and slipped it into the left pocket of his cardigan. He also removed the other tools he would need when Massey showed up.

Walking to the front, Styer looked out the open shades of a window and saw the cruiser at the base of the driveway.

He thought he heard the creaking of floorboards and listened, trying to get the direction of the sound.

119

ALEXA WORKED TO FREE HER MOUTH, REALIZING that if Styer's disguised voice was carrying through the floor that her cheek was pressed against, then he would hear any loud movement from the room above. He was talking to someone, but since nobody had come in, she was pretty sure he was on the telephone.

She looked up at the children and saw that Cyn had stopped crying and was watching her. Hamp continued to wriggle and she shook her head, hoping that he would understand that she wanted him to be still. If he fell off the bed, Styer would come up and see the tape, which was beginning to roll toward her mouth.

She saw Hamp stop moving and look at her. Moving faster, she felt the tape stick fast and she pressed her cheek against the floor and pressed down hard as she moved her head. The tape stuck fast to the floor and remained there as she moved her face as far as she could move without rolling.

"Guys," she whispered. "Hamp, be still. He can hear us."

Hamp shook his head and started wriggling again.

While she was trying to figure out the next step, Hamp sat up and brought his hands around from behind him. Loose cord hung from his left wrist until he pulled it off and removed the duct tape from his face. As soon as it came free, he smiled at Alexa.

"The Great Mephisto," he mouthed, taking a bow.

Alexa smiled.

Cyn nodded. Hamp tore off the tape that was binding his sister.

Okay, Alexa thought, as she watched Hamp in his pajamas and magician's cape slip from the bed, cross the floor carefully, kneel behind her, and start untying the cord knots on the cuffs. Seconds later, she brought her hands through and looked gleefully at the cuffs as she untied her ankles. Hamp reached to the lowest shelf, put something in the pocket of his pajama shirt, and released his sister. She slowly sat up.

Alexa managed to untie the cord around her ankles and stood. Hamp reached out, touched her wrists, took a bent paper clip from his pocket, and in three or four seconds, opened her handcuffs. He bowed again and tossed the impromptu key onto the bed.

Alexa motioned to the children to stay in their places and moved to the window. She heard a door close downstairs and looked out the window, which she unlocked and slowly opened. Looking out through the sleet, she saw headlights approaching from about half a mile away. She knew she had to move fast. The porch roof angled gently away from the house, and she decided that it hadn't yet collected enough ice to prevent an escape down the trellis, which she believed would support their weight. She turned to the children and beckoned them to move toward her. She turned back, slipped out of the window, and found herself face-to-face with a dark figure standing on the porch roof. A firm, wet hand covered her mouth to keep her from screaming.

"It's okay, Lex," Winter whispered.

She saw the headlights of the Jeep that was stopped beside the cruiser.

Alexa climbed outside and Winter handed her his coat. As he climbed carefully and silently into the room, gun in hand, Alexa saw the aluminum bat in Hamp's hands. When he realized there was no danger, he lowered it from a striking position and set it on the bed. He handed his sister a parka that had been hung on his bed-post by its hood.

She whispered to Winter, "Styer killed Roy and the other deputy. And he said there's a remotely triggered bomb planted downstairs in the basement." The children climbed out carefully to join her in the freezing rain.

Winter grabbed the bat and told her, "Be careful, it's slippery. Get the kids down the road to the cruiser. Tell Leigh not to stop until she gets them to Brad's office. Help's on the way out. I'll throw the bat downstairs when I find Styer."

"He's disguised as Dr. Barnett."

"We know," Winter said. "Brad figured his father knew Ruger is a she."

120

AFTER WINTER MADE SURE ALEXA AND THE Gardner children were on the ground, he slipped rapidly down the rear service steps and peered into the kitchen, where the tip of a silencer was visible under an open tabloid on the table. He saw what appeared to be a wide blood smear leading to a utility room, but he couldn't take time to look further. Roy Bishop and the other deputy were dead, and most likely Estelle was too.

With the cocked Reeder .45 in hand, safety off and armed with hollow-points, Winter looked down the hallway and moved back out of sight behind the door to the den. By looking at the mirror on a coat tree, Winter could see down the hallway to Styer standing near the front door. Although he knew Styer's gun was in the kitchen, he figured the professional was armed and that the smaller gun was a backup.

Winter took his cell phone out and waited to press SEND until he was ready. Brad had given him his cell phone with the doctor's number already keyed in as a way to talk to Styer if it became necessary.

When Styer took out the phone, Winter stepped out thirty feet behind him and aimed at Styer's head. He assumed since Styer was wearing a coat inside the house he was wearing a ballistic vest under it.

Winter had a clean shot, and a bullet fired from the Reeder would blow a large hole in the mass murderer's head. He had pictured this moment for years, and he knew he should kill Styer now like the mad dog he was. Winter, standing there, with Styer unaware and empty-handed, could not squeeze the trigger, the reality was so abhorrent.

"Hands behind your head, Styer!" Winter yelled out. "Now!"

"You going to arrest me, Deputy Massey?" Styer asked calmly. "Or shoot me in the back?"

Styer sprang through the living room door, leaving Winter wondering if he'd just made the last mistake of his life.

121

FROM BEHIND A TREE, A SCOPED AR-15 AT THE ready, Brad watched the figures of Alexa, Cyn, and Hamp leave the cover of the bushes and run down toward the cruiser and the Jeep. The young deputy sheriff who'd been at the roadblock was behind another tree on the opposite side of the yard, armed with a riot gun.

Brad used a flashlight to set the deputy in motion, and

then ran to cover the rear of the house from the southwest corner as Winter had said he should. Winter had told them not to enter until he signaled that it was safe to do so, and to shoot Styer down if he left the house. Winter had wanted a clean area of operation where the only other person moving around inside the house would be Styer.

Help was on the way, but the cruisers and EMS were to keep their blue lights off until Brad told them to move up to the house. All he told them was that a killer was impersonating his father.

The deputy outside with the shotgun had been certain that the man in the truck was Dr. Barnett. Now, with Alexa and the children out successfully and all four sides of the house covered from opposite corners, all they had to do was sit tight and wait.

If Brad got a shot at Styer, he would take it, but firing at his father's image, even if the man had probably killed his father, wasn't going to be easy. He sincerely hoped Winter would make that unnecessary.

Brad heard a series of shots fired rapidly inside the house, and clicked off his safety. Watching the kitchen window, he saw a shadow move quickly past the glass. A few seconds later, the interior of the house was plunged into darkness. Styer had thrown the main breaker.

122

WINTER KNEW STYER COULD BE ANYWHERE IN THE rooms that extended along the north side of the house. He had positioned himself at the end of the main hallway where he could see from the front door to the back and down the service hall. With his back to the den door at the base of the service stairs leading up to the second floor, he had Styer hemmed into the north side of the house. If Styer went out through a window to flank his adversary, Brad or the deputy would be positioned at the house's corners to get a clean shot at him.

With his .45 ready, Winter waited, listening for a floorboard to creak, a shadow from the lighted butler's pantry, or Styer's entry into the service hall. Styer suddenly appeared there, faced Winter with a gun in each of his hands, and began firing both at Winter as he moved into the kitchen. Reflexively, Winter rolled back out of the line of sight, but too late, he felt a dull push on his left thigh.

After Styer went in the kitchen, Winter reached down and brought up fingers slicked with his own blood. He could stand, because Styer's bullet had made a through-and-through wound. Aside from the bleeding, the shot wouldn't do anything but slow him down and leave a trail of large red drops.

He was about to change position to cover the back and the kitchen doors when he heard a sharp snap and the lights went out.

Winter slipped off his shoes, and with warm blood running down a leg that didn't want to bear his weight, he started slowly up the rear service steps, holding on to the railing to steady himself.

An explosion followed by the sound of falling glass told him Styer had opened up with one of the handguns, firing at Brad through a window.

If Brad was down, Styer could get away, but Winter knew that fleeing while his arch enemy was alive was the last thing that Paulus Styer would do. Now he had an escape route, which he would use only after he was finished. Winter was going to make him work hard for a kill.

"Gawd alive," Styer shouted in an exaggerated drawl. "I've done gone and kilt my own man-child!"

123

BACK IN THE DARK KITCHEN, STYER REACHED INTO the valise to retrieve his night vision goggles, which he slipped on. He snapped on the power switch and the room came alive. He grinned and looked through the window over the sink to admire his handiwork. Barnett's body was on its back in the grass, the rifle off to one side.

Seconds later, a deputy made the mistake of running to check on his boss. Styer aimed his Glock at the side of the cop's head and squeezed the trigger twice. Thirty feet away, the young man collapsed into the icy grass like a cardboard cutout hit by a sudden wind. His right boot quaked as his neurons figured out they had been disconnected from their command center.

Styer dropped the mostly spent magazines one at a time, replacing one before going to the next gun in case Massey used the pause to attack. Styer went into the eerie green interior of the service hall, aiming the Glocks before him.

Massey was no longer in the doorway to the den, and Styer looked down to see his abandoned shoes and the dark pool of blood. He followed the large wet drops across the floor and onto the stairs where there was more blood smeared on the handrail. He decided Massey would be moving down the hallway upstairs, in an attempt to flank him. When he found the bound-up Keen and the children, it would slow him. Styer could go upstairs and deal with him there, but he would probably get Keen and the kids outside on the roof. Being the valiant idiot he was, Winter would stay inside and keep moving down the hall using the front stairs to flank his adversary.

He had expected more from Massey, and was disappointed in him. Wounded or not, the flanking maneuver was too obvious. Civilian life and a family had slowed his instincts. Styer almost felt sorry for him.

Styer turned and moved slowly down the main hall to wait for Massey to come sneaking along in the dark so he could kill him. Time was getting short. Backup would be coming from town. He would get away, even if an army was surrounding the house, because he had planned for that possibility.

124

WINTER FIGURED STYER HAD CUT OFF THE ELECtricity because it gave him an edge, and since Styer had to figure that Winter knew the layout of the house better than he did, he had to be prepared to operate in the darkness. Only night vision goggles would explain that.

He put himself in Styer's head and stopped in his tracks. He knew that Styer could follow his blood trail. If he moved, he could be heading straight into Styer, who might be waiting for him at a point where he could watch both sets of stairs and the hallway.

He opened Hamp's bedroom door, smiling when the hinges squeaked. Inside, he took out his phone and dialed Leigh's cell phone. After a brief conversation, he left the room and started toward the front stairs, the clock in his head ticking down.

125

IN THE LIVING ROOM WITH THE GLOCKS IN HIS hands, Paulus Styer sat in a wing chair with a view of the front stairs. He had heard a creaking as Winter opened the door to the boy's bedroom and smiled. Three minutes or less to wait. Winter would free Alexa and the brats and stay behind to cover their escape. Styer imagined Alexa and the children straggling across the porch roof, climbing down the lattice, and he figured that Leigh Gardner was probably outside in the Jeep—a frightened sow who would not wander far from her trapped piglets. He didn't care about her. Massey would soon come to keep Styer busy while they got away. But since Alexa knew about the bomb, he would start to look for him immediately, he would have to kill her before he esçaped. Without her to tell the authorities about it, the bomb would take up his pursuers' time and a nice slice of their budget.

Now his entire focus was on Massey—as he had intended from the start. All the rest had just been window dressing. Divine providence, in the form of Kurt Klein, had made it possible.

Styer stifled a yawn with his sleeve, then rested both guns flat against the tops of his legs, ready as a man could be for the next few minutes.

126

WINTER WAS AT THE TOP OF THE FRONT STAIRS, just out of sight from below.

"Hey, Styer!" Winter yelled down. "You ready to die?"

Styer remained silent, not about to give away his position.

"This is what you wanted, right?" Winter called. "All this death and destruction just for me. Man, you are one sick son of a bitch."

His taunts were answered only by the ticking grandfather clock.

"Tell you what," he called. "Turn the lights back on. We stand toe to toe, count to five, and draw. Winner takes all. What do you say? You can't take me in a fair fight, and you know it, you cowardly sack of shit!"

Winter imagined Styer down there listening, wanting to answer. Winter needed only the first gun flash to give him Styer's position. He was betting he could fire the .45 and nail Styer before his enemy could get off a second, better-aimed round. Assuming, as was his custom, that Styer was wearing night vision goggles, that would mean the first flash from Styer's own gun would blind the killer momentarily.

When the grandfather clock started chiming midnight,

Winter raised Hamp's aluminum bat. Five seconds later, the lights in the house came on, and he hurled the bat down the stairs, pleased by the amount of racket it made on the oaken steps. Following the bat's path, gun in front of him, Winter started down the stairs, leaning against the rail. His wounded leg failed him and he fell, his gun leaving his hand and flying down ahead of him, the stainless steel catching the light as it careened off the polished stairs. The sharp wooden edges of each step battered him as he fell. He was aware of Paulus Styer standing up from a chair, dropping one of the guns to the floor, and clawing at the goggles. Despite that, Styer aimed at the staircase, firing rapidly.

127

ALEXA REACHED THE BACKYARD UNARMED, AND spotted Brad and the deputy lying still in the falling rain. She had gone to them, planning to slow only long enough to get a handgun before going inside as Winter had asked her to do. She saw that both of the men had been shot in their heads. A round had hit Brad's head at an angle, taking out Brad's left eye and chipping out a piece of the socket, where rose-colored blood coned down toward the ground. The deputy had two clean holes in his temple. She was lifting the deputy's coat for his handgun when she saw Brad move his hand and blink his right eye. She could see now that the wound had entered his left eye socket and exited at his temple.

"Can you hear me?" she asked him.

He didn't respond.

"Wait here and stay still. Can you do that?"

He nodded and closed his eye. She put his cap over his face to protect him from the freezing rain.

Taking his rifle, Alexa ran to the back door and turned the knob. It was locked. No surprise. Using the key Leigh had given her, Alexa unlocked the door and opened it slowly. Stealthily, she slid into the mudroom, feeling the heat as she eased the door shut. Using her hands to feel, she located the door to the utility room, where the breaker box was, and leaned the rifle against the wall. She heard Winter calling out to Styer at the other end of the house. As she opened the door she stopped when her foot struck something large. Reaching farther, she felt the warm figure of Estelle. Alexa found her neck, felt a weak pulse, stood, and stepped over the woman. Using only her hands, she found the open metal door to the breaker box. She followed the row of breakers with her fingertips, found the larger main button, and hearing the bat clattering on the stairs, she flipped it and was rewarded by white light.

Leaving the utility room to the sound of gunfire, Alexa shouldered the rifle and moved into the main hallway. When Styer moved into view, she realized her scope lens was iced over and fogged. She looked over it and squeezed the trigger, missing wide, the bullet shattering the glass in the front door behind him.

Still facing forty-five degrees from her, Styer swung the gun across his chest and aimed it at her.

Alexa kept firing, adjusting her aim.

Styer was hit and fell, dropping the gun as he went down.

As she came up the hall, her barrel pointed at him, he rolled onto his back and laughed, rose-colored bubbles issuing from his nostrils and mouth. The bullet must have entered his chest after passing through his left shoulder.

As she got to him, she kicked the Glocks away and turned to see Winter getting to his feet and bending down to get his gun.

"You all right?" she asked him. Her ears were ringing from the gunshots.

"No," he said, limping painfully to lean against the handrail.

"Well, I guess you are going to have to arrest me after all," Styer said from the ground below her as he groaned in pain. When he spoke, his words sounded wet, lubricated by the blood rising from his punctured lungs. "You know, Massey—"

His words ended in an explosion from the gun in Winter's hand. Through the new ringing in her ears, she heard the crisp sound of a shell casing click on the floor.

Looking down, she saw that Styer was still smiling despite the new black hole below his chin. Whatever thoughts he'd had were scrambled somewhere in the knot of brains that trailed across the shiny floor beyond the exploded top of his head.

"Jesus Christ, Massey!" Alexa screamed. "Why did you do that?"

Winter shook his head.

Then she saw the small black object in Styer's right hand, his thumb resting on the button. She reached down and carefully took the cell phone in her hands, snapped open the back of it, and, using her fingernail, removed and disconnected the battery.

"The remote," she said. "Cell phone remote."

"The remote?" he asked in total seriousness.

"To detonate the bomb." She stared at him speechless for a long few seconds, shaking her head slowly. "I'd forgotten about it. Thank God you remembered. You *did* remember, right?"

Winter winced, snapped the safety on the Reeder up, pushed it into its holster, and sat down on the bottom stair, his face reflecting only a portion of the agony she knew he was feeling. Alexa walked over, plopped on the stair beside Winter, and put her arm on his shoulder.

"Christ," she said. "Thank you."

It hit her that Winter hadn't seen the phone, nor had he remembered the bomb below them. It came to her as surely as if he opened his mouth and explained it to her. He had shot an obviously dying Styer because he didn't want Alexa to have even a monster like Styer's death on her conscience. As it was, she had merely wounded Styer to save Winter's life. His bullet had removed the killer's death from her gun and her conscience.

Winter had often told her that killing a felon, even in the line of duty, was only a little less damaging than dying yourself.

128

SUNDAY

THE REINFORCEMENTS HAD ARRIVED HALF AN HOUR after Styer died. They took Estelle out to a waiting ambulance and put Brad in another, both headed to a Memphis trauma center. Both Estelle and Brad needed better medical care than they could have gotten locally. Winter rode to Memphis in a cruiser. Alexa stayed at the house.

FBI and ATF agents arrived, fresh from the equipment barn, and everybody waited in a shed away from the house while the ATF found the bomb in the basement, disarmed it, and carted it away.

It was almost noon on Sunday before the doctors at Baptist Memorial in Memphis told Leigh and the children that Brad was going to be as good as ever—except he would only have one eye. Hamp said it was a lucky thing he hadn't lost the eye he aimed with.

Estelle had two .22-caliber bullets removed and the doctors were hopeful of her full recovery if there were no complications like migrating blood clots or infections. One of the bullets had hit her in the back of her head and knocked her out, and the second was stopped by her spine, thankfully not severing her cord. After the operation she had regained consciousness and had promptly asked for a Coke.

The FBI had found Jason Parr's corpse in his suite at the Roundtable. Pierce Mulvane's body was found near the exploded equipment shed. Best they could figure, he was dead from a gunshot wound in his forehead. He had been in the trunk of the limousine when the blast hurled his corpse fifty feet into a pile of tree limbs, where he'd hung across a branch like a Christmas-tree ornament. Woody had located Dr. Barnett's body in a closet in his home.

Kurt Klein had left for Europe that morning after he'd given a statement. All he knew was that Mulvane had missed a planned dinner, and he was asleep in bed when the sheriff from the next county had awakened him.

Winter's hip was sore from the bullet wound and he had three fractured ribs from his fall down the stairs. He ate a late breakfast in the hospital cafeteria and looked at the television screen, where a newscaster was getting about ninety percent of the facts wrong on the events in Tunica County. It was something he was accustomed to.

Sean had wanted to come back to Memphis, but he'd convinced her to wait for him to return to Concord.

Winter suddenly felt a presence over his shoulder and sipped his coffee as a man he thought he'd never lay eyes on again sat down across from him. The cutout put his coffee cup down on the table.

"Been a while," he said.

"A year," Winter said to the man whose name he had never gotten when they'd met at a small airport in Arkansas to discuss Paulus Styer.

"How's the leg?" the man asked.

"I've had worse," Winter said.

"We didn't imagine you'd come out of this in one piece," he said. "You never fail to surprise, Massey."

"I'd sure like to stop doing that. What do I call you?"

"Mike."

"Mike it is." Winter waited.

"Odd you never mentioned you had Styer's DNA."

"You never asked."

"That's fair. I thought I owed you, so we're taking care of the details on this one."

"When have you not?"

"We also know you moved a friend of ours in the SUV. Took a while to figure that one out."

"I don't know what you're talking about."

"Of course you don't. You know, we could use someone like you."

"Work's too hard, it's dirty as hell, and I don't like your management."

"We have new managers now," Mike said.

"Yeah, but you keep getting them from the same sewer." Winter stood. "Try not to burn your mouth on that coffee, Mike. If we're done?"

Mike opened his hands and nodded. "Call if you need anything."

"I won't."

Winter used his crutches to walk over to where Hamp was performing magic for a bald child in pajamas.

Winter placed a hand on the boy's shoulder. "Let's you and me go upstairs and check in with the girls."

"First, my big finish," Hampton said, standing.

Winter waited, smiling as Hampton Gardner seemed

to pluck two playing cards from thin air, placing one in each of the child's small hands.

The child laughed, and his parents applauded.

The Great Mephisto put a hand to his stomach and bowed deeply.

129

IT WAS THREE O'CLOCK SUNDAY AFTERNOON WHEN Alexa finally showed up in Winter's room. "Hey, kiddo," Winter said.

He turned off the TV. After the initial smile she'd been wearing evaporated, his antennae came out. She put the two manila envelopes she was holding on the table beside his bed.

"Is everything okay?" he asked.

"Not really. I turned in your rental, and your gun's in one of these envelopes."

"They released my gun?"

"Nobody's interested in keeping it since the shooting isn't going to generate any inquest. The FBI and Homeland are handling the incidents. You know the 'official' statement drill. Massey, when you think about this, just remember that you did good. Real good."

"You all right?" Winter asked her again, trying to get at what was weighing her down.

"Well, there's something you need to know. When I was at Brad's earlier, a deputy came in with Jacob's coat from the wreck. There was a recorder in the pocket that was damaged and didn't work. I put the tape into another mini and it worked. You need to listen to it. I put another cassette into the damaged machine so they won't know I took it."

"What's on it?"

"Troubling shit. No one else has heard it. I'm headed to the airport, since I've been ordered to join an investigation in progress. I'm going to turn this over to you. You decide how you want to handle it and let me know. I know you'll do the right thing."

She gave him a gentle hug and kissed him on the cheek. He saw that her eyes were filling with tears. She moved to the door and smiled weakly.

"Massey, if it weren't for a few people like you, I'd have written the world off a long time ago. Sometimes I just want to turn in my badge and go live on the side of a mountain."

When she left the room, Winter turned his attention to the envelopes. He reached over to the table and lifted the manila envelope that had *Gardner* written on it.

He took the end of the red string and unwound it from the plastic disk, then poured out a pocket mini-recorder.

Winter pressed the PLAY button. The tape began with Jacob's voice telling the date of the day he was murdered. That was followed by a confession, a surreptitiously recorded conversation with Leigh, and the unmistakable sounds of his flight from the house, which had ended with his death and the recorder's destruction. As

Winter listened, he felt like a trapdoor had swung open beneath him.

Before he closed his eyes, he had listened to the tape three times, and still had no idea how he was going to use the information.

130

LEIGH GARDNER TURNED AND SMILED WHEN Winter walked into the room where Brad Barnett lay in bed, a bandage encasing the left quarter of his head. His left hand was locked with Leigh's right.

"Look who's here, Brad," Leigh said.

"Massey," Brad said, smiling crookedly. His voice was no more than a low rasping. "Leigh told me that German bastard clipped you. Sorry I wasn't more helpful."

"He chewed on me some." Winter shook Brad's free hand gently. "You look a lot better than the last time I saw you."

"Since you were injured in the line of duty, Tunica County has your medical expenses covered. Whatever you need."

"We owe you everything, Winter," Leigh said.

"I asked Leigh to marry me," Brad said.

"I think it's the meds talking." Leigh giggled, squeezing Brad's hand.

"Bullshit," Brad declared. "I didn't really believe it, but you were right about that bastard," Brad said, meaning Styer. "Daddy never had a chance."

"I was lucky," Winter said. "And I had Alexa."

"It's over now," Leigh said, frowning. "We bury our dead, help the wounded as best we can, and life goes on."

"That's that farmer realism talking," Brad said. "Leigh's a rock."

"Yeah," Winter agreed. "That she is."

The door opened and Cynthia came bouncing in with a soft drink in her hand. She patted Winter's shoulder playfully as she passed him, went to the bed, and kissed Brad's cheek. "How you feeling, Pops?" She looked at Winter and her face lit up. "God, is that ever weird or what? I grew up in the same town with Brad and never knew he was my daddy."

"Where's Hampton?" Winter asked.

"Gone to spend the night with an old friend of Mama's," Cynthia said. "She works as a volunteer at the zoo. He's helping her feed animals or some happy shit."

"Cyn!" Leigh snapped. "Language."

"Sorry," Cyn said, shrugging.

"I brought you something," he said, handing Leigh the envelope. "These are Jacob's personal effects from the accident."

"Thanks," she said, dropping the envelope unceremoniously into a shopping bag beside her chair.

Winter's cell phone rang. He opened it and put it to his ear. "Yeah, Billy. Leigh's right here," Winter said, handing Leigh his phone. "He needs to talk to you."

"Yes? I can be at your office in an hour. Address?" she

asked. "Yes, Winter can show me. Cynthia too? Sure, I guess so."

Winter put the cell phone into his pocket and spent the next fifteen minutes making idle conversation with Leigh and Cynthia. He had thought it would be more difficult.

131

WINTER DIRECTED LEIGH TO A LARGE THREE-STORY building in downtown Memphis that housed Lyons, Battle, Cole & Vance, where a dozen attorneys were growing steadily richer.

Winter, Leigh, and Cynthia stepped out of the elevator. Through the glass-enclosed elevator bank, Winter spotted Billy Lyons standing in the reception area talking to a young man dressed for golf. When Billy saw them, he ended the conversation, strode across the space, and opened the door for the trio.

"How's the leg?"

"Stiff and sore."

"The ribs?"

"They're fine as long as I don't inhale."

"I hate to rush things, but can we sign the papers? We need to get back to Brad," Leigh said pleasantly.

"Of course. My office awaits," Billy said, leading the way.

After Billy closed the door to his office, he indicated the conference table and they all sat down.

"What exactly are these papers about?" Leigh asked, looking from Billy to Winter. "I thought everything was done. And why did you ask that Cyn come?"

Winter leaned forward. "Billy is here as your attorney to advise you. After I tell you a few things, you can ask his advice," he said.

"Or you can hire another lawyer if you choose," Billy added.

"That's going to be up to you," Winter said.

"What exactly do I need an attorney for?" Leigh asked. Her face had been captured by a steely frown.

"We'll talk about that," Winter said. "First you need to hear this." Winter took out the recorder and placed it on the table in front of him.

"What's that?" Cyn asked, looking confused.

"This was in Jacob's coat pocket when he was murdered."

Leigh didn't say anything, but the color drained from her cheeks.

Winter snapped on the machine and sat back.

"This is Jacob Gardner," the murdered man's voice said, authoritatively. *"I am making this recording because I think it is prudent for me to have an ace in the hole. It has occurred to me that after this business venture is done, and Leigh does not need me, I will be out in the cold, or worse. I have good reason to believe she's covered her ass nicely and that I will be fed to the wolves. A year ago, I discovered that a foreign corporation was buying land adjacent to a section I was foolish enough to have signed over to my ex-wife as collateral for a loan to repay people I had fleeced. There is no*

way to sugarcoat that, as it is a fact. Leigh has the evidence to prove that as well as other things that would discredit me. When I approached her and attempted to get the land back so I could sell it and regain my financial independence and dignity, she refused. When I discovered that the corporation buying the land owned the Roundtable, I did some research and found out that they owned only high-end resorts, with one exception—the Roundtable. I was convinced they were planning to build another large resort and that my land would be worth a fortune due to its proximity to the resort. This was before I learned from Albert White that my parcel was the sole remaining property in the middle of the whole shebang. I decided there was enough money to go around. Since Leigh was suspicious because I wanted the land back, I knew I had no choice but to bring her in. Leigh's father knew—"

Leigh reached out and turned off the machine. "This is crap," she said angrily. "Jacob was insane." She stood up. "He never once told the truth in his life. He is trying to make me look guilty of something. This is some sort of revenge in case he got caught!"

"We should listen to the rest of it," Billy said.

"Come on, Cyn. We're leaving," Leigh said. "Nothing Jacob Gardner said is worth anything. He never told the truth in his miserable life."

Cynthia stood.

"You'd be right," Winter said. "Except for the fact that he recorded a certain conversation. You can walk out if you like, but if you do, you'll force me to turn this over to Brad."

Leigh and Cynthia sat.

Winter turned the machine on again, rewinded a little,

and Jacob continued. *"Leigh's father knew Albert White from his younger days when he needed a favor done in West Memphis that involved getting his brother out of a possible assault on a whore. He almost beat her to death. For a fee, White framed someone else and Leigh's uncle walked. After that, her uncle sold Leigh's father his interest in the plantation for a pittance because Leigh's father had the goods on him.*

I finally leveled with Leigh because she wasn't going to sell back the land to me. I had quit gambling, but Leigh and White suggested that I lose a lot of money to the casino and other casinos. Albert got ten grand up front, which Leigh paid him, against a percentage of the sale price for his help in getting RRI to pay top dollar. He got me a large line of credit at the Roundtable and two other casinos, and we made Pierce Mulvane think I owned the land they needed. Albert correctly figured they would buy up my other debt from the competition, and pressure me to swap the land for them. When they did that, I admitted that I didn't actually own the land, and that I would have to convince Leigh to sell it. Then Leigh would play the heavy—which is no big stretch—and they would have to pony up really big bucks for it. White and Jack Beals kept us informed as to what was happening inside the casino since those people aren't above using unpleasant means to get what they want, and did we ever have what they wanted. With White on the inside, we thought we could stay ahead of them and be safe."

Winter was watching Leigh's and Cyn's face as they listened, but neither gave anything away.

"Everything was going along fine until the casino manager and people above him felt the pressure. Albert said they

were bringing in a professional to help out and he didn't know who that was. Some mystery man from Europe. They already had a cold-blooded killer—this Tug guy—so we figured this other guy was gathering information. They asked White to supply someone to help the new guy, so White sent Beals in. I believed everything would work fine right up until the babysitter got shot, which nobody knew was going to happen. Beals was helping this new guy and keeping Albert informed, but this guy told Beals shit, and according to White, the guy killed him. Since I didn't fully trust White, Cyn would double-check White's information from Beals. She knew him from when he was a deputy, and she was sixteen, when he stopped her for reckless driving and she had weed on her. My daughter, never one to keep her legs together, fucked Beals to keep from getting in trouble, and from then on she'd meet him for a quickie every now and then. I found out about it when she was staying with me, but figured it wouldn't hurt to see if she could help, pump Beals on the side to make sure White was staying honest. She agreed. Call it insurance. That was between me and Cyn, and I thought it best Leigh didn't know.

"White didn't know anything about the babysitter's killing. Then Beals got killed, and White was freaked, but the money held him tight. That and a threat to tell Mulvane what he'd been doing for us. They'd have killed him for that and he knew it. I tried to get Mulvane on tape admitting to having Sherry killed, but he took the tape. Hell, he was probably recording me. If they were willing to kill Sherry Adams—and I know that Leigh was more likely the actual target—they'll kill me. Maybe White is playing both sides. I can't trust anybody, especially based on Brad's actions, and

what Leigh's been telling him. Now Mulvane's guys have Cynthia and if little Miss Barnett isn't killed, she'll back Leigh up. I sure as hell don't trust those two. Leigh's been talking to Barnett and his buddy and lying to me about what she's telling them sure as I'm sweating. I certainly don't believe she's just playing them to see what they know and what they're up to like she said. She's one conniving bitch, so I'm making this to cover my own ass."

Winter stopped the tape recorder.

"It's all lies. He was jealous of Brad because he knew I loved him. He knew Cyn wasn't his daughter, that I was pregnant with Brad's child when we got married. Can't you see? I love Brad. I've always loved him."

"Jacob was a total loser," Cyn added, her voice rising to a petulant whine. "He ruined everything he could get his hands on. He was a totally selfish asshole. If he'd had his way, the plantation would have been lost, along with everything our family has held on to. He's lying about everything. My mother is totally innocent."

Winter waited until she finished speaking.

"Say I'm willing to believe that you do love Brad, Leigh. That doesn't change the fact that you and Cynthia, to some extent, are directly or indirectly responsible for every death that is connected with this."

"Even if Jacob were telling the truth, nobody could have foreseen that anybody would be harmed," Leigh said. "And I can't believe you are playing this in front of Cynthia. It's too cruel for words. She was a victim of that Beals creature. He raped her. She was a child."

Winter decided to blend Leigh's claim with the truth he suspected. "I have her cell phone records and Beals's too. The text messages they traded are very interesting. Cynthia may have been initially victimized by Beals, but she didn't report the assault, and she kept right on meeting him until very recently. Cyn's car was in that barn when it blew up."

"I lied about where I got kidnapped, but not by who. I didn't know that man."

Winter pounced. "You drove out there."

She nodded slowly, chewing her fingernail.

"Should I get the call record so you can see it and refresh your memory?"

"Yeah, I got a message to meet Jack, but he wasn't there and that man you shot kidnapped me."

Winter picked up the recorder and fast-forwarded to one of the numbers he had filed in his memory. He had doubted there would be any reason to play the tape in its entirety, and it was best they didn't know everything that was on the tape. The secretly recorded conversation be gan with Jacob's voice.

"This is out of control. Brad and Massey grilled me like a criminal. I don't give a shit what you say, they know things they had to have gotten from you, Leigh. They aren't getting it from talking to Albert White. If you think I'm going to take the blame for this pile of shit while you walk away rich, you're fucking nuts."

Leigh's voice said, *"Hold yourself together, Jacob. Cynthia is going to be all right as soon as we do the deal. Why would I be telling them anything that would threaten you? It's paranoia. Brad and Massey are just fishing. Ignore it. Just keep your shit together, your mouth shut, and we'll be out clean with a lot of money. Don't forget who it was turned the couple of hundred grand you would have settled for into millions."*

Jacob said, *"People have died. More could."*

Leigh came back. *"You think I don't know that? We're going to have to live with Sherry's blood on our hands."* Leigh was crying. *"It was that Mulvane who did that. You do what you're told or you will go to jail."*

There was the sound of Jacob hitting Leigh, and of Hamp running in and calling Jacob a bastard.

Winter clicked off the machine.

Cynthia said, "Tell him, Mother. I didn't have anything to do with any of it. Jack raped me when he was a cop and I was a minor. Just because I had a joint on me when he stopped me. I had just turned sixteen. And he made me keep seeing him. I never wanted to, but Daddy told me to see him again or he'd turn Jack in for statutory rape and make sure everyone knew it was me."

Leigh sat up straighter and her expression was one of total resignation. "Billy, are you representing me here?"

"Yes." Billy nodded. "Winter played the tape for me. You have already hired me, so yes, technically you are my client."

"This is just a copy of the tape," Winter told her. "The original is in a safe place."

Leigh asked, "Winter, are you acting in any official capacity as a representative of any police agency here?"

"No," Winter said. "I resigned my commission, so at this moment I am acting on my own behalf."

"I don't want Cynthia involved with this," Leigh said. "It's all on me, okay? She is a victim."

"See?" Cynthia said. "I was only accidentally involved. I've been at school."

"Some. But I bet you've been in town a lot lately," Winter said, guessing. "Okay, get out."

Cynthia grabbed her purse and went to the door.

"Wait for me in the reception area," Leigh ordered. Cynthia smiled weakly at her mother before leaving the room.

132

"I WON'T MAKE EXCUSES FOR MYSELF," LEIGH SAID. "I am guilty of what Jacob accuses me of. It started off as one thing and turned into a nightmare. Cynthia is the way she is because I raised her to be able to take my place, the same way my father raised me. Weakness is for those who can afford it, and we've hung on when few others in our business have. She is strong-willed and, yes, even manipulative. That is what is required of a woman in a man's world. Jacob's attitude toward her was always cold because he knew Cynthia was Brad's child . . ." Her voice trailed off. "I truly did love Sherry and saw her as a member of my family, and . . . poor dear Estelle . . . and Bradley . . . and Dr. Barnett. All the others . . . I deserve any punishment I receive and I will accept any blame."

"Leigh, only you know the full extent of what you've actually done, and precisely what you are or aren't guilty of," Winter said. "You used Brad, Alexa, and me, and we never suspected it. Despite her voluntary participation, Cynthia was in real danger of being killed because you and Jacob involved her. She has problems that probably aren't going to get any better. People are dead, lives are destroyed. You put Hampton's life at risk. As far as I can tell, he's the only one around here that is salvageable. And I want him to be saved."

Leigh interrupted, "Some good did come of it. You killed that monster who killed Sherry and Dr. Barnett. He would have killed my children. I knew I should have come clean, and I really wanted to, but I couldn't without admitting what I had done. And Brad . . ."

"There's one last thing," Winter said. He lifted the recorder, fast-forwarded it until he found the corresponding number, and snapped the PLAY button. Winter watched Leigh's face as Jacob's recorder played his confrontation with Winter, Brad, and Alexa outside the house. The tape was rolling when Jacob drove away. There were two minutes filled with the mad rantings of a man driven by terror as he barreled down the county road. The sound of a horn honking was followed by Jacob cursing, *"Pass me if you can, you prick!"*

The engine roared as Jacob pressed down on the accelerator, laughing and cursing, unaware that the recorder in his coat pocket was collecting the sounds of the car's interior. *"Jesus,"* he cried out. *"Jesus Christ, you're going to kill us both, you idiot. Pizza face! Wait!"*

There was a pop, which was the window glass shattering, some bumping, and a final smacking sound.

"Who shot him?" Leigh asked. "Pizza face?"

Winter shrugged. "Tug Murphy. Alexa checked your home phone records. You called White an hour before

Jacob hit you and left the house. All it took was you telling White that Jacob was going to break. And now of course White and Tug are both dead."

"Jacob believed that Mulvane had Cyn. I knew they wouldn't hurt her if they got the land. I should have admitted everything then, but I knew Cyn would have been killed if Jacob had screwed things up—and he would have. He'd have told you and Brad everything and you could not have saved my daughter. Jacob didn't care about her. That's why I called Albert White."

Leigh's face slackened and her eyes showed fear. "This will destroy Brad. And Hamp . . . Tell me what you want me to do."

Winter stared at her, reading her truthfulness as best he could.

"What if Brad doesn't need to know? He would have to charge you with conspiracy or depraved indifference or whatever the law allows for crimes like yours. I expect he'd quit his job first to let others handle that, and it would absolutely destroy him. I don't think he could live, knowing you were responsible for his father's death and all of the rest of it. Brad is a very good man. I am going to believe that you really do love him. Maybe you just think you do so you can feel better about yourself. It doesn't have to matter."

"I have loved Brad for most of my life. I intend to spend the rest of my life making myself worthy of him. Brad and my children are all that matters."

"If you're truly sorry about what happened, like you say you are, you can prove it easily enough."

"How?" Leigh asked him, hope in her eyes.

"Get rid of the money." Winter took a sheet of paper

out of his pocket and opened it. "Here's a list of the dead and injured, with contributions you can make to each. I'm guessing on your tax liability, but whatever is left over will go to scholarships for underprivileged kids in Sherry Adams's name. You do that and I'll make sure nobody outside this room ever hears this tape. If you aren't being honest about Brad and those feelings, he'll know it soon enough. If you are, it's maybe his only shot at happiness. Maybe Brad's influence can be a counterbalance to what you and Jacob have done to Cyn. You agree to this, Billy has agreed to draw up the papers and handle the financial transfers. Him, I *know* I can trust. That's between you and Cynthia, but you'll do it."

Leigh nodded slowly. "I'll do it."

"I hoped you would see what a good idea it was," Winter said, checking his watch. He stood slowly, knowing his face was reflecting the pain he was feeling. "Truth is, there's a lot worse people than you and your daughter. I think that you're more conniving than evil, but you sure did a lot of evil."

"I didn't think anybody would be killed," Leigh said weakly. Tears rolled down her cheeks.

"But they were. If I thought you hadn't just lost control of this mess, I'd make it my personal mission to see you go to jail. Maybe Brad will help heal you. Leigh, I wish you redemption. I really do," Winter said, lifting his crutches and placing the tape recorder into his pocket. "Billy will let me know when the papers are signed and the money is distributed."

"You won't be sorry," Leigh said, wiping her tears away.

"If I am, you will be even sorrier. This will all be in a

safe place. Now I have a plane to catch. Just remember that I will be watching."

When Winter passed through the reception area, Cynthia kept her eyes on the open magazine in her lap, which was more than all right with Winter. He might regret not handing the evidence to the prosecutor in Tunica County, but he prayed that wouldn't be the case. He had never thought he could let the guilty walk away clean, but he also never imagined he could blow a man's brains out believing that man was unarmed.

He crutch-walked out into the bright crisp Tennessee air, slid into the back of the waiting taxi, and closed the door.

"Airport," he said, leaning back.

After being in the same room with Leigh and Cynthia Gardner, he wanted to take a stiff brush and scrub his skin with disinfectant. He had decided that Paulus Styer would be the last man he would ever kill. Winter Massey knew that going home to the people he loved was the only thing that could make him feel whole again.

ABOUT THE AUTHOR

JOHN RAMSEY MILLER's career has included stints as a visual artist, advertising copy writer, and journalist. He is the author of the nationally best-selling *The Last Family, Too Far Gone,* and three other Winter Massey thrillers: *Inside Out, Upside Down,* and *Side by Side,* and is at work on his next book.

A native son of Mississippi, he now lives in North Carolina with his wife, and writes full-time.

If you enjoyed John Ramsey Miller's exciting new crime novel, Smoke & Mirrors, you won't want to miss any of his bestselling thrillers.

Look for them at your favorite booksellers. And read on for an exciting early look at the next electrifying stand-alone thriller,

THE LAST DAY

coming soon from Dell Books.

The First Day

OUTSIDE CONCORD, NORTH CAROLINA
THE THIRD SUNDAY IN AUGUST

1

SITTING CROSS-LEGGED ON THE COOL CLAY FLOOR, the watcher used the tip of his knife to carve another letter into the wall of his hide. After he inspected the letter—an O—he ran the sharpening stone against the edge, holstered the knife, and set it down gently by his side.

The midday Sunday sun cooked the still, warm air outside the hole. He looked out at the rear of a modern house through a four-inch-tall opening where the trap door was propped up. The large windows reminded him of watching fish in an aquarium. The house's two occupants—a man and his wife—moved from room to room like slow-swimming trout. Rarely were the residents together for more than a few minutes. Their conversations were short ones, and the obvious emotional distance between the husband and his wife gave the watcher great pleasure.

The sound of a motor's purr caught the man's attention, and he looked up in time to see the doctor's Lexus coming around the house as the garage door opened. He felt a rapidly growing sense of arousal as he watched the SUV roll slowly into its bay, the door sliding back into place. The woman was not perfect but nevertheless a beautiful and desirable creature.

The watcher switched off the iPod, opened his rucksack, drew out a jar, and held it so the sunlight illuminated the six large dark-shelled beetles he'd found under a rotten log that morning on his way to the hide. The bugs seemed content, creeping like tanks over the bottom of the jar he had brought to urinate into while he was in the hide. The man knew from experience that the insects would walk around in circles, try to scale the walls, and climb over one another for the rest of their lives, constantly looking for a way out. He knew a great deal about captive behavior. While it was true that the bugs were docile, he had experience with many other creatures whose demeanor seemed fixed . . . until outside forces intervened.

Taking out a drinking straw, the man opened the jar and set the lid aside. He used the end of the straw to jab at the insects, prodding each once or twice before going to the next. After a few seconds, a steady hissing sound, like a leaking tire, erupted from the jar's inhabitants. He smiled, knowing that before long the beetles would attack one another and begin using their powerful jaws to dismantle their mates, leaving a heap of severed legs in the jar's bottom. His grin widened as he likened the interior of the house on the next rise to the bottle of hissing insects.

2

DR. NATASHA MCCARTY EXAMINED THE ABDOMEN OF a four-year-old named Josh Wasserman whose appendix had ruptured early the previous evening. As usual, she'd done a first-class job on both the removal of the defective body part and the even spacing of the sutures. A bright bouquet of tulips stood centered in the window, and Mr. and Mrs. Wasserman sat quietly in chairs on the other side of the bed where the small child lay. Mrs. Wasserman, a small, round-faced woman who appeared to be about eight months pregnant, stared at the child as though he might vanish should she look away.

"How are you feeling this morning?" Natasha asked the bright-eyed boy as she checked the chart hanging at the foot of his bed. His color was good, his vitals strong, and if she hadn't performed the operation herself, she wouldn't know he'd been at death's door less than twelve hours earlier. Children were amazingly resilient.

"My stomach hurts," he replied sullenly.

Natasha watched as the small face twisted in on itself and tears streamed down his cheeks. She set the chart down, put her hand under his chin, and sat on his bed.

"You're going to be fine very soon," she told him tenderly.

"You've been such a good boy," his mother added with forced cheer.

"He's worried that his soccer career is over," his father said.

"That's not a problem, Josh. You'll be back running around and playing ball in a couple of weeks like this never happened." She handed him a tissue from the bedside table and waited until he wiped the tears away.

"Can I have it?" Josh asked.

"Have what?" Natasha asked.

"The palendix," he said. "In a jar. So I can have it to keep."

"I'm sorry, Josh," Natasha said. "We didn't keep it."

"What did you do with it?" he asked, curious.

"We incinerated it."

A look of confusion grew on his face. "What?"

"We didn't know you wanted it. When we remove things from people, we are required by law to burn them in a furnace."

"You *cremated* my palendix?"

Natasha smiled. "Yes."

"We cremated Buster," Josh said. "In a hot, hot fire."

"Buster was our Labrador," Mr. Wasserman explained.

"Mr. Murphy runned over Buster in a car," Josh said.

"Ran over," Mrs. Wasserman corrected.

"He ran over him. I wanted a new dog, but I'm getting a new sister instead. I wanted to bury him, but Daddy said our yard was too little. Our yard is all brown and crunchy because the police won't let us put any water on it."

"It's very dry where I live, too," Natasha said.

"Where do you live?" Josh asked.

"I live way out in the country, north of here," she replied.

"Do you have a dog?"

"We don't have any pets. But we do have deer, squirrels, raccoons, and possums, and lots of birds."

"You live on a farm and you don't got pigs and cows?"

"We don't live on a farm. We live in the woods."

"Do you live with your daddy and mommy?"

"My mommy and daddy live in Seattle, Washington. That's a long way from here. I live with my husband." Natasha braced herself for the next question.

"Do you have any little boys and girls?"

"No," Natasha said, smiling.

"Kids like to live in the woods. You and your husband don't have to live alone, you know."

"Josh," Mr. Wasserman said, "you shouldn't pry into Dr. McCarty's personal life."

"Well . . . she could," he whined nonsensically.

"I'll see you tomorrow morning, Josh," Natasha said, rubbing his head.

"When can I go home?"

"In a few days," she said.

Natasha was near the nurses' station, dictating her notes for transcription, when she saw Dan Wheat in the hallway.

One of her partners, Dan had the bedside manner of a mortician. She didn't know why he'd gone into pediatric medicine, since he seemed to view children as troublesome monkeys. He was rail-thin with a roving eye and a legendary bag of tired pickup lines. Natasha had once overheard one of his young patients tell him he had stinky breath. Dan immediately ordered a spinal tap for the offender before he went off in search of mints.

"Natasha," he said, waving her down. "You see my new wheels?"

"No."

"I broke down and treated myself to a top-of-the line Benz SL550 two-seat convertible in jet-black. It's a bitch to keep clean, so I run it wide open to blow the dust off. Claire is making me buy her a new car as an act of revenge because I won't let her drive the Benz, so I was thinking maybe a simple Lexus SUV like yours so she can haul the kids around in fair style. You buy it, or do you lease?"

"Ward bought it for me."

Daniel barely paused for breath.

"Oh, did Edgar talk to you about my little brother? The boy's got hands like mine, and he aced medical school. We should get him here before he gets an offer he can't refuse in some major city far, far away."

"I didn't know we needed a sixth partner," Natasha said.

Natasha had met Dan's younger brother. If such a thing were possible, William Wheat was half as impressive as his older brother. He was short and stocky, and his half-open eyes made him look like he was in the process of passing out. Natasha hadn't wanted Dan brought on board, but she hadn't opposed her partners. He was typical of what was coming out of medical schools: very intelligent, aggressive, competitive, and greedy. He saw each patient as a business opportunity, and his billings were off the chart because he ordered every test the insurance company would pay for.

"Perhaps we should discuss this at the next partner's

meeting," she said noncommittally. "I hate to break this off, but I haven't slept in two days."

"Does Ward get fed up with your hours? It drives Claire crazy that I'm always working."

"Ward doesn't complain."

"Well, keep William in mind. We're getting busy as hell, and it would help you and Ward to spend some more time together."

After she'd finished in the hospital, Natasha got into her Lexus SUV and headed home. Although it was just after ten A.M., she hadn't been able to fall asleep after the Wasserman surgery, which had finished around ten-thirty the previous evening.

Twenty minutes later Natasha was turning into her driveway. Ward's eight acres had been a wedding present from his father. He and Natasha had selected a ridge, cleared the trees from it, and built a four-thousand-square-foot, split-level modern house. Other than their driveway and the mailbox, there was no sign at all that a house sat back in the woods. The asphalt driveway wound through the trees and curved in front of the house. The home's façade of raw textured concrete and floor-to-ceiling windows had been built with its back facing an elevated ridge.

Natasha used the remote to open her bay in the three-car garage and pulled in. She went into the kitchen, poured herself a glass of pinot grigio, and carried the bottle into the den. She put the bottle on the Noguchi coffee table, took a long swallow from the glass, went into the bedroom, and took a long, hot shower. After slipping into a robe, she got a blister pack of Ambien and went back to the den.

She stood at the couch and stared out at the grounds, feeling again the unease she'd become all too familiar with. Her eyes caught a motion in the shadows and she searched the treeline for the source of the movement. A chill ran up her spine as her discomfort grew. A wild animal, or perhaps someone's house cat foraging for field mice. Of course, with the new subdivision up the road, it was possible that kids were playing in the woods. They'd seen evidence of people having been in the woods over the past two years—soda bottles and candy wrappers—but had never caught anyone close to the house. Ward had the standard posted signs on the property line, but such signs were only suggestions to all but the reputable.

Since the house faced north and the rear overlooked a wall of large trees on the top of the slope, there had been no need for curtains to block the sun or to give the McCartys privacy. For the past weeks, though, she'd been toying with the idea of having blinds installed. She had even gotten an estimate, which had been staggering since the entire forty-five-foot wall was comprised of four-by-eight double panes of thick glass.

Natasha reclined on the couch and chased an Ambien with a quarter glass of the chilled wine.

3

LAS VEGAS, NEVADA

THE HOTEL SHUTTLE DEPOSITED WARD MCCARTY AT the airport to catch his flight home after three days of crowds, bulging tote bags, crowded sales booths, and insincere smiles. He hated trade shows, but had to attend them in order to keep up with new suppliers, new materials, gimmicks, manufacturers, and his competition.

After standing in a long line, Ward showed his North Carolina driver's license and ticket to the female guard; slipped off his shoes, belt, cell phone, and watch; and put them all in a plastic tray. He felt naked in his stockinged feet, and he hated holding up his loose khakis with one hand so the cuffs didn't drag.

At the other end of the conveyor belt, a burly guard with a buzz cut opened his briefcase and had Ward turn on his laptop to make sure it wasn't actually a clever computer bomb. Ward looked over to see an elderly woman standing calmly while a guard ran a wand up and down over her stooped body. Satisfied, Ward's guard lifted out a bubble-wrapped envelope from the briefcase and slipped out a small blue die-cast race car. As he studied the five-inch-long toy, his eyes grew noticeably larger.

"Man," he said, "a 1969 Petty Roadrunner die-cast in near mint. You are one lucky devil. That was a one-year deal, that car." He looked at the underside. "Aw, it's not marked on the bottom. It's a damned nice counterfeit. Isn't that illegal?"

"It's a prototype. It was never produced. One of a kind."

"If you don't mind me asking, where'd you get it?" He placed it back into the envelope.

"It's been in my family for a very long time," Ward said, which was true. The little model car had been in his family several years longer than he'd been on earth.

"Have a good day, sir," the guard told him, as he put the padded envelope into Ward's briefcase beside his computer and closed it.

Ward reached his assigned concourse through a maze of temporary signs, sheetrock dust, scaffolding, plastic sheeting, and constructive pandemonium.

At his gate Ward spent the time waiting for his flight by staring at an open novel he'd bought before leaving Charlotte, trying to absorb the words and make sense of the sentences. When he traveled with paperback novels, he always tore out the chapters as he finished them and threw the pages away, which served to both mark his place and make his load lighter. After he finished the chapter he was working on, he ripped the pages out and put them on the seat beside him, then slowly realized that he had no idea what the discarded chapter's author had tried to convey.

Ward was bothered by the lack of clocks at the gate, which meant that passengers had to have watches, or cell phones, in order to know how long they had until their planes boarded. Of all of the things he didn't like about Las Vegas—and there was nothing he did like—he most disliked the city's denial that time passed there. Sitting in a leather chair with his carry-on bag and briefcase at his feet, he looked out through the windows at the Strip—the city's main street, filled with the best known casinos—easy to spot from the monstrous glass pyramid and the giant sphinx with its lion ass backed up to it.

Opening his cell phone, Ward called Natasha to explain the delay, but got their home answering machine. He had spoken to her only once in the three days he'd been away, when he'd called from the airport upon arrival there for the memorabilia-suppliers trade show. Of the six or seven times he'd called since, he had left short messages. He wasn't alarmed, because Natasha often turned the phone's ringers off, or ignored them. She carried a cell phone but rarely turned it on unless she needed to answer her emergency beeper.

Sudden jazzy notes of youthful laughter froze Ward, and he turned slowly to see not the young boy he expected but a young girl of eight or so playing tag with a smaller child. He exhaled loudly and looked down at his paperback, feeling the sudden tears running down his cheeks. Several times each day for the past year, something brought Barney into his mind, and, with that trigger, a choking gloom descended over him like a wet curtain. It could begin with a familiar odor like iced tea, a flash of a red shirt, sudden movement in his periphery, a flag snapping in a brisk wind, a child with blond hair, a bicycle lying on a lawn—just about anything at all. Any thought of Barney brought Ward back to the memory of clutching a small, limp body in his arms as hell closed in on him.

Barney's given name had been Ward McCarty III, but he chose the name Barney himself at the age of five because he so admired that unidentified person who dressed in an insipid purple dinosaur suit.

Often there were the dreams—some of which included a cameo by Barney, or, if Ward was very lucky, a starring role. Those double-edged dreams were sweet torture, leaving his soul lacerated and leaking some essential nectar. He always woke with an odd feeling of being both full and empty at the same time.

What consumed a great deal of his waking hours was the thought that every decision a creature made led to a path with unknowable consequences. An animal's choice of an action—or path—might find them a mate, shelter, or food—or the possibility of becoming another animal's dinner. By the same token, some bean counter with a sharp pencil might choose to install a less expensive—and less protected—electrical outlet in a garage, which could lead to the tragic death of an angelic child. Ward thought about this faceless man in some generic office day after day. He saw no relief to being forever haunted by the avalanche that began with the simple decision of a budget-conscious man.

Sometimes, when Ward McCarty looked at animals, he wondered if they ever dreamed alive their dead the way people did.

Thankfully, as a contrast to the 116-degree Vegas heat of the day, it was cool inside the wide-bodied craft. When Ward arrived at his assigned row, he found the center seat already occupied by a young girl with blond hair accented with bright red and blue streaks, who was plugged into an iPod. He opened the overhead compartment and somehow managed to wedge in his carry-on.

The girl looked up at him, and when he met her dull green eyes, she smiled, showing small teeth with silver wire braces. Ward pointed to the window seat beyond her, whereupon she unplugged her earphones, got up, and moved into the aisle to let him pass, leaving her cloth tote bag on her seat.

Sitting, Ward pushed his briefcase under the seat ahead of him and buckled his seat belt. The girl returned to her seat and put the iPod's earbuds back in place. He figured her age to be somewhere between thirteen and seventeen. She was barely five feet tall, and the dull yellow too-large-by-a-mile sweatshirt had the famous "Welcome to Las Vegas" sign screen-printed on it, which contrasted with her red shorts and blue flip-flops. He couldn't help but notice that each of the nails on her fingers and toes was painted a different color.

Ward spent the first two hours alternating between watching the movie on a small screen in the ceiling over the aisle and, out of the corner of his eye, observing the electronic activities of the girl beside him.

The black tote bag in her lap contained an assortment of electronic devices, and like a child with a short attention span, she went from her iPod, to a Game Boy, to plugging a set of airline earphones into the armrest to watch the movie, then back to the iPod. Just when he had decided that she was closer to seventeen than thirteen, she took out a DVD player and watched a cartoon clearly geared to very young children. She watched intently, laughing melodiously here and there as the cartoon played.

Thirty minutes out of Charlotte, he dropped his tray, reached into his shirt pocket, and pulled out one of the monogrammed index cards he carried to list things to do. As he lined up his thoughts, Ward began sketching a small, familiar face in one corner of the card.

"Hey," the girl said suddenly, interrupting his drawing.

As she stared down at the card on the tray, she pulled her earphones off.

"Whatcha doing?" she asked.

"Thinking," he replied.

"You're a good drawer," she said. "Could you draw me?"

Ward studied her round face and reproduced her likeness in less than two minutes, all while her eyes moved from his face to the drawing and back, like someone watching a tennis match. Ward had the ability to sketch what he saw, and faces were what he drew best.

When he finished the sketch, she smiled. "Cool. Are you a professional artist?"

He answered, "No. I do some light designing."

A confused look briefly took over her features. "Like what kind of lights do you design?"

"Oh," he said, smiling. "My company makes and markets NASCAR memorabilia. Cars, hats, T-shirts, mugs, key chains."

"No shit?" she said, too loudly. The word earned her a frown from the man beside her. "My mother is a race-car fan."

Ward reached down, took out his briefcase, and opened it, taking out the model car to show her.

"My father had it made in Japan. Nowadays, they are made mostly in China. See, we take pictures of a real car from several angles, and a factory makes the model from the pictures, which they produce, box, and ship to us, and we distribute them from our warehouse. We just change the art on the car depending on whose car it is, since every race team has different sponsors."

"This is so fucking cool. Could I get one?"

"Well, not this one. This one is the first one my father had made," he explained. "This is the prototype. He didn't have a lot of money, and that car raced only one year. As it turned out, he made other models and they did sell and so he ordered more, but this one was handmade. Mostly he used it to show to bankers and investors, who weren't all that impressed. In those days, NASCAR was popular with only relatively few people."

He started to tell her why he had it with him, but didn't. What he did say was, "I can get you a new one—driver of your choice."

"No shit?"

"Absolutely none." He took another note card and scribbled his office number on it. "Call and ask for Kelly, and she'll send one to you for your mother. We have thousands of them in our warehouse."

She narrowed her eyes suspiciously. "How much will it cost?"

"My treat."

"No shit? Thanks. That is so sick."

"Sick?"

"Sick as in cool."

"Who's your mother's favorite driver?"

"I dunno. I can find out." She ran the wheels back and forth on her lap and made a motor noise as she did this. "Is this you on the card?" she asked, meaning the note card he'd given her. "Ward McCarty. That's you?"

"It is," he told her.

"Why were you in Vegas?" she asked. "Gambling?"

"No. Work stuff. You?"

"I fly back and forth a lot," she said. "My dad lives there, and I live with my mother in Charlotte. You married?"

"Yes."

"What's your wife do?"

"She's a pediatric surgeon," Ward said.

"What's that mean?"

"Pediatric means children," Ward said.

"I know that. So she, like, cuts little kids open?" Her eyes were wide, her mouth a circle.

"Yes, but I think it's more complicated than making cuts."

"Y'all got any kids?"

"No," he said.

"You're, like, too old?"

"I expect you're right," he said, trying to smile. This wasn't true . . . as far as he knew.

When she handed the car back, Ward put it back in his briefcase, closed it, and placed it under the seat.

"I need to slip out past you," he told her.

"Why?" she asked.

"Visit the little boys' room."

After the man beside the girl unbuckled his seat belt and stood in the aisle, she tucked her feet up in her seat so he could get out.

When Ward returned to his row, the girl, who was now listening to her iPod, smiled up at him and pulled up her feet to let him get into his seat.

When the plane landed ten minutes later and parked at the terminal, the girl grabbed her bag of toys and was off the plane before Ward got his carry-on and filed out.

He thought about what the girl had said about him being too old to have children, and realized it wasn't true. He and Natasha hadn't talked about having another child since Barney's accident, and the thought comforted him. For the first time in a very long time, Ward McCarty felt a degree of optimism about the future.